Books
I0750351

THE GREEN MOUNTAIN BOYS

A HISTORICAL TALE OF THE EARLY SETTLEMENT OF VERMONT

BY

JUDGE D. P. THOMPSON

Author of "May Martin; or, The Money Diggers," "Locke Amsden; or, The Schoolmaster," etc.

Illustrated by

CARLE MICHEL BOOG

"'Tis a rough land of rock, and stone, and tree,
Where breathes no castled lord nor cabin'd slave;
Where thoughts, and hands, and tongues are free,
And friends will find a welcome—foes a grave."

Cherokee Publishing Company
Atlanta, Georgia

THE GREEN MOUNTAIN BOYS

A HISTORICAL TALE OF THE EARLY SETTLEMENT OF VERMONT

BY

JUDGE D. P. THOMPSON

Author of "May Martin; or, The Money Diggers,"
"Locke Amsden; or, The Schoolmaster," etc.

ILLUSTRATED BY

CARLE MICHEL BOOG

"'Tis a rough land of rock, and stone, and tree,
Where breathes no castled lord nor cabin'd slave;
Where thoughts, and hands, and tongues are free,
And friends will find a welcome—foes a grave."

Cherokee Publishing Company
Atlanta, Georgia

This book is printed on acid-free paper which conforms to the American National Standard Z39.48-1984 *Permanence of Paper for Printed Library Materials.* Paper that conforms to this standard's requirements for pH, alkaline reserve and freedom from groundwood is anticipated to last several hundred years without significant deterioration under normal library use and storage conditions.

Manufactured in the United States of America

ISBN: 978-0-87797-359-1

Cherokee Publishing Company
P O Box 1730, Marietta, GA 30061

INSCRIBED TO THE

HONORABLE HEMAN ALLEN

LATE U. S. MINISTER TO CHILI

TO NO ONE CAN THIS WORK BE MORE APPROPRIATELY DEDICATED

THAN TO THE DISTINGUISHED SON

OF ONE OF THAT

INTELLIGENT, ENTERPRISING, AND FEARLESS

BAND OF BROTHERS,

THE ALLENS,

TO WHOSE ENERGETIC CHARACTERS AND VARIED SERVICES

VERMONT IS SO DEEPLY INDEBTED

FOR HER EXISTENCE AS AN INDEPENDENT STATE

AND FOR THE

FOUNDATION OF HER PRESENT PROSPERITY

PREFACE

The following pages are intended to embody and illustrate a portion of the more romantic incidents which actually occurred in the early settlements of Vermont, with the use of but little more fiction than was deemed sufficient to weave them together and impart to the tissue a connected interest. In doing this, the author has ventured, for the sake of more unity of design, upon one or two anachronisms; or, in other words, he has brought together, or nearly so, some incidents connected with the portions of the two different periods embraced in the work, viz., the New York controversy and the Revolution—which occurred at intervals. Other than this, he is sensible of no violations of historical truth. Without consulting, as perhaps he should, the models to be found in the works of approved writers in this department of literature, he has endeavored to give a true delineation of the manners and feelings of those among whom the scene is laid, together with the deeds and characters of some of the leading actors in the events he has attempted to describe, as gathered from the imperfect published histories of the times, from the private papers to which he has had access, and more particularly from the lips of the few aged relics of that period who actively participated in the wild and stirring scenes which peculiarly marked the settlement of this part of the country. How far he has succeeded in the attempt it is for the public, not for him, to decide.

The Author.

Montpelier, *March, 1839.*

THE GREEN MOUNTAIN BOYS.

CHAPTER I

"And now for scenes where nature in her pride
Roar'd in rough floods, and wav'd in forests wide—
Where men were taught the desert path to trace,
And the rude pleasures of the mountain chase—
With light canoe to plow the glassy lake,
And from its depths the silvery trout to take—
Where nerves of iron grew, and souls of tone
To soft refinement's tranquil scenes unknown."

THOSE who have wandered along the banks of the Otter Creek in search of the beautiful and picturesque, may have extended their rambles, perhaps, to Lake Dunmore, which lies embosomed among the hills a few miles to the eastward of that quiet stream. If so, their taste for natural scenery has doubtless been amply gratified; for there is no spot in the whole range of the Green Mountains that combines more of the requisites for a perfect landscape than this romantic sheet of water and its surrounding shores. Of an oblong form, about four miles in length and one in breadth, this lake, or pond, as such bodies of water are more usually denominated among us, lies extended between the main ridge and a collateral eminence on the west, of a height but little more than sufficient to serve as a secure embankment to this noble reservoir of the hills. From the eastern shore the land rises abruptly into a lofty mountain, which, like some mighty giantess, sits enthroned in the mid-heavens, her head turbaned with a wreath of white mist, and looking down with seeming fondness and care upon the bright daughter that, reflecting back her own rude image, lies quietly reposing in her lap, receiving the rich supply of a thousand pearly rills that come gushing to her opening lips. To the north and south open long and beautiful vistas, extending along over the bright extremities of the lake and terminating among the far off peaks of the Green Mountains; while from the western shore the land, after a gentle rise for a short distance, falls off rapidly toward the Otter, leaving the broad and extensive valley of that stream open to the vision, which now wanders unobstructed to the western borders of the Lake Champlain, where the long chain of mountains that rise immediately beyond lies sleeping in the blue distance, and bounds the view of this magnificent scene.

It was near sunset on one of the last days of April, and in the same year and month as were marked by the opening scene of our great national drama, that four stout and hardy looking men, two of them about the middle age, and two considerably younger, were seen occupying a large log canoe near the eastern shore of the lake just described, and engaged fishing for trout. Their success through the day in ensnaring "the pride of the pure water," as the trout has been appropriately termed, had been ample, as was evinced by the large strings of this beautiful fish lying on the bottom of the boat beneath the feet of their respective captors. Now, however, as the rapidly lengthening shadows of the dark primeval forest that thickly lined the shore had nearly closed over the lake, the party began to manifest a disposition to relinquish the exciting labors of the day. One sat listless and unemployed in his seat; another was taking in and winding up his line; while the third had handled the oars, and sat patiently awaiting the movements of the fourth, who seemed intent on securing, before quitting the station, one more victim, as "a most severe large one," he said, was brushing around his hook. At length the speckled tantalizer, after playing warily around the bait a while, seized it with a desperation that seemed to imply at once his suspicions and his determination to test them, and was drawn flapping and floundering into the boat, amid a shout of exultation from the company, who unanimously declared the fish to be a ten-pounder, and the capital prize of all that had that day been taken. All being now in readiness, the boat was rowed slowly toward the shore in the direction of a spot indicated as the place of their temporary quarters by a slight wreathy line of blue smoke, which had risen from their noon fires, and still hung undissipated along the precipitous cliffs of the mountain above. On reaching the shore the party, after taking out their fish and carefully concealing their canoe in a thick clump of overhanging bushes, proceeded to their retreat, which proved to be a cavern in the rocks at the foot of the mountain, here shutting down within a dozen rods of the lake. The front of this cave consisted of a sort of natural porch eight or ten feet in length, and of, perhaps, about half that number of feet in width, formed by a projection of the rocks above and on each side, so as to inclose the intervening space. From the center of the area thus formed in front, an entrance, wide enough only to admit one person at a time, opened into the interior, or main part of the cavern, a spacious and lofty room branching off in several dark recesses that appeared to extend far into the rocks. This cave had once been a favorite lodge with the Indians, as was evident from the flint arrow-heads and other indications of aboriginal life discovered in and about the place; and in late years it had been the usual resort of professional hunters, and others of the neighboring settlement, when out for more than one day on fishing and hunting excursions on the lake or its vicinity, as it afforded them comfortable quarters for the night, and such as could easily be secured from the intrusion of wild beasts or Indians, small parties of whom, though not generally very hostile at this period, were still occasionally seen skulking among these mountains. The party now present, as before remarked, were four in number. The two eldest of these had nothing remarkable in their appearance to distinguish them from the ordinary run of men except their broad chests and strong muscular limbs, which they possessed in common with most of the settlers. Of the other two, whom we will more particularly describe, one was a young woodsman of very singular and striking appearance. He was full seven feet high and as straight as an arrow. From his trunk, which, though strongly made and quite as large as that of a common stout man, looked like a May-pole, rose a long, slender neck, surmounted by a small, apple-shaped head. His features might have been regular when he slept, but in conversation, in which he was always sure to have a part, they were made to play such antics, by way of acting as gestures to the queer conceits with which his brain was forever teeming, that it would have been difficult to tell what any one of them might have been when reduced to a state of quiescence. His mouth, with a peculiar twist, seemed to move at will in a half circle from one ear to the other; while his nose, playing at cross purposes with his mouth, was seemingly wriggled up to the eyebrows or let down to the chin at the option of its owner. These, with the eyes, which were no less singularly expressive, combined to form a countenance to the last degree comical, though, with all its predominating humor, great good nature and considerable native intelligence were very visibly mingled in its expression. This man went by the name of Pete Jones, or Long-legged Pete, as was his more common appellation among his companions. The other person, the only one of the party now remaining to be described, was evidently far superior in every respect, except physical powers, to the rest of the company. His exterior exhibited a high degree of manly beauty, both in form and feature, while a fine dark eye, with a cleanly turned, rectilinear nose and a high square forehead, indicated tastes of an intellectual character. His countenance was expressive of keen perceptions, and manifested also, like that of the person last described, a strong disposition to wit and mirthfulness; though his disposition, unlike that of his rude companion, had been evidently chastened and trained by education and intercourse with refined society, the advantages of both of which his language and manners showed he had received. His whole appearance, indeed, was such as would induce to the probable conclusion that a romantic turn of mind, with a love of the exciting scenes of the forests or still more exciting strife in which the settlers were engaged with the neighboring colony, had led him to a temporary adoption of his present course of life, and that he was rather an amateur woodsman than one from habit or necessity.

When the party reached their quarters, the person whose description last occupied us separated himself from the rest, and, clambering up the steep, sat down on a commanding cliff some hundred feet from the cave, leaving the duties of the camp to be performed by those who remained below. The latter, after kindling up a fire in front of the cave, proceeded to bring from the interior a light portable kettle and a piece of salt junk, articles with which such parties usually went provided, and soon became busily engaged in dressing and preparing a portion of the fruits of their day's labors for an evening repast.

"Smith," said the tall woodsman whose peculiarities we have before noted, now turning to one of his comrades, as they were proceeding with their culinary labors; "say, Smith, what do you suppose Mr. Selden has perched himself on that old crazy crag up there for? He looks as glum and hazy as a cat-owl winking at the sun with one eye and watching a tree toad with the other."

"Well done for you, Pete Jones!" responded the person addressed; "I rather guess you have hit the nail on the head this time; for Selden, I've noticed, is fond of looking at prospects—scenery, I think he calls it. Well, while he has an eye for that, it's my opinion he is on the lookout for mischief which he thinks may perhaps be brewing for us somewhere. What say you, Brown?"

"Well, I don't know," replied the latter, a plain, blunt, and somewhat dogged-looking man; "there may be something in your idee—and come to think of it, I guess it is so. You know we caught a glimpse or two of a fellow skulking round the shore over yonder last evening, as we were coming across to take up our quarters here; and I remember that Selden seemed to watch his movements as if he had some suspicions that the fellow might be a spy upon us."

"That's it," rejoined Smith; "and if Selden named the affair to the captain when he joined us last night, as I'll warrant you he did, seeing they had considerable private talk together, most likely he got orders to keep a spare eye for breakers to-day. I have noticed several times this afternoon that he seemed to be looking round the lake rather anxiously; and it was that which set me to thinking."

"By the way," interposed Jones; "what in the world can have got the captain that he ain't in by this time? Not a single loud word has his rifle spoken to-day, to my hearing."

"He has doubtless taken a wide range to-day," replied Smith, who assumed to be the best guesser of the trio; "but an eye as keen and an aim as sure as the young captain's never need be exercised a whole day for nothing on these mountains. He don't come home empty to-night, you'll find."

"I wish he would come, however," observed Brown; "I am anxious to know what are to be the orders for to-morrow. I hope he won't make us wait here another day for more to join us before we proceed on the business we came for. We have now been nearly three days, coming and here, without a chance of setting our seals to the back of a single Yorker. I wouldn't have volunteered and left my work at this busy season but for Captain Warrington's promise to let us have right at 'em, and be off again. And I wouldn't at no rate, if he had not fought so like a young lion for me at the time these land sharks turned us, wife, little ones, and all, out into the snow. He did me God's service at that time; so I thought I ought to oblige him by coming. Though, be sure, I was obliging my own feelings about as much; for, so help me Heaven! I would go fourteen miles barefoot in January for a chance to pay off scores upon those same York gentry."

"So would I," remarked Smith, "for what was your case may soon be mine, unless we all turn out and drive the scoundrels from the Grants every time they put foot within them. So we must not grudge a little time spent in paying off our debts in this manner, seeing we shall be doing the public a service at the same time. Only think of Warrington! He has spent more than half his time in this way for the last three years, and all he has ever got by it has been to have a price set upon his head."

"They have set a price upon my head, too," gloomily resumed the other;* "but as for the captain, he will

* The persons outlawed by the New York Assembly, for the apprehension of whom a reward of fifty pounds for each was offered, were Ethan Allen, Seth Warner, Remember Baker, Rob't Cochron, P. Sunderland, S. Brown, J. Smith and J. Brackenridge.

have his reward in heaven; while they have made me so savage and murderous in my feelings that I begin to fear that heaven will be no place for me."

"Well, I owe the scamps nothing in particular myself, I believe," observed Jones; "but not knowing how soon I might, seeing as how I had lately bought a new lot down there near Old Ti, I thought I might as well join you a spell to learn the way and manner of fixing the chaps. And I calculated if anybody could show me 'twas Captain Charley, who, they say, is a trifle braver than Julius Cæsar, besides having a heart as big as a meeting-house."

"What would you say of Ethan Allen at that rate?" asked Smith, laughing.

"Ethan Allen? Lordy! why, two Alexanders, with half a dozen Turks thrown in to stiffen the upper lip, would be used up in making the priming to Ethan Allen! But hoo! what in the devil's name has come among us now?" continued the speaker, pointing to a new figure that had arrived unperceived, and noiselessly taken a station within a few yards of the company.

All eyes were now turned to the spot indicated by the words and odd gesticulations of their companion. There stood a young Indian, quietly looking at the company, or rather, after a peculiarity of his race, looking at everything else but the company the moment they turned and confronted him. He held a rifle in his hand, while his dress differed but little from the ordinary garb of the settlers.

"Umph!" he at length exclaimed in the peculiar, jerking guttural of the native Indian: "Massa Cappen —him no here!"

"Guessed exactly right, Tawney!" cried Jones, awakening from the momentary surprise into which he, as well as his companions, had been thrown by the unexpected appearance of such a visitor; "but what do you want with the captain, my beauty?"

"Umph! you ask; when me tell, then you know," quickly replied the Indian, with the apparent object both to evade the question and retort on the interrogator for the manner in which it was put.

"Right again," exclaimed Smith, pleased at the rebuff thus received by the professed joker of the party; "here, Jones, let me manage him. Where did you leave your company, friend?" he continued, addressing the native coaxingly. "I conclude there are more of your people somewhere hereabouts?"

"Umph!" answered the native with a sarcastic smile; "Now you fraid—scare—why you no run?"

"Righter than ever!" shouted Jones, laughing heartily in turn at his baffled comrade, who had fared even worse than himself in the re-encounter.

Other methods were then taken to draw from the Indian his name and business, but without the least success. He either stood mute, or answered with such odd evasions, that they soon gave over the attempt and called to Selden on the hill, intimating that his presence was needed below. That person, who proved to be second in command of the expedition, as if partly apprized of what was going on, immediately came down and appeared among them.

"Leftenant Selden," said Jones, "they say you can make poetry out of rocks and trees, if you are a mind to—now we want to see what you can make out of this fellow."

"He is very evidently a domesticated Indian," seriously replied the person addressed, who appeared just then in no humor to relish the jokes of the other. "He probably resides with some family in the vicinity. I think I have heard Warrington speak of meeting one of his description in a hunting adventure in this quarter."

"Well, he inquired for the captain," observed Smith.

"Then he has some business with him, I presume," rejoined Selden; "some friendly message, perhaps."

"Umph! that man say it," said the subject of their discourse, pointing to the former with an expressive and respectful look.

"We will try then to hasten the captain's return," observed Selden, and taking from his pocket a sort of whistle, formed from the leg-bone of a deer, he blew a blast whose loud, shrill note was capable of being heard at a great distance.

A strict silence of several moments was now observed by the whole party in listening for a reply from their leader, who, it was understood, carried about him a corresponding instrument. At length, instead of a reply from a whistle, the sharp report of a rifle burst from a neighboring glen and, echoing wildly from cliff to cliff in the surrounding stillness, died slowly away on the distant mountains.

"There he is!" "There goes the captain's rifle! I should know her voice among a thousand," simultaneously burst from the lips of several of the company.

"Just as I told you," said Smith; "I knew he would never return empty. That shot, mark me, brought down a deer, which he had in his eye when the leftenant whistled, and prevented his answering the call, which no small game would."

The event soon proved the truth of the last speaker's conjecture. The heavy, slow tread, as of one carrying some weighty load, now became distinguishable at a distance in the woods, the sounds falling more and more distinctly on the ear every moment as they approached the spot where the expectant and excited party stood, eagerly straining their eyes to catch the first glimpse of their huntsman leader. At length he emerged from the bushes, bearing a noble buck upon his shoulders. Advancing amid the congratulations of his fellows he came up to the spot, and, with the air of one relieved from a heavy burden, threw down his prize to the ground before them. Of the probable age of twenty-six or eight he was a man of a very fine and even majestic appearance. Though tall and muscular, so compactly and finely set were his limbs that his contour presented nothing to the eye in the least disproportioned or ungainly. His features seemed to correspond in regularity of formation to the rest of his person, while his countenance was rather of the cool and deliberate cast, indicative, however, of a mild, benevolent disposition as well as a sound, reflecting intellect. Every development, indeed, whether of his shapely head or manly countenance, went to show a strong, well-balanced character, and one capable of action beyond the scope of ordinary men. His dress, which was that of a huntsman, was neat—not rich—but tastefully arranged and well fitted. A mahogany-stocked rifle, richly chased with silver, with small arms partially concealed in his dress, completed his equipments.

"Heaven save me from another such jaunt," were his first words after he had thrown down his load and recovered himself a little; "a noble buck, indeed, but the chase has been rather a dear one."

"I don't see how it could well have been otherwise, captain," observed Selden, now evidently in high spirits and disposed for a little merriment:

"Your huntsmen, whenever a deer's in the race,
Like your lovers, of course, must expect a *dear* chase."

"Mine has been somewhat dearer, however, I think," replied the former with an appreciating smile, "than was necessary to give zest to those savory trout, which, by the way, I am right glad to see so nearly ready for the partaking."

"Yes," rejoined the other, glancing around at the Indian, who stood demure and silent in the background, with his face partly averted from the company, "and yet I know not, really, Captain Warrington, but you may have other fish to fry first."

"And just about the oddest fish, too, that we have caught to-day, captain," said Jones, instantly understanding the allusion of the last speaker; "I rather think he must be a sort of shellfish, from the difficulty we found in getting his mouth open."

"Oh, ho!" exclaimed Warrington, his eye now for the first time resting on the form of the Indian and his countenance clearing up from the puzzled expression that had come over it for the instant at the enigmatical words of his friends; "a new recruit! That explains your call, the wherefore I was about to ask. A new recruit of doubtful credentials, eh?"

So saying, he advanced to the side of the Indian youth and attentively examined his features; while the object of scrutiny stood perfectly immovable and apparently unconscious of the examination he was undergoing till, perceiving by the hesitation of the other that he was not likely to be recognized, he, without looking up or varying the expression of a single muscle of his face, quietly observed:

"Massa Cappen no remember Neshobee—no remember shoot three wolf?"

"Aha?" said the other, recalled by the last allusion; "the same poor fellow that I so providentially came across and relieved from that savage pack of wolves last year on these very mountains? You may well remember that escape, my friend. But it is strange I did not know you."

"Neshobee hunt all day," resumed the Indian, intent on rehearsing the event, the remembrance of which seemed to light up his countenance to something like the indications of feeling and incline him to unusual loquacity; "hunt, hunt—kill no deer—dark come fast. Now hear wolf 'way out there, howl! howl! Now 'way out here, howl! howl! Now um come together, howl!

howl! Now near off, howl! howl! Now me know what um want, and climb small tree quick. Wolf come, five, six, hungry, and lap um mouth. Me shoot; kill one, and go to load um up again—so no think nothing, and drop um rifle low down—wolf jump high, catch um away—now rifle all gone—no get um—wolf get mad fast—bite um tree, gnaw, gnaw, wolf no do so 'fore. Now tree begin shake, shake, to fall soon. Now bend, bend, slow 'long down—wolf jump, jump, snap um white teeth, and 'most jest catch um Neshobee. Now hoo! bang! one wolf kick over dead—Cappen out there in the bush. Shoot again, two dead! Shoot again, three dead! Now the rest two wolf begin to mistrust to run away afore they dead too. Now Neshobee come down—stay all night in cave with um Cappen—him very good, no forget um."

"Very nearly correct, I believe, Neshobee," observed Warrington as the Indian closed his recital, the longest, perhaps, he ever made in his life, for, unluckily it may be for the romance of our tale, Neshobee was no Logan or Red Jacket, either in length of speech or that peculiar eloquence which most of our writers seem to delight in attributing to the sons of the forest; "very nearly correct; but are you out on another hunt in this quarter, or does other business bring you here at this time?"

"No much hunt, me come for."

"What then?"

"Missus Story talk um on papar for Cappen better nor Neshobee say," replied the Indian, handing Warrington a small dingy scrap of paper.

The latter, after running hastily over the contents of the billet, which caused his eye to kindle with enthusiasm as he read, immediately turned to the company and, with a cheerful, animated air, observed, "It is from our friend, Widow Story, of the Creek down here, and contains news of interest, my boys. Shall I read it to you?"

"Aye, aye, captain," was the eager response.

"Listen then."

"CAPT. W.: I tear out the blank leaf of my Bible to say, *'the Philistines be upon thee, Samson.'* They came over the Creek somewhere north of here, and, after a short consultation near the edge of my clearing, from which I luckily espied them, struck off toward the lake. Munroe, as usual, heads the party, ten in number, as I counted. There are five of you, at least; and that is enough, if you are of the stuff I think you, to attend to confirming our titles in this neighborhood. My messenger is a chance one, but true and friendly, and may be enlisted, I think, for the night's work, if needed.

"God speed you all,

"ANN STORY."

The spirited epistle was received by the company with a loud "Hurrah for the widow!" and, notwithstanding it brought them the startling intelligence that the sheriff of Albany county, with an armed force of twice their own number, was on the march to seize them, two of whom, at least, were known to be under sentence of outlawry for former resistance to the New York authorities while attempting to execute their cruel mandates on the persons or property of the settlers—notwithstanding this, the news was received with the liveliest expressions of joy and enthusiasm. An escape from their pursuers into the forest or on to the water in their canoe, which was the only one in the lake, they well knew might easily be effected. But this was no part of the plan of this resolute little band of Green Mountain Boys; nor was the possibility of their being overpowered and taken deemed by them scarce more worthy of consideration. Their object was the punishment of their foes, for the accomplishment of which this was hailed by them all as a golden opportunity. From the unwonted boldness with which this noted troubler of the Grants was attempting to push so far into the interior with so small a number of men, all of whom were supposed to be unacquainted with the forest in this part of the country, it was rightly conjectured that he must have been apprized by some traitorous settler, not only of the exact situation of the present rendezvous but also of the number of those occupying it; and for similar reasons it was concluded that this person must now be with the approaching enemy, acting as guide in conducting them to the spot, where they doubtless anticipated taking their intended victims by complete surprise, and then hurrying them by night over the country to the British fort at Ticonderoga before the settlers could be rallied for a rescue. In this opinion our band were confirmed by the suspicious appearance of a man who, as we intimated, had been seen the evening before lurking around the shores of the lake, and who, it was now scarcely longer to be doubted, was a spy, dogging them to such place as they might select for their encampment. Next to the sheriff, therefore, and even before him, was this person—whose offense was considered the most heinous of the two—particularly marked for punishment; and it was determined to identify and seize him, if possible, and, whoever he might prove, make him an example to all future traitors. To retain their stronghold, the cavern, however defensible it might be, was no object with our party, as their leader had already determined to leave it the following morning to proceed on the main purpose of their excursion, which was to break up an establishment of their opponents, who had obtained a strong foothold at the lower falls of Otter Creek, and to seize a York surveyor locating lands in that vicinity—from which purpose they had only turned aside for a day or two to give others an opportunity to join them on the lake, the appointed rendezvous, and a pleasant spot for employing the interim in fishing and hunting. Accordingly it was soon concluded to make no regular defense of the cave, but, using it only so far as might best favor them in their object of discomfiting the enemy, the modes of doing which were yet to be devised, leave it to their possession, and quit the place that night. Their game and such movables as were not immediately wanted were therefore now transferred to the boat, which was removed to a secret landing, where the party were ordered to repair at the signal-call of the whistle. These brief arrangements having been completed, and the young Indian, who seemed to enter with great spirit into the enterprise, being employed to stand on the lookout, the company, with their loaded rifles by their side, sat down to their sylvan meal, over which they discussed in gleeful mood the various and ingenious methods which were successively proposed for the reception and chastisement of their assailants, who were expected to make their appearance as soon as it was fairly dark.

CHAPTER II

> "Thus, spite of prayers, her schemes pursuing,
> She went on still to work our ruin;
> Annul'd our charters of releases,
> And tore our title-deeds to pieces;
> Then signed her warrants of ejection,
> And gallows raised to stretch our necks on;
> And straightway sent, like dogs to bait us,
> MUNROE, with *posse comitatus*."

LEAVING our little band of Green Mountain Boys to discuss and settle the manner of receiving their expected visitors, and to make their dispositions for carrying such plan as should be finally adopted into effect, we will now change the scene a little, and, introducing the reader to those visitors themselves, accompany him and them to the scene of action.

In a thickly wooded swamp, near the northern extremity of the lake before described, were assembled a group of ten men awaiting the approach of darkness, which was already beginning to settle in successive and fast increasing shades upon the low lands and glens along the foot of the mountain. They were all armed, though variously—some having muskets, some large pistols, and some only oaken cudgels. Apart from the rest stood their leader, a stern, rough-looking personage, engaged in a low, earnest conversation with another individual, of the apparent age of twenty-five, whose dress and general demeanor seemed to forbid the conclusion that he was either a common follower or one in any command; and yet, from the interest he manifested in the business in hand, it was evident he was in some way connected with the expedition. As the last named person may occupy considerable space in our tale we will pause to note his personal appearance more particularly. He was of about the middle height, well made, though of rather slight proportions. His features, though regular, were commonplace and inexpressive, with the exception of a pair of small, twinkling black eyes, in which an observant spectator might often read meaning considerably at variance with the import of his language, his plausible manners, and the obsequious, smirking smile which he usually assumed while addressing those with whom he had a point to carry. The construction of his head seemed to be somewhat peculiar—his forehead, which was very tall, being nearly in the shape of a triangle, with the base resting on the eyebrows and the sides narrowing to an apex at the hair above; while his head, as far back as the ears, swelling upward into large protuberances, might be better represented by a triangle reversed. His dress was a finer texture than that of any of his present associates, or that ordinarily worn by the settlers, and his whole appearance, indeed, denoted some connection with the more wealthy and fashionable classes of society.

"You say, Sherwood," observed the former of the two last-mentioned persons, at that part of their dialogue which it concerns us to repeat, "you say that, from having been yourself at this cave, you know all the surrounding localities?"

"Exactly—just as I described to you when I reached you last night. There can be no mistaking the place. They are still there, as is evident from the smoke which we saw rising over the spot just now, while passing the head of the lake. The path is now plain, and the game sure, without further guidance; so I think, as I began to suggest to your honor a few minutes ago, that you may now dispense with my further attendance. If I should be seen by any of their party I should be delicately situated here in the settlement."

"To the devil with your delicacy! Why, man, do you think I am going on in the dark, stumbling over logs and through bogs, without a guide? Even you are none too good a one for this cursed hole; but such as you are, in the king's name I retain you; so not another word about quitting us till the scoundrels are secured."

"I am certainly aware, Mr. Munroe, of the importance of securing this Warrington, so great a disturber of the public peace, but——"

"Disturber! doubly d——d rebel! Why, no man in the settlement has caused me so much trouble, considering his audacious assault on me, and all. It will do me more good to see him hung than to sit at the king's banquet."

"Oh, certainly—it would me; and I would by all means aid you even to the capture, if your honor's well-known sagacity and bravery on such occasions did not render my assistance wholly unnecessary."

"Well, well, Jake," replied the sheriff, relaxing a little from his wonted roughness at the flattering expressions of the other, "suppose I am all that you say, it won't serve me in finding a fox's hole in these woods any better than the instinct of any country booby, nor half so well. I tell you, Sherwood, you must conduct us to the place, at least; for we shall then have enough to do to take the fellow, and, what is worse, to get him through the settlement to Ticonderoga. Why, there is not an old woman in all the Grants but will fight for the scoundrel as if he was one of her own brats."

"Oh, there can be no great trouble, the surprise will be so great; but, as your honor desires it, I will go so far as to point out the place, on condition that I then be allowed to keep out of sight."

"Yes; but your half of the reward for taking the fellows, for you say that there is at least one outlaw besides Warrington; you won't claim all that unless you help us through the whole affair, will you?"

"Your honor forgets that I was only to conduct you so far as to point out their retreat."

"Have it your own way, then—but I hate to see a fellow so keen on the chase, and then become so devilish prudent the moment he approaches the game," grumbled Munroe, turning away to give some orders to his men, preparatory to resuming their march.

It having now become sufficiently dark for their purpose, the party were put in motion for the prosecution of their enterprise. And, after striking a light and procuring some materials for torches from the pine knots gathered in the surrounding windfalls, they set forward toward the place of their destination, then about a mile distant. Keeping as far from the shore of the lake as the nature of the ground would permit, lest the gleams of their light, striking across the water to the vicinity of the cave, should betray their approach, they pursued their way along the foot of the mountain with all possible silence and caution; while the glare of their torches, glittering on the points of the crags and thrown back on to the dark forms and eager and flushed visages of the party gliding stealthily along in Indian file beneath the overhanging cliffs, like tigers for their prey, gave them a singularly wild and most unearthly appearance. At length they arrived at the sharp knoll, which, running down from the main ridge above to the water, had so far screened their approach and enabled them to advance with their lights unseen within a few hundred yards of the cavern. Here they made a brief halt to arrange their forces for the onset. As soon as this was effected Munroe and Sherwood crept noiselessly over the intervening rise, followed at short intervals by the rest of the party, with the exception of one man left behind in charge of the torches. Having descended to the level beyond, they again paused to listen and reconnoiter before venturing any farther. All was dark and silent before them. And, concluding that their intended victims had retired within the cave and were probably by this time reposing in unsuspecting slumbers, they now congratulated themselves on a certain and easy conquest, and with freshened impulse once more began to move briskly forward, when the loud *whoo! whoo!—whoo! whoo!* of the "dismal bird of night," or of something strikingly resembling it in note, proceeding from some point above, came pealing through the darkness with fearful distinctness to the ears of the company. All gave an involuntary start. Even the stout-hearted Munroe, for the instant, could scarcely avoid quaking at the strangely dismal notes that thus broke from utter stillness so unexpectedly upon them. The next moment, however, as the consciousness of the insignificant cause of their affright came over them, a half-stifled giggling ran through the company; while their leader uttering a dry "Umph! scared at a d——d owl!" motioned Sherwood to proceed. But the latter, more accustomed to the notes of the supposed animal, and thinking he detected something not quite natural in the sounds they had just heard, became secretly impressed with the fears of an ambush, and, without imparting his suspicions, he hastily pointed out to the sheriff the mouth of the cave, whose dim outlines had now become discernible, and instantly returning to the rear quickly retreated over the hill. With a few muttered expressions of contempt at the flight of the wary and timid guide, Munroe once more set forward with the determined motions of one who is resolved not again to be interrupted by any slight causes. And being now promptly followed by his men, he soon, and without further obstacle, arrived at the mouth of the cave, and, bringing up his forces, immediately surrounded it. Here they all paused, standing motionless and silent, listening long and intensely. Everything within and around was as still as if no living being was within a mile of the place.

"Hallo!" at length sharply uttered the sheriff, after waiting till he began to doubt whether his anticipated captives had escaped, or were all snugly asleep in the cave, "hallo! within there!"

"Hallo, without there!" was the ready reply from the cavern.

"Ha! ye rebel dogs!" exultingly exclaimed Munroe; "you are there, are ye? We have kenneled ye at last, then. Now hear me—I command ye to surrender yourselves to the king's warrant, every scoundrel of ye; but first of all, Charles Warrington. Do you hear the summons?"

"We hear the summons, and well comprehend its import," coolly replied the voice from the cave, which was evidently that of the person especially named by the sheriff; "but touching your last demand, mine ancient friend—for in your voice I think I recognize the person with whom I once exchanged civilities in the southern part of our favored settlement—touching your last demand, I beg leave to observe, that being somewhat personally interested myself in the decision to be made in regard to the requirement, I would respectfully refer you to my friends here, who will doubtless give you such answer as their unbiased judgments shall dictate."

"Do you think to dally with me, scoundrel?" stormed Munroe, nettled at the provoking coolness of his antagonist, and especially at his ironical allusion to a personal chastisement received from his hands the year before; "such attempts will but little avail, you'll find. Nor will it be of the least use, let me tell you all, to think of contending against our numbers: and the longer you hold out the worse it shall be for ye. So yield yourselves instantly, or, so help me Beelzebub, every dog of you shall swing for it."

"Assertions," observed Selden, who, being Warrington's only companion in the cave, now took up the discourse on the hint of his superior; "assertions, sir sheriff, sometimes, unfortunately, are more easily made than proved. You may not find us, perhaps, so entirely unprepared for your visit as you have expected, notwithstanding our warder thought fit, in his owl-like wisdom, to be somewhat tardy in announcing your approach. It may not be prudent in us, however, to speak wholly without reserve in this matter, as we know not how much aid your honor may expect from the friend you last invoked."

The intimations which they gathered from these replies, together with the jeering calmness attending them, which seemed to imply a sense of security in the assailed from resources unknown to the assailants, considerably dampened the ardor of the sheriff and his band; and they began to suspect that their triumphs might not prove so cheaply won as they had anticipated. The men, indeed, now began to show symptoms of fear and uneasiness at standing longer before the mouth of the cave, from which, for aught they could see or know, a dozen loaded rifles might be pointed against them; and their leader shouted loudly to the man left in the rear, directing him to come on with lights, and declaring at the same time, with a tremendous oath, that if the stubborn rascals didn't instantly yield he would send a volley of balls in among them, and if that failed, he would smoke them out like so many burrowed foxes. He was not allowed, however, much time to attempt the fulfillment of his menaces; for the Green Mountain Boys, two of whom only, as before mentioned, were in the cave, the rest being stationed in the nearest surrounding coverts, now deemed it time to begin their plan of operations. Suddenly a fearful screech, something between that of a man and a wild brute, issuing from the thicket above the cave, resounded through the forest, sending its startling thrill to the very hearts of the appalled and astonished assailants. All eyes were involuntarily turned upward to the spot from which these terrific sounds seemed to proceed.

"A catamount! a catamount!" wildly shouted several of the party.

"Where? where?" eagerly exclaimed others.

"There! up there in the fork of that tree!" hurriedly replied the former, pointing to the top of a leaning tree that projected nearly over the mouth of the cave, in a broad fork of which the outlines of a dark body, as if some large animal crouching for a leap upon his prey, with great fiery eyeballs glaring down upon them, was sufficiently discernible to justify their alarm.

"He moves!" cried one, "hark! hear him fixing his claws in the bark! There, he stirs again! look out! he's going to leap down upon us—fire quick, all hands, fire!"

"Hold, hold!" shouted Munroe, the suspicion of a trick now for the first time flashing across his mind. But the command came too late; for while the words were in his mouth, every gun and pistol in the party except his own was discharged at the object of their terror, which was seen in the expiring flash to bound out from the tree directly over the place where they stood; and all, in their eagerness to avoid the clutches of the leaping animal, well known to be terrible when wounded, even if in the last agonies of death, broke away and fled in confusion from the spot, wholly unmindful of their duty in guarding the mouth of the cave, and everything else but their own safety, in the general panic that had seized them. A momentary pause followed the explosion of the firearms, in which nothing was heard save the hasty scrambling of the terrified Yorkers in their eager efforts to escape. In an instant, however, a rushing from other quarters was heard—dark forms were seen swiftly gliding from the cave and the thickets above, in the direction of the retreating party, among whom in a moment more a cry of dismay rose wildly on the air. Munroe and three of his men were suddenly seized round their waists or legs from behind by the iron grasp of grappling arms, and, being lifted from the ground, were upborne with resistless force and rapidity toward the shore of the lake; all of them but their leader verily believing, in the fright and confusion of the moment, that it was the catamount, whose fearful image was still uppermost in their minds, that had seized them and was bearing them off in his grasp.

"Help! help! here! He has got me! for God's sake help me!" screamed one in an agony of terror.

"Murder!" exclaimed another; "oh! get him off—get him off! murder! murder!"

"Oh! aw!" cried the third, in a yell of despair; "he has got his claws in my throat—he'll kill me—he will! he will! yah! yah!"

Munroe alone of all the thus oddly captured party was mute. Rightly judging the character of the foe into whose hands he had fallen, and boiling with silent rage, he made the most desperate struggles to free himself from the vise-like grasp of his captor, who, he at once concluded from his great strength—the effects of which he had before experienced—could be no other than Warrington. But wholly failing in this attempt, and finding himself still carried rapidly onward,—he knew not to what destination,—he next tried to disengage his dirk from its sheath, in which it was confined beneath the grappling arm of his opponent. Before succeeding in this, however, and while intent only on his murderous design, he was borne by his intended victim to the margin of the water, and, with a giant effort, hurled headlong over the bank. The loud splashing that succeeded told that he was now struggling in the embrace of a different, though not a much more comfortable, antagonist; while three more heavy plunges, following in irregular succession along the bank, still further announced that the vanquished sheriff was not without the company of a good share of his friends to console him in the discomforts of the new element into which they all had been so suddenly and unexpectedly translated. The shrill notes of Warrington's signal whistle now sounded the preconcerted retreat. In a moment more the victorious party were assembled at the appointed landing; in another they were embarked; while their boat, by the strong push of the last man springing in, was sent by the single impulse so far into the lake as to put a safe distance between them and their foes, now beginning to rally with cries of rage on the shore. An uncontrollable peal of laughter, ending in three loud and lively cheers, now burst from the Green Mountain Boys, rending the welkin above, and startling the deep recesses of the surrounding forests with the triumphant shout.

"The battle being over," observed Warrington, after the noise of their merriment and exultation had measurably subsided; "let us now turn our attention to the wounded and missing."

"All whole of skin, I imagine," said Selden; "though here is one—Smith, I believe it is—who comes from the fight, as near as I can discover, like the Benjamite of the Scripture, just escaped from the Philistines, with head bare and garments rent."

"I must leave my old otter-skin cap in their hands, I s'pose," coolly replied Smith; "I had to take it to finish off the catamount's head with; for I couldn't fix the fox-fire for the eyes into the end of that bundle of dry grass that I made the body of, so as to look anyhow natural without it, and when I pushed the thing out of the crotch, as I stood behind the tree with my pole, I gave it such a hoist over into the bushes among the scared devils that 'twas out of the question to think of looking for the cap and grabbing one of the scamps too. But as to my coat being tore here a little, I don't valley it a fraction, seeing as how the ragamuffin I hove into the lake got pretty well choked to pay for it."

"Ah, you have done well, Smith," said the leader; "all of you, indeed, have done nobly; but of that hereafter. One of our number I believe is missing—which is it?"

"It is Pete Jones," replied Brown.

"And the Indian chap," added Smith.

"The Indian," resumed Warrington, "after announcing the enemy for us by his admirable imitation of the owl, departed by himself, I presume. As near as I could gather from him, he did not wish to be known as acting against the Yorkers. He probably lives with some family in the vicinity, who are trying to stand neutral in this warfare, and who have cautioned him to govern himself accordingly. His absence, therefore, does not surprise me. But what can have become of Jones? He surely is not a fellow to be easily ensnared or overpowered."

"I rather suspect," replied Brown, "he is after that traitor. As, when the Yorkers were creeping on toward the cave, he whispered to me he thought he saw a fellow pointing out the place and slipping back over the hill, who, he guessed, was the one—and the last I saw of Pete he was working off that way. Suppose, captain, that we row along, so as to stand off the shore, in that direction, to be ready to take him in should he give the word?"

In pursuance of this prudent suggestion the boat was immediately headed round to the north, and rowed noiselessly along the shore in the direction supposed to be taken by their missing companion. They had made but little progress, however, before they were startled by the sudden flash and sharp report of a pistol in a thicket near the shore about a furlong ahead.

"There goes trouble for poor Jones, I fear—the dastard has attempted his life!" cried Warrington, in the varying tones of fear for the result and indignation for the attempt; "but if help be of any further use to him, he shall have it. So, men, pull for it! pull for the spot with every nerve you have got, or the Yorkers will be there before us."

In an instant the canoe, almost leaping from its element at every stroke of the excited and strong-armed oarsmen, was surging through the water with bird-like velocity toward the place. As Warrington had predicted, the enemy on shore, on hearing the report of the pistol, immediately started for this new scene of action. And, quickly perceiving their opponents on the lake making rapidly for the spot, they redoubled their speed and rushed on as fast as the obstacles of the woods and the wet clothes and benumbed limbs of those who had been ducked would permit, to arrive in time to assist or rescue, as the case might require, their absent guide, whom they readily concluded to be an actor in the fracas, and revenge themselves, if possible, on the whole band of their foes for the sad discomfiture just experienced. The race between the two contending parties was a close one. The Green Mountain Boys, however, were again in fortune. Their boat came whirling up to the shore adjoining the scene of action while the foremost of the enemy was yet fifty yards distant.

"You may kick till all is blue," muttered Jones, whose tall form came at that instant peering from the thicket, while with irregular motions he made toward the boat, bearing bolt upright in his arms before him his grappled foe, who was struggling with terrible violence and kicking desperately against every tree within reach of his feet, with the hope of retarding the progress of his captor till succor arrived; "you may kick, and be hanged! but you have jest got to go, my sweet lad, and into a little better company, too, than you hoped for, I guess. No help for it—so in with you—there! now make yourself comfortable, friend," concluded the woodsman, pitching his captive headlong into the boat, and leaping in himself just in time to escape the pursuers, now close at his heels.

"Escaped again, by the pains of Tophet!" exclaimed the enraged Munroe from the bank, as the boat, previously headed round, shot out into the lake beyond the reach of the twice baffled Yorkers. "Fire! fire upon the d——d rascals!"

The command was scarcely uttered before Jones, having as quick as thought again grappled his captive and faced round toward the shore, was holding the deprecating victim before him in the stern, so as to cover the range of the expected volley.

"Let drive there!" exclaimed Pete, with the utmost nonchalance, "you needn't feel any delicacy, gentlemen, for I'll agree to take all the bullets you'll send through this beautiful target I'm holding for you."

"Don't fire! for God's sake don't let 'em fire, Munroe!" screamed the struggling and terrified prisoner.

"You need not be much alarmed, I think, fellow," said Warrington; "the sheriff's pistols must be rather too wet to be very dangerous, and as to the arms of the rest, which were all discharged at the catamount, we shall have but little to fear from them by the time they can be loaded."

"I mistrusted as much myself," observed Jones, releasing the prisoner; "but I thought I would scare the fellow a little, for his scurvy treatment to me."

"The pistol we heard, then, was meant, as we suspected, for you?" asked the leader.

"Oh, yes," replied the other carelessly; "to be sure he showed the best good will in the world to make a hole in me; but I shouldn't have laid that up much, seeing he missed his aim,—which is a sort of punishment in itself, you know,—if he hadn't afterward offered me money to let him go and keep his name and all close. Why, I never was so insulted in my life!"

"His name? who is it? what is his name?" eagerly asked several of the company.

"Mayhap you from down south never heard of him, and don't know him, but I did, the moment I saw his face as he passed the fellow bringing the torchlight. His name is Sherwood, living down in New Haven, and he is jest one of the smoothest fellows that ever wore two faces in a day, asking his pardon."

"Sherwood—Sherwood," said Warrington musingly. "Aha! I now remember to have heard of his having been at Bennington, and also of his having made some suspicious visits to Albany. But we will examine his merits more particularly when we reach the opposite shore."

"See how wishful those fellows are looking after us!" observed Jones, pointing back to the shore, now about fifty rods distant, where the Yorkers, having procured a light, were still standing in a dark group evidently trying to trace the course of the receding boat; "I swan! if I was only bloody minded enough, how I would like to take a shot into that flock of York buzzards!"

"Hold up a little, oarsmen," said the leader, "and we will give them a kinder compliment than that, before entirely parting. So good-night, Mr. Munroe," he continued, rising in the boat, and raising his loud clear voice to a pitch which in the dead stillness of night might have been distinctly audible to a far greater distance; "good-night! my old friend. I hope for the pleasure of many such meetings and partings before we die. Pleasant dreams and a good-night to you!"

"Good-night, sir sheriff," added Selden, in the same strain of mock courtesy; "we humbly trust you will duly appreciate our late reception of yourself and fellows in imitation of the much lauded Oriental custom of regaling friends with the luxury of a cool bath, which, together with the honor done you of being carried, like other immortal heroes, on the shoulders of men, will make out an entertainment, we flatter ourselves, not wholly unworthy of our guests. Good-night!"

"Hallo there, sheriff!" cried Jones, determined to have a parting shot as well as the rest; "hallo, sheriff, won't you jest be kind enough to tell us by way of information, before we go, what kind of a return you calculate to make on that warrant you told us about? We should like grandly to see it when you have got it fixed. That tother poor bothered sheriff's *non comeatibus in swampo,* I guess, would be a fool to it."

CHAPTER III

"Ah, me! what perils do environ
The man that meddles with cold iron—
What plaguey mischiefs and mishaps
Do dog him still with afterclaps."

SHERWOOD, the person we introduced in the last chapter and left a prisoner in the hands of the Green Mountain Boys, a fair candidate for the honor of the Beech-seal or some other of the novel and ingenious modes of punishment, which the settlers were accustomed to inflict on their foes with equal promptitude whether they were foreign or domestic, was a resident of New Haven, in the vicinity of the lower falls of Otter Creek, then embraced within the limits of that town, but now forming the site of Vergennes, the only incorporated city of Vermont. He had here located himself, ostensively to become a permanent settler—to share the fortunes and identify himself with the interests of the New Hampshire grantees; while in fact he was a secret agent of a company of New York land-jobbers, in their pay, and himself engaged at the same time in speculating in the patents issued by the governor of the last named province. Through the influence of his father, a man of reputed wealth living near Albany, he had been taken into the employment of this company.

And they, soon finding him a person well fitted for their purposes, induced him, by opening to his avaricious mind the prospect of making a fortune out of the New Hampshire Grants, in addition to the stated salary to be allowed him, to take a secret agency and locate himself in some part of the settlement where he would most effectually subserve their interests. In pursuance of this object it had been agreed that he should first proceed to New Hampshire, and, taking out a patent from that source, should enter Vermont known only as a grantee of that province, in order that he might thus be effectually secured from the hostility of the settlers and enabled to maintain with them a free and unsuspected intercourse, which at the present juncture could alone insure him any success or safety. This had been accordingly done something more than a year previous to the events of our tale. A single lot of land had been purchased and located by him near the Otter, in the manner agreed on by the company. And so speciously had this wily agent conducted, beginning and carrying on improvements just sufficient to save appearances, while mainly pursuing the objects of his residence in the settlement, that till now he had passed wholly unsuspected of being in the York interest, except in the slight question that had been raised concerning his true character on account of his having been recognized by some settlers from the south part of the Grants, as before intimated, while on one of his secret journeys to Albany. With these remarks, which will apprize the reader with all that may at present be necessary to be known respecting the previous character and employment of this personage, we will return to the thread of our narrative.

Brightly rose the waning moon over the eastern mountains, which cast their broad, wood-fringed shadows far into the lake, while a flood of silvery light, falling on the sleeping waters and towering forest beyond, was gradually unfolding the bold and magnificent outlines of this wilderness landscape, as our victorious band of Green Mountain Boys merrily sped their way to the western shore.

"What a glorious spectacle!" exclaimed Selden, looking abroad over the scene, as the boat emerged from the dark gloomy line of the mountain shadows into the bright and cheerful tract of illumined waters that now met them on their course.

"Splendid! splendid, indeed!" responded Warrington, with equal enthusiasm; "such scenes, one would think, were enough to enamour the whole world of a sylvan life."

"And yet," observed Selden, "those city smoked exquisites, who claim all the taste and refinement of the country, are horrified at the thought of the life we here lead in the Green Mountains."

"I don't think the creturs are so much to be blamed for that," said Pete Jones; "for bringing them here I calculate would be putting them pretty nearly in the plight of frogs that are dug from the bottom of a well—always sure to shiver and die the minute they are brought to the pure air."

"If all this be so," rejoined Warrington, significantly glancing at the dress and comparatively delicate appearance of the prisoner; "I hope that such of this class as are connected with a certain city to the west of us will be less inclined to favor our settlement with their presence hereafter. Let them stick to their mode of life and its luxuries, and we will to our mountains. But I am reminded, lieutenant," he continued, turning gayly to Selden, "of the possibility of our being favored with something on this subject in a more agreeable form, if I rightly divined the nature of your employment and the theme that occupied your mind there at the fire before the cave last evening, after the rest of us had retired to our stone couches for the night. Can you oblige us with the fruits of your vigil, in the shape of a song?"

"Oh, yes, such as it is—that is, if my music will not jar upon the feelings of our friend in durance here, and you are all willing to risk the same effect on yourselves," jocosely replied the other, as he pulled from his pocket a small roll of white birch bark (the soft, smooth inner surface of which he had made, as was in those times not unfrequently the case, his papyrus in noting down his hasty effusion), and turning to the moonlight, commenced:

"In the courts of high life, and in Fashion's domain,
Where Folly is licensed by birthright to reign,
Let the gay idle throng, in their old reckless measure,
Their phantoms still follow, and christen them pleasure.

"But we, who disdain not to follow the plow,
And our livelihood gain by the sweat of the brow—
What have we here to do with the fashions of cities?
Their levees, theatrics, and opera ditties?

"What to do with the trappings around them display'd?
Their half dress, their full dress, their dress promenade—
Their turtle-soup dinners, their port and champagne,
And knick-knacks unnumbered that follow in train?

"All these we will leave, and without one regret,
To the poor pamper'd wights of that butterfly set,
And turn to *our* dainties, the fruits of our mountains,
Our wines sparkling up in their health-giving fountains.

"And wear with just pride, as forever we ought,
Our woolens and checks by our firesides wrought,
While we scout from our country those exquisite goats
Who measure their worth by the cloth of their coats."

As the clear, melodious voice of the singer, floating free and wide over the hushed waters of the lake, died away in the distance, and while the shouts of applause which greeted him at the close of his performance (intended, as was supposed, to hit off the York gentry, and the last couplet to apply to the prisoner in particular) were yet echoing around, the boat of the elated Green Mountain Boys reached its destined landing. And immediately disembarking with their prisoner, they proceeded to a rude, bark-covered shanty, built by former visitors to the lake and standing amid a group of large evergreens a few rods from the water. There, after striking a light and kindling up a cheerful fire, they promptly set about the business of deciding upon the case of the supposed traitor. For this purpose they formally resolved themselves, as was usual in such cases where a resort could not readily be had to a committee of safety, into a sort of tribunal, very nearly resembling, we suppose, a modern Lynch court, a form of dispensing justice which, if ever justifiable, was undoubtedly so in the acts of our early settlers in resisting that system of legalized plunder attempted to be enforced on them by their oppressors. And if the right of defending their homes and possessions from unwarrantable seizures be conceded them, it was certainly not only justifiable but honorable in them to resort, as they did, to such measures as they judged most effectual in shielding from arrest and threatened punishment those of their fellow settlers, who, by their patriotism in the common cause, had rendered themselves obnoxious to the arbitrary enactments of the usurping government. For soon after the settlers had begun openly to resist the authorities of New York in attempting to dispossess them, a law, more despotic perhaps than any to be found in the annals of legislation, had been enacted by the Assembly of that province requiring some six or eight of the settlers, who had been most conspicuous in the controversy, to surrender themselves on the order of the executive within seventy days, to a magistrate for imprisonment and, in case of neglect, to be adjudged convicted and without hearing or trial condemned to suffer death. And not delivering themselves up, as might well be expected, the governor issued his proclamation proscribing them as felons, and offering large rewards for their apprehension, which, while it led to many secretly laid plots and several open though fruitless attempts to seize them by the Yorkers, in concert with a few traitorous settlers, served only to endear them to an indignant and aroused people, who publicly resolved to protect at every hazard their proscribed leaders, and at the same time prepare to defend the general interest of the settlement even at the price of their lives. Of this goodly company of outlaws, embracing some of the first and most talented men of the Grants, two, as before intimated, were among the band whom we have introduced to the reader, and to whom we will now return.

Pete Jones, the principal witness in the case now to be decided, being called on for his testimony, related at large and in his own vein of peculiar drollery what he knew of the previous life and character of the prisoner, who, it appeared, had been frequently absent from home, though his excursions were generally undertaken under the professed character of a sportsman, for the employments of which he pretended a great liking, but for what reason nobody could imagine, as it never could be ascertained that he was ever successful. It also appeared that he had been loud in his denunciations against the Yorkers, and, as far as words could go, a great stickler for the rights of the settlers. The witness then related all the particulars of his detecting and capturing the prisoner. After this the accused was requested to make his defense, when, to the surprise of all, he wholly denied any hostile intention, or any willing participation in the recent attempt of Munroe to surprise and seize the present party at the cave, deliberately stating that while hunting in the woods near the creek that afternoon, he was met, made prisoner by the

Yorkers, and compelled to accompany them on their expedition, the object of which they did not reveal to him. And in confirmation of the truth of his statements, and of his asserted innocence, he cited the general character he had always sustained as a friend of the settlers.

"Do you generally manifest your friendship for the settlers by firing pistols at their heads, sir?" asked Warrington, casting a look of withering contempt on the prisoner.

"Oh, I was trying to escape," replied Sherwood, who had his ready answer to a question he had anticipated; "I was on the point of escaping, and discharged my pistol at this man, who beset me, to prevent being retaken, supposing him all the while to be one of the Yorkers."

"Whew!" uttered Jones, with a whistle prolonged into an exclamation; "now, honestly, friend, I must crave leave to tell you—but that wouldn't be manners, and so I won't—though I should really like to ask you if there was any one Yorker there to-night that a fellow of my short stature—only six foot eleven, in shirt flaps—could be taken for with any sort of conscience?"

"Yes, in the dark."

"But you may remember, possibly, friend, that you had to raise your pistol considerably higher than your head to get aim at mine, which you seemed to fancy shooting at in preference. Besides that, we took what I call a fair measure of lengths on the ground in the bit of grapple we had afterward. Now most folks that I am acquainted with can feel in the dark, if they can't see."

"Oh, I was so confused and frightened that I noticed none of these circumstances, but really supposed it was one of the Yorkers till you had got with me nearly to the boat."

"Well, now," exclaimed Pete, dropping his head in

affected chagrin; "I vow to Jeremiah I never felt so mortified in my life! To be taken for a Yorker! only think of that!"

"A sad mistake, truly," observed Selden, addressing his companions while in a side glance he kept an eye keenly fixed on the prisoner; "but still it was scarcely a more singular one than I made as we struck a light just now, when, turning to look at this man, I could have sworn he was the identical fellow we detected skulking about the shore yesterday—the make, motion, and dress of the two being so very similar."

"That's false!" hastily exclaimed Sherwood, completely thrown off his guard by the roundabout way and designedly incorrect statement of the other, made for the purpose of seeing its effect on the prisoner; "that's false, for this was not the dress I wore yest——" and he stopped short in visible confusion at the thought of the admission he was inadvertently making; while meaning and triumphant glances were exchanged among the company. Soon recovering in some degree his self-possession, however, and seeing how he had been entrapped, he attempted to mend the matter by explaining that he was about to say that this was not the dress he wore yesterday, even had he been here instead of a dozen miles off, as he was, and could prove it, as well as his innocence of all the charges brought against him, if time were but allowed him for the purpose. And this, or his acquittal, he continued for some time to demand, becoming, however, every moment less assured in his tone and more abject in his manner, as he stealthily glanced round and read his doom in the countenances of his judges.

"Well, gentlemen," said the leader, breaking the brief interval of silence which followed the last somewhat broken and confused remarks of the accused; "you have heard the evidence against the prisoner, as well as his defense and avowals of innocence. Will you offer your individual opinions on the question of his guilt? And we will first hear what you may have to offer on the subject, Mr. Jones?"

"Why, I don't know exactly about the chap, captain," said the latter, with a mischievous cocking of one eye, while screwing up his mouth nearly to his ear on the opposite side of his face; "he says he is innocent of the traitor, and it is a poor story if he don't know. But I have two other charges against him, which I consider rather gravus. Firstly, according to his own story, he suffered himself, with that clean pair of legs of his and the woods open for a run, if he chose that; or with guns and pistols if he chose to stand and fight—now while I think on't, I wonder what become of his gun—he suffered himself, I say, to be taken by the Yorkers in a way and manner which is a burning shame to a Green Mountain Boy, if so be he is one, as he pretends. And secondly he missed his aim when he leveled at my head, for which a professed hunter like himself ought to be ridiculous. So I think, considering, I shall vote to have him *viewed*." *

"And you, Smith, what is your verdict?"

"My opinion is," answered the man now addressed, "that the fellow's plausible palaver is all nothing but a made up mess to bamboozle us with. I should like to know how the Yorkers knew that we were here on the lake, or how they happened to find the cave without his help. The fact is, he brought them here to seize us, and was probably calculating to see some of us swinging on a York gallows within a week. My verdict, therefore, will be pretty much such a one as the king gave Haman."

"And what say you, Brown?"

"Guilty! guilty as a dog, and the liar knows it."

"And lastly, your opinion, Mr. Selden?"

* A cant phrase among the settlers, signifying the punishment of offenders.

"Briefly told—that the fellow's guilt is equaled only by his effrontery, and yet, as this is his first known offense, I would recommend a milder punishment than the one which has been hinted at."

"We are unanimous, then, in a verdict, gentlemen," observed the chief, "if I understand your various modes of expressing your opinions. And it remains only to determine in what manner the prisoner shall be punished for his offense. You are all, including the prisoner himself, I presume, well aware that, by a decree of our Convention, the only source of law we feel ourselves bound to regard in cases of this kind, the crime of aiding the enemy to arrest one of our citizens who may have happened to fall under the ban of that despotic edict by which they would terrify us into submission, is made punishable with death. If this were to be inflicted, however, on the prisoner, I should be inclined to grant him a more formal trial before a regularly appointed committee of safety, and allow him time for his defense, as he requests—not that I have the least doubt of his guilt, for I believe him to be the most precious compound of duplicity and villainy that I have seen in the settlement, but I would grant it on the principle of allowing every man the best means to establish his innocence when his life is at stake. Yet, concurring with Mr. Selden, I think we had better adopt one of the ordinary modes of punishment, for which the evidence is abundantly sufficient, administer it on the spot, and dismiss him with the admonition it will give. What this punishment shall be, I will leave to you to designate."

"I should like to have the title of my farm confirmed," said Smith, "seeing the Yorkers still continue to dispute it, and as the Beech-seal is a sort of legal instrument to do it with, they say, I vote that we apply it."

"Just the thing for the double-faced scoundrel, if

we have got to let him off so cheap," bluntly remarked Brown.

"My title to my head," said Pete Jones, "seems to be rather questioned, and as it is an article that would be dreadful inconvenient for me to be without, I motion that it be confirmed too."

"So be it, then," observed Selden; "I had, it is true, thought of a ducking, that he might be enabled to sympathize with his friends over the lake; I also have thought of taking him up into the top of one of those trees and leaving him bound there for the night; but neither of these punishments, probably, would so nearly come up to the fellow's merit as the beechen remedy. I will therefore agree to its application."

The prisoner's doom being thus unanimously settled, preparations were immediately commenced for carrying the sentence into effect. This was understood to be, in the quaint phrase of the times, *"a chastisement with the twigs of the wilderness,"* or the usual number of stripes, forty, save one, faithfully applied to the back of the offender with a green beech rod, termed, as before mentioned, the Beech-seal. Several rods or shoots of that thus oddly consecrated tree were accordingly selected, cut, and carefully trimmed for the purpose. The prisoner was then, in despite of his alternate threats and promises of good behavior in future, stripped of his coat, and firmly bound to the body of a large hemlock, with his face turned to the tree. Everything being now in readiness for the execution of the sentence, the question arose who should be the executioner. For this honor two rival candidates now presented themselves—Brown and Pete Jones—the former claiming it on the ground that no one of the present company had received injuries that so loudly demanded a personal reciprocation as his own, and the latter, with the greatest apparent gravity, contending that it was his peculiar right to do the duty of punishing the fellow for the unpardonable crime of missing his aim, since the shot was intended for his own benefit.

The altercation, however, was settled by the interposition of their leader, who good-naturedly awarded a division of the honors between them, directing that the first twenty stripes should be given by Jones, while Brown should be allowed the privilege of completing the task.

In accordance with this arrangement, the tall woodsman now seized a rod of his own preparing, of dimensions fearfully portentous to the back of the trembling culprit, and giving it a furious flourish in the air, he commenced with a look of terrible fierceness the performance of his allotted task. But malice and revenge formed no part of the character of this jolly and good-natured borderer. The manner in which the blows were given, and the comparatively slight effect they produced on their victim, made it very evident that, notwithstanding all his assumed wrath and fury of countenance and manner, his humanity combined with a natural love of sport, which had doubtless led him to solicit the office, was about to govern him in its execution.

"Well, here is my respects to you, friend," he said, commencing and keeping up a sort of loose, irregular discourse, and counting the blows in a parenthetical tone, as with mighty grins and flourishes he proceeded to apply the typical beech; "there is my respects to you (one), miss your aim again, you lubber, eh? (two) I told you that you shouldn't disgrace the cloth for nothing (three), and then (four) those kicks and (five), I thought at the time (six), that you was kicking against the pricks (seven, eight), so here is two pricks to every kick (eight, nine), scurvy business that of yours, friend, (nine, ten), that kicking against the trees (eleven, twelve), you didn't consider (seven—no, eleven) what a hurry I was in (twelve, thirteen), and then again that offering me money, zounds, sir! (thirteen, fourteen) I should like (fourteen) to know, sir——"

"There! there!" hastily exclaimed the prisoner, who had not been so much hurt amid all this parade of cuts and flourishes as to prevent his taking note of the true number of the stripes which had been administered, and which the mischief-loving woodsman had willfully miscounted. "Hold! you have already struck twenty. Hold, I say!"

"You don't say so?" replied Jones with affected surprise, as he slowly lowered his uplifted arm; "why, I thought I said fourteen—only fourteen last!"

"I care not if you did, sir," expostulated the prisoner, now bold from the consciousness of having at last a little truth on his side; "you miscounted on purpose to prolong my torture—I appeal to the company. You have gone your twenty, I tell you, ruffian!"

"Have? Well, friend, just as you say, not as I care."

So saying, the eccentric but kind-hearted woodsman hurled his rod into the lake, and, bounding off into the woods with the pretended object of procuring some better rods for the use of his successor, but in reality only to avoid the sight and sounds which, from the determined character and exasperated feelings of the man, he rightly anticipated would now follow, disappeared with a finger thrust into each ear in a neighboring thicket.

The flagellation was now resumed. And never was rod more effectually applied to the deserving back of a miscreant spy or traitor than now by the sinewy arm of Brown, doubly nerved as it was by the keen sense he harbored of the injuries he had already received from the hands of those with whom the present victim of his pent vengeance had been found leagued, to assist in dragging him to a gallows, and thus completing on his person the work of destruction which they had before commenced on his property. With a pause at every application of the rod, that no energy should be lost or weakened by the exertion, slow and measured fell the tremendous blows from his relentless arm till he had told out the full number assigned him; while at every lash of the pliant and close hugging instrument of torture the writhing victim sent forth a screech of agony that thrilled through the forest for miles around him.

This painful task being performed—for painful it was to most of the band, while the stern necessity that required it was sincerely regretted by them all—the prisoner was unbound and, with an earnest but kind admonition from Warrington to profit by the lesson he had received, set at liberty; while, muttering many a bitter execration and breathing vows of deadliest revenge on his captors, he sullenly departed from the camp and soon disappeared along the border of the lake in a northern direction.

CHAPTER IV

> "That strain again! it had a dying fall!
> Oh, it came o'er my ear like the sweet south
> That breathes upon a bank of violets,
> Stealing and giving odor."

After the departure of Sherwood our band, not deeming it prudent, without precautions which must necessarily deprive most of them of their rest for the night, to encamp so near an exasperated enemy of double their own numbers, determined on an immediate removal from the scene of their recent exploits. Accordingly they packed up and, without further delay, commenced their march by the beautiful moonlight, which, streaming brightly through the leafless forest, enabled them to pursue their way with as much ease and certainty as by the broadest daylight. Striking off westerly from the lake they directed their course to the nearest part of Otter Creek, where they proposed procuring quarters for the remainder of the night in the log houses of the only two families who resided on the Creek in that vicinity. These two houses were situated nearly a mile apart, while the respective openings around them were separated by a dense wood of evergreens of about half that distance in extent. After proceeding on together for a while the company separated into two parties, three of them bending their course toward the lowest or more northerly opening, where they were to remain till joined in the morning by their leader, to conduct them on their enterprise down the Creek; while the latter, with Selden, taking their venison and a goodly portion of their trout, continued forward directly to the upper clearing. This last was no other than the residence of the fair and spirited friend whose timely notice had not only insured their late escape, but enabled them to gain such triumphant advantages over their foes. And it was this friendly and patriotic act which they were now proceeding to reward, not only with suitable acknowledgment, but with the most valuable portion of their game—an offering that they supposed would be highly acceptable to one in her situation; for this extraordinary woman,* with no other dependence than on her own hands, with the slight assistance rendered her by her boys, the eldest of whom was not a dozen years old, was managing to support herself and her large family of children from the products of a new lot of land which her husband had commenced clearing when he lost his life by the fall of a tree, and which she now with unexampled fortitude persisted in improving, though in the heart of a wilderness infested with wild beasts and not wholly exempt from the hostile or, at least, predatory incursions of the Indians. It was nearly midnight when Warrington and his companions reached the log tenement of this fearless daughter of the wilds. Much to their surprise they found the house entirely deserted. Finding the door unfastened, however, they determined on entering to note appearances within, when it became evident that the desertion had taken place but a few hours before; but whether it was intended for a temporary or final

* An old settler, to whom Mrs. Story and her cave were personally known, described her to the author as "a busting great woman, who would cut off a two foot log as quick as any man in the settlement."

removal they were unable to determine. A bed of coals, yet alive, was raked up on the hearth; while the beds had been taken from the steads and, with all the most necessary utensils of family use, removed from the house.

"What means this sudden desertion of the family?" observed Warrington musingly; "and whither can they have fled?"

"To their neighbor's down the Creek, probably," replied Selden; "the movement has been made, I should conjecture, in anticipation of the return of Munroe and his party, from whose visit to-night a lone woman like this widow would doubtless wish to be excused."

"It may be so," rejoined the other, "but to quit her home from any of the motives which you suggest would be very little like Widow Story; there are few men in this settlement who can handle not only ax, but rifle, with more effect, though woman she be. And as for fear, it is a sensation with which, I verily believe, she is utterly unacquainted. But whatever may have become of the occupants of the house, we may as well, now we are here, make free and remain for the night."

"It will be considered no intrusion, I suppose?" inquiringly said Selden; "I have not the honor of an acquaintance with your heroine, you will bear in mind."

"Intrusion? not in the least; for you must know that we are patriots here—rebels or whatever we were on the lake to-night," jocosely replied Warrington.

"Patriotism," said Selden, following up the train of thought which the last remark suggested, "would seem entirely a relative term, and like beauty, which consists of black teeth, thick lips, and large eyes with one nation and exactly the reverse with another, wholly dependent on the pre-existing opinions of those who claim it for this action and deny it in that. Besides this, as the world estimates actions, success would seem to be quite as essential to constitute the patriot as the merits of his cause or the glory of his deeds. Here, with the settlers, you are indeed called a patriot, and surely there is no one who better deserves from them the appellation; while with the people of New York you are a rebel, outlaw, and hunted like a wild beast. And yet, if our cause prove successful, as Heaven grant it may, the world at large, coming in as umpire, will side with the settlers in establishing your name as a patriot; but if we fail it will join with your foes in declaring you a rebel and reckless factionist."

"Names and definitions, Selden, may be sometimes vague and varying, but principles are immutable. The principles which actuate us in resisting these encroachments on our rights are the same that have animated the bosoms of all those whom the world agrees in calling patriots, from the beginning of oppression to the present time. The disposition to defend our homes and property, besides being implanted in our bosoms as a law of our nature, indispensable to our self-protection, and even existence in the world, seems to have been ordained by Providence also as the natural means by which the rapacity of tyrants should be punished. This, indeed, is the only protection insured to industry and virtue—it constitutes the grand cement of society and the main pillars of all government. This is the foundation of patriotism, which consists only in the defense of justly acquired rights against wrongful aggressions. In our case, the opinions of the world may indeed be various and fluctuating till our rights become fairly understood and the wrongs we have received as fairly developed. But should men of the intelligence to know and the spirit to defend their rights stand tamely still and see those rights wrested from them, to be placed forever beyond their recovery, while hesitating to know whether the world will call their resistance patriotism or rebellion? It is not the name of patriot that I seek, or that of rebel or outlaw that I fear. It is results I am aiming to accomplish, and I will never rest nor cease my exertions till our Heaven-favored cause shall triumph and these rapacious intruders shall be driven from our soil. Could you have witnessed, as I have, the dismay, want, and suffering which these grasping and shameless tyrants have occasioned in this settlement—here, whole families turned from their houses in the midst of winter, with no human habitation within miles of them to flee to for refuge and shelter—there, property, acquired through the severest of toil, hardship, and privation, wantonly destroyed, houses set on fire and consumed to prevent the return of the owners—and then again, females abused, and even the sick roughly ejected and left to perish miserably in the night air or storm, for all these ruthless aggressors could know—could you have witnessed all this you would not be surprised at the exasperated feelings of our people, or the indomitable spirit with which they have persevered in that cause which brought you, till lately a stranger to our wrongs, among us to aid in sustaining. My personal interest, I know, suffers in consequence of devoting so much of my time to the service of the public. Indeed, I have, in common with my chivalrous superior, Colonel Ethan Allan, almost wholly neglected my own concerns while guarding the interests of others. Even now I am the owner of a large tract of land on the borders of Champlain, a part of which, as I have lately been apprised, has been for several years in possession of one of the York patentees, while my duties nearer home have prevented me from ever looking after it or taking, since making this discovery, any steps toward dispossessing the intruder."

"But you surely will neglect it no longer," observed the other; "since we are going into the vicinity, and on similar business."

"We will consider the case after we have righted the wrongs of the houseless settlers at the Lower Falls and fulfilled the other objects of our mission into this region. But let us drop this exciting subject for to-night, that we may obtain a little rest to prepare us for the duties of to-morrow," replied Warrington, now rising to make such scanty preparations as might be required for their repose.

The two friends, after barricading the door and spreading their blankets before the small fire they had kindled on entering the house, now lay down to repose on the floor, which to the hardy and tired woodsman is generally more grateful than beds of the softest down to the pampered sons of luxury and ease. Selden was soon lost in slumber. But his companion, whose mind was oppressed with more weighty cares, and whose feelings had become somewhat excited in recounting the wrongs of his countrymen, courted the drowsy god in vain. And these causes, together with his attempts to account for the absence of the family, for whose safety he was not wholly without apprehensions, continuing for some time to render all his endeavors to sleep useless, he arose, unbarred the door, and without waking his more fortunate companion went out into the open air to try the effect of the cool breath of heaven in allaying the excitement of his feelings and disposing him to slumber. The night still continued bright and lovely. Abroad, nature seemed sunk in deathlike repose; while the deep and solemn silence that pervaded the wilderness was broken only by the low, but far-sounding hoot of the sylvan watchman of the night, or the voices of the inhabitants of the neighboring pools, who were straining their tiny throats in notes of seeming joy and jubilee at their recent release from a wintry thraldom. While contemplating the scene around him, and indulging in the moody reverie which the circumstances were calculated to create in the mind, the young outlaw unconsciously wandered nearly to the bank of the river, which was still bordered by a strip of forest extending from the water back almost to the house. Here, leaning against the trunk of a large tree which some heavy wind had broken off about twenty feet from the ground, he stood some minutes looking listlessly down upon the placid waters, as, sparkling in the moonlight that struggled through the trees above, they moved ceaselessly along on their journey to the deep. Now his attention would become riveted for a moment on some light float of wood sweeping by in the noiseless current. And now he would turn a half listening ear to the sportive plunges of the otter, here once found in such numbers as to have naturally suggested to the hunters who first visited this stream the name which it bears. His meditations, however, were at length interrupted by some indistinct and, at first, scarcely audible sounds, the nature of which he was for some time wholly unable to determine. At last, however, he became satisfied it could be no other than the distinct murmur of human voices; but from what quarter it came he was still unable to decide. He listened intently; and now the sounds became more distinct. Presently they began to swell on the air in the low, melodious voice of a female chanting a tune, which, though not recently heard by him, struck nevertheless familiarly on his ear, awakening in his mind reminiscences of persons, time, and place which formerly occupied a prominent space among the objects of his peculiar interest, but which in the cares and turmoils of the last few years had been almost forgotten. Starting as from a trance, he rallied his doubting senses and made another effort to ascertain whence this mysterious music could proceed, but with no better success than before. Sometimes the sounds seemed to come from the earth or some subterrananeus cavern far beneath his feet. At other times the liquid notes appeared floating high in the heavens above. He now took another position, several paces distant from the one first occupied, to see whether any variation would thus be produced in the sounds.

Here, however, they were scarcely audible. Several other new positions were then tried, but all with the same success; and he returned to the tree where he was standing when his attention was first arrested by these unaccountable sounds. Here he again taxed his powers of hearing to their utmost, when, to his increasing wonder, the same melodious notes fell upon his ear even more distinctly than before. Now, not only the tune seemed familiar to him, but there was something in the voice likewise which his bewildered senses seemed to recognize—something that seemed to touch a chord in his bosom that had never vibrated save under the sweet intonations of one whose words even were once music to his ears; but still one, to heighten his perplexity, who, though her residence had long been unknown to him, could not yet be, he felt assured, within a hundred miles of this spot. Curiosity, surprise, and wonder had now raised his feelings to a pitch of almost frantic excitement; and, without scarcely knowing why, he struck his clenched fist two or three times heavily against the tree, which seemed so strangely the conductor of the sounds in question. A deep, hollow reverberation, indicating a large and extended cavity within, was apparently the only effect produced by the blows. On applying his ear once more, however, he found that the singing had ceased; and every sound was now hushed in silence. He listened a while with suspended breath in expectation of hearing the music resumed. But he listened in vain. He then renewed the experiment of listening from other positions; but being again unsuccessful, he returned to the tree and fell to beating it again, in the absurd fancy that, if there had been any connection between his blows and the ceasing of the sounds the same operation which had caused them to cease might revive them, though deeming it at the same time an utter impossibility that the cavity within the trunk could contain the invisible songstress. All his efforts, however, to gain a clew to the mystery proved wholly fruitless and, after lingering some time near this spot of seeming enchantment, he slowly wandered back to the house, deeply pondering over the singular and incomprehensible incident which had attended his nocturnal ramble. Was it within the bounds of possibility, he asked himself, that the person, the once loved and lost one, whose voice these mysterious notes so much resembled, could now be in this almost uninhabited wilderness? No, no! What other female, then, capable of such execution could be near at such an hour of the night? Surely none! Was it not, then, a human voice that he had heard? Was it the voice of an angel, of "visits few and far between," floating high in the heavens and hymning the stars? What had he done to deserve such special revealment? Or was it, as the traditions of the superstitious would inculcate, the voice of a departing spirit permitted to break on the ear of a distant friend at the instant of departure, for the purpose of apprising him of its exit from earth, or warning him of his own dissolution? Or was it not far more probable, he said, with an effort to shake off these intruding fancies, that his senses had deceived him, and that, after all, the whole was but the work of an over-excited imagination? It must have been so. And, as if determined to satisfy himself with this last solution of the subject, since he could hit upon no other which reason would not sooner reject, he quickened his pace and, like one resolved to end a perplexing inquiry by the best argument he can give, and call it conclusive, bustled forward, now whistling a tune or now affecting to run over to himself the intended business of to-morrow, till he had reached the house, secured the door, and thrown himself down beside his still insensible companion, when exhausted nature soon closed the scene in a profound slumber.

CHAPTER V

"If you had been the wife of Hercules,
Six of his labors you'd have done, and sav'd
Your husband so much sweat."

—Coriolanus.

Real causes of excitement have frequently, and perhaps generally, been found to produce the soundest slumber; while those that are artificial or imaginary have an equal tendency to prevent it, Dr. Young's poetic philosophy to the contrary, notwithstanding. It was thus with Warrington. While the images of the past and the future which fancy had called up were operating in his bosom, he vainly sought the arms of "tired nature's sweet restorer." But after he had found a just cause for excitement, and experienced the utmost of its legitimate effects, that restorer came unbidden and instantly. And the next morning was considerably advanced before he and his companion awoke from the deep and sense-absorbing slumbers which, for many hours, had sealed their every faculty in blank oblivion. They simultaneously arose and went to the window to ascertain from whom proceeded the noise of the ax, whose heavy, resounding blows in the adjoining forest had first awakened them from their quiet repose. At the border of the woods, a short distance to the south of the house and in plain sight of their loop-hole, for the window was nothing more, stood the amazon owner and almost sole creator of this little opening in the dark wilderness, plying her ax with masculine dexterity and effect into the huge trunk of a standing hemlock. In a short time this princely tenant of the Green Mountain forest began to tremble, totter, and bow beneath the supple arm of its life-sapping foe, and at length came down with a thundering crash upon the ground, filling the air around with a cloud of dust, splinters, broken and powdered limbs, and causing the earth and surrounding woods to rebound at the shock. When the obstructing cloud had cleared away from the spot our observant friends beheld the object of their attention mounted on the trunk of the prostrate tree, and proceeding to mark it off into such lengths for chopping as suited her purpose. While thus engaged her attention seemed to be suddenly arrested by something she observed about the house or in a line with it beyond. Hastily descending from her stand on the trunk and seizing her rifle, which stood at the foot of a tree near the stump of the one just felled, she approached with a rapid step and with some appearance of concern till within a few rods of the house, when she slackened her pace and soon halted.

"Tall, stout, and stately," said Selden, still standing with his friend so near the window as to have a fair view of the person of their hostess. "Tall, stout, and stately," he repeated, running his admiring eye over her erect and imposing figure; "face and features even yet handsome, despite the ravages and cares of forty! And then that queenly port! Heavens! what a specimen of Eve's daughters! Surely, Warrington, she must be the very Juno of your Green Mountains! But why not unbar the door and go out to meet her? We shall appear a pretty brace of heroes if she come here and find us hid up like a couple of runaways! She has perceived us, I presume, but is doubtful whether we are friends or foes."

"Stay a moment," said the other, who had been regarding the movements of the woman quite as intensely as his friend, though for different purposes; "I suspect you will soon see that other objects than ourselves are engrossing her attention."

Scarcely had the last speaker ceased when they caught an oblique view of the approaching forms of a number of men, whom they instantly recognized to be Munroe and his party. Hastily retreating from the window and preparing their arms for action, should their use become necessary either for defending themselves within the house or protecting their hostess without, our two friends took positions at small apertures between the logs of the wall, where without revealing themselves they could easily observe their foes, and stood silently watching the progress of events in the yard. Meanwhile the hardy widow had planted herself directly in the path in which the Yorkers were approaching from the main road to her door. And now boldly advancing and confronting them, she demanded what might be their object in turning into a lone woman's dwelling.

"Why, my good woman," said the sheriff, pausing and hesitating in evident surprise at the commanding appearance and determined tone of the person he was addressing; "we are all as hungry as so many kites, after the long morning's march we have had; and now can't you contrive to work up something in the shape of a breakfast for us?"

"I know of but two reasons, sir, why I may not comply with your request," replied the woman, with an air of quiet scorn.

"And what may they be, woman?" asked Munroe, in doubt as to the drift of her discourse.

"The lack of means and the lack of inclination, sir,"

rejoined the other in the same calm and scornful manner.

"Short and sweet," said Munroe; "but I think we can remove your objections easily enough, mistress; my men here have a plenty of salt junk and some bread, which will make out the main materials for a meal; so you will have nothing to do but cook and serve up for us, and if we pay you well for your trouble this will cure both your objections at once, I suppose."

"Think you, sir, I would be hired to serve a Yorker of your stamp?" replied the woman, with increasing disdain. "Why, the money got in that manner would burn through my pockets as quick as if it came at the call of one in league with the arch fiend, and all hissing hot from the burning mint in the regions below! Even the very food bought with it would stick in my throat and poison my children to death in the eating."

"Tut, tut! madam madcap!" exclaimed the sheriff, resuming his wonted roughness and now beginning to chafe under the biting sarcasms of the other; "you show about as much of the Tartar as anything I have met with in my travels for a long while. I wish the rebels much joy in their petticoat champion! But it is time to look a little to such as you. The authorities of the king are neither to be resisted, nor insulted with impunity, you will do well to bear in mind, perhaps."

"Cowards are always allowed the privilege of blustering before women," tartly rejoined the other; "your threats, valiant sheriff, will hurt me about as much, probably, as they frighten me, and if anything further is attempted, you will find I can defend myself."

"We will see, my trooper!" muttered Munroe, making a sudden movement toward the other, apparently to disarm or seize her.

Eluding his grasp and hastily retreating a few steps, the fearless woman cocked her rifle and brought it to her shoulder. "Another step toward me, sir, and your blood be on your own head," she cried, in a cool, determined tone.

"Hang me!" exclaimed Munroe, after standing a moment in mute surprise at this bold and unexpected movement of the woman, who, he began to suspect, could scarcely have been brought to show such singular fearlessness but from a knowledge that help was near; "hang me, if I don't believe the termagant is standing guard to some of these skulking outlaws, whom she has concealed in the house! We must see to this immediately," he continued, moving around his opponent toward the house and beckoning his men to follow.

"Oh, is that all you want," said the widow, taking her piece in her hand and moving aside with the air of one relieved from a personal fear; "you are welcome to all the outlaws you will find here, but you must beware how you attempt to touch me. However, you had better look out for yourself, brave sheriff," she added, in a sneering laugh. "Take care, sir, that some of those terrible Green Mountain Boys concealed within there don't blow you through the head with their rifles!"

"The door is fastened, woman," said Munroe as, stepping up, he tried in vain to open it; "the door is fastened on the inside; see that it is opened, or I will force it!"

"Oh, no, no! why, you would spoil my door, man!" cried the widow, with the utmost apparent concern for the safety of her door; "yes, ruin it entirely; 'twould cost me a hard dollar to get it mended. I forgot to tell you it was barred up inside. We do not stay here nights for fear of the visits of such strolling gentry as yourselves. But if you really wish to handle over my greasy pots and kettles, or crawl under my beds, you can go in as I came out, by going up on the end of the logs at the corner yonder and removing a piece of that bark roof."

"But, honestly, woman, have you seen nothing of Warrington and his band this way last night or this morning?" asked the sheriff, his suspicions seeming to be pretty much allayed by the well managed demeanor and conduct of the other.

"Warrington—Warrington," said she musingly, as if attempting to recall the name of one of whom she might have perhaps heard; "not Captain Warrington? Yes, I have heard of him, I am sure. Is he in this section? Where is he? I should like to see that brave fellow. Why, he was the one that so handsomely beech-sealed one of the York authorities down Bennington way, last year. Now what is his name—I will think in a minute——"

"Oh, no matter, no matter," hastily interrupted the sheriff, unwilling that the story of his own former discomfiture should be made known to his present followers. "Come, boys," he continued, moving away from the house and calling to his men, "we shan't be able to make anything of this crabstick of a woman, so we may as well be on the move again, and as we have lost our guide, instead of going back through the woods we will go up the creek to the ford and then down the military road to Ticonderoga."

"Adroitly done, by heavens!" exclaimed Selden to his companion, as the sounds of the retreating footsteps of their foes died away on their ears; "the woman's tact has saved us, to say the least, captain, from a troublesome contest. But shall I now unbar the door?"

"No; let her continue to manage in her own way," replied the other; "the Yorkers may take it into their heads to stop and reconnoiter the house a while from the woods. And she may deem it prudent to guard against their making any discoveries in that way by remaining a while without, or by entering the house in the manner she pointed out to Munroe."

The woodswoman, if the term be admissible, wary as she was fearless, immediately adopted one of the precautions anticipated by Warrington. And the sheriff and his posse had no sooner fairly disappeared in the forest than our friends heard her mounting the house, removing one of the broad pieces of spruce bark which constituted the rude covering of the roof, and descending into the chamber or garret above them. In another moment she stood before them with a countenance animated with a look of triumph and a smile of congratulation.

"Now a thousand thanks to Mistress Story," warmly exclaimed Warrington, after presenting his friend and exchanging the ordinary salutations; "a thousand thanks, not only for yesterday's timely notice, but for the shield which a woman's tact only could have so successfully thrown over us this morning! But how came you apprised that we were in possession of your castle, as we were without the shadow of a license from its owner?"

"Partly anticipating a visit from some of you," replied the widow, "I purposely left the door unfastened when we left last night. And a peep through the cracks when I returned this morning and found it barred, told me very nearly the character of the occupants. But you don't know," she added jocosely, "how sorely I was tempted, as I saw you lying there on the floor asleep, as helpless as children, to creep in, bind you, deliver you over to Munroe, and claim the reward!"

"When you were praying, 'lead us not into temptation,' at this moment of your trial," said Warrington laughingly, "and thought of the next sentence, 'deliver us from evil,' you concluded it best to take sides with the Green Mountain Boys—did you?"

"Why," replied she, "it might certainly be a matter of some consideration who it were wisest to make friends and who foes, in such a case; and especially so since it now seems that ten Yorkers can be put to flight by one old woman."

"Ay, ay!" gayly responded the captain; "and that

fact, sir," he added, turning with an arch look to Selden, "shows the wisdom of the doubts and apprehensions you seemed to entertain last night in approaching, without leave, the house of one who might become so formidable a foe."

"I should be sorry to spoil the captain's joke," replied Selden in the same spirit, "but in taking possession thus unceremoniously, I think we both depended somewhat on the effect of the peace offering we brought," he continued, pointing to the game suspended on the wall, "in appeasing the household gods for the outrage."

"An ample atonement!" said the dame; "so much so, indeed, that I suspect my nine little hungry household gods will think the obligation wholly on their side. Yes, yes, that mark of your kindness, gentlemen, I noticed when I took my stolen peep in here, and my heart has been thanking you ever since; for my larder, as you may well imagine, is none of the fullest, considering the number depending upon it. It makes my heart ache to put the little tikes on so short an allowance, as I am often compelled to do here, in a place so difficult to obtain provisions."

"But where are your children?" asked Warrington.

"My children? all in *T'other World,* sir!" replied the woman, with a sort of mock gravity.

"In the other world! what can the woman mean?" asked Warrington, turning a puzzled look upon his hostess. "But for the mention you have just made of your children, and your roguish looks, which belie your assertions, one might be startled at the import of your words!"

"Not so much a belying, neither," said the woman; "but come, we will *open Sesame* now," she continued, proceeding to unbar the door, "and after seeing if my brood cannot be conjured back into the world again, for the purpose of assisting me and quieting your apprehensions for their safety, captain, we will see what can be done in the way of breakfast."

"Let me attend you to witness the process of conjuration," said Warrington, who had more reasons for making the request than were known to either of his companions.

"No, sir, no! keep house till I return, or, my word for it, you get no breakfast this time," replied the other in a sportive, yet determined manner, as she quitted the house on her proposed errand, leaving her guests to indulge in such conjectures as they chose respecting the place to which she had gone to summon her concealed family. They were not allowed much time, however, for discussing this curious question; for in a short time their ears were saluted by the mingled sounds of jabbering voices approaching from the woods in the rear of the house, and in a moment more the dame came up to the door with her nearly half-score of hardy little urchins trooping along in noisy glee at her side.

"I will shake hands with the young captain first!" exclaimed one of the boys, endeavoring to outstrip the rest, as they all made a rush at the door.

"You shan't!" vociferated another, springing forward, and eagerly elbowing his way through the throng that was now choking up the entrance. "I say you shan't now, Dick! He likes me best. Ned, you hold him back!"

"I don't care, I will have the first kith!" cried a lisping little image of her mother. "I will—mayn't I, ma?" she added, throwing back her long unfettered hair from before her laughing black eyes with a pretty toss of the head, and entering with high glee into the keen strife going forward for obtaining the first notice of one who, in former calls at the house, seemed to have made warm friends of the whole band of these tiny rivals for his favors.

The next moment the person of Warrington, like

that of Gulliver among the Lilliputians, was almost literally covered by the little beings, two sitting on each knee, shaking his imprisoned hands with all their might; the little Julia standing between, turning up her pretty cheek invitingly for the expected kiss which, for all her declaration, instinctive modesty forbade her to ask for; one or two had hold of each arm, and one more daring and active than the rest, having clambered aloft, was sitting astride the neck, and crowing aloud over the rest from his elevated situation; while all were clinging, laughing, and chattering like a bevy of monkeys exhibiting on an elephant at the show of some traveling menagerie.

Those fashionable misanthropes of the Rochefoucauld or Lacon school, who are forever moralizing and mourning over the selfishness of man; who can see no unadulterated benevolence, no disinterested friendship in the moral deserts of the human heart, might find one oasis, at least, to relieve their jaundiced vision and go to refute the sweeping dictums of their cold and cheerless philosophy, would they but turn their eyes to the artless actions and examine the untutored and guileless hearts of children. How spontaneous their affections! With what intuitive and unerring certainty and quickness they single out those who love them, whether kindred or stranger; and with what confiding readiness and generous ardor is the friendship thus bestowed upon them forever reciprocated; and that, too, with no detracting alloy of selfish feeling, no worldly calculating of results, and no influencing consideration of interest! Verily! while they go to school to *us* for the improvement of the head, methinks it would be well for us if the tables were so far turned that they could become our only instructors in the lessons of the heart.

The dame, now calling off such of her children as she needed to assist her, and dispatching one for water, another for wood, and a third to go to some whispered destination, proceeded rapidly in her preparations for the promised repast. And in a short space of time a tempting meal from the offering of her guests was smoking on the table. The meal, which was enlivened by a recital of the adventures of the band the preceding evening, was no sooner ended than Selden, rising first from the table, departed at the suggestion of his superior to see that the party at the other house were ready to commence their march.

"Now, captain, where are you going with your men?" earnestly asked the widow, as soon as Selden was fairly gone; "I have reasons for wishing to know."

Warrington, after a slight hesitation, imparted the desired information.

"Will you make me one promise?" resumed the woman, "and at the same time receive from me in kindness one caution?"

"On conditions, I will venture to say yes."

"What may they be? If anything that I can properly comply with——"

"I would impose no other terms, certainly—so now for the promise you would exact?"

"Simply this: that the family with whom the young Indian I sent you last evening resides—no question now about their names or residences—that this family, I say, shall not be molested should you or your men ever come across them. They hold under a York title, to be sure, but turned no one off to get possession. Will you promise?"

"For your sake, and the Indian's sake, if the facts are as you state, I will promise my influence in their behalf."

"Now hear my caution. Beware of that fellow you chastised last night—beware of that Sherwood. He will be a serpent in your path."

"Do you know him?"

"I think I do, but must say no more. And now, let's hear your conditions."

"Only that you shall expound my dream, or vision, of last night."

"A dream! vision!"

"Yes! a something, at all events, which conveyed to my ear, as I thought, the sounds of a voice discoursing most heavenly music."

"A sleeping or a waking dream?"

"The latter, I afterward made up my mind to believe, as the readiest way of solving the mystery; but this morning I have begun to suspect——"

"At what time last night, and on what particular spot, did this strange trance fall on you, sir?" interrupted the widow in a bantering tone, which was accompanied, however, with a look betraying considerable curiosity and uneasiness.

"Oh, about the usual time of such visitations—the witching hour of midnight. And the scene should be laid, I think, more particularly than at any other spot, near the foot of a certain charmed tree, or rather the hollow trunk of one, standing not far from the bank of the Creek down here, to which, leaving my companion asleep, I had wandered alone to shake off a fit of watchfulness that the spirits of the air, or something else, had unaccountably sent me."

"And did you relate your adventures to your companion, on your return or since?"

"No!"

"That settles the question with me, then, as to what I should now do," seriously observed the woman. "Captain Warrington, I clearly see that you have accidentally and very singularly hit upon a clew to matters which I thought most prudent to conceal, even from you, friend to the settlers and my family as you are. Follow me, and you shall know more."

So saying, with rapid steps she led the way in

silence toward the Creek, closely followed by her guest, eager to witness the promised development. Passing directly by the hollow tree, to which she pointed with a significant smile as they went along, she conducted him to the brink of the high, steep bank, which was here covered with a thick growth of young evergreen, whose tangled boughs overhung the waters below. Now grasping firmly hold of a projecting root, she swung herself down on to a narrow shelf or offset in the bank, a few feet above the surface of the water. As soon as this position was gained by them both, she proceeded along the shelf a few yards, and, removing a small fir-tree top, which had been to all appearances blown down the bank, disclosed the mouth of a narrow passage running back horizontally into the earth. Into this she immediately entered, still followed by her companion. After groping their way about a rod through the dark zigzag windings of this passage, they emerged into a spacious room formed entirely by an artificial excavation of the earth, which, from a beginning at the outside, had been removed in small parcels and thrown into the stream, till the whole was completed. The walls or sides, which had been cut down perpendicularly from the solid mold and plastered over with thin mud, now presented a hard compact surface. The ceiling, which was in the form of an arch, coming, probably, at the top or center within a foot of the surface above, was supported by the thickly spreading roots of the trees, standing, many of them, directly over the excavation and forming a kind of network, curiously and so strongly interwoven as effectually to prevent the earth from caving in from above. The whole interior was divided into two parts of unequal dimensions by a slight willow-work partition, the lesser of which, being designed for the sleeping apartment, was neatly carpeted with a thick dry moss collected from the spruce knolls in the vicinity; while on one side was extended at suitable intervals a row of little oblong platforms, raised about a foot above the general level by repeated doublings of the same light, springy substance. These, on which were laid such beds as the occupant could furnish, afforded, with or without any further additions, soft and pleasant couches, safely protected against the damps of a ground floor. Beside one of the walls of the larger room was a rude fireplace, constructed of flat stones, and built up several feet high to receive fuel and give direction to the smoke, which, ascending through a sort of retreating flue cut into the bank, escaped through the cavity of the identical hollow stub that Warrington had discovered to be in some way connected with the mysterious melody heard by him the evening before.

"This, Captain Warrington," said the dame, after showing her admiring guest every part of her subterraneous establishment, which she had lit up on entering by throwing a few light combustibles on the fire still remaining on the hearth; "this is my city of refuge—my stronghold, or my *'T'other World,'* as I have accustomed myself and children to call it, fancying, in my wish to keep the secret of its existence to ourselves, that some such name would lessen the chances of a discovery which might accidentally be made, perhaps, by referring to it before others by a proper designation. It was dug out by myself and my little boys, who took to digging as naturally as young foxes, and greatly assisted me. My neighbor below, however, aided me in the most difficult parts of the work; and in case of danger he is to occupy it with me."

"But what were the immediate dangers you apprehended that led you to so uncommon an undertaking?" asked the other.

"For myself I might feel, perhaps, no apprehensions," replied the provident mother. "For my children I feel differently. All parents, captain, however brave they may be for themselves, are always cowards for their children. No real dangers, it is true, might beset us here for years; and then again, they might come like a thief in the night. To say nothing of the heartless Yorkers, who might burn my house, or turn us out shelterless into the snow—to say nothing of the wolves that have been known, in the desperation of hunger, to attack folks in their houses—to say nothing of these, which are sufficiently fearful for most people, what security have we in these outposts of the settlement, even in times of peace, against a hostile visit from the Indians? But when, as now, the rumors of war come floating on every breeze, that danger is daily increasing. The sad experience of my father's family, who were half slain by these hell-hounds of the wilderness at the outbreak of the last war, has taught me the wisdom of precaution. In peace they are even to be distrusted; and the first rumor of war that strikes their ears will put them to whetting their knives for slaughter; while they are sure to anticipate the coming contest by striking the first blow on the defenseless families of the frontiers. Now with these views, is it strange," she added with a smile, "that the mother of nine children, with but one neighbor within miles of her, should foresee the evil and hide herself?"

"Surely not," replied Warrington, struck not less by the forcible language of the woman than by her prudent forecast; "you are right in believing that the storm of a new war is gathering over us; and if you think of remaining here, these precautions are but the part of wisdom, as we know not when or where the storm may burst. But do you occupy this retreat every night, now?"

"We do."

"You enter as we did, taking your children down the bank, I suppose?"

"Sometimes, but more generally by approaching from the Creek in my canoe (which is kept in the bushes a few rods below), lest by coming down the bank constantly we wear a path which might lead to a discovery of our retreat."

"And you all lodged here last night, of course?"

"Yes."

"Part of the mystery, then, stands explained—why should the rest be kept back?"

"What is there more that you do not comprehend?"

"The singing——"

"Might have been my own, if you heard any. You never heard any of my lullaby performances before, I suppose?" said the woman, with an evasive smile.

"No, but I have once heard the performances of another, whose voice is not easily to be forgotten," replied Warrington, turning a keen, searching gaze on the slightly confused face of the widow.

"Warrington, Warrington!" said the woman, resuming a tone of seriousness and intently reading the looks of the other; "as much as I hate deception, I wish I could have misled you. But I saw by your disappointed looks, when you entered and glanced around these empty apartments, that you expected to find here what you have not. And I now see that you still have certain impressions, which I wish could have been done away. But as you seem bent on following up your clew, I will not attempt to mislead you. From what I have gathered from you and others, I have for some time secretly suspected the identity of persons yet supposed to be different, and that I have long known those whose present residence you have little dreamed of: Captain Warrington, there is indeed a rosebud in this wilderness, which I should not have been displeased to see placed in your bosom. But seek it not now—there is a hedge about it too high for your leaping."

"Where is she? I ask but to know where," inquired the other with impatient eagerness.

"Not here, nor near here, now," replied the woman;

"the secret is not mine to reveal: I have said too much already; so question me no further. But come, let us leave for the upper world," she added, rapidly leading the way out, and allowing the other no further chance to resume his importunities till they had gained the top of the bank.

"But surely you will not leave the matter here, after informing me so far?" said Warrington, in an expostulating tone, as he perceived that the other seemed to expect that he would now depart.

"For the present, I surely shall," replied the woman decidedly; "you will urge in vain one who understands her duties to all! Go! your men await you. Good-morning, and God speed you in the cause of the settlers," and imperiously waving her hand for the departure of her reluctant and tantalized guest, she suddenly turned away and disappeared in the forest.

CHAPTER VI

"The sons of our mountains will sheath not the brand
Till the last base intruder is forced from the land."

ONE of the most considerable openings in the wilderness in the northwestern part of the New Hampshire Grants, at the period of our story, was at the Lower Falls of Otter Creek at the head of the lake navigation of that stream, and on and around that fine and fertile swell of land now occupied as the site of a pleasant and flourishing village, to which, as before mentioned, the more dignified name of city has long since been legally applied; though not without sometimes eliciting, probably, from the traveler approaching the place with the expectations which the appellation would naturally raise, a feeling somewhat akin, perhaps, to that which might be experienced on hearing the address of *My Lord* applied to some urchin scion of nobility, at marbles, in his first jacket and trousers. A pitch had been made on this spot, some years before, by one or more of the New Hampshire patentees, a saw and grist mill erected, and a large piece of forest felled and partially cleared; when the whole tract, embracing the Falls and all the improvements, was purchased of some of the York land jobbers by one Colonel Reed. Reed had been the commander of a regiment of Scotch Highlanders that came over with General Wolfe, and was engaged with his army in that memorable battle which gave Quebec and the Canadas to the British crown. This regiment having been subsequently disbanded, the colonel, still continuing in the New World, and in his intercourse between Canada and New York becoming acquainted with the Vermont lands, entered into the speculations then going forward and made the purchases as above stated. Finding his new purchase already in the occupancy of the New Hampshire grantees, and not inclining to be bothered with the delays of a civil process by the York authorities to put him in possession, what should this military land speculator do but repair immediately to Montreal, and, collecting a file of his old disbanded soldiers, go on, armed and provisioned, to conquer and keep and forcibly drive the occupants from the ground, taking possession of the mills, lumber, and all other improvements? After making ample provisions for continuing the improvement of his purchase, he left it to be managed and defended by the men who came on with him, placed under the command of one of his old fear-naught Highlanders, by the name of Donald McIntosh, formerly a brave and trusty sergeant in his regiment, to whom he now delivered written military instructions, setting forth the manner in which the improvements were to be conducted and the post defended against any, or all, who should offer to intrude on the premises. The colonel, being a shrewd man and a close observer of character, national, as well as individual, and well knowing the inherent respect of Scotchmen for discipline and the orders of a superior would insure him more determined defenders of his possessions, as well as more faithful laborers in their improvement, than all the rewards, bribes, or other inducements he could offer, had thrown over the whole transaction the appearance of a military service. And, hiring his men at the monthly compensation they had formerly received as soldiers, and terming it an enlistment during the war, and conducting them to their post under the discipline to which they had been accustomed in the army, he had the address to make these men, not the most intelligent, certainly, honestly believe that they were acting under their old commander in a military capacity only, and were really in the service of the king, to whom this settlement, they were told, was in a state of rebellion. And right faithfully and rigidly did the straight-going Donald, ever continuing to act under these impressions, execute the trust committed to his charge. Immediately proceeding to throw up a large log-house, and inclose a yard around it with a heavy compact fence of hewn timber, he soon gave the post such an impregnable and threatening aspect as effectually deterred the former occupants from attempting, with any force they could rally in the neighborhood, to dislodge the intruders. And, after watching a while and seeing no diminution of the strength of their antagonists or relaxation of their caution, these ejected and plundered settlers, who happened to be among the less spirited of their countrymen, at length pretty much relinquished the hope of regaining their possessions, except in a favorable termination of the negotiation still going forward at intervals between the settlers and the government of New York.

In this manner for nearly two years did the minions of Reed hold and manage these valuable possessions, clearing land, raising crops, and exporting lumber and other products without being at all molested by the settlers, or the attending circumstances being known, indeed, to those who had exercised any general agency in resisting the aggression of the Yorkers. At length, however, the tranquillity of the intruders became accidentally endangered. Ira Allen, the Green Mountain Metternich of after times, and one of the cabinet council of those we are describing, coming through this section on his return to his residence in Bennington from an excursion to the Winooski River, sought lodgings on a stormy December night at the quarters of McIntosh and his men—a call which came near costing the former his life at the outset; for, while he was unsuspectingly knocking for admission, the wary Scotchman, who had been accustomed to consider all his foes who did not give the watchword, noiselessly opened the door wide enough to protrude one arm, and made several desperate lunges at his body, hit or miss, with a naked saber. Providentially, however, the weapon, missing the body, only wounding the greatcoat of the traveler, who, at last succeeding in making the other believe that he wanted nothing more than a shelter for the night, was now admitted and entertained till next morning. This singular reception, as well as the odd and warlike appearance of everything connected with the establishment, awakened the curiosity and excited the suspicions of Allen, who, from the information he obtained by pumping the incautious Donald, and making inquiries of the settlers before leaving the vicinity, returned home in possession of the full history of the case. And the consequence was that before many months a small band of Green Mountain Boys came on from the south, and finding no one about the premises, were proceeding to clear the house and yard of all they contained, when the occupants, who had been at work in the woods, returned, and after holding a council of war a short distance from the house, made such a furious charge with fixed bayonets on the newcomers, that they, little dreaming of so warlike an onset, were fairly routed from the works and were compelled to decamp amid the victorious shouts of the elated Highlanders. Chagrined and vexed on the result of this attempt, the Green Mountain Boys early the next spring set on foot another expedition for dispersing these military tenants of the usurping colonel. And for this, among other objects, Warrington and his companions were now on their way to the spot.

It was not until an advanced hour in the afternoon of the day which commenced by the adventures related in the last chapter, that our band arrived at the outskirts of the singularly guarded possession just described. Their force, swelled by the numbers who had joined them on the last part of their route, now amounted to about a dozen men. They halted in the woods adjoining the clearing for the purpose of consultation, with a view to fix on the best mode of attacking the place, which they were not without hope of carrying by surprise. They had scarcely commenced discussing these points, however, before their attention was arrested by two quickly successive reports of firearms proceeding from a thicket on the opposite side of the creek.

"What will you bate I don't know the bark of that dog, captain?" exclaimed Jones, tipping one of his comical winks to his superior.

"Aha! whom do you suspect, Jones?" asked Warrington, with a look of interest.

"Why, I shouldn't like to make bodily oath of it, be sure," replied the other, "but unless my ear lies like the mischief, one of those popping noises over there was the voice of an old acquaintance."

"To the point, man, if you possibly can!" rather impatiently spoke the leader; "what acquaintance do you mean?"

"The one that I was introduced to up on the lake there last night, asking your pardon, captain," replied Pete, lowering his tone a little under the slightly rebuking manner of his commander.

"You are in the right, Mr. Jones," said the other kindly, though a flash of anger passed over his face at the discovery that now burst on his mind; "I see it all, at last. Those were the reports of a pair of pistols, and in the hands, too, of that traitorous Sherwood, who has been hovering round up on our march, and now fires his pistol as a preconcerted signal to give notice of our approach. It is well for the fellow that he was wise enough to put the creek between us and himself before taking this last step."

"That comes of suffering the scoundrel to go unhanged last night," grumbled Brown. "If I had been the captain, I would have strung him up to the limb of a tree like a sheep-killing dog, and left him kicking in the air."

"It is not always," said Warrington, "nor often, I think, that we find cause to repent of the mercies we have shown; but this fellow—let him beware!" he added, knitting his brow, "let him beware how he is taken again!"

All hope of taking the place by surprise being now relinquished by our band, it was soon settled, as the most probable way of accomplishing their object without bloodshed, which they would gladly avoid, that a feint should be made in the open field with a view of drawing out the enemy from their works, while the part of their force not thus to be engaged should go round in the woods and, approaching in the rear, endeavor to get possession of the house and inclosure. In pursuance of this plan Warrington, taking Selden and two of the men with him, started off for the purpose of carrying the last part of the arrangement into execution, leaving the rest of the force under the command of Jones, whose genius, it was thought, was calculated to conduct the other part of the enterprise now intrusted to his charge, with orders to advance through the open grounds toward the house and adopt such measures on the way as circumstances might suggest for bringing about the desired result.

After waiting a sufficient time to allow the other party to gain a post in the woods in the rear of the works, Pete, the new commandant, put his men in motion, and emerging from the bushes they commenced, in a widespread platoon, their ostentatious march through the field, in order to attract the attention of the enemy supposed to be concealed in their inclosures at the house. It so happened that directly in the course of the advancing party there lay a series of large log-heaps, which, either by accident or design, had been placed in clearing the land very nearly in a straight line, at intervals of about a dozen rods, beginning near the house and extending almost to the woods. When the party had arrived within a few rods of the first log-heap their attention was arrested by the sound of a human voice issuing from behind it, and in an eager, suppressed tone giving off some brief orders, resembling those of military command.

"A'ready? up then, an' gie til the louns!" exclaimed the voice of the unseen leader, in broad Scotch, as a platoon of armed men suddenly rose from behind the logs, and, raising their guns breast high, discharged them full in the faces of the Green Mountain Boys.

"Noo, right aboot face! and rin as if the deevil was after ye, as he is, and mair too," resumed the military Donald, for it was no other than he and his men, who had thus been lying in concealment behind the log-heap, patiently awaiting the approach of their unsuspecting assailants.

The balls, just clearing the heads of our band, whistled through the air and struck with a crash among the dry limbs of the forest behind them. As soon as they had recovered from the surprise into which they had been thrown by the suddenness of this unexpected attack, they all sprang forward in the screening smoke of the enemy's fire, and gained the cover of the log-heap just relinquished by the latter for the next one in the line of their defenses.

"Well, this is what I should call rather a curious

how-d'ye-do, boys," coolly said Jones, when they had gained their shelter; "who would have guessed the scamps were packed away behind this old log-heap? But one thing beats my philosophy—if the bloody dogs really wanted to give us the lead (and they shot dreadful careless if they didn't), why in natur didn't they take aim?"

"They are all regular sarvice men," replied a settler from the vicinity, "and breast-high is the rule of firing in the army."

"Then we may thank the rule for our lives, and not the pesky fools who used it," replied the former. "It would not be a great deal more than right to send our rifle bullets through the whole tote of 'em. But I should some rather not kill the sarpents, if we can get along without; and I guess as how we can, seeing they were kind enough to sound their rattles before trying to bite, as that queer old codger did in giving off word before they let drive at us. And if they will go on as they have begun, we'll just be making our manners when they fire, so that the balls may pass over us, and then follow 'em up as before. But hark! the old chap is at it again! going the motions as regular as the nightmare; there! he has got to *'cock fire-lock!'* Now, down with you, boys!"

Jones and his men had scarcely thrown themselves on to their knees behind their log-heap breastwork before another volley of balls, discharged with the same military precision, whistled over them, and again the old dry hemlocks that skirted the woods appeared to be the only sufferers. Again retreating to their next post, these kilted defenders of the place were followed up as at first by their crafty assailants, who were now becoming highly delighted with the fun of so unique a warfare. And in this manner the fight, if fight it be called, continued through the whole field—one party blazing away at random from every log-heap they reached, and then scudding on for the next, quite satisfied with this way of doing their duty of defending these supposed possessions of the king, since they were conducting their defense, as they believed, according to military rule; while the other party, occasionally discharging their pieces into the air to keep up the appearance of a hostile pursuit, and sometimes raising their hats on their ramrods just high enough above the logs behind which they were ensconced to become visible to their foes when they fired, that they might be thus encouraged to continue the sport, were no less content with this fashion of fighting, as it answered all the objects in view without putting them to the necessity of killing others, and, what was quite as agreeable, without running any risk of being killed themselves.

But leaving these belligerents for the present, we will now follow those who departed to execute the other part of this novel enterprise.

Keeping within the border of the woods, Warrington and his attendants soon made the circuit round the clearing, and arrived at the bank of the Creek in the rear of the buildings, before the attack was made on the other detachment. They had scarcely gained this position, however, before they were aroused by the rattling of McIntosh's salutatory volley on their companions at the other extremity of the opening. And, though the rise of land which intervened between them and the scene of action prevented them from ascertaining by sight the exact situation of affairs, yet readily concluding that the enemy in full force had taken the open field as had been anticipated, they made for the house with all possible speed to get possession of the works before the occupants could find time to return. On reaching the inclosure round the house, Warrington, leaving his men in the rear, went round to the front side and, after a moment spent in reconnoitering from behind a woodpile the parties in the field, crept up and made an attempt to open the gate. But to his disappointment he soon discovered that it was securely barred on the inside; while the noise of some slight movement within apprised him that the place had not been left wholly unguarded. On making these discoveries he immediately retreated to the rear without being seen by the enemy. There, standing beside the wall of the inclosure and eagerly gazing through a small crevice between the timbers, he found Selden, who, now turning with an expressive look, silently beckoned him to approach. Obeying the sign Warrington carefully stepped up to the spot and put his eye to the aperture which the other, now yielding the place, pointed out with his finger, when all that part of the arena within which was in front of the house was opened to his view. And the object that there met his eye struck him with scarce less surprise than what had just been manifested by his more romantic companion. Near the barricaded entrance into the yard, instead of a bearded warrior, stood a young and neatly dressed female of striking beauty, holding a musket and apparently enacting the part of a sentry to fire an alarm gun, or open the gate on the signal of her friends. She had evidently heard the movements of those without, and was now standing, like a startled fawn, her bosom heaving with suppressed alarm, her lips slightly drawn apart, and her head turned in the attitude of intense listening—all combining to give an air of charming and picturesque wildness to her whole appearance. A swarthy-faced girl was timidly peeping from the nearly shut door of the house, to which, on hearing the noise, she had apparently retreated. From the dress and appearance of the latter, Warrington was but at little loss in tracing between these two females the relation of mistress and maid. And now, with a rapid survey of the situation of the whole interior, as far as could be seen, he hastily quitted his stand at the crevice and turned to Selden.

"Isn't she a vision of a creature?" eagerly whispered the latter, his fine dark eyes sparkling with animation. "What in the name of feminine wonders will you show us next, Warrington? But who and what can she be?"

"I am scarcely wiser than yourself, in that respect."

"If the other was a Juno, this, I suppose, must be some warrior sylph of the Green Mountains."

"Not of the Green Mountains, I suspect," rejoined Warrington, "but be she sylph or Satan in heavenly guise, we must pay her a visit, and have possession of the works within ten minutes—the enemy are on the retreat for the gate, and there is no time to lose. Advance, boys, and lend me your shoulders for a stepping stone to scale this wall."

The walls of the inclosure were about ten feet high, exclusive of the pickets which surmounted them, and which were formed of stakes three or four feet long, sharply pointed at the top and set into large augur holes bored in the upper layer of timber.

Taking his men to a part of the wall in the rear of the house which would screen them in their attempt from the view of the inmates in front, and thus afford them a better chance to get over unmolested and without causing an alarm to be given too soon, the leader mounted the shoulders of one of his men, leaped on to the top of the timbers, and soon luckily and without noise succeeded in wrenching out pickets enough to give him a ready ingress. And taking up his rifle from the hands of those below and ordering two of them to follow, and the other, who would have no means of getting up, to act in concert with Jones, he now swung himself down upon the ground. In another moment Selden and the man he had selected having been equally successful, they all three stood undiscovered on the ground in the narrow space between the wall and the back side of the house.

"Well, Selden," said Warrington, with a humorous look, "in what manner shall we proceed with this formidable garrison—by storm or parley?"

"The latter, certainly, unless the storm is to be a storm of kisses," replied the other, in the same spirit; "but seriously, lest the appearance of all of us at once occasion unnecessary alarm, I propose that one of us go forward alone for this purpose."

"Yours shall be the chance, then, of displaying your bravery, gallantry, or diplomacy, as the case may require, in treating with the fair commander."

"Thank'ee, captain."

"But have a caution, sir—remember that other things sometimes inflict wounds besides leaden bullets!"

"Oh, borrow no trouble on my account, on either score," gayly responded Selden, as he disappeared round the corner of the house on his delicate mission.

The merry boast of the last speaker, however, had, but for his good fortune, been a vain one: For the next moment after he passed out of the sight of his friends, the stunning report of a musket saluted their ears, while a bullet whistled by them and buried itself in the wall of the inclosure a few feet from where they stood. Instantly springing forward toward the scene of action, they found Selden standing in mute surprise, but unhurt, a few yards in front of the house and as many rods from the mad girl, who, in the suddenness of the alarm and trepidation that seized her as she accidentally turned round and unexpectedly beheld an enemy within the inclosure and approaching her, had just committed the half involuntary, half frenzied act of discharging at him a well-loaded musket, whose fatal contents he had but narrowly escaped. For a moment there was a dead pause, during which neither of the parties stirred from their respective positions, being nearly invisible to each other in the smoke which was rising in eddying whirls between them. Soon, however, the light and airy form of the warrior damsel became visible to her astonished besiegers. There, pale, agitated, and almost frantic with conflicting emotions, she still stood as if chained to the spot, holding with convulsive grasp the yet smoking musket, and apparently scarcely less frightened at what she had done than for her own personal safety.

After gazing an instant with increasing consternation and alarm as she beheld the now treble number of the enemy, she suddenly threw down her gun and made a desperate push to unbar the gate.

"Nay, nay! lady," exclaimed Warrington, leaping forward to her side and placing his hands firmly upon the bars; "this we cannot suffer now, though we intend *you* no harm," he continued in a gentler tone: "but you had better retire—this is no place for one of your sex. Mr. Selden, will you conduct her into the house?"

"Touch me not!" half shrieked the baffled and maddened girl, shrinking from the touch of Selden, who now approached and offered to lead her to the house; "touch me not, villain—monster!"

"Be calm—calm your fears, dear lady!" said Selden, in a soothing and respectful tone. "Will you hear me? Will you look me in the face? There! do I appear like a villain? Now hear me: although we may try to restore these possessions to their former and, as we believe, rightful owners, yet in doing this we would not willingly injure a single man of the defenders—much less a female. Be prevailed on, then, to retire, and I pledge myself, on the honor of a gentleman, that no hair of your head shall be injured."

During this address, the kind and tender manner of which seemed to strike unexpectedly on her ears, she turned and, looking full upon the manly and handsome face of Selden, a change passed over her agitated countenance. Her overtasked nerves gave way, and her assumed nature melting away into its original softness, like a storm of March dissolving into the tears of April, she burst into a fit of hysteric weeping, and now suffered herself to be conducted unresistingly into the house.

By this time Donald and his men, who, on hearing the report of the musket just fired as they were making a stand behind the last log-heap of their line of defense, hastily discharged a parting round at the enemy and fled for the works, had reached the inclosure; and the former was now vociferating the watchword and rattling away at the gate for admittance. Meanwhile, Jones, with his detachment, being apprised that his friends were in possession of the works by a handkerchief which the latter had, as a preconcerted signal, hung on a corner picket, rushed on after the retreating Scotchmen on their way to the gate, intending to follow them so closely that they could have no time to reload their guns before they should be compelled to surrender.

Looking around and seeing his foes close upon him, McIntosh redoubled his clamor to get in.

"Oh, why dinna ye open the gaet?" exclaimed the impatient and distressed Highlander, still ignorant that any others were within than those he left there. "Thae feckfu' deevils are hard at our heels. Och! oigh! Jessy, Jessy Reed! is it my ain colonel's dochter that wad be doylt at sic a time? An' Zilpah, is your mistress dead, or ye a' fear't an' fasht thegithar, that ye nae ken the coming o' us?"

"Your ladies are all safe in the house, my honest friend," cried out Warrington in reply, "but your quarters are now in possession of other hands. You had better surrender, sir, as it will be of little use to contend against those who are now too strong for you, both within and without."

The astonishment and dismay of the simple-minded Scotchman at the discovery that his foes had obtained a lodgment within his stronghold was unbounded; for, having perceived nothing wrong about his works at the time his attention was arrested by the report of the musket within them, and soon after seeing the man left outside by Warrington running out into the field, he supposed the gun was fired by the bold and wayward girl who had volunteered for the service only to apprise him that someone was around the outside of the works. And he and his men, having given a merry hurrah! for the braw lassie who frightened away the skulking tramper, had come on and reached the gate in the confident expectation that in another moment they should be safely ensconced within their works and beyond the reach of all pursuers.

"Gude guide us!" he ejaculated, looking hurriedly around him, while his countenance exhibited the very picture of perplexity and distress; "Gude guide us! gor't by the rake-hells wi'in and wi'out! Oh, what wad I do! what wad I do!"

"I'll jest tell you what to do, you queer old divil!" sung out Jones, catching the last part of these exclamations, as he brought his men to a halt within two rods of the Scotchmen, who now, mechanically facing about and presenting their fixed bayonets to their opponents, stood glumly awaiting the commands of their leader. "I will tell you what to do," he repeated, "you must knuckle to, old fellow. What's the particular use in your standing out against these six loaded rifles, to say nothing of the captain and his folks inside, if they should take a notion to wake you up a little? So I take it the cunningest thing you can do jest now is for you all to throw down your guns and surrender."

"Hoot awa', mon!" exclaimed McIntosh, aroused by this fresh summons to surrender; "an' I rede ye'll find wese fight and defend till the last drap o' our bluide! Attention, there!" he continued, hastily turning to his men, "prime an' load!"

Warrington now sternly repeated his demand for an immediate surrender; but the obstinate Highlander, knowing no way of obeying the military instruction of his colonel, "to fight and defend," but to fight on at whatever odds or whatever the consequences to him and his men, deigned no other answer to this repetition of the summons than by urging his men to dispatch in loading their pieces.

"What is to be done, captain?" coolly said Jones, calling to his superior, and at the same time giving a nod to his men, at which they all promptly cocked their rifles and brought them to their shoulders. "Speak tolerable quick, if you've any orders, for they are about loaded, and we'd some rather give than take under all the circumstances."

"Neither!" shouted Warrington, "do neither. Knock up their guns! disarm them! grapple with them, and, if too many for you, we'll soon be among you."

A sudden furious rush was now made by the Green Mountain Boys on their astonished antagonists, who, not dreaming of this mode of attack and being busily intent on loading their guns, were taken by complete surprise and to a great disadvantage to themselves. And before they had recovered from their astonishment sufficiently to put themselves in a posture of defense most of their guns were wrenched from their hands, their bodies seized around the waist, and some of them thrown to the ground; while grappling man with man, all were instantly involved helter skelter in the tremendous scuffle that now ensued. And although the Green Mountain Boys were now in the exercise of their favorite athletics, and notwithstanding their great strength and suppleness of limb, they soon found that the entire subjection of these brawny and resolute Highlanders was no very easy task. Though thrown to the ground they had to be held there; though knocked down they again rose to the fight, and though beaten they yielded not. And the victory had, perhaps, been even doubtful had not Warrington now thrown open the gate and come, with a fresh force, to the rescue. Then, indeed, it was not till they saw their leader lying bound and helpless on the ground that the pugnacious Scotchmen could be brought to say that they yielded themselves prisoners.

"I have na yielded yet, ye hogshoutherin' rapscallions!" roared Donald scornfully, as he lay on the ground with scarcely a member of his body, except his tongue, at liberty; "I hae na yielded, an' as muckle victory as ye think to mak it, ye sal never say that Donald McIntosh ca'd himsel' prisoner wi'out first settling the conditions o' the surrender."

"What conditions would you have, brave Scot?" asked Warrington, with great show of respect, as soon as he could be heard amid the shouts of laughter that followed this ludicrous declaration of the vanquished leader.

"What conditions? Why, to be allowed to march out wi' a' the honors o' war, an' a safe passport for the women an a' the gear an' property," replied McIntosh, somewhat soothed by the respectful manner of the other.

"And will you quietly yield up the place and depart, if we will allow you these conditions?" rejoined Warrington, evidently disposed to humor the fallen warrior in his laughable demand.

"We wael bide thae terms of surrender," replied the other, "an' ye hae the word o' Donald McIntosh till the bargain."

"We will let the man have his way for the bravery he has shown," said Warrington, turning to his men. "Take away their ammunition, but restore them their guns, and unbind their leader. Now, Captain McIntosh, arise, parade your men, and conduct the surrender in such manner as suits your pleasure."

Deeply impressed with a sense of what he deemed the honor of his profession required in surrendering so important a military post of the king as he considered this, McIntosh arose, formed his men, marched into the inclosure, halted, faced about, sent a corporal to bring out the ladies and place them in the rear, marched out again, grounded arms, and, with an air of great formality and consequence, pronounced himself and followers prisoners of war, to depart on parole, to serve no more on this coast during the war.

Warrington, from his knowledge of the national character of his prisoners, entertaining no doubts of their fidelity in strictly observing all the stipulations of their leader, now cordially invited them to remain at the post through the night. And the invitation being as cordially accepted, both parties within an hour were commingling in the greatest amity and good feeling, the Green Mountain Boys secretly elated with their success in reducing this stronghold of the Yorkers, and their late opponents resting satisfied with the gallant efforts they had made in its defense.

The next day the vanquished, availing themselves of the permission granted them by the victors, conveyed all the movable property of their master on board several large bateaux which had been kept there for the purpose of exporting lumber or other products of the farm, and set sail down the creek for St. John's or some one of Colonel Reed's possessions on the York side of the lake, near its northern extremity.

Thus terminated this unique and curious contest, which proved to be the last one of any magnitude that occurred between the New Hampshire grantees and the Yorkers for the possession of the soil within the disputed territory. The place being thus left in the hands of the Green Mountain Boys, they immediately reinstated the owners and former occupants, and soon after strengthening and enlarging the defenses into a more regular fortress, they posted a small permanent force there to prevent so important a position from falling again into the hands of the Yorkers or any new set of minions which the late military aggressor might see fit to send on for a second forcible seizure. No further attempt, however, was made to wrest the place from their hands; nor did any of the late offenders ever make their appearance in the place, except the brave and honest, though strangely mistaken McIntosh, who, indeed, after a while returned, but with views not a little altered. For, becoming by some means undeceived as to the nature of his late trust, and being excessively mortified at the development which robbed him in his own estimation of nearly all the glory he had gained in defending it, he seemed to have foresworn the military for a more quiet profession. And, purchasing a farm in the neighborhood, he settled down upon it and in the peaceable pursuits of agriculture spent the remainder of an unusually long life, no less respected for scrupulous honesty than distinguished for the whimsical absurdities that occasionally marked his conduct.*

But there is one of the conquered band whom we have no notion of disposing of in so summary a manner. We mean the heroine of the party—the spirited, wild, wayward, and beautiful Jessy Reed, who was, indeed, no other than the daughter of the usurping colonel. The singularity of the position which our band found her occupying at this place, and the attending circumstances, we will give her an opportunity of hereafter explaining, and content ourselves for the present with a few words respecting her destination and the manner of her departure from the scene where she was introduced to the reader. Instead of going with McIntosh and his men to the north, she had expressed a wish to proceed to the residence of a family with whom her father was intimate, living near the south end of the lake. But the large boats being all required to transport the effects and the hands needed to man them, an

* McIntosh died in the town of Panton, Vt., near the place of the exploits here described, in the year 1813, I think.

open skiff and one man to row it were the only accommodations that could well be afforded her. Still she persisted in her determination. But should she be permitted to embark with no more attendants? The air of extreme novelty attending this singular girl, together with her personal attractions, had from the first made a strong impression on the mind of Selden. He began with playing the soother—succeeded, and became her attendant, the evening after the affray, in a twilight walk along the banks of the Otter, during which he was as much surprised at the exhibition of intelligence and wit, into which he had artfully drawn her, as charmed and interested in her beauty and a certain piquancy and dash of romance which nature and a semi-military education had thrown into her character. But how far this interest was reciprocated he had no means of judging. And should he now offer to become her attendant on her proposed voyage through the lake, would the offer be received? Would she suffer to attend her one of those who had wrested away her father's possessions; one from whom she yesterday recoiled as from the touch of a viper, branding him with the epithets of villain and monster? Sudden metamorphoses are no miracles in this changing world, thought Selden, and a failure in this case shall not happen from the want of an attempt. He delicately made the proposal. She hesitated, blushed a little, and accepted.

"Was ever woman in such humor woo'd?"

CHAPTER VII

"And I, methinks, till I am old,
A fairer maid shall ne'er behold—
The sloping lawn, the cottage small,
The outspread lake, the waterfall,
And thou the spirit of them all!"

A FEW miles from the eastern side of Lake Champlain, and nearly opposite to Crown Point, where now molder the ruins of one of the oldest fortresses in North America, a bald, jagged, and desolate looking peak, known by the ungracious appellation of Snake Mountain, stands frowning over the surrounding levels in solitary and repulsive grandeur. This detached and lofty mountain, being the highest and indeed, the only eminence of any magnitude in all that extensive and beautiful tract of country lying between the lake and Otter Creek for the last thirty miles of its course, served among the settlers, before roads were much opened in this part of the wilderness, as a guide or landmark for all those who had occasion to travel the woodlands in this vicinity. And Warrington, after safely establishing his friends in their possessions at the Lower Falls and dispatching a small band of his forces in pursuit of the York surveyor, repaired with the remainder of his men to the western brow of this mountain, as a rendezvous to which his whole party were to assemble when the surveyor was secured, proposing to employ the interim in making observations preparatory to some contemplated operations in the neighborhood of the place. He was, as the reader has already been apprised, the owner, under a New Hampshire grant, of a considerable body of wild land lying along the shore of the lake, upon a part of which, he had been informed, someone had entered under color of a York title. And as the tract of land in question was situated between this mountain and the lake, it was now his intention to ascertain whether the information he had received was correct and, if found to be so, to take measures for ejecting the intruder, whose name even was unknown to him. With this object in view, our leader, leaving his men to prepare a shelter for their temporary quarters, took his rifle and set off alone through the woods in the direction in which the improvements of the supposed intruder were said to be located. After traveling some miles in this direction he arrived at the top of the last offset in the lakeward slope of the country, before reaching the shore, which now appeared a short distance in front, while an opening of considerable extent became visible on the left. Approaching the skirt of this opening and carefully noticing the natural landmarks around it, he soon became convinced that the whole clearing with all the improvements, was embraced within the boundaries described within his own patent. Having satisfied himself in this respect, he now turned his attention more particularly to the improvements themselves, and felt a degree of surprise on witnessing their comparative extent and superiority over the rest of those of this recently settled country. The house was uncommonly neat and comfortable in its appearance, and very pleasantly situated on the green and graduated margin of a beautiful little brook that meandered, with many a glittering cascade, through a smooth meadow and entered the woods a few rods below the spot where he stood. The outhouse, barn, garden, and everything around were in good keeping—all going to furnish unequivocal indication that enterprise, taste, and some degree of wealth had here been employed. Much did Warrington wonder who could be the enterprising occupant who had accomplished all this in so short a time, and still more, that it could have been done without more particular intelligence reaching him respecting it. But whoever he might be it was not probable that he would part with such fair possessions without a struggle; and, as a garrison was near, the troops of which he understood to be in the York interest, and stood ready, doubtless, to protect the intruder, Warrington at once saw that a considerable force might be necessary to dispossess him, and even should the attempt be successfully made, the same force might be required to be permanently stationed there to defend it. After revolving this subject in his mind a while, he concluded to defer it for further consideration, and perhaps for a consultation with his companions; and now dismissing the matter from his mind he again gave his attention to the inviting prospect around him. The day was bright and tranquil; the balmy breath of spring, wafted over flowering field and budding forest, was dallying with the whispering pines above, thus gratifying one sense with delicious odors and soothing another with the soft and dying murmurs of Æolian melody. The long tract of the far stretching waters of the lake, sleeping in the rays of the descending sun, shone with dazzling brightness, which at intervals was beautifully relieved by the dark green islands which studded the glittering expanse. The sloping uplands beyond, which reanimating nature was just beginning to clothe in the green vesture of summer, rose up from the long line of nodding pines that lined the western margin of the lake in beautiful perspective, each individual feature of the landscape becoming more and more indistinct in the mellowing distance, till the view was terminated by the last long ridge of climacteric mountains, whose tall ice-clad peaks fiercely flashing in the sun were marked in bold outlines against the cloudless blue of the heavens. A solitary flag was waving over the massy and frowning walls of the opposite fortress, on which the *Mene Tekel* had already been traced by the Unseen Hand that writes the destinies of nations: for the emblem lion, that there now proudly floated on the breeze, and glorying in his strength and prowess, seemed bidding defiance to the world, was doomed, before many revolving suns had finished their daily course, to be plucked down by those who were alike fearless in their resistance to oppression whether coming from a sister colony or a parent country.

While Warrington, who was an enthusiastic admirer of nature, with whom he particularly loved to commune in the solitudes of the forest, where her empire was undisturbed by the works of art, was giving his soul to the magnificent prospect before him, he was recalled from his reverie by the light plashing of oars in the waters below. And turning his eyes in the direction of the sound, he indistinctly discerned through the trees a small skiff approaching the shore of the lake, rowed by a single person who, on reaching his landing, drew up his boat and, taking out of it a gun, ascended the bank. As he emerged from the thick underwood that skirted the shore into the more open forest and advanced into the higher grounds, Warrington soon discovered from his uniform that he was a soldier or some subaltern from the fort, who had come over, he concluded, in search of the partridge or other light game with which the woods here very plentifully abounded. The man still continued leisurely to advance into the forest till he had reached the runlet before mentioned; when something on his right in the direction of the clearing seemed suddenly to attract his notice. And, after pausing a while in apparent doubt and indecision, he began somewhat cautiously and with an air of hesitation to move forward toward the object which had arrested his attention and which he still appeared to keep anxiously in view. Our leader, who in the meanwhile kept his stand unobserved, supposing the other had sprung some game at which he was endeavoring to obtain a favorable shot, continued with a sort of listless curiosity to watch his motions till he had passed out of sight behind an intervening copsewood of low firs that thickly extended along the slope some half dozen rods from the clearing. In a few moments, and as the former yet stood patiently listening for the report of the expected shot, the voice of a female, coming from the quarter to which his attention was directed and uttering a slight cry as of mingled surprise and alarm, reached his ear. The voice of the man was next heard in the earnest, though flurried tones of seeming entreaty, which appeared to be followed by a hasty movement toward the object addressed—and in a moment more a piercing shriek rose wildly from the spot. Grasping his rifle and plunging into the thicket Warrington bounded down the hill with the speed of a wild deer toward the scene and in another instant the parties were revealed to his sight—a young lady of the most interesting exterior, with her hair loosened and falling in disorder over her neck and shoulders, and her flushed countenance eloquent with indignation and alarm, as with half-averted face she struggled to free herself from the fellow who, by a grasp of one hand on her garment, was endeavoring to detain her in her attempted flight. One glance at the victim of this rude assault sufficed to tell the unexpecting and astonished Warrington that the fair original of that picture which had been so long engraven on his heart was before him, requiring his instant aid and protection.

"Back! ruffian, back!" exclaimed he, as with leveled piece he rushed upon the soldier, who stood mute and confounded before so unlooked for an apparition; "back! I say. Unhand the lady, or you die on the spot!"

Quailing beneath the stern and withering glances of the other, the abashed aggressor immediately relinquished his hold on the girl and, muttering a denial of any intentional wrong and a few curses at the interference of Warrington, slunk away and disappeared in the woods.

"I am much indebted to you, sir," said the still agitated maiden, scarce audibly, her eyes timidly bent on the ground, as her protector now gently advanced to her side.

"Miss Hendee," said Warrington hesitatingly, after an awkward silence of a moment; "do I not behold my former acquaintance, Miss Alma Hendee?"

"Mr. Howard?" exclaimed the girl, as with deep surprise she now for the first time lifted her eyes to scan the features of her before unrecognized deliverer.

A slight flush passed over the face of the other on hearing himself addressed by that name, and he opened his lips as if to correct his fair friend, but a second thought seemed to repress the expression of the first, and, quickly recovering from his hesitation, he observed, "I little thought to have met you here, Miss Hendee. I could almost forgive the wretch who caused you this fright, since he has been the means of my meeting again with one whom I have never ceased to remember with pleasure. But you have companions here, surely?"

"No nearer than the house, from which I wandered down the run just now and, tempted by these flowrets peeping up along the banks, extended my ramble, perhaps imprudently, thus far into the woods."

"And is this fair situation, then, your home—the residence of your father?"

"Certainly it is," replied Miss Hendee, resuming her natural cheerfulness. "Why, surely, Mr. Howard, you did not suppose I had turned wood-nymph to wander in the forests and house in the caves, did you?"

"I hardly knew what to think, for it never occurred to me that the father of Alma Hendee could be in possession of this beautiful opening."

"And why not, my dear sir? Why, we have been here these three years. And if we have not made the wilderness blossom like the rose we have at least gone so far as to make the rose blossom in the wilderness. Come, you shall attend me home and see what a pretty flower garden I have in progress."

"To the opening, at least," responded Warrington, obeying the motions of his fair companion.

"And now, sir," resumed the latter gayly, as they proceeded on their way, "having answered your questions, let me be the catechist a while, will you? And, in the first place, from what cloud so opportunely dropped my gallant deliverer, just at the particular moment he was wanted?"

"I, too, am an inhabitant of the Green Mountain settlement, though not of this vicinity," answered the other; "and, you see," he continued, smilingly pointing to his rifle, "that my old propensities still hang about me; and for the present you must take this as an explanation of my wandering into this section of the country. I had just arrived at the border of the woods up yonder, and was viewing your delightful situation, when your cries brought me to your side."

"I am half ashamed of the noise I made," rejoined the lady, "and I presume it was unnecessary. He has occasionally been at our house; and how far he considered himself warranted on such an acquaintance to obtrude himself as he did, I know not. But, being startled by the fellow's unexpected appearance, and uncertain from his hesitating and equivocal manner what might be the nature of the proposals which he said he wished to make, and which at last he seemed determined I should stop to hear, I became much alarmed, I will confess; though I should feel excessively mortified to have any stir made about it. I hope you will not mention the affair to my father when we get home?"

"Certainly not, if it is your wish—that is, I would not, if I were to see him," replied Warrington, pausing, as they now came into the open field.

"But surely, sir, you will go to the house? My father will be very much pleased to renew his acquaintance with his Doctor Hunter, as he would always persist in calling you."

"Your kind invitation, believe me, Miss Hendee, is most gratefully received; but I think it would hardly be advisable for me at this time to accept it."

"And why not? So near and not visit us? I know my father will be delighted to see you and have you spend several days with us—particularly so, I imagine, at the present time, when he is not without apprehensions of an attack from the Green Mountain Boys, as they call them. Why, did you know that a band of these men have, for several days past, been ravaging the settlement along Otter Creek, headed by that terrible fellow, Captain Warrington?"

"I heard," replied the other, confused and stammering at this unexpected question and the commentary on his own character which he perceived it involved in the mind of his fair companion, "I heard—that is, I was aware that the person you mention had come into this part of the country. But your father need be under no apprehension on that account," he continued, regaining his composure, "for I think I can very safely answer for Warrington that neither he nor any of his followers shall ever disturb the father of Alma Hendee."

"You can! can you? But why couple my name so very oddly with that of this fearful man? I do not fully comprehend—I know there are two parties in this settlement, and I suppose he and his company pretend to be acting for the New Hampshire party. Perhaps *you* belong to this party, and know him, and can influence him in our behalf? Oh, if you would! But come, do go to the house with me and assure my father of this."

"Not now—another time—perhaps to-morrow, I may visit you—that is if——" And Warrington paused and hesitated, as if doubtful whether to proceed, while, with a waiting and wondering expression, the girl stood earnestly looking him in the face. "Miss Hendee," he at length resumed, somewhat pensively, "you left the place which afforded me the pleasure of your acquaintance unexpectedly—quite so to me. On my return a day or two after our last interview, to my great disappointment I found you were gone—whither, I was never able to discover."

"We intended you no disrespect, however, Mr. Howard, in leaving thus unceremoniously," replied the girl, exchanging the free and cordial, for a more guarded and distant manner, as if she instinctively anticipated what was to follow. "My father, who, as you are aware, had then become able to resume his journey, gained some information from a traveler who called in your absence, which led him to determine on leaving the place the next morning. I should certainly have been happy *at that time* to see you again and apprise you of our departure."

"'*At that time,*'" rejoined the other, catching the emphasis, and slowly, and with a tone of disappointment, repeating the expression, "'*at that time*'; and have

Miss Hendee's feelings, then, changed since I last saw her?"

"I then esteemed you, Mr. Howard, much—very much, indeed," she evasively replied, looking down, while her fingers were busy in tearing a flower that she had plucked by the way. "I thought highly of you—very; and I still know not why I should not regard you with the same respect."

"*'Respect,'* my dear Miss Hendee, is a term that falls coldly on the ears of those who are looking, or, at least, hoping, for a warmer expression. You were sensible, were you not, that at the time to which we have been alluding, I was cherishing for you a tenderer sentiment?"

"I had no right to understand so," tremulously replied the lovely listener, the quick heavings of whose bosom plainly told the tumult that had been awakened within; "you certainly made no professions that would warrant me in such a belief."

"Miss Hendee," resumed the other after a pause, "you were, if I rightly understood your character, as I presume you are now, a frank and ingenuous girl. May I then not hope that in kindness to me you will give a frank answer to a question which I would ask you?"

"If a proper one."

"If, then, a profession, which I intended to have made you had opportunity been allowed, were to be made now, are there more obstacles now than then to prevent it being favorably received?"

She made no reply, and Warrington, stealing a glance at her averted face, perceived that her eyes were suffused with tears.

"There is, indeed, then, one between us," at length said the other sadly.

"There is," was the reply, in a tone of regret, which should have satisfied even the monopolizing heart of a lover. But love with men, oftener than otherwise wholly blind to policy, is rarely content to rest satisfied with those indirect expressions and delicate intimations, which are a surer proof of its existence in the female heart than the most open declarations, and, absurdly craving more, is not unfrequently compelled to put up with less. It was thus with our lover as he rejoined:

"May I not have the happiness to hear those lips declare that my affection has been in some measure reciprocated?"

Still there was no reply.

"Am I to understand," resumed Warrington, "that Miss Hendee has pledged her hand irrevocably? And can it be that she has pledged herself, too, for a union into which her heart can never enter?"

"What have I said, Mr. Howard," replied the girl, looking up with the air of offended pride, "to warrant such questions? With some, perhaps, I might not be slow to resent your intimation. And as it is," she continued with great dignity, "you will hold me excused, I trust, for declining to commune further on a subject which should now be as uninteresting to you as it is embarrassing and even painful to me."

"Surely, surely! dearest lady, you cannot believe that I would intentionally offend?" said the disconcerted lover. "We will, however, dismiss this subject for the present, if so unpleasant."

"For the present, and forever!"

"If it must be so—and yet——"

"No more, no more! I know not even that I have done right in listening to what you have already said—or remaining here so long. You will now receive my adieu, and excuse my immediate return."

"One moment yet. You will not deny me another interview."

"At my father's house and in my father's presence, most certainly not."

"Even on these hard conditions I will, then, soon seek it. Cruel one, adieu."

"Adieu!" responded the beauteous girl, as, tripping lightly away, she looked back with a smile so eloquently sweet that it erased in an instant the effect of every frown she had given and every negative she had uttered, from the mind of her repulsed, but not despairing lover.

The progress we have now made in our story makes it necessary to recur to some incidents of an earlier date, connected with several of our leading personages, and having a bearing on the events yet to follow.

Some three or four years previous to the events just related, and when the settlers were first meditating an open resistance to the authorities of New York, it became an object with the former to ascertain how far the government of that province was there sustained in its attempted aggression on the Grants by the feelings and opinions of the people at large—whether, indeed, there did not exist among that people, especially those living near the disputed territory, a considerable degree of sympathy for the settlers in their unrighteous persecutions. For in the event of such a sympathy, the latter believed that the meditated resistance might be ventured upon with safety, or with safety, at least, when compared with a case where the feelings of the people were enlisted on the side of the government. It was therefore determined that an emissary should be sent into the part of New York lying contiguous to the Grants who, traveling in disguise or with disguised objects, should endeavor to ascertain the true sentiments and feelings of the people on this subject: and Warrington was the person selected for this delicate, though important enterprise. Accordingly setting out alone with his rifle, and traveling on foot under the assumed name of Howard and in the character of a hunter and herbalist, he traveled all that section of the country into which he had been particularly sent, calling at almost every house in his course and mingling with all companies and classes in pursuing the objects of his secret mission. And it was while on this excursion that he accidentally formed the interesting acquaintance of which the reader has already been apprised. Happening on one of the main roads leading from the east to Albany, he was overtaken by a gentleman and a lady in a carriage, traveling toward the last mentioned place. They had passed by him but a few rods, however, before the horse suddenly took fright and overturned the carriage, by which the man was seriously hurt, though the lady fortunately escaped with little injury. Springing forward to their aid, Warrington, after securing the horse with no little difficulty and danger, turned his attention to the travelers, who proved to be a father and daughter of the name of Hendee. Assisting the wounded man into his vehicle, and placing his daughter by his side to support him, he attended them, leading the horse, to the nearest habitation, which was a poor inn not far from the place of the accident. And having formerly been placed in circumstances in which he had gained considerable practical knowledge of medicine, he, in the absence of a regular physician in that thinly settled country, undertook the cure of the invalid himself, closely attending him till he became convalescent, and repeating his visits at short intervals during the two or three weeks that elapsed before the patient was able to resume his journey. And it was during these visits, in which he had evidently found great favor in the eyes of both father and daughter, by the kindness and delicacy of his attentions, that he had contracted an intimacy with the latter which soon passed the ordinary bounds of friendship, and ripened into that blissful state of the affections which constitutes perhaps the most surely happy period in the course of love—when the feelings of parties are tacitly understood and appreciated by each other before an open avowal occurs to throw with its business-like aspect the first shade of earth over this paradise of the heart. It was at this interesting stage of the intimacy that Warrington returned one day after a longer absence than usual, and found, to his great disappointment and regret, that Hendee and his daughter had departed the day before, without leaving any note or message, as he then could learn, explanatory of their unannounced and to him unexpected departure. Believing from this that he might have been perhaps deceived in regard to the nature and extent of the interest which he flattered himself he had created in the bosom of Miss Hendee, and feeling a little piqued at this appearance of neglect on the part of both father and daughter, he soon ceased his unavailing inquiries concerning the family. And he had never heard anything further respecting them, or received the slightest information of the place of their subsequent residence, except the vague and uncertain information which he gathered in his adventure at the subterraneous abode before described, from that time to the present hour, when to his utter surprise he found them located on his own land. And now having no suspicion that they were conscious of intruding on the rights of another, and least of all his own, in taking up this place under a York patent, and still cherishing all his former sentiments for the daughter, whose heart he believed he still retained notwithstanding the claims of another to her hand, he resolved to relinquish his right to the land and even keep his ownership, if possible, a secret from the family while he should prosecute his suit with the girl, at least till he had unraveled the mystery that still seemed to hang over her, and become better satisfied of the hopelessness of his case.

Revolving this subject in his mind he returned to his encampment and announced to his wondering companions that he should have no occasion to employ them in the affair which, as they were apprised, he had been to investigate.

CHAPTER VIII

"Let us be conjunctive in our revenge."

"'Tis lucky! I can work my purposes,
While seeming but to do the State a service."

PERHAPS there is no kind of hatred that finds harbor in the human breast more deadly and inveterate than that which is entertained by the perpetrators of base actions against those who have detected them in guilt. Nor does the degree of inveteracy with which this fiendish feeling is secretly cherished by the former, appear to be very often lessened by any forbearance which may be exercised by the latter in not exposing their baseness or bringing them to punishment. We will not detain the reader, however, with any speculations of our own on this dark and somewhat singular leaf in the history of the human passions, but leave the subject to be illustrated by those incidents of our story by which these remarks were here suggested.

When the discomfited soldier retreated from the presence of Warrington and the rescued maiden he concealed himself in a thicket, from which he could espy the movements of the couple till they separated. And when this had taken place he proceeded directly to his boat and entering it, pushed for the opposite shore, plying his oars with a sort of nervous and spiteful energy, as if impelled by the commingling feelings of chagrin and revenge that were working within him at the thoughts of his defeat, and the consciousness that he had disgraced himself forever in the eyes of the girl, as well as exposed himself to the contempt and abhorrence of her deliverer.

"Fool! fool!" he angrily muttered to himself, as he urged his skiff through the waters, which, as if in mockery at the dark turmoil of his breast, were now sparkling in cheerful brightness in the rays of the setting sun; "stupid fool, to think a timid girl would listen to me in such a place! and more fool still to manage so blunderingly as to alarm her, when, if I had begun right, I might have told her all, or at least found out whether she would have made it to my advantage to do it. And then to mend the matter, I must try, in my eagerness, to stop her! which brought down that cursed interloper upon me, as if the Old Boy sent him just at that moment to make an affair out of the trifle! I wonder what they supposed I wanted to do? that is plain, however, what they thought; but they were mistaken: Bill Darrow for once is accused of what he is not guilty! Ha! ha! ain't that a curiosity! Well, the plan, like every woman plan I ever laid, is all blown to the devil now, I suppose; though I can yet bring it about with the old man if I choose. But that scoundrel, d—— him! whoever he may be, I'll dog him to the death, but I'll pay him for his rascally interference!"

While thus reasoning and raving by turns, in the way of soothing his smarting feelings, he had nearly reached his destined landing, a small cove about a furlong north of the fort, when he caught a glimpse of a man standing among the bushes on the shore apparently awaiting the approach of the boat.

"Ah! who have we here?" resumed the desperado, as, shading his eyes with his hand from the blinding rays of reflected light that fell in his face, he threw a scrutinizing glance at the person of the other. "Why! can it be? it is—Jake Sherwood himself! What in the devil's name brought him here just at this time? Ah! my dear fellow, you may thank your good stars, and evil ones, that you are not by this time pretty devilishly well dished! But can he have mistrusted my good will? No, no! the secret is still my own, and for the present shall remain so, as my best stock in trade. Yet what can he want with me? Some Beelzebub errand to be done, I'll warrant me! Well, he shall pay roundly for doing it, besides shelling out something more than promises on the old score, or I'll yet put him in a spot he will little relish, I am thinking."

"Well, Darrow," said Sherwood, as the former now reached the shore, and, pulling up his boat, mounted the bank; "sporting a little over yonder this afternoon, eh? What luck? None! Well, that is the way sometimes. But come, take a seat on this old log here in the bushes. I should like a little talk with you; so lay aside that grim scowl of yours and be sociable once, if you can."

"Sociable! hum! I should like to know who in h——l could feel sociable, or wear a decent face, while his conscience is loaded down with such soul-damning secrets as these of yours."

"My secrets! Ha! ha! as if they were not yours, too!"

"And they may be somebody's else, too, unless you mend your manners, and show yourself a little more liberal than you have been lately, Jake Sherwood. But what brings you here now, and what would you have with me?"

"Oh, nothing very special—nothing of any great consequence——"

"Nothing very special, hey? When did Jake Sherwood, or his father before him, ever call on Bill Darrow without a special object, I should like to know?"

"Well, well, supposing I have an errand, what then?—what is there so out of the way in that, you surly one?"

"Why, nothing out of the way, but exactly in the way, as I said. But what is the use of puttering with your roundabout moonshine?—out with it!"

"Darrow," said the other, after glancing about him as if to make sure that there was no one within hearing; "there are several of the York outlaws prowling about Otter Creek. We came near seizing them a few days ago at Lake Dunmore, though they escaped us, and that was not all—but no matter—they, day before yesterday, went down the creek to the Lower Falls, and took and laid waste Colonel Reed's plantation there. And their leader, one Warrington, with part of his gang, has since moved off somewhere in this direction. Now there is a reward of about two hundred crowns to be had for taking this fellow. I have had my eye on him some time, and now I have some particular reasons for wishing him secured."

"What kind of a looking fellow is he?" asked Darrow, with considerable interest. "Do you know him by sight?"

"Yes—a tall, square built, and rather good-looking fellow—that is, he might appear so to one who did not know him for a scoundrel."

"The same, by heavens!" exclaimed Darrow, after musing a moment. "Yes, he must be the very fellow I saw not two hours ago, as I was skirting along Captain Hendee's clearing over yonder. He was walking with a woman near the woods."

"How! what woman—not Alma Hendee?"

"Can't say."

"No, no, it must have been the maid—and yet—but confound the audacious scoundrel, how came he there, and so soon acquainted with either maid or mistress, unless my suspicions are right?"

"All that you can answer as well as I—though come to think more about the woman's make and gear, I'll be hanged if I don't believe that it was the old man's daughter."

"Fire and furies! it must be so."

"Why, what are you so wrathy about?" said Darrow, with a malicious smile. "You are not afraid the fellow will run away with your girl, are you, Jake?"

"My girl! who told you so? Not mine, unless I please, I would have you to know! No, no, sir, no fear of this poltroon in that. But still I can't exactly comprehend the movement. If he was reconnoitering with a view to ousting the old man, would he be walking out so familiarly with his daughter? It don't look like it—no, it means something else, which must the sooner be seen to. And thanks to the rascal's boldness, he has put his fate in my power quicker than I expected."

"How—in what way?"

"Why, don't you see, Bill?" said Sherwood, turning with a familiar and coaxing air to the minion, "don't you see how easily he can be entrapped, if he remains at Hendee's to-night, or repeats his visit?"

"Ay, but how would you manage the business?"

"You are a sergeant—take a file of men, go over, surround the house, and take him. Your superior won't object."

"But how am I to know when he is to be found there?"

"I will go over myself, reconnoiter, as soon as dark, without showing myself to alarm him, and if I find the game be there I will make a torch signal at the landing. You must keep watch, and as soon as you see the light come over with your men. If he is not there to-night, he will be soon; Alma Hendee is not a girl to be once seen and draw no second visit. Yes, by the powers of darkness, I have him at last! But supposing he does not come into this trap; he certainly is prowling somewhere near; and you can prowl, too, Bill. And—at the last pinch—you are a good rifle shot, I think, Darrow?"

"Ha! ha! out at last, then! I thought it would finally come to that. Jake Sherwood, you are a book that I can read by looking on the cover."

"Then you know what I would have you do."

"Yes; but where would be the reward in that case? The Yorkers don't pay for heads that have been bored, do they!"

"The Governor's proclamation don't say delivered *alive*, but only delivered. But whatever question there might be about that in some cases, there shall be no failure in this. I have influence enough at headquarters to see that your bill is footed if you bring this about in any shape."

"And you will do it?"

"Upon honor."

"Upon interest, you mean."

"Upon both, if you please."

"That will do, and for this d——d good reason—if the security *is* weak, I know of that which can easily be made to enforce the bargain. Jake Sherwood, I am your man."

"Now, that looks like a cheerful good will, without your usual drawback of grumbling. Well, we understand each other, do we?"

"Hum! a d——d sight too well, Jake!"

"Why, we part friends, don't we?"

"Yes, and it rests with you whether we remain so. But I must be back to the fort. And, as it is getting dusk, you go directly over, I suppose?"

"Soon; but you understand that we are to try to cage him at Hendee's first. Remember to look out for the signal!"

"Ay, ay!"

"Yes; my suspicions were right about him and the girl," soliloquized the plotting agent, after the departure of his reckless minion. "But never mind, I have put the bloodhound on the scent; and if the animal don't forget his own nature, in addition to putting a stop to this business, I shall soon have the pleasure of seeing that haughty leader of these savage rebels atone for every blow which he caused to be inflicted on me at that accursed lake! And that jeering lieutenant and all the rest, reward or no reward, shall have their turn next. And then their executioner, if I can contrive to make the hated scoundrel such, must be made in some shape to follow them. Perhaps, however, he may be disposed of in the war said to be brewing. At all events, he is too dangerous a fellow to my interests to be suffered to remain here long, to say nothing of the insults which I am compelled to bear, and seem to take in good part, from his devil's tongue. I wonder, though, what made him undertake this dangerous business so readily? The reward, I suppose. Well, let him have it; revenge is dearer to me than money. But perhaps I can contrive to get both; if I could but manage, after securing this renegade captain, to make Darrow and some of the rest mutual executioners! Ha! that would be glorious! But of that hereafter; now for the first object."

So saying, and partially arousing himself from his reverie, he proceeded along the shore a few rods to a point where he had left his skiff, and, entering it, began to pull slowly for the residence on the opposite shore, already described, to which we will next take the reader for the purpose of introducing some new characters, and making the place the future scene of a large portion of the incidents to follow.

CHAPTER IX

"I prythee, daughter, do not make me mad."

It was on the second evening after the incidents related in the two preceding chapters occurred that an elderly gentleman sat at the door of the pleasantly situated cottage before described, quietly indulging in the habit-made luxury of puffing the Indian weed, as, enjoying the bland breezes of the evening, he calmly looked out upon the broad expanse of the lake and the diversified objects of the landscape around, over which the shades of night were now rapidly gathering. Now his eyelids would droop and his head sink slightly toward his breast, under the sedative influence of the narcotic fumes he was imbibing, aided by the ceaseless croakings of the frogs, whose evening choruses rose from the marshy shores of the lake in drowsy monotony on the ear. And now he would partially arouse, and his eye would light up for an instant with returning consciousness, as his ear caught the new note of some bird of passage just returned from his hibernal flight to the warm south, and now for the first time heard, marking the progress of the season. The man might have been sixty, though his appearance indicated a greater number of years; for his head was nearly white with the frosts that the fatigues and privations of the camp, in which the vigor of his manhood had been spent, had prematurely sprinkled on his head. And yet his erect figure and keenly flashing eye, as his attention became aroused to objects around him, betokened a spirit still unbroken, and intellect still unimpaired, in spite of a shattered constitution and the ravages which hardships and time had depicted on his thin and war-worn visage. Though, at the same time, the rapid play of the muscles of his face, and the combined expression of every feature of his countenance, evidently denoted that, with fine sensibilities, and much that was generous and noble, he naturally possessed a sanguine temperament and a fiery disposition, which his growing infirmities had rendered still more irascible. And such, indeed, was the case with Captain Hendee, the person whose appearance we have been endeavoring to describe. His life had been one which had been checkered with no ordinary vicissitudes. He had been an officer in the Colonial army, and out in most of that fearful struggle with the French and Indians, that, with little intermission, spread death and desolation through all the borders of the English colonies in America from 1744 to 1760; and he had suffered imprisonment, sickness, and all but death in that terrible warfare. He had also known the extremes of affluence and poverty in his pecuniary affairs, while great felicity and uncommon bereavements had marked his domestic relations. He had buried two wives; each, while she was spared him, the charm of his existence. And, to add still more to his cup of sorrows, a darling son, who had been intrusted to the care of an uncle in his father's absence, soon unaccountably disappeared, having been abducted and murdered, it was supposed, by some lurking band of Indians. One daughter, the child of his last wife, was now all that remained to him to smooth the pillow of age and prop his declining years. And well did that beloved and truly lovely daughter fulfill the filial trust thus imposed. Aware of her parent's infirmities, as well of temper as of body, she became the gentle soother of the one and the watchful nurse of the other. And ever manifesting the most affectionate solicitude for his welfare, and always assiduously attentive to his slightest wants and wishes, while readily overlooking the harshness which in his fits of petulance he occasionally showed her, and which she generally answered only with a tear, she gained over him by this, and the superadded influence of his affection for her and his sense of dependence on her for happiness, a control for his good that the whole world united would have failed in attempting to obtain.

A discreet and demure maiden of about thirty, an old servant, who lived with them in more prosperous days, still remained with them, and with one more person, scarcely less regarded, completed all the permanent members of the family. That other person was no other than Neshobee, the young Indian, with whom the reader has already had a partial acquaintance, without having been before apprised, however, we believe, of his residence. He was one of Captain Hendee's trophies of war, having been captured in an onset on an Indian lodge, to which a band of murderers had been traced after one of their massacres on the frontier settlement. The Indians being taken wholly by surprise and nearly all slain by the first fire, this lad was found burrowed unhurt in a pile of dry leaves in one of their haunts, and secured by the victors; when the captain declared, with a sort of melancholy jest, that as the hell-hounds a year or two before had deprived him of a son of about the same age, he would for once follow their custom of supplying the place of the slain by adopting one captured from the enemy. And accordingly he took the boy, then six or eight years old, back with him to his post, and finally to his family, with whom the captive had ever since resided.

The domicile of this strikingly contrasted family was a common cottage, constructed, after the fashion of the better sort of houses in the settlement, of hewn timber, so exactly squared and laid together in the present instance as to make smooth, compact walls, neatly whitewashed without and tightly ceiled with boards within. The interior, which was divided into two principal rooms, parlor and kitchen, with a range of bedrooms and other small apartments abreast, exhibited an odd mingling of the relics of refined life with the crude substitutes for furniture and the various articles usually found in the houses of a border settlement. On the high mantelpiece of the best room stood the wide-spreading antlers of some noble buck, the tips of the various branches being ornamented with curious sea-shells, the egg-shells of rare birds, and other devices of the tasteful young mistress of the establishment. Rich mahogany chairs were cushioned with the feathered skins of the loon, a large water-fowl abounding in our northern lakes, and remarkable for the thickness and tenacity of its skin, as well as for the downy softness of its feathers. A light stand, of exquisite workmanship, was supplied with a curiously beaded miniature Indian canoe for a tray, containing a pair of small clam-shells for snuffers. On wooden pegs in the wall were suspended the remains of a once superb mirror, the broken parts of which were artfully concealed by festoons of the creeping evergreen; while on one side a small, but well-selected, assortment of books, arranged on broad shelves, completed the list of all the prominent articles by which the room was furnished. The furniture of the kitchen was mostly of the roughest kind, and the whole room abounded with evidences of the woodman's life, the walls and ceiling above being hung with implements of hunting, furs, pieces of drying venison, and other trophies of the chase, taken by Neshobee, the young Esau, or red Nimrod, if the reader please, of the family.

"Come, father," said Miss Hendee, with a look of affectionate solicitude, as, rolling up her needle-work, she rose from her seat by his side, "had you not better take a seat within; I fear you are exposing yourself too much to the night air to expect quiet from your rheumatic shoulders to-morrow."

"No, Alma," replied the old gentleman, knocking the ashes from his pipe; "I know just what I can bear; old Fahrenheit himself could not make an instrument that would indicate the state of the air, whether hot or cold, dry or humid, more exactly than these sensitive fluids in my old shattered frame. No, the atmosphere is peculiarly soft and warm this evening. I think old Boreas has nearly lost his claws for this season. I just heard a whippoorwill, or muckawis as the Indians call it, which they say never appears here in the spring till winter has got so far toward the big ice-pond on his return to the north that he will no more come back."

"I knew it was very mild to-night, father, but I thought perhaps you were not aware how late you were remaining in the open air, since you appeared so deeply engaged in cogitation."

"True, girl, I have been thinking over matters a little."

"What matters, father, may I know?"

"Yes," replied the other, now rising and following his daughter into the room we first described; "yes, Alma, you shall know, for you are yourself one of the parties concerned."

"I, father?"

"Yes, you are, girl; but in the first place, let me ask you if you did not think your cousin Sherwood's manner, in his visit last night, rather singular?"

"I might have thought so, perhaps. In what

respect did you imagine his manner was singular, however?"

"In several. What was it that he seemed to be hinting about so mysteriously? And did he not have the air of one who is secretly suspicious of something?"

"Does my father," replied the other, evading a direct answer, "does my father think that anything very singular in Mr. Sherwood?"

"Why—why—" said the captain, surprised and staggered at the question—"why, yes, I had hoped so; for these secretly suspecting characters I dislike, Alma, you know. Confound them, yes, I detest them!"

"And I," rejoined the girl, with a smile, in which the jocose and serious were significantly blended, "I am too much my father's daughter, I confess, to think otherwise myself."

"Why? what? how?" hastily exclaimed the captain, puzzled and uneasy at the remark of the other. "Why, what on earth can all this mean? No rupture brewing between you and Jake, is there?"

"Not that I am aware of, as far as there are any ties to sever; or, at least, none that I, as yet, have been the just cause of; though——"

"Though what?" sharply demanded the father, with increasing irritation. "Zounds! you don't think the fellow is trying to claw off, do you? Curse the hollow-hearted—— Humph! what was I going to say?"

"Nothing but the truth, father, I presume," answered Alma, looking up with a faint smile and a sort of cool desperation in her manner.

"Yes, I was," quickly rejoined the other, hitching about in his chair. "Blast it! girl, why didn't you tell me I lied?"

"What! tell my father he lied?" said the girl roguishly; "no, no! that would have been the worst of manners."

"Yes, yes," pettishly returned the captain, "but

why don't you stand up for him? I don't like this *don't care a fig* sort of way you have about the business. Hang me if I don't believe you are the one, after all, who wishes to be off!"

"And would you object to my trying to get the start of him," again evasively replied the girl, "if I believed he was intending to desert me?"

"Why, no," answered the other, "not that I know of; no, that would be, perhaps, a decent *finesse,* if that was the case; but it is not. Then, what is all this bothering and teasing me for?" he continued, in a vexed and expostulating tone; "this supposing things that are not so? You will work me up to a fever; make me mad—March mad—without letting me know which of you to be mad at. 'Tis provoking, insufferable, girl! Why not tell me in your usual direct, offhand way, at once, how the matter stands between you and Jake?"

"Father," said Alma seriously, "I most certainly would tell you if I knew myself."

"Well, if that don't cap the whole, now!" said the captain, eyeing his daughter with an incredulous and somewhat contemptuous expression; "a courted girl know nothing of her own courtship! Your caged squirrel, that hangs in the kitchen yonder, knows nothing of nuts, does he?"

"Now, father, you wrong me," said the other, a little piqued at the taunt, and now perceiving the necessity of being a little more explicit on the subject which she felt reluctant to discuss, lest she should, by such frankness as she could wish to use, displease her sensitive parent. "Mr. Sherwood once certainly made me proposals; and I, knowing how much you had the project at heart, acquiesced—or, rather, I did not reject him; since that time he has not often reminded me of the subject. His own affairs he keeps to himself; and a few silly compliments on his part complete the whole story of what you call our courtship."

"Beggarly account!" muttered the captain, with an air of disappointment; "beggarly account, as the fellow says in the play. Cold business, this, for a love affair, or I am no judge; I'll be shot if I am! But, zounds!" he continued, again kindling up, "why I thought it was all a settled business! And it was settled—and would be now if your powers of winning were exerted to have it so! What will become of us the Lord only knows, if this falls through."

"Oh, I would borrow no trouble on that score, sir," observed Alma.

"But I shall, though," rejoined the other. "The truth is, Alma, we are poor—poor as Job, when the devil had done his damnedest! We owe Jake's father—which, as he is sole heir, is the same as Jake himself—for nearly all we have. If my little Edward could have been spared to me—but the noble boy is gone; and that family have been the vortex in which all my property and expectations have been swallowed up. I do not say that the property went wrongfully; but it went. Even before Jake came here I had thought of the possibility that you might become the channel by which this property would be diverted back again into my family. And when he made proposals to you, and I understood you accepted him, I confess I was gratified. It gladdened my old desolate and despairing heart with the thought that it would insure my comfort in my decrepit and helpless old age, while it would give you the home and wealth which I never could furnish you. And now to have the only bright streak I have seen for years in my dark future suddenly blotted out—to have the only pleasant cup that has been presented to me for so long thus dashed from my very lips! And by whose hand?" he added, with startling fierceness, as, trembling with rising passion, he shook his clenched fist before the face of his unoffending daughter. "By whose hand, I say? Girl, girl, if I really thought——"

"I will marry him, father," replied the girl, bursting into tears, which were drawn forth more, however, by the picture he had drawn of his hopes and sorrows than by his menaces. "Oh, I will—I will marry him, for your sake, dear father, if it breaks my heart!"

"Hang it! no, you shan't!" exclaimed the excitable old man, touched to the quick by the sight of his daughter's tears, and his whole feelings undergoing a revulsion as sudden as rose the tempest of his passion. "No, you shan't! Brand me for a brute if you shall! No—no—no!" he repeated, till his increasing emotion fairly choked his utterance, and he could articulate no more.

The tide of passion having risen to its height, was now left to subside in the pause that followed.

"Let us now dismiss this painful subject from our thoughts," at length said the daughter, the first to recover her composure, "and do not let the matter further disturb your feelings, my dear and generous-hearted father; for whatever be the final result, rest assured that I will never marry without your full consent."

"Dutiful, noble girl!" sobbed the old man, dashing away a tear; "God has left me a consolation in you, my dear daughter, which I ought to be thankful for, and which, but for my accursed temper, I should repay with better treatment."

"Oh, do not name it, father; do not name it," replied the daughter, with a sweet and cheering smile; "if we should go upon faults, I may have scores of them, any of which, perhaps, would outweigh the solitary one you tax yourself with."

Miss Hendee had never before ventured so far in manifesting a disposition to thwart the known feelings and wishes of her irritable father. But her late accidental interview with Warrington, whom she never again expected to see, had forced upon her mind a comparison between her two lovers which made her more painfully sensible than ever how much she must sacrifice in becoming the wife of Sherwood, whose true character, as deeply veiled as he had endeavored to keep it with this family, she had in some measure penetrated, and she could not forego this opportunity of letting her father see how heavy upon her heart hung the chain that she was wearing only out of regard to his happiness; and yet scarcely more now than before did she meditate on throwing off this chain, by which she had passively suffered herself to be bound. But determining to defer any consummation which might, for the present, be urged upon her, she suffered herself only to hope the event of circumstances more auspicious for reconciling the now conflicting duties which she owed herself and, with all his faults, her still loved parent.

After the conversation just detailed the parties soon repaired to the kitchen, where, in his great armchair before the cheerful fire, the captain was accustomed to spend his evenings, sometimes listening to the silver-toned voice of his daughter, as she sang some favorite song or read some favorite author, and sometimes recounting the thrilling incidents that had marked his adventures while battling the subtle foe of the wilderness. One of his most attentive auditors, when engaged in the latter employment, was Neshobee, with whom the veteran also often amused himself in conversation, either imparting information to the native, or listening to the shrewd and original remarks made by the latter in answer to the various questions by which he was purposely interrogated. Perceiving now, however, that the place of this almost necessary adjunct to his happiness was vacant, the captain immediately inquired of Ruth, the servant-maid before mentioned, if she knew whither the Indian had gone.

"He is out in the field, captain," replied the person addressed, with some signs of uneasiness in her looks, "and I wonder what strange thing he sees or hears to-night that makes him act so oddly? I have been out and called to him, but he paid no attention to me, and kept on his pranks, sometimes listening with his ear to the ground, and then dodging or crawling from one stump to another."

"Aha!" said the captain, with a look of interest; "those are generally pranks that mean something with an Indian. I wonder who can be prowling about us now?"

"Mercy!" exclaimed Ruth in alarm; "if it should be the Green Mountain Boys!"

"The worst would be their own, I think," coolly observed the captain, "that is, if they come to show us such play as it is said they have shown some on Otter Creek."

"What would you do, father, in case they should come on such an errand?" asked Alma, with an air of mingled curiosity and concern.

"What would I do, child? Why, I would put a rifle bullet through the first one who should attempt to enter, even if it should be Warrington himself. Be sure, I know but little of this cursed dispute about titles. They may have as much right to lands that they have bought, and first improved, as the Yorkers, for aught that I know; and I was never for hanging them for fighting in such a case. But here—why, zounds! do you think when I have got the first possession, and done so much upon the place, that I am going to give it up to the greedy dogs? No! not if their great devil and all generalissimo, Ethan Allen, should come on with all his forces, would I give it up without a fight! Hoo! they shall have my heart's blood first!"

"I trust there will be no necessity for bloodshed anywhere, father," rejoined the daughter, quite composedly; "I have reason to—that is, I do not believe the Green Mountain Boys will make the least attempt to molest us."

"Well—well, girl," said the captain, scanning the other closely, and at first with rather a puzzled air, which soon, however, gave way to a look of approbation; "I must say that does not seem much like borrowing trouble, as most of you women do in such cases. However, I have been taught by the Indians, and sometimes have paid dear for my schooling, too, that this borrowing trouble is not always so bad a thing after all, as it generally keeps us well guarded against a surprise. But here comes our scout; so let us hear his report. Well, Neshobee, they say you are scouting to-night—what is in the wind?"

"Me hark um, but no tell um," replied the Indian, quietly taking his place by the fire.

The dog in the yard now gave one of those faint, indecisive sort of yelps usual with the animal when doubtful whether he has heard something that should require his notice.

"Beagle thinks pretty much as you do, Neshobee," said the captain, comprehending the tone of the dog. "But hark!" he added, as the animal barked again, and in a more decided manner; "I can't read that so easily. What do you make of it, boy?"

"Beag say that no four-foot coming, cappen," said the native unconcernedly.

"Is the rifle well loaded, Neshobee?" asked the captain, glancing at the firearms suspended by hooks on the wall.

"Yas!"

"And the fowling-piece?"

"Me spose um."

"Very well, down with them, then! Alma, step and bring me my pistols! and in the meantime we will bar the door. Ruth, lend a hand! If these fellows," continued the captain, coolly assisting to execute the several commands he had so rapidly given to his household, "if these fellows had any honest errand they would come up to the house at once, like men, instead of skulking around at a distance, as they evidently are. We may as well be prepared for them."

"Father," said Alma, returning with the required pistols, and now manifesting the most lively concern; "father, I do beg of you not to think of firing on any-one rashly. Ascertain what they want, at all events. Your apprehensions, I think, are wholly groundless—I cannot think—indeed I am very sure——"

A gentle rap, rap, rap! on the outside of the door caused the speaker suddenly to suspend. All now stood hushed in silence till the rapping was repeated in several louder and more distinct knocks.

CHAPTER X

> "But who was he, that on his hunting spear
> Lean'd with a prouder and more fiery bearing?
> His was a brow for tyrant hearts to fear,
> Within the shadow of its dark locks wearing
> That which they may not tame—a soul declaring
> War against earth's oppressors."

"HALLO, there!" called out Captain Hendee, in no very gentle tones, as he cocked his pistols, and threw himself into an attitude of defense. "Hallo! who comes?"

"No enemy, to say the least," answered the voice without.

"Let him in, father, do let him in!" said Miss Hendee, in a low, beseeching tone.

"What, without giving his name!" said the captain. "Why, child, I don't know that voice from Adam's! No, no, friend or foe, he shall undergo that ceremony."

"Well, father, you can just ask him without being so rough, can't you?" interposed the daughter, in an earnest half whisper, quietly placing her hand on the arm of the other.

"Friend," said Captain Hendee, softening down at the entreaties of his daughter, and as it occurred to him that the tones of the voice he had just heard were entirely of a pacific character: "friend, will you favor us with your name?"

"Captain Hendee," said the man, seeming to hesitate about complying, "I am wholly unattended, your dog here seems to acknowledge my acquaintance, and if you will not do the same, when I am admitted," he added in rather a jocose tone, "I will agree to depart as peaceably as I came."

"Humph! me know that man talk! Him no bad!" said the Indian, with a low chuckle.

The captain now, evidently a little chagrined at the suspicions he had entertained and the parade he had made, immediately drew out the bar and opened the door, when the visitor entered, but quickly paused, after entering the threshold, to receive the scrutinizing look of the other.

"What! no—yes, 'tis!" exclaimed Hendee, between perplexity and surprise, after looking a few seconds into the face of the newcomer. "Well, now, by the great Jupiter! if I am not absolutely ashamed of myself! Mr. Howard!" he continued, advancing and cordially shaking the other by the hand, "Mr. Howard, God bless you, sir, how do you do? Apologies by the dozen are yours!—or should be, if such moonshine concerns were ever worth offering. But walk in, walk in, sir. Here are my family—all together now—they were not when you saw us, I think. Alma, you are acquainted with—Miss Ruth, this is Mr. Howard. And here is another, Neshobee, we call him, a native, as you perceive, but for all that an adopted member of our family."

Miss Hendee, though much embarrassed at this meeting, in spite of all her attempts to appear composed, managed, nevertheless, to exchange the customary salutations in such a manner as to conceal her embarrassment from all except her lover; between whom and herself it seemed to be tacitly understood that they should meet each other as for the first time, without making the slightest allusion to their late interview. There was another of the family group, also, that came in for his share of surprise, at least, at some of the circumstances attending the meeting. And that was the Indian. Not expecting to see Warrington here till he heard his voice at the door, and never dreaming till this moment but that the latter and his master's family were entire strangers, the poor fellow, when he saw them meet as old acquaintances, and, above all, when he heard Captain Hendee address the other by the name of Howard, looked perfectly confounded, and expressed as much unfeigned astonishment as an Indian countenance, perhaps, ever exhibited. The instinctive prudence of his race, however, prevented him from betraying, by words, his surprise and perplexity, or exposing Warrington in the disguise which he supposed was for some good reasons assumed.

"Well, Mr. Howard," resumed the captain, after the usual salutations were over, "I am right happy to renew my acquaintance with you, and have the opportunity to express, personally, my obligations to you for your many kindnesses to us at the time of my accident on the road. You probably thought our departure rather abrupt on your return. But you received my note, did you not?"

"No, sir, neither note nor message."

"What! Then that old heedless poodle of a landlady forgot it, or more probably lost it, and, to mend the matter, thought she would conceal from you that I gave her one. Well, well, you must have thought us rather singular beings, as well for that as for some other things you perhaps noticed in us. For, I remember, we kept you pretty much in the dark about our affairs. The fact was, Mr. Howard, and I care not now who knows it, that I was then under the apprehension of being pursued and taken back by creditors before I could reach my connections in Albany, where I expected to obtain the means of satisfying them, as I did before making this purchase."

"You did not return then?"

"No! When I arrived there, finding that sales were making in these lands, I concluded on a life in the woods, made a purchase, came on here the first season with hired men, and then sent for Alma from Albany and the rest of the family and goods from Connecticut."

"And what directed you particularly to this location?"

"My own knowledge of the country obtained in the wars when I was campaigning with Put and Rogers along the borders of this then bloody lake. I remember the spot well. A pitch had been made here by some Frenchmen, who cleared up several acres, lived here a few years, and then deserted the place. This was the first opening made this side of the Connecticut River, all the rest of the country being, at the time I first saw the spot, one broad, unbroken wilderness. Many a weary march, and many a cold, wet bed have I had on these dark and tangled shores. I have often wondered how we could have outlived such hardships. With the constitution and spirits I then possessed, however, I had but little dread of the woods, or the red imps that infested them. But my days of fighting are now over, Mr. Howard."

"Some in my situation, with these evidences around, might feel disposed to doubt that, captain," smilingly observed Warrington, motioning to the firearms, which had not been yet replaced.

"Ah, you have me there," gayly responded the other; "but, honestly, we were expecting visits of a different character. If those rough-dealing devils, the Green Mountain Boys, had beset us, instead of our peaceable old friend, Dr. Hunter, there is no telling but even so broken down an old Trojan as I am, might have shown some fight on the occasion."

"Perhaps, sir," replied the guest in the same spirit; "I should tender my condolence at your disappointment in not being allowed the chance to exercise your old vocation."

"Not a whit, not a whit, sir. For I should extremely regret to be forced into a quarrel with my countrymen in defense of what I consider my rightful possessions. And I hope it may never be the case. But we have had some reason to believe otherwise within a day or two past. A friend apprised me that a band of these fellows was abroad and probably on their way to this part of the lake shore; and our two scouts here, Neshobee and Beagle, having successively made their reports in their respective fashions, to-night, that there were skulkers in the bush, I, for one, began really to expect that we had got to do battle for our home. Alma here, however, I am half ashamed to own, was less apprehensive, and bore herself more coolly than any of the garrison, not excepting the old soldier of forty battles at their head! Hang me! if I don't believe the girl, like old Falstaff, knew by instinct who was coming! Come, child, now be honest, was it not so?"

But Alma, whose head suddenly dropped at the remark, and whose fair cheek glowed like the fire before which she was sitting, was too busy with her pretty fingers in tumbling over the contents of her work-basket for a thimble or some other article that became, just at that moment, unaccountably missing, to heed the question or think of answering it. Even Warrington appeared to be a little discomposed at this close, though random shot of the old captain; but he did not forget to throw a glance of gratitude toward his fair friend for the confidence which the captain's statement seemed to imply that she had placed in his assurances at their late interview.

Captain Hendee, without seeming to notice the sensation which his last remarks, intended only for a passing joke, produced on some of his auditors, at length resumed:

"You wandered round the borders of the woods some time before you found us, I conclude, sir, from the noises that Neshobee heard previous to your arrival?"

"Oh, no, sir; I came direct, and without stopping."

"I don't see, then, but we have as much reason now as before to expect a visit from the enemy to-night," musingly observed the captain.

"Me guess um what I hear no Mountain Boys," said Neshobee, looking significantly at Warrington, as if he considered the latter to have the most interest in the information thus imparted.

Neither the remark of the Indian, nor the meaning look that accompanied it, was lost on Warrington, as was evident from the expression of uneasiness that for an instant became visible on his countenance; but he remained silent.

"Which way did you come, Mr. Howard?" resumed the captain; "I believe you have not told us, nor, indeed, how you became apprised of our present residence?"

Warrington, catching a forbidding glance from Miss Hendee, was hesitating, on her account as well as his own, what answer he should frame to the embarrassing question, when he was suddenly relieved from his dilemma by a bold, heavy rap at the door.

Captain Hendee, feeling more assured this time from the reinforcement received in his friend Howard, who, as usual, had his rifle with him, immediately rose, and, with but a slight hesitation, opened the door, when he suddenly paused and stood a moment gazing in mute surprise at the figure before him. Soon recovering, however, he, in a sort of hesitating and doubtful tone, invited the man to enter.

Acknowledging the proffered courtesy with a stately bow, the stranger advanced with a bold, free step and a fearless air into the middle of the room, where he paused and bowed slightly to each of the assembled group, most of whom, however, were too much surprised and overawed at the singular and formidable appearance of the man to return his salutations. And, indeed, his appearance was of so unique and striking a character as well to warrant the sensation which his presence seemed to produce. Of an uncommon height, and with an extraordinary breadth of chest, supplied with large, brawny limbs, his whole frame constituted a figure of the most Herculean cast; while his large, darkly bright eyes, and the air of intelligence that marked the general expression of his coarse, lion-like features, gave evidence that his intellectual powers were not, as frequently occurs in such instances, wholly incommensurate with his physical proportions. A modern phrenologist, indeed, while comparing his high and remarkably expansive forehead with the vast volume which composed the back part of his head, might be much puzzled to decide whether his intellectual or animal nature would most predominate in his character. His dress, which was likewise somewhat singular for the times, consisted of high, heavy boots, buff breeches and doublet, with a high-collared, white shag coat of the frock kind, all of which was surmounted by a fine, though much worn beaver, slouched, except the front part, which was turned up so as to give an additional boldness to his large features, and to impart somewhat of a bandit aspect to his appearance. This, to ordinary observation, completed his outward equipment; though a closer inspection might have revealed the shape of a stout pistol swelling the smooth and snugly setting leather over each of his breeches pockets, while the buckhorn handle of a large war knife might occasionally be seen protruding from its sheath attached to the side lining of his coat.

Placing the heavy rifle which he bore in his hand in a corner, the stranger now advanced, and, with an air of easy unconcern, seated himself by the side of his host, in the family circle round the fire.

"My name is Hendee," at length said the captain, evidently not wholly at ease in the presence of this bold and fearful looking visitor; "my name is Hendee, and being no great stickler for ceremony, I hope I shall be excused, sir, in saying that it always affords me pleasure to know by what name I may address my guests."

"That's right!" bluntly commenced the stranger in reply, "and you got at it ingeniously, too, by George!"

"I meant no offense, sir."

"Oh, no; but let me see—it is now May, is it not?"

"Yes, sir."

"Well, then, for the month of May my name is Smith."

"Sir? Did I rightly understand you, sir?"

"I presume so. I said Smith, because there are more of that name than any other."

"Yes, sir, but what follows from that?"

"Why, of course, sir, that you stand a better chance to get my right name; men will lie like the devil, sometimes, you know!"

"Really, sir?" said the captain, his eyes beginning to shoot fire at this apparently intended insult, "really, sir, I cannot understand your drift, if you do not mean to offer us an affront."

"Ha! ha! ha!" roared the stranger, in a voice that shook the house. "Well, now, if that ain't a good one—ha! ha! ha! Why, no, friend," he continued, familiarly turning toward the other and giving him a rough slap on the shoulder, "no, no, friend; but you just said you was no great stickler for ceremony—nor aint I, as you see. So let us be honest, and live up to our professions."

"Agreed to that. And yet," rejoined the captain, perfectly at a loss what to make of his strange guest, and though still vexed, yet now half ashamed of the feeling he had shown, "and yet, sir, I have met, in the course of my life, but with few honest men who were afraid to tell their names."

"Why, the truth is," replied the other, with an air of much seriousness, "that you are all such quarrelsome cusses down here in the Grants, that a stranger, like myself, can't safely travel among you by any other name than Smith, if he had one. As to myself, I don't exactly know, in the strictly legal sense of the thing, that I have any name—to *speak* of, except Smith; for I still stick to Smith, mind ye—this is for the month of May."

"Well, well, have it as you will, man," observed Hendee, now softening down, and beginning to be amused in spite of himself at the blunt drollery of the other. "But I must say you are the greatest oddity I have met with for many a day."

"That may be, friend," said the stranger, his countenance assuming the cast of sincerity; "but as you, like a wise man, have concluded not to be offended at nonsense, let us talk sense a little: Captain Hendee, a man of your intelligence and observation cannot but have long since noticed the quarrel that has been brewing between us colonists and the mother country?"

"I have, sir; and with the most painful regret," was the guarded reply.

"And those Bostonians and Virginians, who have taken the lead in the resistance to the king's authority," resumed the stranger, again assuming an equivocal look, and fixing his eyes keenly on the countenance of the other, "those fellows are a set of Christless knaves, for their rebellion, you agree?"

"Knaves? How so, sir?" replied the captain hastily, and with a look that betrayed more of his feelings than he intended should have been revealed to a stranger, and especially to one who apparently entertained sentiments on this subject so different from those which he had long privately cherished.

"Aha!" eagerly exclaimed the stranger, with evident delight, "sits the wind in that quarter, really and truly? Well, I am not disappointed in you, after all, thank God!"

"Yes, but you, sir?" said the captain, again confounded at the seemingly contradictory language and manner of the other, "what did you say but a moment since?"

"What did I say? Oh, pooh! that is nothing!" replied the stranger. "But again, and seriously, Captain Hendee (for I am now satisfied that it will do to ask you the question), should matters proceed to open hostilities in an attempt to burst these accursed fetters, how far could your countenance and support be depended on?"

"Stranger," said Captain Hendee, looking the other full in the face, "as singular a man as you appear, you nevertheless have an honest countenance, and would not, I think, try in my own house to lead me into a snare. But granting that your sentiments and mine coincide on this subject, what could you ask or expect from an infirm old man whose only home and property lie under the very mouths of the guns of Fort Frederick?" *

"I see, I see!" answered the stranger. "But it may be worth much to us to know that your heart is in the right spot. For the times are coming when even what such as you can do may be of incalculable importance to the cause. Indeed, sir," he continued, with increasing

* The fort at Crown Point was, in the old French wars, denominated Fort Frederick.

earnestness and with deep and startling emphasis, "indeed, sir, those times are already at the door: *Blood —American blood has been shed!*"

"Where? where?" simultaneously burst from the lips of Hendee and Warrington.

"At Lexington," resumed the stranger, with clenched fist and eye of fire. "Fifty American citizens have been shot down like wild cattle by a foreign soldiery! and their blood has gone up to the great God in cries of vengeance! All Massachusetts is in arms! And are we here of the Green Mountains to remain idle?" he added, and with a look and a tone of almost frightful energy; "by all the thrones of heaven and hell, *no, no!*"

"Oh, for the renovation of one year of my manhood's vigor!" exclaimed the captain, springing from his chair and hastily striding round the room.

"All that is well enough, but useless, my friend," observed the stranger, after a silence among the company of a few moments, in which he seemed to have brought his feelings back to their usual current: "so instead of calling on Hercules, like the man of the fable, in prayers that never can be answered, be thinking what you can do. This Indian," he continued in an undertone, approaching close to the captain, "he is domesticated in your family?"

"Yes, brought up by us, mostly; a cunning, prudent, and faithful fellow," replied the captain, in a voice too low to be heard, as he supposed, by the rest of the company.

"And may be made a useful friend for some emergencies, with your permission, captain?"

"You have it, that is, for an occasional runner, scout, or the like. I should not like to part with him for any great length of time, however."

"Here, my friend," said the stranger, approaching the native, and presenting him with a valuable pocket knife, "will you take this as a gift to remember me by? Now look me in the face."

"Yas—umph! Ah, him good—one very good!" said the Indian, quickly pocketing the knife.

"Now, captain," said the stranger, putting on his hat, and giving other indications of his intention to depart, "I have only to say that I am sorry I could not have been more frank with you in some particulars; but circumstances forbade it. Now I must be off; and I have some notion," he continued, looking at Warrington, "of inviting your guest here to accompany me as a guide."

"Mr. Howard is an old acquaintance, sir, just called after a long separation," said the captain. "We should be sorry to part with him so soon."

"Mr. Howard will remain through the night with us, surely?" interposed the musical voice of Miss Hendee.

The stranger gave a scrutinizing look at the father and daughter, and ended by exchanging with Warrington looks of intelligence which very clearly showed that the two were by no means strangers to each other. Seeming to satisfy himself he was about to remark further, when the tramp of men, now heard approaching the door, arrested the attention of the company. The rattling of guns announced them to be armed men, among whose voices the quick ears of Miss Hendee recognized that of Darrow. Instantly rising, she hastily invited Warrington to take a seat in the other room; and, the latter complying, the lovers disappeared through one door just as the newcomers entered the other.

CHAPTER XI

"Ha! here come those we counted not on meeting."

The company whose arrival was announced at the close of the last chapter proved to be a small detachment of soldiers from the opposite fort. They were seven or eight in number, under the command of their sergeant, Darrow, who, with three others, after knocking, though scarcely waiting for a bidding, unceremoniously entered the kitchen, the remainder of the force having been posted at the doors and windows without, to prevent all escape from the house. As an ostensible reason for calling at this time Darrow carelessly observed that, being out in pursuit of a deserter, a part of their company had gone up the lake with their boat, thus depriving them of the means of recrossing, and leaving them no other resort but to crave a shelter of Captain Hendee for the night, or, at least, till their boat returned. Calls of this kind by the officers and soldiers of the garrison being of no very unfrequent occurrence at the house, the present visit, therefore, occasioned the captain little or no surprise, and, being of a hospitable turn, and fond, as might be supposed, of having those for company who belonged to a profession in which a great portion of his own life had been spent, he appeared to feel quite at ease with his new guests. Not so, however, with all the company assembled. The meeting between the soldiers and the stout stranger before described seemed to be mutually unexpected, and evidently but little relished by the latter. For, though they were all personally unknown to him, yet he was aware that he might not be so to them; and should the last supposition be true, as, from certain sly looks which he saw exchanged between the soldiers he thought highly probable, he was sensible that he had a part to play for himself and Warrington, of whose co-operation he felt assured, that would require all his tact, and, perhaps, put to the severest test the powers of both to extricate them from the threatened difficulty.

Nor were the stranger's suspicions by any means groundless. Darrow had before seen the man, and at once recognized him as one who, if taken, would prove a far greater prize than the person whose seizure constituted the particular object of the present visit: but one, at the same time, well known to be the most formidable and difficult of capture of all the Green Mountain outlaws.

"That aint the fellow we came for," whispered Darrow to the soldier nearest him the first opportunity that occurred for so doing unobserved. "He must be with the girl in the other room, I think. But this big chap is one of the same kidney, only worth two of him, if taken; secure him as well as the other and your pay shall be doubled. So keep your eyes on him for the present, and we will wait till they go to bed and get to sleep, for the other is no baby for a tussle; and this one," he continued, with a significant look, as he cast a fearful glance at the giant-like person of the stranger; "and this one, to say nothing of the ugly instruments they say he carries under his clothes, he is—he's the devil and all—he's thunder!"

This information, with the orders accompanying it,

being soon passed around to all the band, every movement of the stranger was regarded with the most suspicious vigilance. But he, contrary to their expectation, made not the slightest movement which indicated that he was meditating any attempt to escape. On the contrary, the more he was watched the more unconscious did he seem that he was an object of suspicion or vigilance with any of the company; and with the utmost unconcern he soon began to mingle in the conversation, commencing with those blunt cordial kind of advances to Darrow, and as many of his men as he could find excuse for addressing individually, which are generally the surest, if not the only road to the soldier's heart. Nor was it long before he had succeeded in putting himself on a familiar footing with the whole band, whose feelings and senses, in spite of the distant restraint and the guarded watchfulness they had imposed upon themselves, were fairly captivated by his bold sallies of wit and the irresistible drollery of his manner. Captain Hendee, with his war stories, was completely thrown into the shade by the extraordinary convivial powers of the stranger who, having now fairly become the hero of the company, continued to pour forth, from his seemingly inexhaustible resources, sally upon sally, with increasing brilliancy, and anecdote upon anecdote, each of which was more ludicrous or striking than the preceding one, till the whole party became convulsed with merriment and the house shook with the din of laughter. And now, satisfied with the success that had so well crowned his efforts in this respect, he called on Captain Hendee to bring on glasses and a gallon of spirits at his expense, declaring that, "of all God's cattle, he preferred soldiers for companions. It was not every day that a hunter, whose next door neighbors and common acquaintances were bears and wolves, and whose sweethearts and select friends were wolverines and catamounts, had the rare luck to fall into such glorious company. He could well afford to treat, and he should hold it a privilege to have a bout with his military friends, helping them, while he could, to drink health to the king, confusion to all enemies, and shame to the devil."

Leaving this bold, sagacious, and singularly gifted outlaw and his companions to the merriment he had infused into them, and the boisterous and drunken revelry that followed, we will now repair to the other room, where a far different, though no less interesting, scene was in progress.

When Miss Hendee, on recognizing the voice of Darrow among those of others about to enter the house so abruptly, invited Warrington to take a seat with her in the other room, she did so from a sudden impulse, arising out of her secret dread of encountering one whose recent conduct had filled her with the deepest dislike, coupled with a sort of vague apprehension that the visit of these soldiers, with Darrow at their head, at this particular time was in some way to affect the safety of her friend, whom she thought thus to shield from the impending danger. And it was not till they became seated in the room by themselves that it occurred to her that she had voluntarily afforded her lover the very opportunity which, at their recent interview, he had earnestly requested, but which she had so promptly and pointedly refused him. Blushing deeply at the thought of her apparent inconsistency, and fearful that this act would be misconstrued by the other, she suddenly commenced uttering an apology or explanation, but perceiving some worse dilemma from so doing, she stopped short in the midst of a sentence, blushing more deeply than at first, while an embarrassing silence ensued which neither party for some moments was able to break. Warrington, however, comprehending the cause of her embarrassment at a glance, and anxious to relieve it, soon rallied, and observed:

"Fear not, Miss Hendee, that I shall misinterpret

this act of yours in inviting me to a seat with you here; I believe I can appreciate the motives that led to it, and I certainly feel very grateful for the deed."

"You were ever generous, Mr. Howard," replied Alma, with a grateful smile, "but do you comprehend all the motives that might have influenced me in this?"

"I may not all, but will Miss Hendee state wherein she supposes I may not understand them?"

"Did you recognize any of the voices of these last visitors while they were at the door, or have you since?"

"I can scarcely say I have, though I conclude them to be soldiers from yonder garrison."

"They are—all that will appear, at least, I presume, and among them is that suspicious fellow from whose intrusion you so kindly relieved me the other day. He went away at that time, I think, harboring revengeful feelings toward you, and does not this visit involve some design against your safety? Though, I confess, I can hardly see how you should be sought here with any purpose of revenge."

"You may be right, Miss Hendee," said the other thoughtfully, after a silence of a moment; "you may be right in supposing me the object of this visit. I have had some suspicions from the first that it was so; and I have noticed some indications, indeed, since we have been in this room, which go to confirm me. Yes, you may be right in this, but wrong, I think, in judging of the motives that have led to the visit."

"What other motive can there be but the one I assigned?" at length asked Alma, with an air of perplexity mingled with some uneasiness.

"Miss Hendee," resumed Warrington, with considerable embarrassment at the effort, "your question leads me to a declaration which my painfully conflicting obligations as a citizen, and as a gentleman who has received much kindness from your family, will be some excuse, I hope, for withholding till now; but which my feelings will allow me to withhold no longer. Miss Hendee, my name is not Howard!"

"Not Howard!" exclaimed Miss Hendee, with a look of unfeigned surprise. "Not Howard!" she repeated, the tall arches of her beautiful brows slightly contracting with an incipient frown. "Surely, surely, sir!"

"Nor is that, I fear you will think," resumed the other seriously, and now with perfect composure, "the worst of the avowal; I am aware what I risk—what, indeed, I shall probably forever lose in your esteem, fair lady. But duty to you, and respect to my own character, compels me to disclose. I am Charles Warrington!"

A sharp, inarticulate exclamation burst from the lips of the astonished and recoiling girl at the announcement of the name.

"What is the matter, there, Alma?" asked Captain Hendee, in a tone modulated somewhere between the jocose and anxious, as he thrust his head partly through the door, beside which he was sitting, on the opposite side of the partition, in the other room, "what is the case there, girl? Doctor Hunter is not pulling a tooth for you, is he?"

Perceiving, however, nothing but dumb shows going on between the parties, and satisfied with the shot he had given them, he left them to another embarrassing silence, which for many minutes was broken by neither.

"I am so surprised at this strange and unexpected development," at length observed Miss Hendee, though with mind and feelings still unsettled and balancing between the former high opinion she had entertained of her companion as Howard and the preconceived picture of the ruffian-like character with which she had been accustomed to associate Warrington: "so surprised that I hardly know what I should say, or how I should act toward you, sir, in the new character in which you now stand before me. Am I to understand that our quiet home, here, is now to be made the theater of contention in a dispute for possession?"

"Heaven forbid!" replied Warrington eagerly; "you have, Miss Hendee, my pledge already in this respect, given to you at our last interview. Can you doubt my will to redeem it? And you now perceive with what authority I could make the assurance. But though you can have no apprehension of this kind of me, or my people, for whom I can safely answer, yet what will be your opinion of one who made and has since sought your acquaintance under a disguised name? It is that which troubles me, dear lady. And in that you have an apparent right, at least, to condemn me, though not acting for myself, but for those who assigned me the part in which disguise was deemed necessary."

"You need not forestall your sentence, sir," said the other, something very like a smile again lighting up her sweetly expressive countenance; "I know too little of the merits of this unhappy controversy, I freely confess, to feel sure of doing justice to either party in any opinion I might now express. I believe I can still put trust in you—at least, I will for the present believe so—for it would indeed be humiliating to us all to find ourselves so much mistaken in one whose character we had so highly estimated. Yes, in you," she repeated with emphasis, "but in your party——" And she paused, but soon, and without finishing the sentence, resumed: "Can you inform me who is that fearful-looking and singular stranger in the other room? or was I mistaken in judging from some appearances I noticed that you and he were acquainted?"

"Your conjectures were true. His name, however, I cannot disclose. But this I may say, that he is not all that he may have appeared here to-night; and yet he is far more—a man of many high and noble qualities, combined with extraordinary powers of body and mind, though now placed here in circumstances as inauspicious as my own. These circumstances, as they will make up an answer to the question you asked before I announced my true name, I will now, with your permission, briefly explain."

His fair auditor signifying a willingness, at least, to listen to the explanation, Warrington, taking a comprehensive glance at the true grounds of the controversy between the settlers and their opponents, drew a vivid picture of the wrongs and consequent sufferings which the former had endured, and which led to the part he had taken in their behalf; explained the necessity of the disguise he had assumed, related his subsequent career, and the consequences to himself and all those who had taken a conspicuous part in attempting to defend the poor settlers against the rapacity of their oppressors.

"Is this, Mr. Howard—excuse me, Mr. Warrington, I should say," observed the other, evidently interested, and even touched by the recital she had just heard; "is this, indeed, an impartial account of this hapless contest? And are these armed men here to drag you to prison and an ignominious death for acting a part like this? Why, oh, why did you venture here into the very jaws of the lion? and now, why do you a moment linger? Why not escape while they are at their noisy carousals in the other room? That door —these windows——"

"Have all been guarded; each by a soldier with a loaded musket, from the moment we entered this room. An ear, practiced in the forest, has not failed to catch the sound of their cautious and stealthy tread, the occasional rubbing of their muskets against their buttons, and indications of their presence and object not to be mistaken."

"Oh! I do wonder how you can be so calm. What

hope—what resource is there left you, in which you can now trust for escape?"

"Many! Be not concerned. They probably think we shall remain through the night, and will deem it safest to defer any attempt to seize us till they suppose us asleep. I trust much in my friend, ever fruitful in expedients, and now acting a part in the other room, as nigh as I can judge from what occasionally reaches my ear, with reference to effecting this object. Neshobee is a friend; and may I not hope an acquiescence, at least, from you?"

"Most certainly the latter, and if I could—but what could I do?"

"Perhaps nothing—perhaps much. We must act on circumstances. But had we now not better part. I feel anxious to be co-operating with my friend," said Warrington, rising and moving toward the door.

"One moment longer—that is, if you are not too anxious to go," observed Alma, motioning him to remain.

"What would my fair friend say?" asked the other, perceiving her to hesitate.

"Should you escape this danger, as I hope you may," at length replied Alma, "I trust—I pray, that you will not be so thoughtless as to venture here again. There may be other hazards in repeating your visits here, besides the fearful one you have already incurred of being seized in behalf of the public authorities."

"Indeed! But in what way, lady?"

"There may be those," she answered with evident reluctance, and with severely conflicting feelings, "who would look on your visits here with—with suspicion; and who, I fear—who, perhaps, I would say, might have a disposition—that is, he may——"

"I did not understand the name," said Warrington, with the appearance of wishing to relieve the embarrassment of the other, and assist her to proceed.

"I did not name him, and I would gladly avoid doing so," replied she, still hesitating.

"But of what avail will be your caution, unless I know against whom to be on my guard?" asked he, with a little spice of the lawyer in the question, he being more anxious to learn the name of his unknown rival, to whom he rightly conjectured she alluded, than concerned on account of any danger he apprehended from his jealousy or malice.

"But if you kept entirely away—unless, perhaps, you should be sought out for the crimes you have already committed," said the girl half playfully. "I much wish you could have received this information from others," she continued, after a pause; "but as you might not, and as I have ventured, perhaps unadvisedly, to give it, I know not but you have a just right to require the name. It is Sherwood—one Jacob Sherwood."

"Sherwood!" said Warrington, in utter surprise; "Sherwood! That then explains several things that to me were mysteries. Sherwood!" he repeated, musing, and speaking as if to himself; "yes, I know the man, and the heart of the man. But is it possible, with Sherwood for a rival and Alma Hendee the object, that she for him would——"

"Trespasser!" exclaimed the other, shaking her head with a look in which menace and roguishness were quietly blended. "Trespasser, beware!"

"Cruel! cruel! I must not, then, even ask if there is hope, even one ray of hope, in the future!" rejoined Warrington, with an air of tender reproach.

"Oh, how can you ask?" replied Alma, her countenance now changing to a serious, even a sad expression. "How can you ask or expect this when I see no hope for myself? And how can you think of entering into a discussion so useless, at such a moment as this? Go, go!"

When Warrington, at the close of the interview above described, entered the room of the revelers, he found them at the height of their boisterous carousals. The health of every known potentate on the earth, and some under it, was proposed and drunk by the huge stranger, now the undisputed master of the ceremonies, who, at each rapidly succeeding toast, tossed off his glass with as little apparent regard to its effect on himself as if the beverage had been water; such, at least, was there every appearance of his doing, for he always lifted a full glass to his lips and returned it empty to the table, while he made this his boast on urging the same on his companions of the revel, all of whom, with the exception of Darrow, seemed little disposed to refuse a compliance. The latter, however, after drinking a few stinted glasses, contrived constantly to evade a repetition which would unfit him for the enterprise that he, at least, had by no means lost sight of; while it was with increasing uneasiness that he perceived the fearful inroads which the liquor was making on the faculties of his men. This, however, might not have alarmed the wary sergeant had both of his intended victims been in the same condition, since, so long as they drank as freely as the rest, the difficulty of their seizure, he knew, would be diminished in the same proportion with the powers of the men upon whom he depended for its accomplishment. But Warrington, he soon noticed, though mingling gayly with the rest at the board, seemed inclined, like himself, to drink but lightly, making the excuse, when urged to take more, that he wished to keep sober in order to take care of his brother hunter, who seemed in a fair way to require his assistance. And the appearance of the stranger, indeed, soon well confirmed the truth of the observation. His wit fast grew vapid; and some of his remarks were so silly that none but the very drunkest of the soldiers would join him in the maudlin roar of laughter which he raised at each of his efforts to be witty. He began to sway to and fro, and his huge frame to totter at every step, like a sapped tower about to fall to the earth. All of which was observed by Darrow with a look of malicious satisfaction.

Warrington now proposed that the company should break up, and all retire for the night. This proposal was seconded, though from far different motives, by both the captain and Darrow. A question, however, now arose in regard to the accommodations which could be furnished for sleeping. The captain stated that he had but two spare beds, which might be made to answer for four of the company. He should have been extremely happy to be able to accommodate all his guests with beds; but as it was, they must agree among themselves who should occupy those he could furnish. The sergeant immediately proposed that Warrington and his drunken friend should take one of the beds, and himself and one of his men should occupy the other, while the rest should seek lodgings in the barn. At this moment the drunken outlaw, roused from his stupor, into which he seemed to have fallen during the discussion, so far as to appear conscious of the point of debate, and hiccuping at every word, swore, with a big oath, that his military friends should have the best. They should have both the beds, or he would fight them like h——l. And that other scurvy hunter, who was not man enough to drink like a gentleman, should go to the barn with him, and sleep on the hay, or he would fight him, too, and be d——d to him.

To this Darrow, for some reasons of his own, strenuously objected, and the debate was growing warm when Miss Hendee entered the room, and, after asking the cause of their dispute and looking a moment with an air of disgust at the now helpless stranger, earnestly begged her father to let the creature have his way, and by no means suffer him to occupy a bed in the house.

"I think, Captain Hendee," remarked Warrington, now for the first time offering an opinion, "that the man's notions, as bad off as he appears to be, are correct. He will probably keep the house in an uproar half the night if he remains. It is more suitable, I think, that he should be taken to the barn. And it is my duty, I suppose, to attend him."

"I by no means intended to exclude you in my prohibition, sir," said Alma, addressing Warrington.

"Oh, no, certainly not, I presume. But I think I ought to go with him," rejoined Warrington. "And a bed of hay," he added gayly, "is far better than has sometimes fallen to my lot."

"Hoy! there, cap—cap—capting!" stammered out the stranger, lifting his head, though nearly falling out of his chair at the effort; "say, you Cap—Capting Handy, Hindy—dev—devil knows what; take good care—care my rifle; cost ten pounds, king's lawful cur—cur—curren—cyation; God d——n—bless him!"

"And of mine, too, captain, if you will. We will leave them in the house till morning, with your permission," observed Warrington, exchanging a significant glance with Miss Hendee.

Darrow, who till now had manifested a determination that our two outlaws should remain in the house with him, on hearing that the valuable rifles were to be left behind, seemed no longer to entertain any suspicion of the arrangement last proposed, and conceded the point without further objection.

Captain Hendee then ordered Neshobee to take the rifles into the next room, and, pointing out the beds to be occupied by Darrow and his men, took leave of his guests for the night, and with his daughter retired to the other part of the house. Everything being now settled to the apparent satisfaction of all parties, it only remained to get the helpless and unwieldly outlaw to his lodging in the barn. And Darrow and his men all declaring that they would by no means consent to quit their generous entertainer till they had seen him safely disposed of for the night, Warrington and the soberest soldiers to be found in the company now assisted him in getting on his feet and bracing out his legs so that he could be kept from dropping on the floor. When this, with considerable difficulty and no little noise and merriment, had been effected, they planted themselves firmly under each arm, and at the word of command, sportively given by one of the company, trundled, or rather pushed, his huge and staggering carcass forward toward the barn, attended by the whole company, reeling, jostling, and shouting along by his side. After they had arrived there, and succeeded in getting their charge over the threshold, they unceremoniously tumbled him on a pile of hay on the barn floor; when, after exchanging mock ceremonies of parting politeness, Darrow and all his men, now feeling sure of an easy and safe capture as soon as their intended victims were asleep, departed for the house.

"Charles!" said the big outlaw, raising himself on his elbow as soon as the sounds of the receding footsteps of the soldiers had died away; "Charles!" he repeated, in a low, though perfectly sober, tone, "you creep carefully round to those side windows, and see if some of these cusses aint still lurking round the barn to watch us."

The other, silently complying, soon returned and reported that no one was visible.

"Well, now, Charles," resumed the first speaker, "you get down there at my feet and see if you can pull off my plaguy old boots. There is more than a quart of rum in them. I can neither run nor fight worth a copper with my feet in such a devil's pickle."

"Upon my word, colonel," said Warrington, while complying with the request just made, "you would make no slouch of a juggler. I saw no chance of succeeding in any way short of drinking or openly refusing. And I was not a little puzzled to decide whether you were stark mad in taking such quantities of liquor, or whether you had some way of otherwise disposing of it which I could not detect. Indeed, for the last half hour I have been perfectly at a loss to know whether you were drunk or sober. How did you contrive to cheat them so cleverly?"

"Buttoned up my high collared coat, so as to come up over my chin, at the outset. Then, minding to stand so as to admit no side views to that hawk-eyed sergeant, or to the others, till they were too far gone to see straight, I dashed every glass down my bosom. Not a spoonful has gone down my throat to-night! so help me Peter! who never lied but three times, as I recollect. But come, we must be thinking of something else now. And the first question to be settled is whether we shall go off without our rifles, and perhaps lose them entirely, or whether we shall hatch up some scheme to get them out of the house."

"I have strong hope, though I may be disappointed," said the other in reply, "that we shall soon get hold of them through other agency than our own. I think we had better venture on remaining here for a few moments longer, to wait the result of an effort which I feel quite confident will be made for this purpose."

"Aha, Charley—been plowing with the captain's heifer, hey? Well, we will wait a little. Yes, yes; I see now what the sly jade was at when she set in so plausibly to have 'the loathsome creature' carried off to the barn. And, indeed, Charles, I suspected, soon after I arrived, that you was in for it there. But how in the name of Cupid, and Hymen, and Venus, and all that sort of heathen cattle, did you happen to pounce upon such a superb piece of housel stuff? I thought you never strayed so far down here to the land's end?"

Warrington then related to his companion all the circumstances connected with his acquaintance with the different members of the Hendee family, his late discovery relative to his ownership of the land, and the course which he had and still intended to pursue in that respect, without revealing, however, the uncertain and somewhat peculiar attitude in which he stood with the daughter.

"Right nobly said and done!" exclaimed the other, who had listened with the appearance of much interest to the recital, and who seemed highly to appreciate the delicate generosity of Warrington; "nobly, indeed, though with a higher touch of the chivalrous, I fear, my dear fellow, than you would often find reciprocated in this wooden age and country. However, you will one of these days be rewarded, I suppose, by receiving the same lands, and an article with them that will richly repay you for your forbearance; for, by all the saints, from St. Paul down to ragged St. Patrick, I swear that if there be any angels of clay—that, though, is nonsense for a married man. But, seriously, Charles, I don't know when I have seen the like of that girl! A form and a face the mold of which, I think, must have been broken with but one cast; eyes with the rich and lustrous hue of good old indigo, though pure and clear as the mudless crystal to the very depths of the soul beyond them. And then, her smile, Charles—enough to craze an anchorite, by heavens!"

"Really, colonel," rejoined Warrington jocosely, "you would make me jealous if I had but a tithe of the title to the girl that you suppose. She is engaged, man, to one Sherwood, the very fellow, as I this night ascertained from her own lips, whom we caught and beech-sealed for a spy and traitor, on our way down the creek, and to whom, doubtless, we are indebted for this concerted plan for our seizure."

"I heard of your doings with that scoundrel as I

came along a day or two after. And the only fault I find about it is that you did not string him up, according to the decree of convention in such case made and provided. But can it be possible, Charles, that God ever made this girl for such a fellow? I swear I don't believe it! And if there is not enough to you to set him aside——"

"Well, what then?"

"Why, you don't deserve her, that's all—but whist! I thought I heard a footstep. See to your pistols, Charles!"

"All handy, colonel. But what is your plan if they beset us here?"

"Why, fight 'em, most likely, I think. A d—— poor story if we two aint a match for those four half-fuddled devils!"

"Certainly; but there were nearly or quite as many more, posted round the house in ambush, or my ears deceived me sadly."

"No, were there?"

"Yes, I am positive, colonel."

"Well, well, Charles, the trifling addition of three or four more of them aint worth speaking about. But hush again!" continued the speaker, his voice sinking to a whisper; "I was right; I just caught the glimpse of a head peering in at that side door."

The senses of the big outlaw had not deceived him. And the object of his suspicion now appeared several times before the partly opened door, though at each time suddenly and for a moment withdrawn. At length the door was cautiously opened considerably wider, and the questionable head thrust fairly in, where it remained stationary as a block for a full minute.

"Umph!" at length uttered the object, in a low, but distinct tone.

"All right," said Warrington; "it is Neshobee, as I expected."

"Umph! Me come—got um your rifles," said the latter noiselessly advancing and handing the guns to each of their respective owners.

"You have done us no fool of a favor, my fine fellow," said the elder Green Mountain Boy. "How did you get the guns out of the house?"

"Missus Alma contrive um all," replied the Indian. "She put um out her sleep-room window; then say it; so me go bring um."

"A glorious girl, that, by Jupiter!" resumed the former. "You and she, both, my red friend, deserve a pension at our hands. Here, take hold of this crown piece, to begin upon."

"Him good! cappen; him good afore," said the native, taking the proffered coin.

"And I will try to continue so," said Warrington, thrusting another crown into the Indian's ready hand. "But anything more, Neshobee?" he continued, judging from the other's manner that he had something further to impart.

"Missus Alma say me tell um go; saw the rest sogers come in house now, drink rum more again; say go straight, quick; better no stay minute."

"Good advice, too," said the big outlaw, "and let us lose no time in following it. Charles, lead the way!"

Cautiously emerging from the barn and clearing the yard fence, our two friends now proceeded with silent but rapid steps through the open field till they gained a knoll about sixty rods from the house, when the nameless outlaw paused and looked back.

"Clear of the rascals at last, I believe," observed Warrington.

The other made no reply, but stood as if debating some point in his mind which he was unable to decide.

"Well, which way now, colonel?" resumed the former, thinking his companion might be hesitating about the route they should take.

"Get thee behind me, Satan!" at length exclaimed the other, violently dashing back both his hands. "Give me joy, Charles," he added, without paying the least attention to the question that had just been asked him; "give me joy, for I have conquered."

"Indeed, sir, it is quite impossible for me to comprehend you."

"Not comprehend me! Oh, true, how should you? It only passed through my mind. Well, Charles, I have been sorely tempted—never so tempted in my life."

"About what, pray?"

"Why, about going over and taking yonder fort to-night. According to your account of the numbers now on this side, there cannot be over ten or a dozen left in the garrison. You and I could have taken their boat here, while they were waiting for us to get to sleep, slipped over, and made the attempt. I think we could carry it. And, ah!" continued the speaker, rubbing his hands in ecstacy, "there would have been glory, glory in it, Charles! But duty forbade; for a failure certainly, and success probably, would have defeated an object of twofold importance to the country. And conscience told me I should forego my private wishes for public good. That object, as stone walls have ears, they say, I will not name here. But it was that which brought me into this section. Hendee's situation here, so near one of the enemy's strongholds, made it important that his feelings should be known. And it was for that purpose I called to-night, when I unexpectedly found you. I intended to have been at half a dozen other places before this; and I should, but for this cursed bother with these minions of hell and New York. We will now on to your encampment. I called there at sunset. Your lieutenant had returned. The party sent to seize the surveyor had just been heard from, and were expected to arrive with their prisoner to-night. He must be tried and disposed of in a hurry. But have you made any further discoveries about the York justice in this section?"

"I have ascertained his residence, and discovered the bearing of his feeling toward the enemy—nothing further."

"Enough! I have received since we parted papers which settle the case. We must have him up, and do off all this York business in a batch in the morning; for there is much to be done to-morrow in preparation of a general meeting of the trusty to-morrow night, in the vicinity of the Middle Falls. Ah! Charles, there is something afoot to which this petty warfare we have been engaged in with New York is as a rush light to the meridian sun! I burn to be in it, for it will be great, daring and glorious!"

Leaving our two Green Mountain Boys to proceed to their present destination, with hearts swelling at the thought of the future, and somewhat elated withal at their fortunate escape from a danger of certainly no small magnitude, when the vicinage of the fort and the small chance of a rescue are considered, we will return for a moment to the company we left at the house. It would be difficult to describe the rage and chagrin of Darrow and his men when, after waiting till they supposed their two intended victims were helpless in sleep, they proceeded stealthily and with undoubting assurance of an easy victory to the barn, and discovered that their birds were both flown. They saw at once that they had been fairly outwitted by the wily outlaws. Solacing themselves, however, with a promise of seizing the fugitives another day, they gave up the project for the present, well knowing that any attempt at pursuit would now be utterly useless. And at the command of Darrow, who kept his future purposes, whatever they might be, to himself, they all silently withdrew from the house, and immediately crossed over to the fort.

CHAPTER XII

"They came not from the head, it was the heart that wrote them."

THE next morning after the affair at the Lower Falls between our Green Mountain Boys and the hired minions of Colonel Reed, a separation, as the reader will readily remember, took place among the former, the several individuals who had occupied a conspicuous place in our story departing in different directions, and with objects as diverse as their various destinations. Some of these individuals, still designed to sustain a close connection with the events we have undertaken to delineate, have been neglected through several of our last chapters, in order to preserve, as unbroken as possible, the chain of the leading part of the narrative, in several scenes we had commenced, so nearly connected as to render a break alike disagreeable to both reader and writer. But being allowed a short respite before following those with whom we have just parted, we now hasten to bestow, in the first place, some attention on our friend Selden and his new charge, the volatile but not ungifted Jessy Reed, by following them to the destination for which they were on the point of embarking when we left them. This was at Skenesboro', near the south end of the lake, so called from the name of the proprietor of a large body of land at this place, Colonel Skene, who, being not only a wealthy landholder, but the commander of one of the king's regiments, had here constructed a large, strong stone house, and made it a sort of military post as well as the residence of his family and various dependents. The whole of this curious establishment, not a little resembling that of one of the ancient feudal lords, was, at this time, under the command of Major Skene, a son of the proprietor, the father having been some months absent, engaged in negotiations for his own aggrandizement at the British court. It was to this place that Miss Reed had so fearlessly undertaken a voyage in an open skiff with one oarsman and Selden, her volunteer knight attendant. But a description of this voyage, together with many circumstances which preceded it, we will now, agreeably to a previous intimation, allow the fair young voyager to give in her own language. And for this purpose we present the following letter sent by her a few days after her arrival at Skenseboro', and received on the morning following the events recorded in the last chapter:

"To Miss Alma Hendee:

"I have most serious doubts, my dear Alma, whether I am exactly myself. And should you be equally dubious, as I expect you will, when you have perused all that I shall now, under the rose, impart, you may set it down, if you please, as the relation of a pretty dream which has passed through the brain of Philip Skene's half-courted highflyer, while dozing under the soporific thoughts of a matter of course, all very suitable sort of a match, with his grave and calculating majorship. One thing, however, I imagine is certain; and that is that I am here at Skenesboro', snugly immured in the major's stone castle. And why I am so positive of this is that I feel so sleepy and have felt so ever since he left us. He! Who? Ah! that sets me afloat again! But I will begin at the beginning, and, dream or no dream, you shall have the whole of my adventures with (now be making up your mouth for interjections!) those horrid, brave, dear, ugly Green Mountain Boys.

"Accompanying my father from Montreal with my half Indian girl, Zilpah Wampum, under the arrangement that we should be left and stationed at Skenesboro' during his contemplated sojourn of some time in the city of New York, I besought him right earnestly on the way to let me go with him to visit his possessions up Otter Creek, to which he intended to return for a day after landing us at the major's. After a few of those not very alarming affairs, pshaws! pishes! etc., I carried my point, as I generally do, with my, I fear, too indulgent parent. And what was still greater victory and certainly much harder to be won, I prevailed upon him at last to let us remain there for a *few* days after he had proceeded on his journey, under the condition that I was to take a *very* fair, warm, and *very* calm day within a week at farthest, and, with our best boat, and two of our most careful men there, proceed to our original destination.

"Well, there we remained at that wild, romantic place, happy as larks, by day rambling round the fields for flowers, skirting the woods for spruce gum, boxberries, and bird's nests, and at night listening to the adventures of the men, or quizzing the honest old McIntosh, the commander of the post, as he calls himself. There we remained, I say, till the fourth day after father had left us, when, who should make his appearance but that plausible and oily-tongued beau of yours, Jacob Sherwood, announcing that a band of Green Mountain Boys, headed by Warrington, the outlaw, was in full march to lay waste, burn, and destroy our possessions, and murder every soul to be found on the premises, or, at least, to carry us off as captives to their dens in the mountains! My heart beat like a young drummer! And as for Zilpah, though mute as a fish, her complexion wonderfully improved about that time, I assure you. However, being a soldier's daughter, as well as yourself, I soon made up my mind not to die of fright, at least; so I flew round, helped the men to make cartridges and whatever else I could do in preparation for the expected visit. Sherwood was invited to aid in putting the garrison in a state of defense, and remain with us through the coming siege. But, oh, no! He couldn't possibly! He must be off to the woods to watch the enemy's approach, and give us signal guns when they arrived at the clearing. Well, after the whole establishment had resounded with the din of preparation about an hour, and everything was prepared for their reception, McIntosh called us together, women and all, for a council of war, to hear the different plans that might be offered as to the best mode of conducting the defense, though doggedly determined, all the while, that none but his own should be adopted. And what think you that was? Why, that all the men should take the field against the enemy and fight their way back, under cover of log heaps, to the works, leaving us poor women entirely alone, to unbar the gate to receive them when they should reach it and give the watchword. This sage plan of operations, as you may well suppose, did not at all strike my fancy. But, finding opposition useless, I submitted with the best grace I could, demanding, however, as the terms of my compliance that they should leave me a good musket (a major's wife at one of our stations, some years ago, having taught me how to load and fire one) for our defense, in case I should have occasion to use it. This settled, McIntosh marshaled his men, sallied out, and lay in ambush till the enemy appeared, when a battle commenced in which powder enough was burned to have slain a regiment, though, strange to tell, not one drop of blood was spilled on either side.

"Now comes my part of this queer drama. While I stood at the gate listening, with palpitating heart, to the thunders of the musketry in the field, and anxiously awaiting the signal to open to our men, I heard steps outside the inclosure, which I knew could not proceed from any of our party. Almost desperate with fear, I seized the loaded gun which had been left for me, and stood on the defensive, while poor Zilpah, still worse frightened, fled into the house. All for a few moments was quiet, when, happening to look round, I beheld, to my utter surprise and consternation, one of the enemy approaching me, three of them, it seems, having already scaled the walls behind the house. Heaven forgive me! In the desperation of the moment I fired my gun at him, though, thanks to the same Heaven, without hitting him. He proved to be the lieutenant of Warrington, who now, with the other man, rushed forward from behind the house, when all stood confronting me. But what do you think they did? Seize me like ruffians, as from Sherwood's tale of the horribles I expected? No, they came forward, and in the most mild and gentlemanly manner advised, nay, entreated me to retire into the house, to which I now suffered myself to be conducted by Lieutenant Selden, who had just providentially escaped death by my hand! I think I must have appeared like a fool. I certainly felt like one.

"I need not inform you that our men now soon surrendered to the Green Mountain Boys, who took possession, claiming, however, none of the moveables, and asking only that the men should leave the place the next day. The treatment I received and the explanations given me by Warrington (who, by the way, is a noble-looking fellow; Alma, I wish you could see him) in regard to this war about titles, soon overset all my preconceived opinions of the Green Mountain Boys. Indeed, if we can rely on their statements, I hardly know how our people can be justified in driving these poor settlers from their farms.

"But what shall I say of him?—Mr. Selden, I mean. Who would credit—I would not a week ago, I am sure—that, after having called him a ruffian and monster to his face, as I did when he first approached me, I was found in the twilight of the same evening rambling arm in arm with the handsome, quizzical, audacious rogue, along the freshly flowered banks of the Otter, quoting poetry with him, or listening to the better poetry of his own brilliant conceptions, which sometimes flowed from his lips in bursts of surprising eloquence, and sometimes in sallies of wit, so original and irresistibly humorous that I would defy the gravest puritan in the land to keep his risibles from breaking loose on the occasion. He volunteered to attend me to Skenesboro' the next day, and I—now don't suspect me of being captivated with the fellow, Alma—I accepted the offer—how could I do less? Well, the next morning, with Zilpah, bag, and baggage—the bag, you will say, perhaps, should have been given to him—and with one of my father's trusty and strong-armed Highlanders for an oarsman, we shipped aboard boat and proceeded down the creek. The day was most serenely fair. And our voyage to the mouth of the stream, as we glided along the gently flowing current in its meandering course, was indeed delightful. The forest-lined banks were beautifully frosted with the white wood violet, or blushing with beds of wild tulips; while the budding branches of the overhanging trees above seemed fairly vivified by the thousand melodious duets that were joyously bursting from the happy little hearts of these minstrel lovers of the grove.

"After we had reached the open lake we found a pretty breeze blowing freshly from the westward. And the gentleman fixing up a blanket for a sail, our little craft swept through the lake right merrily, I assure you. We were soon abreast of your charming situation. And I could hardly consent to pass you without hauling up for a short morning call; but the men urging that, by improving the breeze, we could easily reach our destination by night, when otherwise we might fail of so doing, I reluctantly agreed to forego the pleasure of seeing you, and introducing my Green Mountain Phœnix—not that I am particularly charmed with him myself, but I think you would have been gratified in beholding so rare an avis, as a gentleman, as he really is, from so wild and savage a region as this Green Mountain country.

"At noon we dined quite romantically from off the middle seat of our boat, on edibles furnished from our store basket, and neatly arranged by Zilpah. I never partook with greater zest; and what with the keenness of our appetites, the novelty of the affair, and the thousand spicy things said on the occasion, I don't believe I should have enjoyed the banquet of a princess with half the pleasure that I did this meal.

"After we had taken our refreshment and again got under way, for we had run into a little cove beautifully overarched by a cluster of whispering pines, the saucy rogue so managed as to get Zilpah and the oarsman into one part of the boat, and himself and your humble servant into the other, with our blanket sail forming an impenetrable screen between. Here, after sentimentalizing and poetizing a while over the ever changing views of scenery, alternating with the majestic and beautiful, as we rapidly glided by them, he began a set of compliments so very pointed and squinting loveward, but at the same time so oddly framed, that I knew not whether to laugh or be angry. I should have severely chided so much boldness in a stranger, however, on one or two occasions, had not the provoking creature, carefully watching my countenance, thrown in some remark that gave an entirely different turn to the whole meaning of what he had begun to say. So you see, Alma, how far I am from anything like the tender passion in this strangely begun and no less strangely maintained acquaintance.

"The remainder of our voyage was now mostly occupied by him in giving me a history of his life as far as he knew it himself, relating the singular and certainly very romantic adventures through which he passed, from his childhood to the present hour. Having neither time nor space to detail them now, I will only say, briefly, that he was born somewhere in New England, as he supposes, for he neither knows his birthplace nor the name of his parents. But by some means or other falling into mercenary hands, when a mere child, he was sold as a slave,—passed through several hands, and at length carried over the waters,—taken into the protection of a philanthropic nobleman in England, by whom he was liberally educated, and furnished with a handsome outfit to purchase a commission in the army, or seek his fortune wherever he could find it. He then, after wandering a while in Europe, obeyed the impulses of his own heart and came to visit his own country; when, being enamored of a sylvan life, and thinking he should enjoy the excitements usually to be found in a border settlement, he soon found his way to the New Hampshire Grants, and enlisted in the controversy which he here found going on between the settlers and the New Yorkers.

"By the time he had closed this very interesting and delightfully told autobiography, we hove in sight of the castellated establishment of the Skenes. It was then, almost for the first time, that it occurred to me that, attended as I was, my meeting with the family must be an extremely awkward one, since the feelings of the major, as well as those of his father, the colonel, are known to be hostile to the Green Mountain Boys, and I could not forbear hinting this to Selden, and suggesting, at the same time, the expediency of withholding from the family, till he had gone, all knowledge of the late affair at the Falls, or his passing incog. among them.

" 'Oh, no!' was the prompt reply, 'mince no matters on my account, fair lady. Having made my peace with her who is most interested, and obtained an absolution for my offenses—have I not? at least,' he continued, with a tone and smile so sweet, so tender, and yet so imploring that I found my head nodding an assent before I knew it, 'at least, may I be permitted to hope I shall, my dear Miss Reed?—having done this they must be singularly disposed, indeed, to espouse the quarrels of others if they offer me any personal disrespect. No, no, fear it not, and should *you* feel disposed to countenance my remaining at this place through the night, I shall gladly risk all consequences to myself from so doing.

"We had now reached the landing, and in a moment the inmates of the house, who were expecting me about these days, and had conjectured who we were, all rushed out, and Marge and Mary Skene, with their brother, came flying like two paper kites with a lubberly boy at their tails down to the boat to receive us. I don't know how I made my tongue do its office in returning their salutations, for my heart certainly leaped right up plump into my mouth, and I cannot conceive how that poor little member, so shamefully belied in our sex, could have possibly found room to wag! It did, however, and I introduced Mr. Selden by name to them all. The girls, I thought, seemed rather pleased that I had brought them a new candidate for their toils, and so fine a looking fellow in the bargain. But the major, reckoning on the possibility, I suppose, that the other might become a candidate for the toils of somebody besides sisters, looked rather askew at my gentleman; nevertheless, not knowing exactly what might be a safe conclusion on such uncertain premises, he soon brought himself to behave quite decently, and escorted us all to the house without further ado. But further trials were in store for me; for Mr. Seldon, as soon as we had all got comfortably seated, to my surprise, broke the ice at once; and, after craving their attention for a moment, while he relieved Miss Reed, as he said, of a task which he could readily conceive would be an unpleasant one for her to perform, very coolly related the whole transaction which led to his acquaintance with me, and the consequent responsibility that devolved upon him of seeing me safe to my friends.

"I felt, though I could scarcely tell why I should, like a criminal while Mr. Selden was making this development, which, I had many fears, would involve his personal safety; notwithstanding he had done nothing, as yet, he tells me that the York government consider worthy of death or bonds. All seemed much surprised at what they heard, and in the major's face—that is, as soon as he could comprehend the matter, for it takes an idea some time, you know, to get through his cranium, and no great wonder, neither, considering how far it has to go—in the major's face I saw evident signs of a gathering storm. But knowing that, on reasonable calculation, Mr. S. might count on two days at least before a cloud engendering in so cold a climate would become sufficiently charged to be dangerous, I did not feel greatly alarmed, and especially so as the girls seemed disposed to laugh at the affair. And Marge, on Mr. Selden's playfully proposing to submit himself to us ladies to pass sentence for his crimes, quite smartly observed that we would sentence him to an imprisonment of a week in their stone jug, as she termed their house, and be let out to attend us on horseback or in a boat ride each day.

"We now passed the remander of the evening very pleasantly. And for the next two days we almost literally inflicted on Mr. Selden the sentence which had been so queerly imposed. We read, walked, sailed, and rode alternately; and a right merry time we had of it, I assure you—Mr. Selden, in the meantime, becoming a great favorite with the girls, especially with Marge, to whom I thought he was rather more particular than he should have been in strict politeness to the rest of us. He had an object, however, I presume, in conciliating the girls by his attentions. Do you think, Alma, that Marge Skene is so very handsome as some pretend to think her?

" 'But where was my doughty major in the meanwhile?' you will ask. Why he was so unaccountably busy with the workmen in the fields just about those days that he could not, on any account, attend us on any of our delightful excursions. And when he joined us at our meals, he was as grave as a Turk. Mr. S., however, I thought, was less alarmed than amused at his awfulness of countenance.

"After two days thus spent, and on the morning of the third after our arrival, Mr. S. suddenly announced to us his intention of an immediate departure. The girls were evidently touched with regret and disappointment at this unexpected announcement, thinking, perhaps, that their work was but half complete. But if ever Margery or Mary Skene is selected by him for a cynosure I have mistaken his taste; and yet, I confess, his conduct has sometimes not a little puzzled me. He thanked me for the consideration I had shown him under the unpleasant circumstances of our first acquaintance in a manner so handsome and feeling, that it made me feel like a condemned and guilty one, when I thought of that mad act of mine which marked the introduction to which he alluded. He then very politely thanked the girls for their kindness and hospitality, and was about to depart when Marge found tongue to invite him to renew his visit.

" 'I know not,' he answered, somewhat pensively, 'that circumstances will ever permit me that pleasure in person, but if you know of any way, fair ladies,'—he continued, glancing quite meaningly at somebody, as the girls in their jokes would afterward have it—'any way of receiving the visits I may pay you in dreams, I doubt not that you will often be favored with the repetition you have so kindly invited. Adieu, ladies, aideu.'

"I do not, certainly, know the reason of Mr. Selden's abrupt departure, but from what I can gather I suspect the major had that morning dispatched an express to the authorities at Albany, with a view to get the former arrested. This, I presume, he by some means or other got wind of, and I am glad of it, if for no other reason than that it defeated Philip's jealous meanness. He gave us all quite a lecture that night for being so familiar with one who was so much a stranger, and threw out many ill-natured remarks about Mr. S. that helped his own cause, perhaps, less than he imagined. I wish Heaven had made him such a man.

"I must now close this long, and, I fear, very foolish letter. I dare not read it over for fear I should burn it. I shall remain here for the present—I must, I suppose, till father returns. Oh, what will he say when he hears what they have done with his possessions! For myself I care nothing about it. He loses only what he paid for the land—a mere trifle. As for the labor and improvements bestowed there, he has been more than twice paid by the profits received. Besides, he is wealthy enough without this property, which, I really suspect, he cruelly took from the poor settlers, who had as good a right to it as himself—perhaps better.

"P. S.—I said I must stay here till father's return, but should he tarry some months, I might contrive, perhaps, to come and spend a few weeks with you. If I should, as Mr. S. will be somewhere in your vicinity probably, and may claim me as an acquaintance, you might possibly have an opportunity of being introduced to him—that is if he knew that I was there. Now, my dear girl, I must bid you good-by, with the charge—now lift up your hand and swear—that you will neither show this, nor breathe aught of its contents, to mortal ear! Remember! Write soon. Adieu.

"JESSY."

CHAPTER XIII

> "You shall be viceroys here, 'tis true,
> But we'll be viceroys over you."

> "Wait not till things grow desperater,
> For hanging is no laughing matter."

A FEW miles to the southward of the encampment of the Green Mountain Boys before described, stood the tenement of a settler whose improvements were somewhat in advance of the rough beginnings of those who had resided in the immediate vicinity. And the owner and occupant, having gained that point of comparative thrift from which he could look down upon his less fortunate neighbors, had lately begun to manifest an ambition to outshine them also in the civil distinctions to which he believed himself now entitled. But his solicitude for preferment not allowing him to await the tardy honors which his fellow-settlers of the New Hampshire party might be inclined to bestow, he had lately turned his longing eye to other dispensers of these coveted favors. And the prayer of his heart being secretly made known in the right quarter, was soon answered in the shape of an offer of the office of justice of the peace from the government of New York. Though aware of the dangerous nature of such an honor to an inhabitant of the Grants, yet the temptation which was now set before him, and which, indeed, he had indirectly sought, was altogether too great to be resisted; and in an evil hour he privately accepted the office, in defiance of a decree of the Convention of his countrymen, which had placed the acceptance of such an office from such a source, by a settler, high in the calendar of punishable offenses.

To the tenement of this aspiring dignitary we will now take the reader, in anticipation of other visitors. It was the next morning after the adventure of Warrington and his friend, the stout stranger, at Captain Hendee's; and the dawning light was just beginning to appear in the dapple east. The freshly made squire was already awake, reflecting with peculiar inward satisfaction on the honors of his new station, as he lay beside his loving rib in a small bedroom adjoining the kitchen. He had only the night before received his commission, and his heart was full of the pleasing subject. He not only dwelt on the present consequence which the office would confer, but his expanding thoughts began to stretch forward to the future; and he counted over the probabilities of his advancing, on a stepping stone like this, to much higher distinctions under a government which he was now ready to believe —nay, secretly to wish—would soon exercise the entire control in the settlement.

"They will call me squire, now," he soliloquized, half aloud, "and once squire, always squire; so I shall get the title, let what will come of it."

"Come of what, Mr. Prouty?" asked his helpmeet, with a yawn, awakening just in time to catch the last part of the sentence.

"Why!—why, I thought you was asleep, Polly. Come of what, did you say? Oh, nothing in particular; only I have been thinking over things a little. And I'll tell you what it is—there will shortly be a great overturn in this settlement. There will, you may depend on't."

"What, the Yorkers get the upper hand?"

"Sartain as you live, Polly!"

"Then where will go the title to our farm? That was what you was talking to yourself about, wan't it, now?"

"No, it wan't. And that aint a thing, neither, that troubles me a mite."

"Why not?"

"Because the office I have just got under the York government I consider amounts to a security against that. And if the Green Mountain Boys will let me alone—but I don't intend they shall know about my office yet a while."

"Yes, but what good will it do you to be a justice, if you can't be squire?"

"Why, what does the woman mean?"

"I mean if you darsen't let folks know, so as to call you squire."

"Oh, I can do some business, even now, among the York party, without much danger. And it won't be long before all that trouble will be over; for, as I told you, there is about to be a complete overturn here. The Yorkers are preparing to come on with a strong armed force. Now don't say anything to the neighbors about this, Polly, as I had it in confidence from Mr. Sherwood."

"Oh, did you? Well, that Mr. Sherwood is a complete gentleman—how perlite he is! Don't you think so, Mr. Prouty?"

"Yes, perlite enough, forzino. Well, as I was going to say, if they come on, Ethan Allen, Warrington, and Member Baker, with all they can raise, will stand no fag at all with a regular York army. And all who stand out then will be indicted and informationed against. There will be plenty of warrants called for about those days, you may depend on't. And I, being the only government justice in this part of the Grants, shall have the making of them. It will be money in my pocket, I tell you, Polly. And then, when——"

"Well, I hope you will then feel like getting me a new silk gown. You know, Mr. Prouty, that my white dimity is now the only dress that I have fit to see company in."

"Oh, fudge!"

"I say there is no fudge about it, now! The neighbors call us rich, and still it is a solemn fact, Mr. Prouty, and I don't care who knows it, that you dress your wife a great deal worse than——"

"Well, well, don't bother me now; but hear what I was coming at: When the York government gets well established here, as it will be, they will want two or three judges in this quarter, I guess, and I being the only one in all this section that had courage to accept the office of justice of peace, shouldn't you think, Polly, they would kind o' naturally hit on me for one of them?"

"Why, bless me! will they? So they will, won't they? And then, certainly, Mr. Prouty——"

"Hush! hush! I hear somebody coming up to the door. Who on earth can they be, I wonder, that's started out so early?"

A smart rapping now being heard at the door, Justice Prouty leaped from his bed, seized his—inexpressibles, modern dandyism would term them, we suppose, but finding no authority for believing our fathers made use of any garment the appropriate appellation of which they considered it indecent to express, we will venture to call things by their right names—seized his breeches, hurried them on, together with the other parts of his outward equipment, and emerged into the kitchen, after having twice gone back, at his wife's hasty and imperious call, to close, and more tightly close, the door behind him. After the customary "walk in," distinctly pronounced by the squire, the door was opened and two men entered, both unknown to the former, though not so to those who have followed us through all the different scenes of the preceding pages; for, in the striking altitude of one of the visitants, which compelled the civility of bowing, *nolens, volens,* as he entered the door, like a boy coming into a country school, and in the comical leer of his countenance, as with one eye he seemed to be measuring the affectedly dignified person of his host, while the other was busily employed in taking an inventory of the various articles about the room, the reader will find no difficulty in recognizing our jovial friend, Pete Jones. The other, whose dress and gentlemanly bearing formed a striking contrast with that of his rustic companion, was no other than Selden, who, as before intimated, having arrived the previous evening, had volunteered with the former to make this early call on the justice, to procure his immediate attendance at their encampment in the woods.

"Be seated, gentlemen, pray be seated," said the squire, bustling about, and setting chairs for his guests with one hand, and finishing the buttoning up of his vest with the other; "make yourselves comfortable; no ceremony here; just turned out, you see. Called on business, I take it, gentlemen?" he added, meaning official business, on which his mind was still running, and the wish in this case, as often happens, proving father to the thought.

"We have, sir," answered Selden, bowing with well-assumed respect. "You are a justice of the peace, we are told?"

"Why, as to that, sir," replied Prouty, hesitating, and glancing with a doubtful air alternately at Selden and his companion, "perhaps I may have heard—that is, I can't sartainly say, but I have heard that I was appointed to the office; though as to accepting—— You are of the right party, I trust, gentlemen?"

"We certainly think we are, at least, sir," rejoined the former gravely.

"That's as true as preaching, squire," said Pete; "for if we aint on the right side, I would give my old jack-knife to know who are."

"All right, I presume, gentlemen; but rather ticklish times, you know; thought it no hurt to be a little particular. But what business did you want done? No harm in asking that, I s'pose, gentlemen?" said the squire, adding the last question by way of opening a door for a retreat should one be necessary.

"Oh, no!" replied Selden; "but I know not that I can state precisely the nature of the business which those who sent us for you wish done; but it is something, I believe, that they think requires your presence."

"Oh, ho! not to be done here, then, gentlemen?" observed the squire, a little doubtingly again.

"No, sir; the place is several miles from here, I should think," responded Selden, with an air of indifference.

"Is Mr. Sherwood there?" asked the squire, rather anxiously.

"I believe not, squire," answered Selden, with the same indifference, "but they are anxious he should be, and hope he will come before closing the business."

"I'll swear to that, squire," said Jones, with a ludicrous effort to keep mischief from showing itself in his countenance.

"Aye, all right, then, gentlemen," rejoined the squire, still stupidly determined to understand the indefinite and evasive language of his visitors in the way that his wishes pointed. "But I thought I would make sure. You sir,'" he continued, addressing Selden, "I thought from the first glance must belong to the right party. This other gentleman here I didn't know so well about; but it makes no difference what I thought, as I see you agree. I will attend you, gentlemen. But hadn't we better stop and get some breakfast first?"

"Oh, no," replied Selden; "they expressly told us to come on immediately, and the folks would have a good breakfast prepared for us all by the time we could arrive there."

Esquire Prouty, after notifying his wife of his intended absence, now signified his readiness to depart; when all three set forward toward the encampment of the Green Mountain Boys, the former, without further question or any apparent distrust, putting himself under the guidance of his attendants. And, wrapped up in self-consequence and dreaming only of the important figure he was shortly to make in the first exercise of his new vocation, he unhesitatingly followed his guides as with rapid steps they silently led the way, sometimes proceeding in the road, sometimes through a piece of woods, and sometimes through open fields. At length they reached the border of the dark, continuous forest within which, at the distance of about half a mile, was the encampment to which they were destined; when the squire, now for the first time hesitating or seeming to entertain any suspicion that they were taking him to a less agreeable destination than he had anticipated, paused in his steps, and threw a doubtful and apprehensive glance around him.

"Never mind, squire," cried Jones, who, having with difficulty restrained himself from giving vent in some shape or other to the secret merriment he had been indulging on the way at the squire's credulity in suffering himself to be so foolishly lured from home, thought it would now do to begin to banter the obtuse justice a little. "Never mind, squire; you needn't look so streaked; we belong to the right party, you know."

"Yes; but if you would but just inform me, gentlemen," said the other imploringly, and with visible perturbation, "only just inform me——"

"Oh, push ahead, man!" interrupted Jones, who, purposely dropping in the rear, now urged on the reluctant squire with a show of pettish impatience, as if detained by excuses too frivolous to merit a reply. "Push ahead; my stomach is getting fairly wolfish for that breakfast. I'll be blessed if I don't almost think I begin to smell it at this distance!"

Somewhat assured by the other's manner of treating his scruples, and, though not quite satisfied, yet feeling a little ashamed of his fears, the squire now passively suffered himself to be conducted forward till, reaching the foot of the mountain and turning closely round a projecting ledge of rocks, he suddenly, and to his utter dismay, found himself in the midst of a group of sturdy men, whom, from their appearance, he at once knew to be a band of Green Mountain Boys. Instantly comprehending the nature of their business with him, he stopped short, and stood confused and trembling in mute alarm before them. Nor were his fears at all diminished by the array of well-known names which his conductor the next moment announced by way of introduction, the ceremonies of which the latter now commenced performing very formally with those nearest at hand.

"Esquire Prouty, allow me to present you to Captain Remember Baker," began Selden, pompously waving his hand toward a keen-eyed, determined-looking man who stood in front of the others.

The confused squire nodded his head mechanically, but his tongue refused to do its office except by a half-articulated "How'd do, sir," as he heard the name of one of that famous trio who had so long been the terror of the New York authorities.

"Again, Esquire Prouty, will you permit me the pleasure of presenting you to Captain Charles Warrington?" proceeded Selden, as the latter advanced to favor the introduction.

"Warrington!" gasped the squire, with increased trepidation; "Warrington, too!"

"And yet once more," continued the imperturbable lieutenant, beckoning to the Herculeon hero of the shag coat, who figured so conspicuously at Captain Hendee's in his adventure with the soldiers the night previous, and who was now here and came forward at the intimation. "Once more, Esquire Prouty, shall I have the *very great* honor of introducing you to Colonel Ethan Allen."

"God have mercy on me!" involuntarily burst from the lips of the affrighted justice as the announcement of the last name capped the climax of his terror and despair. "Oh, God have mercy! I am a lost man!"

"Pooh! you cowardly fool!" exclaimed Allen, with a look of mingled pity and contempt; "rouse up and bear it like a man; and if you promise no more to betray your injured and bleeding country by becoming the tool of tyrants, it shall go the lighter with you. At all events, you need not fear that you will be punished to the extent of *half* your deserts. But, come, boys, set on the breakfast. It might be hazardous to our prisoners, the squire and surveyor here, to proceed with them with the inward man in so ravenous a plight; for Hunger and Mercy never got near enough to each other to shake hands since the fall of Adam. And even the awards of Justice herself might be of questionable rectitude if made under the irritations of an empty stomach."

The breakfast, which consisted of a plentiful supply of roasted venison, partridges, and other small game, with such trimmings as the settlers living near, and in the secret of the encampment, had sent in, was served up on a rude kind of platform, composed of smooth white pieces cleft from the freely rifting basswood, and supported on cross-pieces laid upon forked stakes, or crotches, as they are usually denominated in the woodman's phrase. Around this temporary table benches of an equally rude construction were placed sufficient for the accommodation of all the company, including the prisoners, now consisting of the squire, the surveyor, and his assistant, all of whom were respectfully shown places at the table. The meal was generally partaken in silence, the officers seeming to fear that too much sociability might have a tendency to unnerve them for the task on hand, and the men respectfully followed the example of their superior, with the exception of Pete Jones, who could not forbear occasionally throwing a sly joke at the chopfallen squire.

"Now, gentlemen, for business," said Allen, rising from the table the moment their meal was finished, as, ominously knitting his dark, heavy brows, he pulled from his pocket and in a loud, commanding voice commenced reading a decree of the Convention forbidding *"Each and all of the inhabitants of the New Hampshire Grants, to hold, take, or accept any office of honor or profit under the colony of New York,"* and requiring *"All officers and others acting under the Governor or Legislature of that province to suspend their functions, on pain of being viewed."* He then produced a letter from a secret agent of the settlers at Albany, giving the date of Prouty's commission, and inclosing a letter from the squire himself accepting the office in question. He also sent a copy of a notice sent some weeks previous to the surveyor, warning him to quit the Grants without delay.

"And now what have ye to say?" sternly demanded Allen, turning to the prisoners as soon as he had finished reading the documents. "What have ye to say, ye minions of York, why ye should not be *viewed* to the full extent and meaning of the decree made and provided for the like of ye?"

Quailing under the withering gaze of Allen, the justice could not muster courage to lift his head or utter a single word in reply. But the surveyor, who was a man of more firmness, and bore himself quite collectedly on the occasion, attempted an argument with the leader of the Green Mountain Boys, denying all right of the settlers to arrest him, protesting against being tried by any but a court acting under the authority of New York, and appealing to that authority for his justification.

"The authority of New York!" scornfully exclaimed the other; "appeal to the authority of New York! Why not appeal at once to the chancery of hell, the fountain head of that stream of corruption which comes to us under the name of New York law and justice? We, sir—we, the poor and insufferably abused settlers of these Grants, have often appealed to that source of justice—appealed for protection against the lawless aggressions of your cormorant speculators, who have attempted to wrest from us our rightful possessions, to seize with the grasp of plunderers our hard-earned pittances, and turn us out houseless and destitute into the wilderness. But we have appealed in vain, and only to learn our own folly in expecting that sin would ever be rebuked by Satan. No, sir, we will suffer no such appeal, but will ourselves give you a conclusive judgment in the premises; and such an one, too, as shall give you the wages of your iniquities. What say you, my merry mountaineers?"

As soon as the hearty but variously expressed responses by which the men testified their approbation of the remarks of their leader were over, Baker, Warrington, and Selden, who during the discussion had been engaged in a low conversation apart from the rest, beckoned Allen to approach them. The latter, obeying the intimation, advanced, and after listening attentively a while to some proposal or plan which the others appeared to be imparting to him, snapped his fingers with delight, and exclaimed:

"Capital! Capital, by Jupiter!" he repeated, bringing down his huge palm upon the snugly fitting buckskin covering his broad thigh with a slap that echoed through the woods like the report of a pistol. "Member, you shall announce it to them, and I will see that it is carried into execution."

Baker accordingly stepped forward, and, addressing the surveyor, gravely informed him that it had been determined to accede to the wish he had expressed of being tried, if he was to be tried at all, by a court of his own colony; and that Justice Prouty, who had lately been commissioned by the government of New York, would therefore now immediately proceed with the trial.

"Oh, gentlemen! oh, sir!" began Prouty beseechingly, as Allen now came forward to attend to the part he had proposed to assume in the business.

"Now, don't, Justice Prouty," interrupted Selden, with provoking irony; "don't, I beg of you, suffer your diffidence to deprive us of the aid of your acknowledged abilities in this important case. Having had the honor of introducing you to this company, I am very anxious that you should acquit yourself creditably on the occasion."

"Yes, sir; but, then, my situation——" again began to expostulate the troubled justice.

"Come, your worship," interrupted Allen, with a spice of the comic mingled with the determined expression of his countenance, "you are to try and to sentence this York interloper, and no two ways about it, neither, I will swear to you. There," he continued, seizing the reluctant and trembling squire, with one hand, grasping the seat of his breeches and the other his collar, and lifting and placing him on the side of the platform, with the apparent ease of one handling an infant; "there! sit on the edge of this table for a King's Bench. You did not think to arrive to that honor so soon, did you, squire?"

"Now, squire," said Peter Jones, with one of his

mischievous looks, "may I be eternally happy if I don't think you a considerable dabster of a prophet! Don't you see how cute it is all coming to pass, what you told your old woman this morning about your getting to be a judge soon? Though I must axe your pardon, squire, for listening under your bedroom window a little before we rapped to come in."

"Well, is the court ready to proceed?" said Allen. "Now for my opening, as the lawyers say. I am for the prosecution, recollect?"

"Now, I do protest, I beseech you, sir——" once more began to stammer the confused and dreadfully perplexed justice.

"Shut up, sir!" fiercely exclaimed Allen. "Hell and furies! who ever heard of a court before so despotic as to refuse to hear the statements of counsel? No, no, Mr. Court, that will never do; so now hear me."

The squire, thus awed into silence, hung his head and sat as still as his agitation would permit, while the other produced and again read the documents by which he had first introduced the subject; and, after briefly summing up the evidence, demanded that a sentence be imposed upon the surveyor of forty lashes of the beech rod.

"I dispute the authority of your pretended Convention, and I protest against the whole of these proceedings as illegal and riotous!" exclaimed the surveyor, with considerable spirit.

"Well, very well, sir," said Allen, with the utmost composure; "you have had your say and made your defense, as you had an undoubted right to do. I am always for liberty of speech when a man has really anything to say, and also for allowing a fair hearing in all cases, though that is more than your infernal York tribunals will permit, in nine cases out of ten. But let us now attend to the decision of the court. Boys, you may as well be getting a brace of genteel beech-sealers, for I feel very confident of a decision in my favor. Now, Mr. Justice, proceed with your sentence. Forty stripes with a green beech rod is all I claim, recollect; quite moderate, certainly; but it is always best to lean toward the side of mercy. Proceed, sir!"

"Anything else, gentlemen," groaned the distressed squire. "I will do anything else you say. But this, now, I cannot, and dare not do."

"Hark'ee, Mr. Court," rejoined the other, placing his arms akimbo and looking at the justice with the air of one resolved to have no more words on the subject, "a sentence out of you I will have, as sure as the devil delays his coming for your soul long enough for you to pronounce it. Will you proceed, sir? No answer, eh? Well, we will soon see whether Ethan Allen has got to eat his own words or not. Jones, bring me that surveyor's chain in the camp there."

Allen, taking out his pocket handkerchief, very deliberately made a slip noose and adjusted it round the neck of the trembling squire. He next carefully tied the tail of this noose to one end of the chain, throwing the other end, at the same time, over the large limb of a tree which projected directly over their heads at the height of twelve or fifteen feet from the ground.

"There, Jones, catch that end, and just straighten her out a little," he observed, with a cool, business-like air. "I have heard say that hanging was intended to bring about justice. Let us see if a little of it won't have that effect in the present instance."

Obeying with mischievous alacrity, Pete, now running the chain rapidly over the limb, brought it up just "taut enough," to use a sea phrase, to make the noose sensibly felt by the squire; upon which the latter, staring and glaring wildly around, as a slight sense of suffocation came over him, leaped upon his feet, and stood upright. This shift, however, afforded him but a momentary relief, for Jones quickly followed up the movement, straightening the chain with a jerk that brought the victim on to his toes; in which position, grappling the chain above his head with both hands, and begging, like a half-whipped schoolboy, for mercy, he was suffered to remain for a moment, to give him one more opportunity of complying with the requisition which had been made upon him.

"Your last chance of salvation!" exclaimed the leader, in a tone that testified his growing impatience at the man's obstinacy. "You will comply in one moment more, or, by the horned Lucifer, the next shall find you dangling within a yard of yonder limb!"

"Now I would, gentlemen, sartinly would if——" again began to splutter the struggling, though yet unconquered squire.

"String him up, Jones!" cried Allen, with startling energy.

The next instant the body of the poor justice was spinning round on one toe, with the tip of which he was barely able to touch the platform.

"Oh, I'm choking!" screeched the now really suffering wretch. "Oh! ugh! ugh! ugh! I will—will—I'll do it!"

"Ease away there, Jones!" said Allen, "he has come to his senses at last, and I think there will be no further trouble; so you may give him full play now."

After being again questioned as to the reality of his intentions to proceed with the required task, the subdued squire was let fully down, and permitted to stand at ease on the platform; when, as soon as he had recovered his breath and composure sufficiently to allow him to speak, he mumbled off the sentence which he had run such risks to avoid pronouncing.

"Now, Mr. Court," said Allen, with a slightly roguish curl of the lip, "as you have been brought to a sense of your duty and given the sentence which justice required of you, it is no doubt incumbent on you, sir, to see it executed. And, as all my men, here, stand sworn never to execute any sentence of a York magistrate, it follows, of course, that you must be the executioner yourself in the present case; so now dismount, sir, if you please, take this rod, and, after I have unnoosed you of this marvelous prompter of justice," he continued, taking off the noose, and placing a beechen rod in the hands of the other, "you will proceed to apply it in a way that shall show the sincerity of what you have just said and done. Boys, you may now take off the surveyor's coat, and then form a ring, with a few switches in your hands, if you will, to see that justice is duly administered on the occasion. There, that will do. Well, squire, we are now ready to proceed—what! hesitating again! Jones, seize the end of that chain, there, and be ready, while I replace the noose."

But Prouty, having had quite as many of such promptings as he felt willing to receive, did not wait to be noosed again, but, lifting the rod, moved forward, as if ready to perform the required task without further resistance. Allen then advanced and threw another rod down at the feet of the surveyor, gravely observing:

"There, Mr. Surveyor, supposing from what you have thrown out here that you think the court has sentenced you unjustly, we have concluded that, while he is executing the sentence on you, we will give you a chance to avenge the injury. You have, therefore, our free and full permission to return, blow for blow, through the whole of it. Indeed, sir, I should rather advise you to do it; for our boys, here, who are great sticklers for fair play, may take it into their heads, perhaps, to say that it would be unjust for one Yorker to receive all the honors of the day, without imparting an equitable share to his fellow. And in case you should neglect to do what they think is about right, I know not what may happen to you. And now, Mr. Justice," he continued, turning sternly to Prouty, "now, Mr. Justice, be lively, and with the fear of God and Ethan Allen before your eyes, lay on, sir!"

It would be difficult to conceive anything more strangely ludicrous than the scene that followed. The reluctant squire, daring no longer to delay, now gave two or three faint and harmless blows across the legs of the surveyor; when he was admonished by Ethan Allen, in a tone which experience had taught him pretty well how to interpret, to lay on more seriously. Spurred up by his fears, the justice then began to administer the applications of his rod with about that medium degree of violence, which, producing all the smart of heavier blows without the benumbing antidote of bruising, is always far more irritating, and is generally, perhaps, even more intensely painful to the victim than blows of double the severity. At all events the squire's applications soon produced a very visible effect on the surveyor, who, till this stage of the business, had stood eying the proceedings in dogged silence. But now leaping about, and being no longer able to stand the pain which the squire's applications began to impart, he hastily caught up the rod at his feet, and, swearing with spiteful bitterness that he *would* put it on, to punish the other for suffering himself to become the tool of a mob, gave back the blows with so much interest that it soon roused, in turn, the ire of the justice, who, now beginning to dance to the same tune and from the same cause which had put his opponent in motion, fell to, and laid it on in good earnest. Becoming thus mutually incensed, and the anger of each rapidly kindling at the increased pain of his adversary's applications, every blow of the one was followed by a heavier blow from the other. And, the blows falling heavier and thicker every instant, it soon grew into one of the most severe and furious flagellations ever witnessed in the settlement, and one that was amply satisfactory to our band of Green Mountain Boys, who stood by, sending forth shout after shout, and peal after peal of laughter that fairly shook the slumbering wilderness with the deafening reverberations. And so deeply engaged had become these unaccustomed dignitaries in administering to each other this whimsically conceived and queerly conducted punishment, that it was not till they had exceeded the prescribed number of stripes by nearly a dozen that either of them thought of yielding. Prouty, however, being of a less obstinate disposition, and possessing less nerve than the other, at length gave over, and cried lustily for quarter, which, even then, so implacable had the surveyor become, was only granted him on the interposition of the Green Mountain Boys.

"Well, squire," said Jones, the only man who seemed disposed to make any comments at the close of this curious scene, "don't you think these Yorkers most cruel, bloody fellows? Ah! jest as I told you, squire, we belong to the right party."

The business of the morning having been thus brought to a close, Justice Prouty, with an admonition to go and learn wisdom from folly, was released and sent home. The surveyor's instruments were next broken to pieces by Allen, and the fragments hurled into the bushes. The surveyor himself, with his assistant, who had not been considered of public consequence enough to be punished, was then put in charge of Jones and Brown, who were ordered to escort them to the New York line, and there leave them.

Within half an hour from the departure of the prisoners the encampment of the Green Mountain Boys under Snake Mountain was broken up and the place deserted, the different individuals composing the band, after a brief consultation, having been dispatched by their enterprising and impetuous leader in various directions, on secret business connected with the important events which were in train, and the new and untried scenes which were now soon to follow.

CHAPTER XIV

"Strong hands in harvest, daring feet in chase,
True hearts in fight, were gathered in that place
Of secret council."

If there is a town in Vermont whose first set of inhabitants deserved the appellation of high-minded and worthy, it was the early settlers of Middlebury. Distinguished, from their first pitch on the fertile banks of the Otter, for enterprise, firmness, and intelligence, they were among the foremost to resist the aggressions of a government which, unwittingly, perhaps, had lent itself to aid the unprincipled schemes of a few rapacious land speculators; while the opening scenes of our revolution found them ready to engage, with the same alacrity, and with the best of their means, in the greater work of achieving the independence of their whole country. And scarcely had the storm of war passed over, and the sunlight of peace began to break in on their infant settlement, before they united, with a zeal as extraordinary, considering their circumstances and means, as it was commendable, in rearing, by private munificence alone, a collegiate institution which for many succeeding years did more, probably, toward elevating the moral and literary character of Vermont than any one cause operating within her borders. And her alumni, now many of them in eminence at the bar and in the pulpit, and found gracing not only every station in their own favored country, from the humble schoolroom to the Senate chamber of the nation, but nobly dispensing her light among the people of every clime upon the face of the broad earth, whither, in the fearless and enterprising spirit of their fathers, they have scattered themselves—now to teach the arts to the boorish Russ or besotted Turk, now to assist the enslaved Greek or South American in his struggles for freedom, and now to rear the standard of the Cross among the degraded pagans of the East—her grateful alumni, often, often turn back in fancy to their beloved Alma Mater,

"To linger delighted o'er scenes recall'd there,"

and admire and bless the noble and self-sacrificing spirit of Painter, Chipman, Storrs, and others of her munificent founders, who made themselves poor in pecuniary estate that the children of their country might become rich in knowledge.

With these remarks, suggested by the location of the scene about to be described, and their expression here prompted by the personal interest which the writer of these unworthy pages must ever feel in that institution in which he was taught at once his weakness and his strength, and to which he is mainly indebted for the schooling and chastening of a wild and untutored imagination, and for the formation of whatever mental character he may possess; with these remarks, we say, let us now proceed to the narration of our story.

Could one of the fabled scenes drawn by the immortal Homer have been so far realized, on the 4th of May, 1775, that Mars, the supposed supervisor of every military enterprise, had sat in his cloud-begirt chariot over that tract of country lying between Lake Champlain and the Green Mountains, to take note of whatever in his line of business might be on foot below, he might have perceived, on looking down from his lofty car near the close of that day, movements among the inhabitants of the particular section just named, so simultaneous, and yet so apparently unconcerted, that even his godship himself, unless previously in the secret, would have been sadly puzzled to decide in what manner to account for them. Nearly every man could have been seen leaving his home for some point not far to the south of those falls on Otter Creek around which the flourishing village of Middlebury now stands. Though all would have seemed gradually centering to this spot, yet this would have been the only point of agreement discoverable in their movements or apparent objects. Some carried axes on their shoulders, some hoes, or other instruments of husbandry, and some had guns, with which they appeared to be amusing themselves, as they passed along, by shooting squirrels, or whatever small game might fall in their way. And in no instance were two men seen traveling together; and, if by chance any two happened to come across each other, they immediately separated, one stopping till the other had passed out of sight, or both diverging into different, though parallel routes. The exact point of their concentration was at length seen to be an opening in the wilderness, on a gentle swell of land commanding a view of the devious Otter from its western side. Nearing the center of this opening stood a log house tenanted by a hardy and enterprising settler, a confidential friend of the master spirit of this clandestine gathering. A barn, also of the same construction, and of dimensions ample enough to hold half a regiment within its walls, was standing some rods in the rear of the house. This huge fabric, as it finally appeared, had been selected, both on account of its size, and the central position which it occupied in the northern part of the Grants, for the approaching meeting of the Green Mountain Boys. And as the shades of evening began to gather over the wilderness, and individual objects grew indistinct to the view, many a dark form might be discovered emerging, one by one, from every point of the surrounding woods and stealthily taking their way in silence toward the building appointed for their rendezvous.

But, leaving this company to finish their noiseless gathering, we will now recur to note the adventures of one of our heroes on his way to the scene of action. We speak in the plural, here, as we do not pretend to fix on any one of the several leading personages of our story as the particular hero of the work. But should the reader deem such an one to be essential in the performance, we leave him to make his own selection from all the characters we have introduced—a privilege to the reader, which, we trust, will prevent any question in his mind whether the author himself has selected the one for this honor who is the most worthy of the appellation: and a privilege, too, that we the more freely accord, since we have often wished for the same favor ourselves while reading works of this kind, and bored with the everlasting recurrence of "*our hero,*" applied, not infrequently, to the worst drawn, and by far the most spiritless character in the book.

After the separation of our band in the morning, the leaders, as before intimated, were actively engaged through a good part of the day in calling upon the settlers to sound their views and feelings in regard to the approaching struggle between the colonies and mother country, and to apprise them, if found right in sentiments and ripe for action, as was generally the case, of the contemplated meeting, and the precautions deemed important to be observed in conducting it.

Warrington, having performed the task allotted to him as his share of the delicate and sometimes difficult duty, set out, late in the afternoon, for the appointed rendezvous of the evening. After leaving the vicinity of the lake, to the borders of which his duties had been principally confined, he soon entered the woods, and having decided on the course to be taken, proceeded onward with rapid step several miles toward his destination without pausing. But at length feeling somewhat wearied with the exertions of the day, he sat down to rest him for a few moments, on the trunk of a fallen tree, and was dreamily running over in his mind the singular events of the past few days when his attention was arrested by a clicking sound, resembling that which attends the cocking of a musket. While looking around him in doubt whether his senses had not deceived him, in respect to the impression they conveyed of the sound, he distinctly heard the snapping of a firelock in a thicket at no great distance from the spot he occupied. Springing upon his feet, he brought his own rifle to his shoulder, and, stepping behind a tree, awaited in silence the result, which, he supposed, whatever the cause of the movement, would soon be disclosed. But hearing nothing further, and concluding that the sound came from some hunter, who, having gained sight of game, and, snapping his piece at it, had noiselessly crept off after it in another direction, he thought but little more on the subject at this time, and soon leisurely proceeded on his way. The walk of half a mile now brought him to that dead and desolate stream, whose name, at the present day, "Lemon Fair," has so often proved a puzzler to the stranger traversing this section of the country, and led him to ask the cause of so singular an appellation. The explanation that follows, however, reconciles the apparent incongruity in a way as simple and curious as it is generally unexpected. And the inquirer is soon enabled to trace this before unaccountable name from "Lemon Fair," through "Lamen Fair," to the *lamentable affair!* which is said to have burst from the agonized bosom of a traveler, who once, in attempting to ford the stream, was doomed to the pain of witnessing his noble steed become inextricably mired, and, sinking deeper and deeper at every effort to clear himself, finally disappear with fearful death struggles in the bottomless quags of this Styx of Vermontane rivers. Warrington here paused to note the air of peculiar dreariness and gloom which, even at this day, seems to brood over this paradise of eels and owls—the former finding their Elysium in the stagnant, muddy, and root-tangled pools of the stream, and the latter on the decayed limbs of the long colonnade of dead and leafless trees lining the banks, where they sit moping and gloating over the inexhaustible storehouse of countless reptiles swarming in the dark and turbid waters beneath. And while standing upon the banks of this stream, with his mind thus engrossed, he was startled by the sharp report of a rifle, bursting from a fallen tree-top on a knoll at the distance of some eight or ten rods behind him; while at the same instant a bullet, passing through his coat between his arm and body, struck and buried itself on the dry and barkless surface of a tree standing a few yards before him. Whirling suddenly round toward the covert from which the shot issued, as now plainly indicated by a light cloud of diffusing smoke, he again quickly brought his rifle to his shoulder and stood for a few seconds straining his vision for a sight of the invisible foe. But being unable to discover any object with such certainty as would justify his returning the fire, he suddenly changed his purpose and leaped forward with all possible speed toward the place. In one moment he stood on the spot just occupied by his dastard assailant, when he succeeded in catching a glimpse of a dark form rapidly retreating over another swell into a thick and tangled swamp. His first impulse was to recommence the pursuit; but a second thought told him that it would probably be in vain, while it uselessly exposed him to the hazard of another shot of his enemy from some concealment which he would have time to gain unperceived. He therefore reluctantly turned and retraced his steps to the stream he had just left.

From the form and motions of the assassin, although in disguised dress, Warrington was but little at loss in identifying him with Darrow, whom he had twice met and as often frustrated in his base, or, to say the least, very questionable designs. And coupling the improbability that the fellow was acting from his own promptings in his murderous attempt with the friendly hints of Miss Hendee, he no longer doubted that Sherwood was indeed bent on his destruction, and, finding a willing instrument in Darrow, had instigated this method of accomplishing it. But abandoning all thoughts of any measures to punish or circumvent either the base tool or his still more dastard employer till his public duties should allow him more leisure, he now hastily crossed the stream and proceeded with rapid steps toward the rendezvous of his assembling companions, which he only reached just as the last glimmerings of departing daylight were fading in the western horizon.

"Charles, how is this!" exclaimed Colonel Allen, breaking away, as soon as he noticed Warrington's arrival, from a group of several of the most influential settlers in the vicinity, with whom he appeared to have been engaged in a low confidential conversation. "How is this that you are the last man to come on the ground? Why, I thought the devil had got you, or, what is the same thing in Dutch, that you had gone over to the British to apprise them of our project. But, come, sir, as I suppose we must allow you the credit of having done rather better than that, I have concluded to make you my right hand man for the evening. So now for business."

"In that case, colonel," replied the other, "let me suggest to you the precaution of placing a few sentinels around us while in convention. There may be those abroad to-night who, if permitted to look in upon us here, would render our enterprise as vain as the Crusades. Were it not too dark I would show you a hole in my coat through which one of these prowlers a few miles back, by a small mistake, put a bullet, instead of through my heart as evidently intended."

"God bless you, Charles, what do you mean?" asked Allen, with surprise and emotion.

"I mean as I say."

"But who could it be?"

"That despicable sergeant, instigated by Sherwood, I suspect."

"And what was you about not to return the compliment on the spot?"

"He escaped me in a thicket, and I had no time to spend in the cautious pursuit which would be safe or successful. Would to Heaven I could have more leisure!"

"Well, by the blessing of God, Charles, within a week we will have our heels on the nest of rattlesnakes. But it is time to organize. You were right about a guard. Will you attend to placing it while I assemble the company in the barn and see that each has the watchword?"

Allen now ordered lights to be brought, and, placing himself at the door of the building, he called to the company to advance and enter singly. Each man as he presented himself, and before suffered to pass in, was strictly required to give the watchword, which, as a precautionary measure to prevent anyone being present whose views had not been previously ascertained, had been confidentially imparted by Allen and his associate leaders since the meeting was in agitation. The word chosen for this purpose was Carillon, an appellation by which fort Ticonderoga was designated by the French while in possession of their government. After every man had passed this test of admittance, and thus proved himself entitled to mingle in the deliberations of the assembly, Colonel Allen called the meeting to order, and after stating that important business was in contemplation, the successful result of which might depend upon the secrecy with which it was conducted, proposed a sort of oath or affirmation, binding all present by a solemn promise not to divulge the proceedings of this meeting, and its consequent measures, till the reasons which made the secrecy necessary should cease to exist. This proposition was acceded to and the oath taken by rising. Allen then, as the acting chairman of the assemblage, declared the meeting open for remarks on the subject which they had met to discuss.

The dead silence which was now for a few moments observed by the expectant assembly was broken by Warrington, who, calmly rising, proceeded, after a few preliminary observations, to give a brief history of the commencement and progress of the quarrel between the colonies and the mother country. He then enumerated the wrongs and aggressions which the former had suffered, while meekly and vainly petitioning for redress, and closed by a vivid picture of the recent massacre at Lexington, and with an eloquent appeal to the settlers to join the inhabitants of the sister colonies in avenging the death of their slaughtered countrymen.

As he closed his harangue, which had been listened to with the most profound attention, a visible excitement ran through the assembly. And the hasty changing of positions, as they sat upon their rude plank seats ranged in rows round a small table, on which dimly burned a small taper, the glistening eye, the indignant glance, the firmly compressed lip, and the silent working of the muscles of the faces of these hardy mountaineers plainly told the speaker that he had been addressing men who neither lacked the intelligence to comprehend, nor the spirit to act, as soon as a definite object for action was set before them.

Remember Baker, one of the most shrewd, sagacious,

and coolly calculating men of the settlement, next arose and addressed the meeting. With a few observations, for he was not a man of many words, going to confirm the statements and fortify the positions of Warrington, he told them that although he doubted not in the least that principle alone with them would be sufficient to excite them to action in the coming contest, yet their policy, as settlers engaged in a controversy with New York for their homes and property, demanded that they should take a bold and decided stand against the British; for by doing this they would at once enlist the sympathies of the other colonies in regard to their wrongs, draw upon themselves the attention and respect of Congress, to which, if backed by the considerations of a meritorious service in the common cause of the country, they could successfully appeal for protection against the aggressions of New York, and thus place themselves in an attitude in which they could not only command justice, but finally secure the privilege of becoming an independent State.

"Member is right!" exclaimed one of that class with whom this artful, and as the event afterward proved, by no means ill-grounded argument, was calculated to operate with particular force.

"Ay, ay!" responded another, "give me Member Baker for foresight! The more birds we can kill with one stone the better."

Although the argument of Baker was not probably without its effect on the minds of all, situated as the settlers were with respect to their controverted rights, and when added to the manly appeal of Warrington to their patriotism and principles, had wrought up the assembly to a high pitch of feeling, yet Allen, conceiving that something more was needed to ripen them for action and raise their minds, as he was desirous of doing, to a level with his own high-toned enthusiasm, now rose, and, after looking for a moment fearlessly and confidently around him, as he stood towering with his giant form, like Saul among the people, began:

"MEN OF THE GREEN MOUNTAINS:

"In the struggle in which you have been for many years engaged, you have won among the people of these colonies a name of valor and patriotism. But have you gained this proud distinction in surmounting the difficulties of the past, to lose it now by inaction in the more important stake of the present? Have you so long, so nobly, so triumphantly resisted arbitrary power in the shape of little tyrants near home, to submit, now, to the lawless dictations of great ones from abroad? Are you, who have just saved your homes and possessions from the grasp of these, now willing to yield them tamely to those?—to those whose despotic dominion will soon render them but possessions in name, to be transmitted to whom? to whom I say? To slaves in the persons of your own children! yes, your own children, who, if suffered to retain their own inheritance at all, must retain it with a foot of a lord on their necks and the hand of a priest in their pockets! Green Mountain Boys! could you who have drank in liberty from the very air of your green hills, never yet contaminated by the breath of a tyrant, could you witness this and live? And, above all, can you now look idly on and see a hireling soldiery swarming your country, enforcing the accursed requisitions of their masters at the point of the bayonet, shooting down your countrymen and brothers by scores, as if they were wild beasts, for exercising but the rights which God and nature have given them—can you look upon a scene like this, and lift no hand for your rights?—strike no blow to avenge the cold-blooded murder of your countrymen at Lexington? Great God forbid! No! no! my brave mountaineers, you were never born to be cringing slaves! Your bold hearts and sinewy arms were never made to be listless and idle at a time like this! Come, then, come on! follow me, whose heart is laboring and leaping for the work of vengeance, and whose arm is nerved and aching for the blow! Follow me, and I will lead you to deeds which shall cover the Green Mountain Boys with imperishable glory, and make their name the watchword of liberty while a tyrant shall remain to disgrace the image of his God, or pollute the earth with his presence."

During the delivery of this brief and exciting appeal the expectant audience at first sat in their seats as silent and motionless as a group of statues. Before the speaker had proceeded through many sentences, however, the whole company had noiselessly risen in their places, where they stood as if spellbound in their tracks, every head eagerly bent forward, and every eye, gleaming with the kindling fire within, riveted upon their idolized leader, to catch the bold and inspiriting thoughts that fell burning from his lips, now with looks of fire and scorn, and now with the intonations of thunder. And as he went on, rising in energy and power at every sentence, eyes were seen to flash brighter and brighter with indignation, tears of excited and overflowing feeling to gush over many a rough cheek, while many a clenched and brawny fist was brandished aloft, in mute response to the heart-stirring words of the speaker. And, when he closed, "Ethan Allen forever! Ethan Allen forever!" rose in one loud convulsive shout to heaven.

All being now ripe for action, and many loudly demanding the object which might immediately require their services, Allen laid before them the project of marching at once upon the British forts at Ticonderoga and Crown Point, with the object of surprising and capturing these two important though now weakly garrisoned fortresses. The settlers being in general well apprised of the state of these garrisons, and entering with great zeal into the views of their leaders respecting the importance and feasibility of the proposed plan, the latter now made a call for volunteers, and immediately commenced an enrollment of names, which, when completed, was found, to the joy and surprise of Allen and his colleagues, to embrace more than three-fourths of the assemblage now present; while even the rest expressed an earnest wish to aid in the enterprise so far as it could be done without leaving the neighborhood of their homes, where their presence was demanded. All necessary measures preparatory to the expedition, as far as regarded the forces raised in this section of the Grants, were then discussed and settled, and a sufficient number of men were selected to guard every road by which any information of the contemplated movement could be conveyed to the enemy. These were ordered to enter upon their duties next day; while the main body were to equip and otherwise prepare themselves in the best manner the circumstances would admit, and assemble at Castleton on the fourth day from the present time. After these arrangements were completed Allen ordered his horse to be brought to the door, and announced his intention of departing that night for the south part of the settlement, to superintend the mustering of the forces enlisting or enlisted in that quarter.

"Well, my brave boys," said the colonel, mounting his horse, while his devoted followers were crowding around him, "remember to meet me at Castleton on the 8th. Captain Warrington and Lieutenant Selden will muster and take charge of you. Captain Baker goes to Winooski river to raise what force he can there, and come in boats to join us on the lake. As to myself, before to-morrow's sunset I must be at Holy Hill.* And

* An appellation by which Ethan Allen was in the habit of calling Bennington.

now, my fine fellows, go home and prepare yourselves without letting your left hands know what your right are doing, and may the Lord bless you all till I see you again."

So saying, and putting spurs to his horse, he rushed down the road to the south and disappeared.

CHAPTER XV

"Now be thou strong! Oh! knew we not
Our path must lead to this?
A shadow and a trembling still
Were mingled with our bliss!"

THE following epistle from Miss Hendee to Miss Reed, an answer to the one from the latter inserted in a previous chapter, was written in the interval between the meeting of the Green Mountain Boys last described and the general mustering of their forces for their contemplated enterprise.

"Forgive me, dear Jessy, but really I could not help laughing, on the receipt and perusal of your vivacious and very interesting letter, to see the desperate attempts you there repeatedly make to conceal from me and yourself, by naked, unmasked assertion and inferences without premises, the heart-hidden secret which your every third sentence, at least, most palpably discloses. Yes, my lady, whether you believe it or not, yourself, you are but little better than a gone girl, and your doughty major will find it out, too, as sure as jealousy has eyes and love none. But never mind it, my dear girl, nor turn up that pretty slender nose in a miff at what I say, since the same letter that gives you cause of displeasure, if cause there be, will furnish you also with the means of an ample revenge; for I, too, have adventures to relate, of the past week's occurrence, scarcely less extraordinary than your own. When you said, Jessy, in that little parenthesis which you threw into your letter concerning Warrington, '*A noble-looking fellow; I wish you could see him,*' you little thought that your wish had been granted ere expressed; and far less did you dream, when you added, '*I think you would like him,*' how much of a prophetess you was likely to become; for Charles Warrington I have seen, Warrington the Green Mountain Boy, Warrington the York outlaw, and Warrington the generous, high-minded, and, as you truly say, noble-looking fellow! And in what estimation I secretly hold him, you will better understand, when I inform you that my old acquaintance Howard, of whom you have often heard me speak, and Warrington are one and the same person! You cannot be more surprised at this news than I was myself at the discovery. And not small was the confusion of thought and feeling I experienced at first, I confess, in reconciling the warring conceptions I had previously entertained of these two, as I supposed them, different and almost diametrically opposite characters. In this, however, I have at length succeeded, and even to that degree that I cannot but feel that the character of Howard, pure and exalted as I ever thought it, receives an additional luster from the noble and disinterested part he has taken in behalf of these poor, and, as I am now satisfied, unjustly treated settlers.

"And with this avowal of opinion you will, of course, understand that I think none the worse of him for being a New York outlaw.

"We have had three interviews. The two first I must pass over lightly, as I have much of a more interesting character to communicate. I first encountered Warrington in the border of the woods adjoining our opening, where I wandered, a fatalist would think, but to be frightened by the questionable appearance of a sergeant from the fort, and to be relieved by the opportune arrival of my knight-errant Green Mountain Boy. Our next meeting was at our house, where in the course of the evening he made known to me for the first time the identity of which I have spoken, and where also he came near being seized by this same sergeant and his soldiers, who, I feel sure, came here for no other purpose, being prompted by the reward, and instigated, as I cannot but suspect, by one who shall be nameless. But Warrington and another of the leaders of the Green Mountain Boys who happened here that evening, and who, by the way, was a most extraordinary man, fairly outgeneraled their mercenary enemies, and, by a little favoring from a quarter which you are at liberty to guess at, both luckily made their escape. Our last interview has been to-day, and a most important one, too, I fear it may prove to the destinies of your perplexed and, in some respects, truly unhappy friend. But before entering upon particulars I must recur to some events which transpired in the interim. The next day after W.'s visit and fortunate escape, Sherwood came here and raised a storm in our quiet family, which has not yet wholly ceased raging. It seems this sagacious lover of mine, who has often heard my father recount the Samaritan kindness of Howard, and perhaps suspected my own secret partialities, had discovered, by worming himself into the confidence of the settlers, that Howard and Warrington were the same, but, for reasons of his own, had kept the discovery entirely to himself, though he had been for several months in possession of the secret. It appears also, that he had been apprised of each of my interviews with Warrington. And, coming armed with all this annihilating array of facts, as he believed it, he, without saying a word to me, called my father aside, and poured the whole story into his ears, with such additions and embellishments as he conceived would best subserve his purpose—the amount of which was, as near as I could gather, that my father had been harboring a branded villain, who, in the guise of a gentleman, had been aiming at the seduction of his daughter and the eventual seizure of his possessions. Trembling from head to foot with uncontrollable rage, my father immediately hastened to my apartment. I will not, I cannot even attempt a description of the painful scene that followed. You are not unacquainted with my father's unfortunate infirmities of temper. You can, therefore, in some measure fancy, perhaps, how he would feel and act under such a representation of things so nearly affecting his wishes and interests—a representation in which fact and falsehood were so artfully blended that a much cooler temperament, under the circumstances, might have been thus wrought up to anger. He swore and wept alternately. I wept freely also, but only at witnessing his distress, and at the thought of my own luckless destiny, which had placed me in a situation where I must sacrifice my own happiness for life, or probably be the means of destroying that of a parent, who, with all his faults, is still dear to my heart. I said but little, however. Delicacy as well as prudence forbade my disclosing the state of my feelings. And as to all other charges, I could only assert my innocence, for I had then given Mr. W. scarce a word of encouragement.

"After my father had exhausted his store of reproaches upon my poor head and left me, Sherwood entered and took up the discourse. I could not but feel amused, in spite of my indignation and contempt at his despicable course, to see all the doubling and shiftings he went through in his desperate attempts to regain my favor, which my manner probably pretty plainly told him he had put in considerable hazard. After protesting, flattering, apologizing, and arguing, with the sycophancy of a Frenchman and the sophistry of a Jesuit, he finally departed, leaving me to myself and the negative happiness which his absence has not very lately failed to afford me.

"The next morning I reminded my father, whose madness seemed to have something more of method in it than the day before, of a visit which had a few days previous been projected at his own suggestion. This was a ride, on horseback, to Otter Creek, to carry a few necessaries to a distant relative of ours, Aunt Story, as we call her, whose curious subterraneous abode I have before described to you, I believe. No serious objection being made to the proposal, I accordingly set out with Neshobee, my usual attendant on these excursions, who, on another horse, accompanied me in the capacity of baggageman and squire. We had a pleasant ride, and arrived without any particular adventure at the creek, opposite her wood-begirt residence. Oh, how delightful is a morning ride at this season of the year through these flowering forests! How fragrant the viewless odors that regale your senses at almost every step! And, in the present instance, as you near the Green Mountains, how pure and invigorating the breezes that, seemingly uncontaminated by a contact with earth, come wafting down their dark sides fresh from the mid-heavens! I never approach these green-hilled monuments of sylvan magnificence but my physical powers receive an impulse, and my moral nature becomes sensibly exalted. No wonder the Green Mountain Boys should be men of such high-toned character!

"On reaching the banks of the creek Neshobee set up his shrill whoop (not war-whoop) to make known our arrival to this fearless woman of the woods. This being heard and understood by her, she quickly made her appearance, came across with her boat, and ferried us all safe over the stream, our horses having been left tied to saplings on the bank behind.

"I must not stop to describe the cordial reception I met with, as I always do in this singular yet interesting family; nor my romp with the curly headed brood of children that thronged around me, capering in wild glee at my arrival, and their eyes fairly sparkling with joy and gratitude at the sight of the tit-bits I had brought them. After the rumpus and romping with the joyous little creatures had somewhat subsided, I took the bright-eyed and lisping little Julia in my lap; when the pretty rogue immediately clambered up and, putting her arms around my neck, in the sweet, pleading, and playful tones of infantile eloquence exclaimed:

" 'Now, Couthin Alma, mayn't I kith you again? There, I did! I will again! There! ha! ha! Now I have kithed you ath many timeth ath I did the young captain.'

" 'And who, pray, my pretty one,' said I quite innocently, 'who is this young captain with whom you appear to have been so familiar?'

" 'Oh, he ith the young captain,' replied she, hesitating in her childish simplicity how to define her favorite by any other appellation than the one by which she had been accustomed to hear him called; 'he ith—he ith a good young captain. I kithted him three timeth. And wouldn't you kith him, too, Couthin Alma, if he'd let you? Wouldn't the young captain let Couthin Alma kith him, ma?'

"Puzzled and confused at I scarcely knew what, I turned to the mother for an explanation; when, to my still greater confusion, I beheld her holding her sides, while her eyes were fairly dancing in the bright tears of suppressed risibility, to which she now gave way in a right hearty fit of laughter.

" 'Excuse me, Alma,' said she, as soon as she could command her merry emotions sufficiently to speak; 'excuse me for laughing at the child's ludicrous introduction of a subject which I was at the very moment thinking how I could myself break to you. The young captain, as some of the settlers call him, is no other than the well-known leader of one of the bands of the Green Mountain Boys, Charles Warrington. Why bless me!' she continued, with a look of surprise, as she now lifted her eyes from her work to my features, 'what ails you, Alma? Why, your face is as red as—oh! ah! aha! you knew all this before, did you? And you have seen him yourself, you rogue?' she added mischievously, shaking her finger at me and fixing her keen eyes on my face. 'You have, Alma, and you need not attempt to deny it.'

"'I have not denied it, aunt, have I?' I replied, rallying as well as I could.

"'Well, now, Alma Hendee,' she rejoined, with a gratified and serious air, 'I have not heard anything this long while that has done me more good than this news. Indeed, for the past week in particular I have actually prayed that you might meet him, though I dared not be the means of bringing it about. And the reason why I wished it is because I think so much of the man, and feel such an interest in the cause which he has done so much to sustain; and also because I knew that you, from your intercourse and connection with the York party, and from your hearing, as you naturally would, nothing but slander and misrepresentation on the man and curses on the cause in which he has been so nobly engaged, that you, I say, must have almost necessarily imbibed wholly erroneous opinions of both him and his cause. Now, has it not been so?'

"'Such,' I answered, 'was once, I confess, too much the case.'

"'I thought so,' she resumed; 'and but for the fear that I might displease you—for I never know how to hold up when I begin—and perhaps be led into a quarrel with your fiery old father, who has been so good to me, I should before this have spoken to you on these matters. Why, this same Warrington and a party of his followers were up on Lake Dunmore the very day you were last here; and while you were here in the house playing with the children I discovered, as I was out to the edge of the woods to get cedar boughs for a broom, a gang of Yorkers going in pursuit of them. Don't you recollect I came in and proposed sending Neshobee out to kill us a partridge?'

"I remembered it, and assented.

" 'Well,' she continued, 'it was for no other purpose than to dispatch him to Warrington with a note that I scribbled in that closet. Neshobee, I knew, was a friend to the captain.'

" 'Neshobee!' said I in surprise, 'why, I never heard him so much as utter the name!'

" 'It is true for all that,' she rejoined. 'Warrington once did him a service when they happened to meet on a hunt, and Neshobee, being made acquainted with the other's situation, and knowing yours, has been as prudent as he is faithful.'

" 'But what became of the Yorkers?' I asked.

" 'The Green Mountain Boys threw them into the lake and returned to this neighborhood,' she answered. 'The captain and his lieutenant came and slept that very night in this house, and were here asleep on the floor when I came up to the house after helping you off the next morning. Do you remember singing us a song that night, just before going to bed, and how you were interrupted by a noise in the woods above us?'

" 'I do; but what of that?' said I, somewhat startled.

" 'Why, nothing,' she replied, smiling, 'only Warrington, who rambled out after his friend fell asleep, heard your performance.'

" 'You astonish me, Aunt Story,' I replied. 'But surely he could not have distinguished my voice in that underground abode?'

" 'Not exactly,' answered she, 'and yet he was strangely puzzled, and seemed when telling me of the affair the next morning to have some suspicions of the truth.'

" 'But did you tell him who it was?' I eagerly demanded.

" 'No, Alma,' she said; 'I kept your secret for reasons which I have before named, and sent him off worse puzzled than before. But how did he introduce himself—as Howard or as Warrington? For that the two are one and the same is a riddle that I guessed out long ago.'

"I told her the circumstances, after which she resumed:

" 'So you have a hurricane at your house. Well, Alma, let it blow on, and overturn, till it levels falsehood and corruption to the ground, and brings truth and justice uppermost. And when that takes place, if you will believe me, Jake Sherwood will be swept into the gulf of infamy, where he ought to be now, instead of being here among men, with the pretensions of a man, but with the real character of a spy and hypocrite!'

" 'You are very severe, aunt,' I remarked, not so much offended, however, as I might have been.

" 'I hold, Alma,' she rejoined, 'that the boldness of a truth is no reason for suppressing its utterance. Why, Alma Hendee, whether you know it or not, whether you will believe it or not, it is God's truth that with all his smooth manners and gentlemanly appearance, the heart of that same Jacob Sherwood is as black as the outside of my dinner pot!'

"I began to say something which she took for a qualified assent, when, cutting me short, she went on:

" 'You know that it is so, Alma. And, now that you have again met with Warrington, I know where your heart is, or I should not venture to say so much. Far be it from me ever to interfere with matches—matches that are truly such. But mis-matches, patched up on earth, and accursed of heaven, I should feel myself honored in being the instrument of breaking. And knowing, as I think I do, all the motives and circumstances which led you to acquiesce in this entanglement with Sherwood, and knowing also that a match between you would be yoking darkness to light, I stand prepared, as your friend, acting in the place of your sainted mother, now in heaven, to advise you to say—even in despite of the favorite schemes of your mistaken and blinded father—to say to Sherwood, as Peter said to Simon Magus, who would buy the sacred gift with money, "Thy gold perish with thee!" '

"A long conversation then ensued between us, in which all the information possessed by either, relative to the York controversy, and the part taken in the same by Warrington, Sherwood, and others, was mutually imparted and received, and our opinions and feelings on these subjects freely exchanged. While still engaged in this engrossing theme one of the children came running into the house with the cry, 'The young captain is coming! the young captain is coming!' I was struck dumb by this unexpected announcement, and so surprised and fluttered that, had I been a bird, I believe I should have instantly clapped my wings and flown away. But, as it was, I had nothing to do but prepare to meet the half-dreaded, half-courted danger as unconcernedly as possible. We had little time allowed us for preparation, however; for scarce had the announcement been made before Warrington entered the door attended by—whom think you, Jessy? I wish you could have been there. In that case, to follow up that odd comparison of yours, the brisk little drummer in your heart would have found his match, I think, to keep up the accompaniment with the lively performer at work in my own; for Captain Warrington's attendant was no other than your favored knight, the gay, witty, and handsome Selden. An hour spent in his company was sufficient to make me feel that these flattering epithets, and even more, might be justly applied to him. Now, don't be jealous, girl, for though peculiarly pleased with him I certainly was, yet my feelings were anything but those constituting what we define to be that undefinable concern called love; no, no, not that, but a singular sort of a flowing away of the heart toward him, which I can neither describe nor account for, unless the solution be found in the prepossessions of him that your letter had implanted.

"We were now summoned to dinner, which our freehearted hostess had done her best in preparing for us. The meal itself, as you know it must have been, considering the limited store from which it had to be prepared, was certainly a plain one. But partaken in such company, how could it be other than a delightful one! With me, it forcibly exemplified the proverb of the wise man, 'Better is a dinner of herbs where love is, than a stalled ox and hatred therewith.'

"After dinner Warrington, with his peculiar delicacy of manner, proposed a ramble. My tongue would have declined the proposal, but my heart, rising in rebellion, suppressed the utterance, and I silently and with a palpitating bosom assented. All seemed to understand the object of our walk, and no one, not even a child, offered to accompany us. I felt, indeed, myself that my destiny for life hung on the events of that hour. We proceeded in almost unbroken silence to the bank of the river, when I soon found myself seated, I scarcely know how, by his side upon a flowery hillock. The quiet waters, sparkling in the rays of the meridian sun, were gently gliding along in soft murmurs at our feet; while a spreading thorn-tree, loaded with blossoms of snowy whiteness and filling the air with delicious fragrance, formed the canopy for our heads. I cannot describe what now passed. My heart soon overflowed with contending emotions. I found myself able to prevail against its stronger dictates no longer; and my feelings found vent in a flood of tears. My head involuntarily rested on his shoulder while he advocated his cause with all the tender pathos of love, which found a chord in my own bosom so powerfully responsive to its eloquent pleadings that

> "Then our hearts together run;
> And like kindred drops of water,
> Met and mingled into one."

"The winged moments flew by unheeded; and when, at the end of an hour, which in this sweet trance of the affections seemed as a moment, we rose to return, our mutual vows of unchanging love and eternal constancy had ascended to the registry of Heaven.

"Soon after our return to the house the gentlemen apprised us of the necessity of their immediate departure; when, after an affectionate adieu, they proceeded on to their destination. This destination I am not at liberty to unfold, and shall consequently be debarred from some particulars connected with my parting with W. which awakened a solicitude alike new and painful to my feelings. I did not tarry long after they left us. But, after a shower of thanks, praises, and blessings from our hostess for the step which I apprised her I had taken, I soon set out for home, where I arrived before sunset.

"On another page of this letter I styled myself your perplexed friend. I am so, though not because I regret the step I have taken, but on account of the difficulties which must soon beset me. I have also many painful apprehensions of the effect which my engagement may have when it becomes known, as ere long it necessarily must, on not only my father's happiness, but his property, owing to the peculiarities of our situation. As these cannot be understood without a knowledge of some former events connected with our family,

I will in confidence briefly relate to you the leading particulars of our family history. My paternal grandfather's family consisted of my uncle, Gabriel Hendee, and my father, James Hendee, with their half-sister Mary, who married John Sherwood, father of Jacob Sherwood. To these three was left a considerably extensive property, which was increased as far as regarded the shares of Gabriel and his brother-in-law, Sherwood, who, becoming partners, engaged in the lucrative trade and commerce of the Connecticut River, on the banks of which, within the borders of Massachusetts, you are already aware, we all once resided. But my father, who was of a different disposition, and less inclined to confine himself to the details of business, entered into uncertain speculations which, instead of increasing, diminished his original inheritance, involved him in some pecuniary embarrassments, and finally led him to abandon trade, for which he seemed neither to have much tact nor inclination, and seek a commission in the army destined for the French and Indian wars, then beginning to rage along our borders. Obtaining the commission he sought, he was soon called into active service, having intrusted Sherwood to arrange his affairs and take charge of our property; while Uncle Gabriel, having no family and becoming an invalid, retired from business and came to reside with our family in father's absence. Several years thus passed away, father at intervals returning home to see his wife and son, the darling little Edward, and spend such time with them as his public duties would permit, scarcely troubling himself to look into the state of his property, which he believed to be in hands where it would be husbanded to the best advantage. My Uncle Gabriel in the meanwhile still continuing to live in the family, and appearing much attached to it, especially to his little nephew, made his will, bequeathing his whole property to the child when of age, and all the income till that time, and certain portions of it after, to my father. But it so happened not long after this that Mr. Sherwood, who had taken a temporary residence further up the river, paid our family a long visit, at the end of which he took my uncle home with him, where he soon grew worse and died; not, however, as it soon appeared, till he had added a codicil to his will, making, in case of Edward's death, Mr. Sherwood's son, Jacob, legatee, and placing that family where the will placed ours. From that time misfortunes seemed to fall fast and heavy on our devoted family. My mother soon sickened and died, leaving me, her youngest child, about a year old. Our family establishment was then broken up. Edward was placed in the family of Mr. Sherwood; and I was sent to a relation of my mother in Hartford. But father, already borne down with sorrow at the loss of two wives (for my mother was a second wife by whom he had no other child), was doomed to another blow scarcely less fatal to his happiness, and more so to his future prospects, in the further loss of that son on whom all his hopes and dependence had been placed. The boy had been allowed, as the story was told, to accompany a reckless young man, then in Sherwood's employ, many miles into the interior, and there strayed away and never could be found. There was a rapid river running through the woods, in which he might have been drowned and swept down into the Connecticut. But it was considered more probable that he had been seized by some small, lurking band of Indians (traces of whom were discovered in the vain search for the boy), and by them murdered, as it was supposed, since no tidings of him ever reached us. My father, when he returned and learned the fate of his son, was inconsolable. And Mr. Sherwood seemed deeply to sympathize with him, and, moreover, to manifest great regret that uncle had so altered his will as to take all his property from our family, assuring my father that he would make such provision for us as would be a recompense. After this visit my father remained abroad to the close of the war, when, being discharged from the service, he began to bethink him about the means of a future livelihood, and called on Sherwood to account for his property, which, to his dismay, had dwindled to a mere pittance. And, receiving it, he commenced a small business in Hartford, where he resided till I was about seventeen, living in good style and bestowing on me the best education the place afforded. But again becoming embarrassed by expenses beyond his income, and his pride revolting at the thought of being a bankrupt in this place, he took me, and secretly left town for Albany, to avail himself of the many promises of Mr. Sherwood, who had removed to the latter place many years before. We were kindly received by Mr. S., who furnished father with money to pay off his creditors in Hartford, and subsequently to purchase our present residence, though most of the improvements have been made through the means of the half pay which he receives from the government.

"You will now, Jessy, be able to appreciate the difficulties of my situation, and perceive the reasons which actuate my father in the strenuous course which he has pursued, and will be likely, still, to pursue in urging a connection between me and Jacob Sherwood. Jessy, adieu. A. H.

"P. S.—When I closed, as above, last night, I expected the letter would have been taken early this morning by Major Skene's colored man, Jack, who said he should go up with his boat to-day; but he has just called and says he shall not go till to-morrow morning. The main object of this postscript is, however, to say that if you thought it so important that I should keep your secret, you cannot but see how much more so it is that you keep mine. I know not but Mr. Warrington's life may depend on it—I did not mean to say this, but my fears and forebodings have compelled me. You do not know Mr. S.—would to Heaven I had never known him. Farewell. "ALMA."

CHAPTER XVI

"They came, impatient for the fight,—
Burning to rush into the slaughter,—
Ready to pour their blood like water
For what they deem the right;—
Like men, preferring glorious graves
To life if it must be the life of slaves!"

It seems to be universally conceded that the first settlers of Vermont were men of an iron mold and of an indomitable spirit. And it is no less true, we apprehend, that with corporeal frames unusually large and muscular, and constitutions peculiarly robust and enduring, they possessed, also, intelligence and mental energies which, considering what might naturally be expected of men of their condition in life, and their situation in a wilderness, affording none of the ordinary means of intellectual culture, were equally remarkable. The proof of these assertions is to be abundantly found, we think, in the unequaled stand taken by them for their rights in their memorable controversy with New York, and in the multiplied documents that grew out of it in the shape of resolves and decrees of conventions, addresses to the people, memorials and remonstrances to the governor of that province, and to the British throne itself, all drawn up with great clearness and cogency of reasoning, and evincing a knowledge of natural and constitutional rights in a people among whom law, as a profession, was then entirely unknown, which are generally to be found only in the courts and councils of old and highly civilized countries. And even were these testimonials to their character wholly wanting, ample evidence that they were a generation of no ordinary men may still be seen in the scattered remnant of this noble band of heroes yet lingering among us, like the few and aged pines on their evergreen mountains, and, though now bowed down by the weight of nearly a century of years, exhibiting frames which would almost seem to indicate them as men belonging to another race, and which are still animated by the light of wisdom and intelligence and warmed by the unconquerable spirit of freedom yet burning unwasted within them.

Those who have treated on this subject, when alluding to the facts we have stated, have generally coupled them with observations upon the invigorating effects of mountain air, etc., leaving us to infer that these peculiarities of the early settlers were attributable only to such causes. It is, indeed, doubtless the case, that the wild scenery and the pure, elastic air of mountainous countries are the most favorable, under the same degree of culture, to the formation of the highest grade of physical as well as moral and intellectual character—imparting, in the one instance, that health and peculiar vigor which brings the human system to all the perfection that it is capable of attaining, and, in the other, engendering, with firmness of nerves and firmness of purpose the usual attendants of great bodily powers, a healthy and high-toned imagination and those lofty aspirations that exalt the character, and prompt to great and noble actions. But whatever influence the peculiar climate and scenery of this Switzerland of America, as Vermont may, perhaps, be appropriately termed, may have had, in this respect, on the descendants of these hardy settlers, little of this influence, probably, would have been perceptible on the settlers themselves; they, it must be recollected, were not natives of these mountains, but recent emigrants from other New England colonies. And whatever peculiarities they possessed must mainly have originated in other causes—from the very nature of the enterprise, probably, which brought them together, that of settling a wild and rough frontier country, known to be attended by a thousand difficulties and hardships, and beset by a thousand dangers, in which men of ordinary stamina would never think of engaging. They, indeed, may be looked upon in the light of picked men, or more rightly, perhaps, in that of volunteers, stepping boldly and confidently forth for some extraordinary enterprise, of which the hazard and difficulty are so great, that nothing but an uncommon union of courage and strength can accomplish it, and of which the success, or even the attempt, it may be, furnishes the best evidence of these qualities in those who voluntarily enlist in the undertaking. And as regards the intelligence and mental character of these settlers, their educations were generally equal to those usually received among the better classes of the old settlements where they were obtained, and superior, probably, to what the same were able to furnish to their immediate descendents. And this fact, together with the emergencies, which not only called all the energies of their minds into action, but constantly improved them, and enlarged their information by the investigations they were induced to make for the successful prosecution of their cause in the New York controversy, will sufficiently account for their intellectual superiority over the ordinary settlers of other new countries.

With these observations, here thrown in by way of showing our warrant for many of the descriptions of character which we have introduced, and which we thought it not impossible might otherwise subject us to the charge of indulging in improbabilities, we will now proceed with the incidents of our story.

The morning of the 9th of May broke brightly upon the encampment of our troops at Castleton, disclosing to the view, now for the first time, an organized band of about three hundred as brave and hardy men as ever assembled for deeds of daring and danger. Of this number more than three-fourths were Green Mountain Boys. The remainder were men collected from the nearest parts of Massachusetts and Connecticut, and led on by several enterprising militia officers of these colonies, who had actively co-operated in getting up the expedition. A council had been held the night previous, for the purpose of organizing these united forces, which had been dropping in irregularly through the day and a greater part of the night, and also for making all other necessary arrangements to march for their destination the following morning. At this council Ethan Allen had been unanimously appointed the commander in chief of the expedition. Colonel Easton, one of the Massachusetts officers, was placed second in command. And the third grade was assigned to Warrington; while Selden, in making the subordinate appointments, was raised to the post of captain to supply the place left vacant by the promotion of his superior. Even our friend Pete Jones, though now absent, was not forgotten in the distribution of honors, but named to take charge of the scouts, provided he joined the expedition. All these arrangements having been made the night before, as just stated, the troops by sunrise had breakfasted, and were now under arms and undergoing a review preparatory to marching. All were in high spirits and animated at the thought of being immediately led to the important object of their enterprise. Their gallant leader, now dressed and equipped in a manner appropriate to his rank, and mounted on his own noble charger, was riding proudly along their imposing front

—now pausing to give some directions to an officer, now to inspect the equipments of a company, and now backing his curvetting steed to take a view of the whole; while his towering form seemed to dilate, and rise still higher to the view, his bosom heave with pride, and his eyes glisten with delight, as they ran along the lines of his stout and broad-chested Green Mountain Boys, and read in their hardy features, lit up with enthusiasm, and eagerness for action in a cause which every man had made his own, the same high resolves, the same burning desires to signalize themselves that animated his own bosom.

At this moment a stranger, who, with a single attendant in the capacity of a servant, had but a short time before arrived, came on to the ground and took a conspicuous stand in front of the troops. He was of about the middle age, stout, well made, and handsomely featured, while a Roman nose, a thin, curling lip, and a black, flashing eye, with the peculiarly contemptuous and even sinister expression and reckless air which they combined to give his countenance, denoted no ordinary degree of self-esteem and a fiery and impetuous disposition. He was richly and fashionably dressed, and wore a sword, epaulet, and other insignia usually worn by field officers of the times.

"Captain Blagden," said Selden, turning to a Connecticut officer near him, and pointing to the stranger just described, "can you inform me who that proud and scornful-looking fellow yonder may be? He belongs not to us of the Green Mountains; nor does he appear to have any connection with the troops from Massachusetts, or with those from your own colony; and yet his demeanor and showy military appendages would lead one to suppose that he came here to take command of the whole of us."

"I have been looking at the man myself," replied the person addressed, "and, though not quite certain, yet I believe I know him. I think he must be one whom I well knew when we were boys, and of whose singular career I have since been often informed. And, if my conjectures are right, his name is Arnold, Benedict Arnold of New Haven."

"But what do you imagine has brought him here with these apparent assumptions?"

"Well, now I bethink me, sir, I remember that the day I left home a townsman of mine, who had just returned from New Haven, reported that, when the news of the battle of Lexington arrived at that place, Captain Arnold, who is the commander of an independent company there, started with several other military men post haste for the scene of action. And as he is said to be a good officer, having been a soldier in the army (into which he run away and enlisted in his youth), I should not be surprised to learn that he had received a commission from the Massachusetts Committee of Safety. And, further, as he was stationed, while a boy soldier, at Ticonderoga, and knows, doubtless, considerable of its situation, I will hazard a bottle with you, Captain Selden, that he has craved and obtained permission of that committee to take charge of the troops which they probably heard were collecting for this expedition."

"Aha! Colonel Allen, I imagine, will have a word to say to that bargain. It would fairly break his heart to be deprived of the chance of receiving the first charge of grape or canister that shall salute us from the wide-mouthed war-dogs of Old Ti. And if your surmises are correct, a collision, I fear, is unavoidable, unless Mr. Arnold should, as I think he certainly ought, waive his pretensions to the command."

"A collision it will be, then; for Arnold, it is said, was never yet known to yield to anything when his purposes were fixed. A more reckless dare-devil, I suppose, never trod the footstool. Why, sir, when we were but boys, I have known him spring upon a large water-wheel in full motion, grasp one of its arms, with his head toward the circumference, and there remain till he had been dashed through the back-water beneath during forty revolutions! I have known him, singlehanded, seize and overcome a mad ox, which had broken away from and nearly killed a dozen men. One or more duels he has fought abroad; while scores of bullies have been cudgeled and conquered by him about home. Indeed, if one-half that is told of him is true, the wild bulls of Bashan had not a spirit more untamable, nor scarcely more bodily strength to back it."

"All that may be, sir, but those who know Ethan Allen will laugh at the very idea of there being found a man in New England who can outdo him in feats of either strength or courage. And when they tell you, as they truly may, that they have seen him bite off the heads of board nails by dozens, seize by his teeth and throw over his head bags containing each a bushel of salt, as fast as two men could bring them round to him; grasp two opponents who had beset him, one in each hand, and, lifting them clear off the ground, hold them out at arm's length and beat them together till they cried for mercy; engage alone with a York sheriff and his posse of six common men, rout the whole, and leave them sprawling on the ground, you will probably allow that such a man will not be very likely to succumb to your hero. Let this Arnold but offer to assume the command, and, unless I am sadly mistaken, you will see what kind of stuff our old Green Mountain lion is made of. But see! the fellow is beckoning the officers to approach him. Let us move up to the spot and hear what he has to offer on the occasion."

Understanding and heeding the intimation of the stranger officer, who was, indeed, no other than Benedict Arnold, afterward so infamously conspicuous in the annals of our revolution, most of the officers, including

Allen, who had dismounted for the purpose, immediately advanced and formed an irregular line before him.

"Gentlemen," said he, with a perfectly assured and confident air, after waiting till all had approached and assumed a listening attitude, "I am personally unknown, I presume, to most, or all of you, but having been clothed with the proper authority, and directed to proceed to this place for the purpose, I have the honor to announce myself to you as the commander of this expedition; consequently, it is now my duty to take charge of these troops."

"Sir," said Allen, taking a step in advance of his fellow-officers, placing his arms akimbo, and turning up his ear, as if the better to catch the words of the speaker, whom he eyed askance with a look of queerly blended doubt and scorn: "Sir, did I hear aright? Did you say that you thought it your duty to take charge of these troops?"

"I did, sir, and still so consider it," replied Arnold rather restively.

"Do you, indeed, sir?" rejoined Allen, with a look of cool derision. "Then it was altogether a mistake of mine in supposing that the reverse of your proposition would have made out a more probable case?"

"I know not what you mean," said Arnold, his voice trembling with stifled anger at the biting significance of the other's remark. "You may learn, however, that I am not a person to be trifled with, sir."

"Well, I can't pretend to say what or who you are not," replied Allen, waxing warm, and giving token of a direct onset, "but I should like to know who the devil you are that come here from another colony to take the control of men who now own allegiance to no power short of that of the God of heaven?"

"My name is Arnold," replied the other, biting his lips in suppressed rage, "and I hold a commission of colonel, with the orders I named, from the Massachusetts Committee of Safety. There! examine it for yourselves!" he added, pulling out a parchment and disdainfully hurling it at their feet.

The roll was instantly picked up and attentively examined by several of the officers; while Arnold stood aloof in contemptuous silence, scarcely deigning to bestow a glance on the company thus engaged. It indeed proved, as he had stated, a colonel's commission from the source above mentioned, enclosing another document signed by the same Committee, authorizing Arnold to raise troops in Massachusetts or elsewhere, to the number of four hundred, and march them for the reduction of Ticonderoga.

"Now, sir, where is *your* commission? I should like to see it in turn," said Arnold, addressing Allen, and advancing with an air of triumph, as soon as the examination of his credentials, which he supposed must silence all further question of the right he had assumed, was completed.

"My commission?" promptly replied Allen, by no means disturbed by this unexpected demand, though in fact he had no paper commission to show, as the council appointing him had not deemed such an instrument essential; "where is my commission do you ask? There, sir!" he continued, pointing to his troops, who, understanding Arnold's claim to take command of them, already began to exhibit visible tokens of displeasure at the thought of having their idolized leader superseded by a stranger, "there, sir, it is, engraven on the hearts of these two hundred and thirty Green Mountain Boys! Trace it out there for yourself! Read it in their eyes, in every lineament of their countenances! And if that is not enough for you, then ask them whether Ethan Allen, who is getting gray in their service, is to be thrust aside for a commander whom they have never before seen?"

"Never! no, never!" fiercely burst from a hundred

lips along the lines, while many indignantly threw down their arms, and all, either by word, look, or gesture, gave unequivocal indication of their determination to allow no man to usurp the place of their chosen leader.

The countenance of Arnold, with all his assurance, instantly fell at so decided and to him so unexpected a manifestation of the disposition of the troops; and he bit his lips in vexation and mortified pride at his defeat.

At this crisis of the affair Warrington, fearing in common with the other officers that the altercation might prove ruinous to the enterprise, stepped forward and interposed. He first respectfully, and in a manner calculated to soothe the irritated feelings of Arnold, set forth the doubtfulness of his right, even under the instructions and commission he had received, to assume the command of troops who had not been enlisted by him, but who had volunteered without any knowledge of him or his instructions, and with the implied condition that they should be left to the choice of their own leaders. He then appealed to him as a gentleman, a patriot, and friend to the common cause, whether he would do well to insist on his claim, since doing so, as he must see, would prove destructive of their expedition. This courteous and well-timed appeal, which opened a door by which Arnold might honorably retreat from his awkward position, seemed to produce on his mind an instantaneous effect. The dark and angry frown which had settled on his countenance gave way to a bright and cheerful look. With one hand he instantly tore the epaulets from his shoulders, while with the other he drew his sword and threw it on the ground, gallantly exclaiming:

"Gentlemen, I most cheerfully waive all pretensions to the command, which of right, I am now convinced, belongs to the brave leader of the far-famed Green Mountain Boys. But as to going with you on this glorious enterprise, it is a privilege which, by ——,

I won't relinquish! Gentlemen, will you furnish me with a common musket and accept me as a volunteer soldier of your gallant band?"

Allen appeared to be taken completely aback by this sudden declaration of Arnold. His naturally forgiving and noble disposition and quick feelings were instantly touched with this mark of magnanimity, as unexpected to him as it was remarkable in the man, being the most striking, and perhaps the only instance of the kind ever displayed by this brave, but unprincipled officer in his whole public career.

"Done like a man, by Jove!" exclaimed the chivalrous leader of the Green Mountain Boys, advancing and cordially proffering the other his hand, while the tears of admiring and grateful emotion fairly started out on to his brawny cheeks. "Done like a man and a hero! Here, God bless you, give us your fist! There is about the right kind of stuff in you, after all, my friend. Will you accept the post of my aide-de-camp, with the rank your commission gives you?"

"Most cheerfully, sir," replied the flattered Arnold, waving his hand with easy and grateful courtesy.

"Pick up your sword and badges, then, sir," resumed Allen. "Call for your horse, and we will on together, like brothers, in the cause of God and the people. Officers and soldiers!" he continued, in a loud and cheering voice, that rang like a deep-toned trumpet far and wide over field and forest around, while he sprang upon his impatient charger and waved his sword on high; "prepare to march! Ethan Allen still commands you. Peace is in the camp, the Lord on our side, and victory before us! Forward, march!"

Three loud and lively cheers told the satisfaction of the men at this double announcement; and in another moment the whole corps, wheeling off to the brisk and stirring notes of shrieking fife and rattling drum, were sweeping down the road in full march toward the object of their destination.

The route of the troops was along the military road which, in the French war of 1759, had been opened from Charleston on Connecticut River, across the Green Mountains to Lake Champlain, by a New Hampshire regiment acting under the orders of General Amherst. This road, leading directly through Castleton and taking a northerly direction, branched off within a few miles of the lake, one fork running down to the shore opposite to Ticonderoga and the other proceeding onward to Crown Point. Although this, at the period, was perhaps the best road in the settlement, still it was little more than a roughly cut path through the wilderness, abounding at this season with deep sloughs, fallen trees, and other obstacles calculated to prevent much expedition in traveling. But such was the spirit and constitutional vigor of the men that a march of four or five hours brought them over half the distance from their late rendezvous to their destined landing on the lake, the former place being about thirty miles from the latter. They had now for several miles been passing through a heavy unbroken forest, and the mounted officers, riding a short distance in advance of the men, were anxiously looking forward for a clearing, or some suitable place to halt for a midday refreshment.

"There," said Allen, turning to his companions, as the sound of a falling tree came booming through the forest from a distance, "did you hear that? We are nearly through these endless woods at last, it seems."

"Is that so clearly proved by the falling of a tree?" asked Arnold, who was but little of a woodsman. "Old trees, I thought, like old men, often fell without human agency."

"True, sir," rejoined Allen, "but human agency brought that tree to the ground; and it stood beside some opening, too, or I will agree to be reckoned, like the prophets of old, without honor in my own country."

"Colonel Allen is right," observed Warrington. "The falling of a green tree always produces a dull, heavy, lumbering sound, such as we just heard, occasioned by the air it gathers, or, more properly perhaps, disturbs in its course; while the sound of a dry tree in falling is sharper, and comes with a single jar to the ear. That this tree stood near an opening is sufficiently evident from the echoes that followed the sound, which, in this flat land, could only be produced by the reverberating woods-wall of an opening. Yes, the colonel is correct: I can now hear the chopper's blows quite distinctly."

The falling of another tree in the same direction here interrupted the conversation; while the axman's blows, sounding in the distance, and in the tranquil medium through which they were conveyed to the ear, like the ticking of a clock in the stillness of night, could now plainly be heard by all. In two or three moments a third tree came thundering to the earth. Another, and yet another followed at equally brief intervals—the noise attending each successive fall, as well as that of the fast repeating blows of the chopper, who was causing such destruction among the sturdy tenants of the forest, all growing more loud and distinct as the party approached.

"There must be more than one of them," observed Colonel Easton, "to level so large trees at that rapid rate."

"No, sir," replied Warrington; "the regular, and non-interfering sounds of those blows indicate but one axman. You have not witnessed so much of the execution of which our Green Mountain Boys are capable as I trust you will within twenty-four hours, colonel. At all events, the fate of a tree under the sinewy arms of one of them is very soon decided."

"This fellow, however," remarked Allen, "does indeed lay to it with a will. I think he must make a good soldier; and as such he shall go with us, if of the right way of thinking, if not, as a prisoner; for it behooves us now to know pretty well the character of every man who is permitted to remain behind."

The party now soon came in sight of the man who had been the subject of their conversation. He had made an opening in the forest of about two acres, which he was rapidly enlarging. Having just leveled one large tree, he was now bending his tall frame in an attack upon another, a giant hemlock standing near the road, and had struck two or three blows, sending the blade of his ax into the huge circumference up to the helve at every stroke; when the tramp of the approaching party reached his ear, causing him to suspend and look around him.

"As I live, it is Pete Jones!" exclaimed Warrington, "just beginning upon his new pitch, which he mentioned to us."

"Good!" said Allen, "I am glad we have come across the droll devil. But we will furnish him with business a notch or two above that: the Red Coats need leveling a cursed sight more than the trees, at this crisis. If nothing more, he shall lend us that everlasting long body of his for a ladder to scale the walls of Old Ti! Jupiter! if Frederick of Prussia had a regiment of such chaps, how the fellow would brag! Hallo, there!" he added, dashing forward toward the woodman, who stood gazing with an expression of quizzical wonder, now at the approaching cavalcade of officers nearby, and now straining forward his long neck to get a view of the lengthened columns of men, just beginning to make their appearance in the distance.

"Well, hallo it is, then, colonel, if there's nothing better to be said," responded Jones, after waiting an instant to see if the other was going to proceed. "But now I think on't, colonel, where did you get so much folks? By Jehu! how they string along yonder! Why, there's more than a hundred slew of men coming! And then what pokerish-looking tools they've all got! Now I wonder if they aint a-going a-visiting over to Old Ti, or somewheres?"

"I should not be surprised if something of that kind should prove the case," replied Allen, laughing. "But what are you about, that you have not joined us in the proposed visit?"

"Why, I calculate to be about this old hemlock till I get it down, colonel."

"Nonsense, you ninny! Why were you not up to Castleton last night?"

"Now, don't fret, colonel—I did think of it, honestly; but knowing you must all come this way, I thought I might as well be making a small beginning here till you got on. And so I put in yesterday a little, and have now let in heaven's light on something over two acres, I calculate. But if you are expecting to have pretty funny times of it over there, I don't much care if I—that is, I'll think of it, after I have brought the top of this old hemlock a little lower——"

"Your most obedient, Captain Jones," gayly exclaimed Warrington, now riding up.

"Captain of what?" asked Jones, a little puzzled to know whether he was to receive this address as a joke, and let off one of his own in return, or whether something serious was intended by it: "captain of what?—of the surveyor, that I sent over the York line a day or two ago, by a gentle touch with my foot on his northerly parts?"

"No, seriously, Jones," said Allen, "in organizing last night, we deemed it best to have a small band of scouts, of whom you was fairly voted in the captain, or scout-master, if you like the name better. No man in the settlement can go before you in performing the duties of this post. Will you, without more words, accept it and join us?"

"Can't you let me stop to cut this tree down first? 'Twon't take scarce a minute, colonel."

"No, the men are at hand. We did think to find a spot to halt and dine here, but as I see neither place nor water, we must on till we find them. How soon shall we meet with such a place?"

"Let me see, as the blind man said. Oh! there is a cute little beauty of a brook, with smooth banks, that's just your sorts, not half a mile ahead."

"Fall in here with the troops then. But where is your rifle?"

"Hard by there, under a log," replied Pete. "I'll warrant you never catch me far separated from old Trusty, with a good store of bullets to go on such errands as she and I have a mind to send them. Well, old ax," he added, in an undertone, as he took up the implement to which he seemed addressing himself, and carried it round to the back side of the tree, "the colonel thinks it best that you and I should bid each other good-by for a short time; and there! you may sit in that nook between those two roots till I come back again.

" 'So now in the wars I go, I go,
All for to go a-sodjering.
Trol, lol, lol de larly.' "

And thus, in the prompt spirit of the times, and with the characteristic sangfroid of the man, this jolly and fearless woodsman, drawing out his rifle from under an old log and cheerily trolling the above quoted catch of some homely old song with a chorus of his own making, fell into the ranks of the troops then passing, having left his favorite ax, for which he seemed to have contracted a sort of fellow-feeling, standing behind the tree on which we found him engaged, where it was destined to remain unregarded by its owner during a great part of the Revolutionary War—and where, on returning, after many years of hardship and danger, spent in bravely battling for his country's freedom, he found it in the same place and position, safe and uninjured, except in the thick coat of rust that had gathered over it—an incident of olden times well-known as a historical fact by many in that section of the country where it occurred.

The spot described by Jones being found and appropriated, the troops partook of a dinner from the provisions of their packs, after which they were allowed an hour's rest, which was enlivened, as they were seated along the mossy banks of the gurgling rivulet, with song, tale, and jest, till the deep recesses of the forest rang with the sounds of their merriment. While the officers, who were seated in a group by themselves, were consulting their watches and awaiting the moment set by them for resuming their march, a horseman, approaching from the west, suddenly rode up, dismounted, and stood before them.

"Ah, Phelps!" exclaimed Colonel Allen, springing up and shaking the newcomer heartily by the hand. "Is it possible—a spy returned unhung from a British fort? Well, sir, what news from the camp of the Philistines?"

"Almost everything we could wish, gentlemen," replied the person addressed, a Connecticut gentleman of considerable shrewdness and address, who had been dispatched a day or two previous to go over to the fort, enter it on some feigned errand, and gain the best knowledge of its situation the circumstances would permit. "I have been within the fort—mostly over the works; stayed there last night, and came away unsuspected this morning."

Phelps then proceeded to give an account of the manner he had effected his discoveries at the fort without exciting the suspicions of the garrison relative to the object of his visit; how, in the assumed character of a green country bumpkin, he made it his ostensible errand to see a war cannon, and also the strange man that shaved other men, called a barber; how the soldiers laughed at his pretended ignorance, and the officers, coming to see the green Yankee, amused themselves by questioning him and listening to his replies, at which they were amazingly tickled, and then ordered a twenty-four pounder to be fired, for the fun of witnessing the prodigious fright into which the report appeared to throw him. And finally, having induced him, after many entreaties, to permit the barber to shave him, how they all stood by to see the performance, laughing heartily at the wincing and woeful countenances he assumed and the fears he pretended of having his throat cut.

After finishing his diverting description of this part of his adventures, he detailed with great accuracy the situation of the fortress, the names and grades of the officers, and the number of the garrison.

"But, gentlemen," said he in conclusion, "there is one question which I will no longer delay to ask you. Have you made provision for boats to transport the troops across the lake? There is not a single craft larger than a skiff on this side, just now, within ten miles of the fort."

"God forgive me the oversight!" exclaimed Allen. "We must instantly set measures on foot for repairing it. Douglass—Lieuteant Douglass, step forward here a moment! What boats are there this side the lake to the north of this?"

"An excellent scow for our purpose is owned by the Smiths, a few miles this side of Crown Point," replied the blue-eyed and broad-shouldered descendant of his Caledonian namesakes, stepping promptly forward and comprehending at a glance the emergency that produced the question.

"The Smiths? Good! They are with us, too, in heart, and should be also in person," rejoined the colonel.

"Well, their scow we must have at all events. And you, Douglass, are the very man to go and get it. Will you do it?"

"I am the very man who is willing to try, Colonel Allen," answered the other.

"And you can reach the landing against Ti with it by nine o'clock this evening?"

"Hardly, I fear. It is nearly a dozen miles. But I'll do my best, colonel."

"Go, then, as if the devil kicked you on end. The salvation of our project may depend upon your getting back in season. But stay! We must have more boats than one. To the south I know of none. Perhaps you may meet with some going up or down the lake which might be pressed into the service; or, as the last resort, one might possibly be got away from Crown Point without a discovery which would endanger us. Another man, however, will be wanted for any of these purposes, besides the oarsmen you will pick up on your way. And —Jones! this way! Have you heard what we are at? Very well. You are just the chap to go on this hap-hazard errand. What say you? Can you bring anything to pass if we send you?"

"Why, I can't exactly say, colonel," replied Jones, placing his feet astride and looking up with one eye queerly cocked on his interrogator, while the other was tightly closed. "I aint so much of a water-fowl as some; but perhaps I mought make fetch come a little."

"Pack up, then, and be off with Douglass in two minutes; and remember, both of you, if you fail us——"

"Then what?" asked Jones, suddenly stopping and looking back. "I don't calculate to be over-particular, colonel, but if it wouldn't be too much trouble I should like to know that before we start."

"You shall be doomed to sit forty days and nights in sackcloth and ashes," humorously said Allen.

"By Jonah!" exclaimed Pete, "the boats shall be there by the time, colonel!"

While the latter part of this dialogue was going on Warrington stood with his back to the company, with one foot on a log, busily engaged in writing with his pencil on a blank leaf torn from his pocketbook and placed on his knee.

"Aha, my lad!" said Allen in a playful undertone, as he approached the former and significantly placed one finger on his shoulder; "more faith now than when we two were lying on the hay in the captain's barn waiting for our rifles, eh?"

"I really wish you would mind your own business, colonel," replied Warrington, with affected anger.

"Well, well," resumed Allen, laughing, "send it, my boy. Mars, they say, never prospers so well as when he has Cupid in his train, in any case. But with such a piece of God's handiwork as yours to incite to action—heavens! if the knights of old had been blessed with such lady-loves they would never have needed to carry half a hundredweight of old iron on their lubberly carcasses to make them heroes."

Stripping off their coats to fit them for a rapid march, these athletic and resolute woodsmen now seized their rifles, took a glance at the sun for a hasty calculation of the bearing of the course to be taken to lead them to their proposed destination, and, plunging into the woods, were soon lost to the sight of their companions.

A small guard was then sent on in advance, with orders to pick up and detain every man on the road not in the secret of the expedition. Scouts, to range the woods on the right and left, were also dispatched for the same purpose; after which the main body of the forces quietly resumed their march for the lake.

CHAPTER XVII

"There are strange movements among all the troop,
And no one knows the same."

Leaving Allen and his companions in arms to make their way to the lake shore, we will now, by way of marking the progress of the two active foresters who had been dispatched northward for boats, change the scene, for a short time, to the quiet residence of Captain Hendee.

It was a little past sunset on the evening of the day on which the events last described transpired. It had been a day of unusual stillness in the northern part of the Grants. The lively sounds of the plying axmen, which were usually heard ringing through the forests in every direction, were all hushed. The women went a-visiting, and were seen to whisper in the corners apart from the children. The boys finished their tasks by noon, and for the remainder of the day were sauntering round the brooks with their fishing-poles. All the active men had disappeared; though no one mentioned aloud the cause of their absence. And a sort of Sabbath-day quiet and inaction seemed to prevail over all this section of the settlement. Captain Hendee was sitting in his open door, enjoying as usual his evening pipe, and wrapped in that placid and contemplative mood to which this indulgence usually disposes. His daughter was seated near him at a window in an attitude equally calm and contemplative though engrossed with reflections, probably of a far different nature; for her fair white hand rested on a small volume lying on the window-sill before her, opened upon those heart-melting strains of the hapless Eloise, which Pope, that master of rhyme and marrer of reason, sung with such seductive sweetness; and her tear-moistened eye was fixed, pensively and unobservant, on the slumbering waters of the outspread lake; while occasionally a gentle sigh, betokening the inward conflicts of hope and fear, was heaving her snowy bosom. While the father and daughter were thus seated and their minds thus absorbed in their different trains of reflection, their attention was suddenly arrested by the sounds of advancing footsteps.

"By all the saints in the calendar!" exclaimed the captain, after gazing an instant in surprise at the striking proportions of our young Anak of the woods, for it was no other than Pete Jones, who, at the distance of eight or ten rods, was now seen stalking toward the house, "what a cloud brusher is there, Alma! Can you imagine who he may be?"

"No, father," replied Alma, who was also looking at the approaching visitor with an expression of mingled wonder and curiosity; "but I just noticed that young Tyler and Wilcox of this neighborhood passed beyond the barn yonder, and I conclude that this man is some friend of theirs. They are probably all going on some fishing excursion. The man, I presume, wishes to get a little fire for this purpose."

By this time Jones had reached the door in which the captain was sitting.

"Good-evening! Will you walk in, sir?" said the latter in an indifferent tone and without moving, as if he expected the other would decline the invitation and announce his errand at his door.

"Why, yes, I may as well," replied Jones, offering to pass in without appearing to notice the hesitating and inquiring look of the captain, who now at once yielded the space to his guest. "You see I was bred to manners," continued the woodsman, jocosely bowing, so as to enable him to enter the door.

The captain, smiling good-naturedly at the remark, handed Jones a chair, took another himself, and waited in silence, and with the same expecting air as before for the stranger to name his business. This, however, Jones did not seem ready to make known, but continued sitting in silence, with a puzzled and undecided air, as if greatly at loss what to say, or how to bring about some object he had in view, now glancing at the captain, now at the different objects about the room, and now at Miss Hendee, on whom his eyes lingered with an expression of unfeigned admiration.

"Very fine weather, this," remarked the captain by way of breaking the silence, which he seemed to think was becoming a little awkward.

"Very; considering the times and the state of the nation," responded Pete dryly, and with the manner of one who would show that he is too busy in thought to engage in conversation.

The captain then made some other commonplace observation, which met with no reply of any kind; when, finding himself thus defeated in every attempt to draw the other into conversation, and tired of waiting for him to name his errand, he withdrew his attention and sunk into his own reveries.

After Jones had sat a while longer chewing his cud of perplexity, a change appeared suddenly to come over him. A flash of intelligence and decision lit up his countenance. And after dropping his head an instant, as if settling the details of a plan which he appeared to have hit upon, he slowly drew up his features into a sober and troubled air, and began to catch his breath and shiver all over, like a man taken with an ague fit. He then rose, tottled across the floor to the hearth, raked open the fire, and spread his shaking hands over the coals, at the same time attempting to speak as he observed the eyes of the captain and his daughter were turned upon him with a look of lively concern.

"Oh, nev—never mind!" he said, articulating with great apparent difficulty, in his attempt to quiet their alarm; " 'twill s—s—soon be o—o—over now—though the—the—these swamp ag—ag—agues are bad while they last. You, you don't—keep—keep great fires—here—I—I—I see."

"We will have one in a moment, my friend," said the captain, leaping up at this hint, and hobbling out of doors after wood with unwonted activity.

No sooner was the old gentleman fairly out of sight than Jones' malady entirely disappeared. He quickly drew out a billet, and turning, tossed it into the lap of the astonished Miss Hendee.

"Here, mum," said he in a low, confidential tone, "there's no time to be polite; but read that, and if you want to scrabble off two lines or so in answer, contrive to get it into my old hat there on the table, in almost no time, as I'm in a taking of a hurry. But stay, where's the Indian?"

"He has gone to take a letter for me to Major Skene's colored man, now lying with his boat down here at the landing, I believe," replied the blushing girl, already on her way to her apartment to read and answer the billet, which a glance at the handwriting told her was from her accepted lover.

"That's lucky," said Jones; "now I want that chap to go with us. We have got a trifling chore to do to-night somewhere in the neighborhood of Old Ti. Had I better speak to the old gentleman about his going or not?"

"My father should be consulted, and yet——"

answered Alma, hesitating lest the suggested application to Captain Hendee might in some way lead to a discovery of her own secret—"I heard him promise Neshobee's services to Colonel Allen for such an emergency. Perhaps you had better consult no one but Neshobee himself, and if he is willing to go, I will stand his friend in defending the delinquency, if such it be."

Captain Hendee now returned with the wood, and found Pete's ague much as he had left it. But as the fire blazed up from the light combustibles which had been thrown on to it, the attack seemed gradually to subside. Meanwhile, Alma had retired, read the brief outpouring of her lover's heart, and penned in answer:

"From my heart I thank you for your kind note. All as yet remains undiscovered—painful, painful exigency! which compels concealment of so important a step from an only parent! And yet I regret not my troth; and whatever of sorrow it may cost me, I will not repine at the fruit of a tree of my own planting. Heaven preserve you, my very dear friend, in the hour of peril, and crown with success your efforts in the cause of freedom.

"Yours, but too truly,

"A. H."

By the time Alma had completed her note and managed on her return to the room to slip it, unobserved, into the designated place of deposit, Jones had so far recovered from his pretended indisposition that he announced himself in a condition for proceeding on his way. And taking a coal of fire between a couple of chips, by way of accounting to the captain for his call, and stopping a moment to listen to the sage nostrums recommended by his host to prevent the recurrence of his ague, he departed and joined his two newly enlisted associates, who were impatiently awaiting his coming in the adjoining field. It being now sufficiently dusk to prevent all observation from the opposite garrison, they proceeded immediately to the landing, which they found guarded by two Green Mountain boys, who, making fishing their ostensible business, had in pursuance of the arrangemnet before mentioned closely watched the place during the two preceding days. Here also they met Neshobee, who had just returned in a skiff from Major Skene's scow, in possession, as before intimated, of a stout negro, who, with two low, sottish fellows under his command, having spent that day at the fort to take in some loading and visit the soldiers previous to starting for home, as they intended to do the next morning, had come over just at night and taken a fishing station near the landing. Jones and his companions hesitated not to open their project of obtaining this boat to Neshobee, who very cheerfully agreed to co-operate with them in duping the negro, and to assist in rowing the boat up to the landing where they were to be met by Allen's forces. The boat was lying about a dozen rods from the shore; and Black Jack, as he was called, and his men, having pulled up their anchor, were now on the point of putting back for the fort, when the party on shore, their plan of operations being all arranged, hailed the black commander and desired him to haul up to the landing.

"Who the debil you, who want me do all dat for notting?" replied Jack in a swaggering, consequential tone.

"Oh, pull up to the shore," said Wilcox, "there are three or four of us here who are wishing to make a bargain with you."

"Bargain, hey? you shackaroons, you! You tink for play some deblish trick, don't you? Guess you find out you no catch weasel sleep so easy as all dat come to!" responded the negro, chuckling at his own wit and sagacity.

"No, now, honestly, Captain Jack," rejoined the first speaker, "we want to go to Shoreham landing to-night, to be ready to join a wolf hunt which they are going to start there early to-morrow morning."

"Gosh all fire-lock!" exclaimed the black, whose opinion of his own importance was greatly raised by being addressed as captain: "You tink I row my boat all de way op dar in de dark jest for commodate you? No! see you all dam fus!"

"Now you are too bad, captain; but you won't damn our jug of old Jamaica, that we intended to offer you for carrying us up there, will you?" said the other, taking a jug from under his coat and swinging it over his head, so that the black, whose taste for liquor was well known to the young men, might catch a view of it in the twilight.

"What you say dere?" eagerly said Jack, stretching forward his neck to see and make sure of the existence of the tempting implement.

"We say," replied the former, "that here is a gallon of as good rum as ever run down your throat, which is at your service if you will close the bargain. Come, give us your answer, for if we can't make a trade with you, we must be off for a boat somewhere else. What say you?—and mind ye, we will lend you a stiff hand at the oars to boot."

"You help row de boat, you say?" answered Jack in an altered and yielding tone. "Why de debil you no say so fore? Dat be a case dat alter de circumstance. You werry much to blame, gemmen, dat you no mention so portant a difference in fus place," added the negro, while he and his men headed round the boat, and handled the oars with such effect that nearly the next moment she was lying at the landing.

Within five minutes from this time, the magic jug, which had effected such a wonderful change in the aspect of affairs, having been well tested in the meanwhile by Jack and his associates, all hands were stripped and bending to the oars of the old scow, which, under the forceful strokes of Jones and his party, aided by the rum-power of Jack's two besotted boatmen, was surging through the waters toward the south as fast as their united strength would drive her.

They were soon met, however, by puffs of south wind, against which they found it possible to make but a very slow headway. And it was not till considerably past midnight that they came to the last reach and hove in sight of the destined landing. But here, overhauling Douglass with the other scow, and the party he had enlisted to help man it, both boats, with renewed efforts of rival speed, pushed forward for the appointed shore.

"Boat ahoy!" called out Allen from the landing, where, as the boats neared the place, his huge tower-like form, rising in bold relief over the stationary group of officers around him, could now plainly be discerned by the approaching crews; "boat ahoy! who comes there?"

"Douglass and friends, in this," was the reply from the first boat, coming in about its length in advance of the other.

"And who in the next?" asked Allen.

"Jones and a thunder cloud!" responded the well-known voice of the jolly woodsman. "Now you needn't think I am fibbing, colonel; for you will see it lighten when we get ashore."

"All is well, then," said Allen, without heeding the remarks of Jones further than his announcement of himself with a boat, "all is well, and glory to God in the highest, that you have got here at last! I thought you would have never come. Why, it has been an age since dark! Some old sun-stopping Joshua must be fighting on the other side of the earth, or I swear it would have been daylight long ago!"

By this time the first boat had struck the shore, and the crew, leaping out, were all readily recognized by the leader, who then turned to the other boat, at that instant driving up with the astonished and frightened negro (now for the first time mistrusting a trick) gibbering and sputtering aloud:

"What de hell all dis?—who all dese? what pretty dam scrape you got me into here, you shackaroon debils, you?"

"What in the name of all that is black and red have you got here, Jones?" cried Allen in surprise, stepping up and peering into the boat on hearing Jack's exclamations.

"Why, just what I told you, colonel. Here! don't you see it lighten, now?" said Pete, pointing to the negro's eyes, which, glaring wide with fear and astonishment at what he saw and heard, glimmered like fire-bugs in the dark. "But the English of it is, colonel, that we came across Major Skene's scow commanded by Captain Darky, with his two oarsmen here, who for a gallon of rum were kind enough to bring us along to join the hunting match at Shoreham, where we have now arrived, safe and sound," he continued, turning to the black; "so now, Captain Jack, you have fulfilled your bargain with us; and we have nothing more to say, so far as we are concerned. If these rough-looking chaps here want to employ you further, they will let you know it, likely."

"Jones, you deserve a pension for life!" exclaimed Allen, comprehending the whole affair in an instant. "You and your friends here have killed more birds with one stone than you dreamed of yourselves, perhaps. But we have not a moment to lose, so leap out, my lads. And as to Major Skene's boat, it is my lawful prize; and Major Skene's negro, and Major Skene's negro understrappers here, are all my prisoners!"

"Oh, no, totally unpossible to stop, gemmen!" said Jack in a good lord, good devil sort of tone, being doubtful whether they really intended to make him prisoner or engage him and his boat to carry them to some other place. "I have provision for de major's family aboard. Day all out ob supply for dere necessity. Quite unpossible, gemmen."

"We will take care of the provisions. So out with you in no time, you black Satan!" said Allen impatiently.

"Oh, it be out ob all question I stop!" persisted the negro with increasing alarm, "I have odder portant business—I have letter from de young leddy at Captain Hendee's to de young leddy ob Colonel Reed at de major's dat I oblige for deliver early in the morning."

"We will undertake the delivery of the letter," said Selden and Warrington simultaneously.

"Tumble them out, boys!" sternly commanded Allen.

"Oh, lordy, I den be ruin! totally, foreber ruin!" groaned the distressed and frightened black, as the men seized him and his two drunken associates, and led them to the rear to be put under guard.

The boats were now instantly headed round, the oars muffled, careful oarsmen selected and placed in their seats; when, after each boat had been filled with as many troops as their respective burthens would safely permit, they pushed off from the shore, preceded a short hailing distance by a skiff occupied by Allen and Arnold, with Phelps to pilot them to their contemplated landing on the opposite shore. The wind had some time since died wholly away; and the elements were now all hushed, as if in the slumbers of death; while the deeply freighted crafts glided slowly on, impelled by the light dip of the feathery oars which, in the hands of the experienced and careful men who plied them, unitedly rose and fell as noiseless as the feet of fairies on beds of flowers. At length the dark, massy walls of the fortress, looming up and marking their broad outlines against the western sky, became discernible to the men. And yet, as they drew near these frowning walls, pierced by a hundred cannon, over which, for aught they knew, the lighted matches were suspended, awaiting but the signal to send their iron showers of death to every man of their devoted band, no misgivings, no weak relentings came over them; but at a moment like this, and that which followed at the onset,—moments furnishing, perhaps, a more undoubted test of courage than those of the half-frantic, half-mechanical charges of the disciplined legions of Napoleon at the later fields of Austerlitz and Marengo,—at a moment like this, we say, their stout hearts, nothing daunted at the dangers before them, beat high and proudly at the thought of the coming encounter, and with stern determination gleaming in every eye, and with the low, whispered words of impatience for the moment of action to arrive, they moved steadily on to the daring purpose.

Passing down obliquely by the works, they landed some distance to the north of them. The instant they touched the shore the troops leaped on the banks; and scarcely had the last foot been lifted from the boats before they were backed, wheeled, and on their return for another load, leaving those on shore to await in silence the arrival of a re-enforcement from their companions left behind before marching to the onset. Those companions, however, were not destined to share in the glory of this splendid achievement of the eighty Green Mountain Boys who had landed; for in a few moments, to the dismay of Allen, the faint suffusions of dawning day became visible in the east. Cursing the luck which had caused such delays, and chafing like a chained lion held back from his prey, that impetuous leader for a few moments rapidly paced the shore before his men in an agony of impatience—now casting an eager look at the fort, still silent and undisturbed, now straining his vision after the receding boats, which, to him, seemed to move like snails across the waters, and now throwing an uneasy glance at the reddening east, whose twilight glow, growing broader and brighter every instant, plainly told him that before another detachment of troops could arrive his forces would be discovered, and the enterprise, in all probability, would thus be defeated. Maddened at the thought, he stopped short in his walk, paused an instant, and brought his foot with a significant stamp to the ground, showing that his resolution was taken. And quickly calling out Jones and Neshobee, he dispatched them to go forward, cautiously reconnoiter the fort on all sides, and return as speedily as possible to report their discoveries. He then formed his men in three ranks and addressed them.

"You see, my friends and fellow-soldiers," he commenced, pointing his sword toward the east, "that daylight will reveal us to the enemy before a re-enforcement can possibly arrive. But can you, who have so long been the scourge of tyrants, bring your minds to relinquish the noble enterprise, and with it the proud name you have achieved, by turning your backs on the glorious prize when it is now almost within your grasp?"

He paused for a reply; when "No! no! no!" ran through the lines in eager response.

"I see—I see, my brave fellows," resumed the gratified leader, "I see what you would do. I read it in your deeply breathed tones of determination—in your quick and short-drawn respirations, and in your restless and impatient movements. But have you all well considered? I now propose to lead you through yonder gate; and I fear not to tell men of your stamp that we incur no small hazard of life in the attempt. And, as I would urge no man to engage against his own free will, I now give free and full permission to all who choose to remain behind. You, therefore, who will voluntarily accompany me, poise your guns."

Every man's gun was instantly brought to a poise with a motion which told with what good will it was made.

"God bless you, my noble fellows!" exclaimed Allen proudly, and with emotion. "Courage like that," he continued in tones of concentrated energy, "courage like that, with hearts of oak and nerves of steel like yours, must, will, and, by the help of the God of hosts, shall triumph! Come on, then! follow me—march while I march—run and rush when I set the example; and, if I fall, still rush on, and over me, to vengeance and victory! To the right, wheel! march!"

When the band arrived within about a furlong of the ramparts they were met by the scouts, who reported that all was quiet in and about the fort, while the open gate was guarded only by one sluggish and sleepy-looking sentinel. Halting no longer than was necessary to hear this report, Allen, placing himself at the head of the center column, silently waved his sword to the troops as a signal for resuming the march; when they all again moved forward with rapid and cautious steps toward the guarded gateway. And so noiseless and unexpected was their approach that they came within twenty paces of the entrance before they were discovered by the drowsy sentry, who was slowly pacing to and fro with shouldered musket before it. Turning round with a start, the aroused soldier glared an instant at the advancing array, in mute astonishment and alarm; when he hastily cocked and leveled his piece at Allen, who was striding toward him several yards in advance of his men. It was an instant on which hung the fate of the hero of the Green Mountains and, probably, also the destinies of Ticonderoga. But the gun missed fire. The life of the daring leader was safe and the garrison slept on, unalarmed and unconscious of their danger. Leaping forward like the bounding tiger on his victim, Allen followed up the retreating soldier so hotly that, with all the speed which fear could lend him, he could scarcely keep clear of the rapidly whirling sword of his fiery pursuer, till he gained the interior of the fortress; when he gave a loud screech of alarm, and, making a desperate leap for a bomb-proof, disappeared within its recesses. Meanwhile the rushing column of troops came sweeping like a whirlwind through the gate; when fairly gaining the parade ground in front of the barracks they gave three cheers which made the old walls tremble with the deafening reverberations and caused the slumbering garrison to start from their beds in wild dismay at the unwonted sound. Scarcely had the last huzza escaped the lips of the men and their leader, who disdained not to mingle his own stentorian voice in the peals of exultation and defiance, which rose in thunders to heaven, before the latter was rapidly threading his way through flying sentries and half-dressed officers toward the quarters of the commandant of the fortress. Pausing an instant on his way to chastise a dastard sentinel whom he caught making a pass at one of our officers with his bayonet, and whom, with one blow with the flat of his sword he sent reeling to the earth with the cry of mercy on his lips, the daring leader bounded up the stairway leading to the commandant's room, and thundering at the door, called loudly to that officer to come forth. Captain La Place, who had just leaped from his bed on hearing the tumult below, soon made his appearance with his clothes in his hand, but suddenly recoiling a step, he stood gazing in mute amazement at the stern and threatening air and the powerful and commanding figure of the man before him.

"I come, sir, to demand the immediate surrender of this fortress!" sternly said Allen to the astonished commander.

"By what authority do you make this bold demand of His Majesty's fort, sir?" said the other, almost distrusting his senses.

"By what authority?" thundered Allen, "I demand it, sir, in the name of the Great Jehovah and the Continental Congress!"

"The Continental Congress?" stammered the hesitating officer, "I know of no right—I don't acknowledge it, sir——"

"But you soon will acknowledge it, sir!" fiercely interrupted the impatient leader. "And hesitate to obey me one instant longer and, by the eternal heavens! I will sacrifice every man in your fort!—beginning the work, sir," he added, whirling his sword furiously over the head of the other, and bringing the murderous blade at every glittering circle it made in the air nearer and nearer the head of its threatened victim, "beginning the work, sir, by sending your own head dancing across this floor!"

"I yield, I yield!" cried the shrinking commandant.

"Down! down, then, instantly!" exclaimed Allen, "and communicate the surrender to your men while any of them are left alive to hear it."

Scarcely allowing the crestfallen officer time to encase his legs in his breeches, Allen hurried him down to the scene of action in the open parade below. Here they found the Green Mountain Boys eagerly engaged in the work of capturing the garrison, who were making considerable show of resistance. Two of the barrack doors had been beaten down, and about a third of the enemy already made prisoners. And the fiery Arnold was on the point of blowing a third door from its hinges with a swivel, which he had caused to be drawn up for the purpose; while a fourth was shaking and tottering under the tremendous blows of an ax, wielded by the long and powerful arms of Pete Jones, who was found among the foremost in the contest.

"Cease, cease ye all!" cried Allen, in a loud voice of command, as he appeared among them with La Place by his side.

"Now, raaly, colonel," said Jones, suspending his elevated implement and holding it back over his head in readiness for another blow, "I wish you would let me settle with this devilish old oak door before I stop. Why, I never was so bothered with such a small potato in my life!"

"No, no!" answered the other, smiling, "let us have silence a moment, and we will save you all troubles of that kind."

"Well, then, here goes for a parting blessing!" exclaimed the woodsman, bringing down his ax with a tremendous blow, which brought the shattered door tumbling to the ground.

The British commandant then calling his officers around him, informed them that he had surrendered the fortress, and ordered them to parade the men without arms. While this was in performance a second detachment of Green Mountain Boys reached the shore, and, having eagerly hastened on to the fort to join their companions, now, with Warrington at their head, came pouring into the arena. A single glance sufficed to tell the latter that he was too late to participate in aught but the fruits of the victory. With a disappointed and mortified air he halted his men and approached to the side of his leader.

"Ah, colonel!" said he, "is this the way you appropriate all the laurels to yourself, entirely forgetful of your friends?"

"Pooh! pooh! Charles," replied Allen, turning to the other with a soothing, yet self-complaisant smile at the half-reproachful compliment thus conveyed, "you need not mourn much lost glory in this affair. Why, the stupid devils did not give us fight enough to whet our appetites for breakfast! But never mind, Charles, there is more business yet to be done; Crown Point and Major Skene's stone castle must both be ours to-night. The taking of the first shall be yours to perform. And after breakfast and a few bumpers in honor of our victory, we will dispatch you for that purpose, with a corps of your own selection."

"Thank you, thank you, colonel," replied the other with a grateful smile. "But the expedition to Skenesboro'—may I not speak a word for our friend, Selden!"

"Aha!" replied Allen, laughing, "then this offer to take charge of the negro's letter had its meaning, eh? I don't know exactly about that chip of a British colonel for a Yankee patriot. Now, yours, major, I acknowledge to be a true cynosure. But his, I fear, will prove a dog-star. However, this is his own hunt; and, as he is a finished fellow, and doubtless brave and true, I think I will give him the command of the expedition, unless claimed by Easton. But hush! the commandant is about to go through the forms of the surrender. I must away, but will see you again."

The brief ceremonies of the surrender were soon over, when, as the fortress was pronounced to be in full possession of the conquerors, the heavens were again rent by the reiterated huzzas of the Green Mountain Boys, while British cannon were made to peal forth with their deep-mouthed thunders to the trembling hills and reverberating mountains of the country round, the proclamation of victory!—the first triumph of Young Freedom over the arms of her haughty oppressor.

CHAPTER XVIII

"A thousand evil things there are that hate
To look on happiness; these hurt, impede,
And leagued with time, circumstance, and fate,
Keep kindred heart from heart, to pine and pant and bleed."
—MRS. BROOKS.

IT is time, perhaps, that we should recur a little, to trace the operations of some personages of our story whose agency, though unnoted by us through several of the last chapters, had yet in the meanwhile been actively exercised in bringing about the events that were destined to follow. And it is with a sort of reluctance of feeling that we turn from the soul-kindling task of describing the noble exploits of Allen and his patriot companions, to the low and despicable plottings of the base Sherwood and his still more execrable associate in crime. Though twice foiled in his attempts to procure the destruction of Warrington, under the sanction of a despotic law, of which advantage was taken mainly to cloak the true motives of the act—though signally defeated in this, and the bolder attempt at assassination which was subsequently made at his instigation, yet still restless as the dark spirit of evil, this plotter of michief, instead of relinquishing his object, was now only the more intently engaged in devising and putting in practice new ways of accomplishing his nefarious designs.

On the evening that Darrow had attempted the life of Warrington in the woods, Sherwood was sitting in his house, which was kept by a simple couple wholly in the interests of their employer. He had just arrived from a visit to the house of Captain Hendee, where, as the reader has been apprised, he had been sowing the seeds of discord in that hapless family. And the chilly reception with which his parting advances had been met by the indignant girl whom they were intended to soften and deceive more than ever confirming him in what his jealousy had long since suggested, that her inclinations were setting strongly toward his hated rival, and foreseeing that something must speedily be done to counteract the current, he was now revolving over the different schemes that rose in his teeming brain for effecting his purpose, in case of the failure of his minion to remove the object alike of his hatred and his fears. While thus occupied in mind, Darrow, whose coming was not wholly unlooked for, arrived and sulkily entered the apartment.

"Ah, Darrow!" exclaimed Sherwood with his usual hypocritical smile, "very glad to see you. I knew not whether you would come to-night or return to the fort."

"Why," replied the other, "when I concluded to give it up for a d—— bad day's work, I found myself nearer your house than the fort; so I came, that's all."

"Glad you did. So come, unrig and sit down. The old woman in the other room will have us some supper ready soon. But no luck with your rifle to-day?" said Sherwood with a significant smile.

"None—except getting half tired to death, in this cursed wild-goose chase of yours," petulantly replied the surly minion.

"What! not even get a sight of the game, after so much beating about the bush?"

"Yes, twice; and failed both times, as the devil, who sent me on the errand, would have it," answered Darrow with an equivocal glance at the other.

"Failed! how!" said Sherwood, without appearing to notice the half-intentional sarcasm of Darrow.

"Why, the first time, the devilish rifle missed fire, for a rarity—the second, its owner missed his aim, and had to take to his legs to save his bacon."

"All this is very singular, Mr. Darrow," observed Sherwood, with a disappointed and somewhat incredulous look.

"Yes, but true for all that. Believe it or not, just as you please, I care not a groat."

"What mean you now, Darrow?"

"Exactly what I say; and I am beginning to mean something more, too."

"You are a strange fellow, Darrow. But let us have all your meanings, wants, and wishes in a lump. I am in no humor for riddles."

"Nor I neither. Well, then, though the fellow escaped my bullet by no intended fault of mine, yet I am not sorry I missed him. I have been thinking of the business coming along, and for all your talk about his life being forfeited, I can't make it out much better than killing—not to use a worse word—which they say gives a fellow ugly dreams. So I have made up my mind to let you do your own jobs of this sort in future. And if you persist in urging me further——"

"Killing! who asked you to kill him?" interrupted Sherwood in feigned surprise.

"Curse you, Jake! you know well enough you meant that. But I am still willing to help take the fellow and hand him over to the Yorkers to punish, or lend you a hand to carry any other point, if you will do the clean thing by me. But in the first place you must tell me what you fear from this fellow, and why you are so specially set on having him taken, more than Allen or any other outlaw?"

"That is more than I intended to tell anyone; but as I suppose you will better serve my interests by understanding this, you shall know the whole business: well, after I had been here a while, I noticed that the girl, when the captain said anything in praise of this Howard, as he supposed his name was, never joined her father in praises of the fellow, though she never had any ears for anything else while the slightest mention was made of him. And if I so much as asked a question implying a doubt about the fellow's perfection, she would show resentment as plain as looks could do it. Now, Darrow, if you would discover whether a girl entertains any secret liking for a man, just introduce his name in her presence, contriving both to praise and censure him, and if she refuse to join you in either, but is all attention when you praise and grows restless when you censure him, you may safely set it down that love is secretly lurking about her heart. It was something like this that led me to think that this Howard had made an impression, which I little relished. This suspicion caused me to obtain from the old captain a minute description of the fellow, and having before had one of Warrington, it occurred to me that this favorite might be no other than the outlaw himself. And being determined to ascertain whether my conjectures were correct I made a secret journey to Bennington, where I got a sight at Warrington, and where, by professing great wrath against the Yorkers, I was let into secrets which confirmed me in my suspicions. There, also, I made arrangements for being apprised of Warrington's future movements, with one Willoughby, who sent the word which enabled me to ferret out him and his band at Lake Dunmore. All this, however, I kept secret from the Hendees, but took especial pains to inspire the old man, and more particularly his daughter, with a horror of the character of Warrington. And now, Darrow, after the insufferable scoundrel has caused me to be tied up and whipped like a dog, and, to cap the climax, has found his way into this family and attempted to beguile from me my betrothed, can you ask why I wish to see him brought to justice?"

"Why, you seem to make out considerable of a case of it, to be sure," replied the other carelessly, as he rolled his tobacco quid in his lips. "But, 'betrothed,' do you call her? Why, I thought you cared so little about the girl that you was quite undetermined whether you would have her or not?"

"Well, whatever I may have said before, I am not undetermined now—for the girl, in spite of men, or devils, I swear I will have!"

"What mighty object is there, Jake, in breaking your neck for her? Be sure, she is a snug piece enough, but you can catch other fish as fair, and those, too, who will bring you hundreds to her none."

"I have plenty of objects to answer: one is to defeat this hated scoundrel—another, to punish her for presuming to like him. I don't say now I will marry her. But she shall be mine, to do with as I choose. I will have her, and keep her in a spot where it shall be mine, not hers, to decide whose wife she shall become. That, indeed, was mainly my motive in drawing her into an engagement in the first place; for you know, Darrow, that in case the old concerns should happen to be ripped up, a matrimonial plaster would cure all. And so long as I kept things in this posture, I should have the remedy at hand."

"Yes, but what chance do you consider there is of ripping up old matters?" asked the sergeant, throwing a keen, inquiring glance at the other.

"Why, such a thing is possible, you know. The old man, my father, I mean, as he grows weak and childish, may repent and kick over his own kettle, and, of course, mine. Indeed, I have great fears of this; for, though he never said anything to me of the kind, not dreaming that I ever met with you here, or discovered by any other means the secrets of his former management, yet I have lately observed in him a sort of growing uneasiness, a whining melancholy way, which, with his great anxiety that I should marry this girl, has made me rather jealous that his firmness is giving way in this quarter. Besides this, there are other dangers: that boy, who, you say, the old man still thinks was done for, may yet be alive and return to make me trouble."

"Well, if he should, he would be a no very lousy foe for you to contend with, Jake—that is, if he is as smart for a man as he was for a boy. I tell you, he was a bright one for a four-year-old. I liked him and never had the least notion of harming a hair of his head."

"What object had you, then, in making the old man believe as you did?"

"Why, I mistrusted that that would please the old man best, and I'll be hanged if I don't believe it did, Jake, if he is your father."

"Well, there are these chances against me, and then——"

"And then Bill Darrow may leak, you was going to say, was you, Jake?" sneeringly asked the minion.

"Oh, no!" quickly responded the consummate dissembler with a gracious smile and a surprised air, as if such a thought never entered his head. "No, indeed. I should as soon fear myself. But I was thinking, and about to say that, besides these chances, Warrington's communication with the girl will prove dangerous to my plans, and that they must be stopped."

"Well, how are you a-going to do it, short of following up the plan we have already been acting on to so little purpose?"

"Why, I have already taken one step to-day by informing Hendee that his friend Howard was no less than the outlaw Warrington in disguise. This was touching the fire to his gunpowder temper; and has pretty effectually blown the fellow up as regards any open communication with the girl."

"That may be, but it has also blown up your best trap for taking him, you see, don't you?"

"Perhaps so, but I dare not risk his visits with the standing he evidently held in their minds. And now, having broken off all open intercourse between the girl and the audacious rascal, we must go to work to sunder those ties which may yet secretly remain."

"Hum! That, I should think, would be like trying to cut off sunbeams with a jackknife. I should like to know how the old boy you calculate to do that?"

"Oh, easy enough, though my plan is not quite made up. I will tell you in the morning. But will you assist me in carrying it out?"

"Don't know but I will. But supposing I do, and see you fairly through the whole scrape, what do you finally intend to do for me?"

"Anything almost that you may ask, Darrow. You will own that the earnest money I gave you the other day was a handsome affair?"

"Hum! Yes, decent."

"Well, from the late news, I suppose we shall have war. Warrington and most of these rascally settlers will be with the rebels. I, from several motives, shall go for the king. And I have made up my mind to get a captain's commission and raise a company to act in this quarter. You shall be my lieutenant. And then we will use up these refractory settlers in a way they little dream of. But hark! The old woman is rapping for us to come to supper. I will mature my plans, and open them to you, as I said, in the morning."

CHAPTER XIX

"I something fear my father's wrath; but nothing
(Always reserv'd my holy duty) what
His rage can do on me. You must begone:
And I shall here abide the hourly shot
Of angry eyes; not comforted to live,
But that there is this jewel in the world
That I may see again."

THE development made by Sherwood at his late visit seemed to produce on Captain Hendee, whose mind had been previously prejudiced and poisoned for the purpose, all the effect which the former could have desired. The captain's feelings of pride were deeply touched at the thought of having entertained and welcomed in his family a man acting under the disguise of an assumed name, and consequently harboring, as he reasoned, no honorable purposes. And these views going to confirm all the falsehoods and dark insinuations by which that Iago in malice and subtlety had accompanied his disclosures concerning Warrington, the mind of the irritable old gentleman had been wrought up to a pitch of exasperation and bitterness which he pretended neither to disguise nor control, and which he failed not to vent on all around him, but more particularly upon his unhappy daughter. To her, indeed, his whole demeanor became changed; and his treatment was marked by a distrustful coldness and continued austerity of manner which she had never before for so long a time experienced from her passionate, but hitherto quickly relenting, parent. And yet she, who was happily the very reverse of her father in temper, had neither manifested nor felt the least wish to resent the unkindness; but calm and amiable in disposition, as she was fearless and spirited in action, she had borne all with the most forgiving patience, prudently awaiting the subsiding of the tempest of his passion before she should attempt, as she was resolved to do, to exculpate Warrington, and gradually bring about a change in his views and feelings in regard to and connection with Sherwood. She well knew that he was now laboring under many false impressions, which she felt conscious of her ability to remove as soon as he should become sufficiently calm to listen to the voice of reason. Day after day, therefore, she had anxiously watched for some appearance of relenting, some more softened mood, which should afford her an opportunity of making this attempt with a reasonable hope of success. But till the evening on which Jones called at the house she had observed nothing that indicated the least relaxation in her father's feelings. And being then interrupted by the woodsman's call, at an hour which usually afforded her the only opportunity she had through the day of conversing with her parent alone, she deferred her purpose to another day. But the next day brought along with it events which so engrossed her time and attention that this desired object was not again sought to be obtained, till circumstances intervened which destroyed every motive and wish she could entertain for accomplishing it.

Such was the state of feelings and such the relative position in which the father and daughter stood toward each other on the day which proved so triumphant to the American arms on Lake Champlain. In the early part of that day the attention of this family, as well as that of all the inhabitants of the vicinity of the lake, was aroused by heavy and repeated discharges of cannon in the direction of Ticonderoga. Little dreaming of the fact that the cannonading, which was filling the whole valley of the lake with its echoing thunders, was the harbinger of a victory already won, the whole neighborhood was instantly in commotion—some riding post-haste into the interior to carry the news or rally volunteers, some flying from house to house to interchange the expressions of their fears and sympathies, and the greater number rushing down to the nearest landing on the lake shore to gain the first tidings of their friends engaged in the deadly conflict which they supposed was at that moment raging round the walls of the hostile fortress. In a short time the dooryard of Captain Hendee's cottage was filled with a group of excited boys and anxious females. And agonizing were the sensations of many an affectionate wife and sister, and oft and fervent their trembling ejaculations to Heaven for the preservation of husbands, brothers, and lovers in this hour of danger. And not the most indifferent among those thus oppressed with painful solicitude for the event, which they believed involved the fate of all they held dear on earth, was Alma Hendee. To her, whose lover might be expected to be among the foremost of those engaged in the perilous assault, every gun that came booming over the waters brought with it a pang for her agitated bosom. Nor was her anxiety the less painfully felt, because circumstances compelled her to endure it in silence. The firing at length ceased, and all awaited in trembling solicitude some arrival which should bring them information of the result. This, however, continued for several, and to most of them, long and tedious hours, to rest in uncertainty. But at length a horseman, covered with dust and lashing his foaming horse to speed, came furiously galloping down the road to the south. All, with beating hearts and breathless expectation, awaited the announcement of the rapidly approaching messenger. The next moment, as he neared them, he swung his hat round his head, exclaiming "Victory! victory! hurrah for the Green Mountain Boys! Ticonderoga is taken, and not a man killed! hurrah! hurrah!" and, without scarcely checking the speed of his horse, on he dashed to carry to others the joyful tidings. The cracked voice of the war-worn and veteran Hendee was the next instant mingling with the shrill and high-keyed cry of the boys around him in the responsive hurrah that now involuntarily burst from their lips. With tears of joy and thankfulness gushing over many a fair cheek, the females hurried on such habiliments as they had laid aside, and the company, immediately dispersing, hastened to their respective homes with the gladdening news, leaving Captain Hendee and his daughter again by themselves, and their cottage to relapse into its usual quietness. The day, however, was not destined to close upon them without the occurrence of other events of stirring interest. Toward sunset several bateaux filled with armed men made their appearance on the lake, approaching from the south, and as they neared, were soon discovered to be bearing down upon the fortress of Crown Point.

"Bring me out my old spyglass, Alma!" cried Captain Hendee, hobbling from the garden where he had been to work toward the house, and turning round every few steps to look at the little armament which he had discovered approaching. "Here comes more trouble for the British—or else that fellow fooled us with his news, and these are a re-enforcement for the garrison. Come, step quick, girl! I can't make them out with certainty."

"Would British troops be likely to come in that

direction, father?" said Alma in accents tremulous with emotion, as she approached and handed the required instrument to the other.

"Why, no; I should hardly have expected it; but let us see," replied the captain, adjusting his glass and placing it to his eye. "By Heavens, the girl is right! Those boats contain anything but British regulars. No, they must be Green Mountain Boys, about to make an onset on the fort. See! how stiffly they bear down toward the old walls!" he continued with animation. "Gad! they are bold fellows, to say the least, to be sailing directly in the teeth of yonder war-dogs! But here, child, your eye is keener than mine; take the glass and watch their movements."

The girl took the glass, and bringing the boats within its field of vision, looked long and intently without speaking.

"They are coming to a halt now, are they not?" asked the captain.

"Yes, they have nearly ceased rowing now," replied the maiden. "Why, how plainly I can see even their features! Now there is one, who has mounted a bench and appears to be giving commands to the rest. Now he has turned his face this way, as if—as if——"

"Why! how unsteady the girl's hand is! Nonsense, child! you need not be frightened—they are not coming near us," half pettishly, half encouragingly exclaimed the captain, supposing his daughter's very visible agitation proceeded from an apprehension that the commander was about to order the boats to cross over the lake toward the house.

"I am not afraid, father, only—but see! their boats are turning to the shore. They appear now to be putting into a small cove."

"There is where they are cunning," observed the other. "They don't think it altogether safe to approach much nearer in the range of those murderous long guns.

If I had been there in command of the fort, I think they would have seen trouble some time ago. Thank God, however, the stupid fools within there have lost their best chance! But what are they doing now?"

"They have landed, nearly all landed now, and seem to be forming on the bank."

"Good! now, Alma, you will have a chance to see a little of your father's old trade—that is, if the garrison have sense and courage enough to make use of the advantages they possess for repelling their assailants. Are they moving forward yet for the fort?"

"No, the commander appears to be addressing two men apart from the rest, one of whom seems to be unrolling something white. Ah! I see, now; it is a white flag. The two now advance along the path leading to the fort, while the rest appear to stand in a waiting attitude, anxiously watching the motions of their two companions as they approach the gate."

"It is a summons from the commander, girl—a summons for the surrender of the fort. Now you will see whether they will obey it, and yield without a blow the prize that cost the king so much toil and blood in the winning, as my sad experience can well attest. Many a dark and fearful night, Alma, have I ranged these woods, while the savage foe were lurking around us in every direction. Old Major Put, as we used to call that dare-devil, and myself once——"

"There! there! father," interrupted the other, "the messengers have now approached near to the walls. A man appears on the top. They are conferring together. The messengers point to their companions. The man on the walls seems to hesitate. They now seem to direct his attention to something down the lake. Look, father, and see if anything is to be seen coming in that direction."

"Now the lord be with the assailants for a sudden rush, or their game is up!" exclaimed the captain, as, in compliance with his daughter's request, he turned and threw an inquiring look along the lake toward the north. "Two boats filled with armed men are coming up the lake rowing for life—British, no doubt, hastening to succor the garrison."

"No, father, no!" joyfully exclaimed the girl as with trembling haste she turned the glass to the armament in question. "You are again mistaken. These, too, are Green Mountain Boys, coming on to join their companions."

"Green Mountain Boys! from that quarter? where should they come from?"

"From the Winooski River, father. Captain Baker has been on there, and——" eagerly replied the other, but stopping short and blushing, as it occurred to her that the remark would lead to the discovery of the source of her information.

"Really, girl! one would suppose you had been to the council of war where this campaign was planned," said the captain with an air of surprise; but being too much occupied with present objects to trace the association, he, to the great relief of his confused daughter, reverted to the scene before him and said, "You may be right after all—if so, victory is certain. But turn now to the fort and see what is going on there."

"I will—I am, father," replied the flustered girl. "Ah! I have a view again: now the conference between the commander, or the man on the walls, and the two messengers seems to be broken off. The latter are departing. But now the man seems to be calling them back. They turn to him again and hold parley. Now the messengers turn quickly round, and wave their flag to their companions, who seem suddenly to be put in motion. And, see! see! their whole body is rushing toward the fort. How their guns glimmer through the trees as they pour along the path! How their commander's sword flashes in the sun, as half turning he whirls it about his head to motion them on! There! there! father, they mount the swell!—they approach the walls—the gate is thrown open; and now they disappear within the works, and all is still."

"And all without a single gun being fired in defense of Old Frederick! impossible!" exclaimed the captain, with mingled feelings of joy for the success of his countrymen, and shame for the garrison, who would surrender, without resistance, a fortress which years of his life had been spent in helping to wrest from the Frenchmen.

"Here! look, look, father!" again exclaimed the excited girl, "the lion flag goes down! another of a lighter color goes up! Have they not conquered, father? They have! They have! and oh! how thankful!"

"Yes! 'tis all over!" responded the captain, rubbing his hands in ecstasy. "Quick work, by Heavens! Not a gun fired!—not a man killed, and the old Lion is flat on his back! The command of the whole of Lake Champlain is ours! Huzza for liberty!" he shouted, leaping from the ground, forgetful of his lameness in the excitement of the moment, and throwing his hat into the air: "Huzza for the Green Mountain Boys! They deserve a hecatomb for their victories!"

At this instant a dozen columns of smoke shot out fiercely from the walls of the fortress, and the deafening peal of cannon which followed announced to the shuddering hills around the surrender of the last controlling foothold of British power on the waters of Lake Champlain to the prowess and patriotism of the Green Mountain Boys.

Alma, now delivering up the spyglass to her father, hastened into the house, and took a seat in her window, where, unobserved by any, she could observe what further movements might transpire at the scene of action, and at the same time freely indulge in her emotions of joy and gratitude for the preservation of her lover, whom she had distinctly made out to be the leader of the victorious party.

An hour or two after the surrender a skiff, containing a single individual, put off from the shore under the fort, and directed its course to the landing below the cottage. The individual, on reaching the shore, came directly toward the house, and was soon ascertained to be Neshobee by the captain, who, still remaining in his garden, had been watching the coming boat. The Indian rather sheepishly approached his master, conscious, perhaps, that as far as regarded the captain, he had played the truant in joining the expedition.

"Well, Neshobee," said the captain, as the other with averted face came carelessly along, "where have you been all this time?"

"Umph! me been go learn fight um."

"I thought it likely enough they had got you away for that, as I suspected from several things I noticed yesterday that this business was afoot. But how did you know I should be willing you should join in these doings?"

"What you tell big cappen—colonel, who make believe drunk todder night?"

"Well, well, my lad, I don't mean to scold you much for joining in so good a work, though you might have talked with me a little before you went. But have you been with the big captain, who is no other than Ethan Allen, Mr. Sherwood informed me?"

"Me have."

"Well, he was commander of the expedition, I suppose. What did he and his men do there at Ticonderoga?"

"They take um redcoats,—pile up their guns for no let um have um more,—fire big guns, more fifty—hoo! bang!" replied the Indian with significant gestures.

"And was it the big captain who come on with the men to take this fort?"

"No, young cappen, major, what you call Misser Howard."

"Well, you may go now," said Hendee impatiently, motioning the other to go on to the house.

"How proud I should now be of that same Warrington, outlaw though he be, but for this accursed business!" muttered the captain to himself, after the Indian had departed, with a tone and manner in which admiration and dislike, kindness and resentment, regret and bitterness, were strangely blended. "Hang me! if I don't almost think the better of the girl for liking him. Though if Jake's stories be true!—I wonder now if the fellow did not lie to me?—would to God things had been different! But they are not different, and won't be; and hell town! what am I talking about? It can't go—no, no! and by the powers of earth! it shan't go, an inch further, or I will make the house too hot for her!"

While the passionate and unhappy father was thus giving vent to his conflicting feelings, the Indian entered the house and proceeded to the apartment of the daughter, who had also noted his approach and beckoned him from the window to come to her room.

"Now tell me, in the first place, Neshobee," said she eagerly, "whether Mr. Sherwood was over there to be taken prisoner with the rest?"

"Me no see him."

"You said yesterday he was then there."

"Me see him, as me say, then,—no there to-day when we come—guess him run."

"Very likely; but Darrow was there of course, was he not?"

"Him no there, too."

"How unfortunate!" exclaimed the maiden with an air of disappointment and regret. "Not even one of them, then, is secured! Well, well, Heaven knows best; and in that I will still put my trust. But what have you there?" she added, as her quick eye caught the hand of the other fumbling for something in his pocket.

"Cappen send um," quietly answered Neshobee, pulling out a billet, which was instantly snatched from his hands by the eager girl.

"Oh, why not have told me, before! But you may go now, Neshobee;" and with a quick, impatient waving of her hand, she motioned him away.

With a beating heart and glowing cheek the happy girl read and re-read many times the precious note; when, after pondering anxiously and deeply a while, she took her sheet and wrote:

"Your few lines, my dear sir, have been received, and read, I know not how many times over, and with an interest which I dare not acknowledge. Your propositions, too, have been all candidly and even anxiously weighed. And it is with many, very many regrets, my more than friend, that I am forced to the conclusion that at present it were better that they be not complied with. You first propose to come here openly, explain to my father the reasons which compelled you to that course which he pretends so much to censure, and claim the privilege of addressing me—all the explanations which it may be needful to make would, I am satisfied, with my father's present feelings and impressions, be better listened to from me than yourself. And most assuredly they shall be made to him as soon as his mood shall be such as shall warrant the belief that they will be received without passion or prejudice. And before you take the step you propose, I could wish also to see some change in his views relative to the match he has marked out for me. And changed, believe me, they sooner or later will be. Reason will at length resume her sway; and, to say nothing of your character, the character of one of whom I would not willingly speak my opinion must soon be better known to him. And he will see and feel for himself that his present requirements are neither wise nor generous. But do not, for my sake, for your own sake, beloved friend, attempt to accomplish all this now under circumstances so inauspicious: for I feel it would be useless; and not only so, but lead probably to the defeat of the objects and consequently the happiness of us both. No, Warrington, be patient, trust in Heaven to expose guilt and reward innocence, and rely on the constancy of her who is resolved to bring about a state of things when her lover can be received in her father's house with the kindness and respect to which he is entitled.

"As an alternative, in case I disapprove your first proposal, you request to be favored with secret, or stolen interviews,—Warrington, Charles Warrington! would you recommend such a course to a beloved sister? With your delicacy of sentiment, with your admiration of exalted virtue, I know you would not. Why, then, ask it of one whom you propose to make more than a sister? Again, dearest friend, I must say to you, no! I have ever disapproved of clandestine meetings—there is an air of guilt about them—a something that seems to imply a consciousness of wrong, which innocence and rectitude of purpose should never stoop thus tacitly to acknowledge. And the same views which have led to the disapprobation of these have in most respects an equal application to the measure that you hint it may be expedient for us, as a final resort, to adopt—a private elopement. In some countries, and in some states of society, such a measure may, perhaps, be sometimes justifiable; but is it so in a land like ours, where force is rarely, if ever, used to defeat the engagements of lovers? While armed with the panoply of virtue and reason, and possessed of the moral courage which these should ever impart, few females, I apprehend, need here resort to this questionable practice. And were I to be wed to you to-day, Mr. Warrington, it should be done openly, and, if permitted, in the presence of my natural protector. But if the ceremony were forbidden, I would then, after frankly apprising him of my intentions, as openly depart with you to a place where it would be allowed. And if force were employed to restrain me I would then throw myself on the protection of him who would defend or deserve to lose me.

"You know not how rejoiced is my heart to hear of your personal safety—how proud to learn your brilliant successes and how gratified at the promotion you have received. You say you are about to proceed south, to make enlistments for an expedition into Canada. Go! Deserve well of your country, be true and constant, and, while you remain what I now believe you, count me so, and be assured that all the reward that this poor heart and hand can confer shall be eventually yours. My prayers will attend you amid the perils of war. Apprise me often—as often as possible—of your situation. And, notwithstanding I have declined your present proposals, oh, do not believe me now, do not hereafter think me less devotedly yours.

"ALMA."

When Alma had finished her letter she sought her trusty messenger and confined it to his charge, with instructions to convey it to Warrington at the fort that night, or as soon as he could absent himself without exciting the observation of her father; after which she again returned to her solitary apartment, and soon sought her pillow, to escape the perplexities of the present in the bright visions of the future. During the next day her time and attention were more than usually occupied by calls at the house, from those passing to and from the fort. And it was not till nearly night that she found an opportunity to escape from the company with which, in successive parties, the cottage had been thronged through the day. But being relieved at length from these hospitable duties, and wearied with the bustle in which she had been engaged, she threw a light kerchief over her head, and wandered into the fields to indulge in those solitary musings so grateful to separated lovers. The golden sun was just sinking behind the western hills. The earth was a variegated carpet of flowers beneath her feet; and tempted by the beauty of the evening, she continued her course almost unconsciously down the little vale toward the woods; and before she was aware how far she had wandered she had arrived at the border of the field, and was standing by the tree beneath which Warrington had first breathed to her the word "love." After indulging a while in the associations which this sequestered spot awakened in her mind, she turned and was retracing her steps homeward when she was startled by the sharp, rattling voice of someone a few rods below her, and turning, she beheld Pete Jones making his way up the slope toward her.

"Hold up a little bit there, lady; that is, if you're a mind to," he said, respectfully approaching and holding up a letter between his thumb and finger. "There's a little concern of a letter, which Captain Selden handed me to give you."

"Indeed! an answer from Skenesboro' so soon?" said Alma with a subsiding blush, which was raised by the thought first occurring to her mind that the message came from another quarter.

"Answer to the letter the nigger had—d'ye mean? —why, yes, rather spose so. Anyhow, I believe it came from that little hum-bird of a girl that we caught at that small scrape we had with the old podunk of a Scotchman and his folks at the Lower Falls a week or two ago."

"You mean Miss Reed, probably. Have you been up to Skenesboro' since you were here?"

"Oh, yes, a lot of us went up there yesterday, after things had been pretty well fixed at Old Ti."

"For what purpose, if I may ask, sir?"

"Why, only just to let the major there know that the Continental Congress had kinder taken a fancy to his stone house. At all events, Captain Selden told them something of that sort, as we made them all prisoners there."

"What! the ladies and all? I trust they will have no reason to complain——"

"Ah, you needn't borry no trouble there, mum, I guess. The ladies won't be very likely to cry their eyes out, at falling into the hands of such a chap as Captain Selden—now you see if they do! For instance, mum, by way of a similar," continued Pete, beginning to look mischievous, being no longer able to keep down his ruling propensity for joking, "for instance, suppose now, that Major Warrington should come over here with men enough—and 'twouldn't take over a thousand neither, mayhap——"

"You need not trouble yourself to explain, sir," interrupted Miss Hendee rather flurriedly. "The letter will inform me of all particulars, doubtless. You will now excuse me, as I must return. But perhaps you will go to the house for some refreshment, or to remain with us through the night?"

"Why, no,—thank'ee, mum," replied the other, a little abashed at the dignity which the girl assumed. "No, I must be off to my traps: I am a sort of a water-mail to carry orders to-day. Captain Selden sent me on this morning, with dispatches to old thunderbolt—Colonel Allen, you know. Well, the colonel, he sent me with my little bird of a canoe a-going again, like a football, down here to Crown Point, to notify the major to come up to a council there, to-night or in the morning. So you see I must put on with my errand, as I haven't been to the fort yet. You may just tell the old captain at the house, if you're a mind to, that my ague, since I was there, hasn't been very desput, considering."

So saying, the jolly borderer turned and bounded down the slope like a young colt, giving vent to the exuberance of his animal spirits, as soon as he was fairly out of the restraining presence of the lady, in his favorite old chorus, "Trol, lol, lol de larly!"

Hastening to the house and then to her room, Miss Hendee eagerly tore open the letter just received, and read as follows:

"Be astonished, O ye heavens! and Alma Hendee, be you thunderstruck! as I know you will be, when you learn that we are—every man of us,—the major and all, prisoners of war! Yes, I am a second time prisoner to Mr. Selden! What means it, Alma? There is some strange fatality about it that passes my poor comprehension. Oh, for someone deeply skilled in scanning the future—someone gifted with the second sight which is claimed by our Highland seers in Scotland, to divine to me the portent of this singular happening! How very surprised we all were when they landed—a body of armed men—and marched up, taking possession of the yard and disarming our soldiers.

"The major was in the house, and never mistrusted, I really believe, what could be their object, till they had seized the sloop and bateaux, and by their rapid movements in surrounding the men put it out of his power to make any resistance. All this was, seemingly, the work of a moment. And before we had recovered from the first shock of the surprise, Mr. Selden, who appeared to be chief in command, had entered the house, and with drawn sword stood before us. The major then, indeed, began to show some symptoms of uneasiness—more, however, even then, I thought, at the presence of one whom he evidently has both feared and hated since the former visit, than because he really supposed he was in earnest about capturing the establishment. After Mr. Selden had politely saluted us ladies, he bowed formally to the major, who returned the compliment only by a vain attempt to get his organs of speech in motion.

" 'Who?—what? Hem!' he stammered, stepping restlessly about the room, and looking daggers at the other. 'Why, sir—I should like to know, sir,—yes, sir —let me tell you, sir, what I think of you, sir!'

" 'Oh, never trouble yourself, major,' replied Mr. S., with a satirical smile, 'it might take you a longer time than I could possibly spare to devote to so unimportant a purpose.'

" 'Why, sir!' resumed my doughty warrior of a lady's parlor; 'd—— you, sir! do you mean to insult, sir? I'll just let you know, sir—you'll just please to walk out of the house, sir!'

" 'Oh, be patient, major,' rejoined Selden with the most provoking coolness. 'Let me explain to these ladies the nature of our call, lest they be unnecessarily alarmed.'

"He then informed us of the outbreaking of the war, the capture of Ticonderoga, and the determination of the Americans to possess themselves of this post also; and consequently the necessity of our removal to some other place, to which he assured us of a safe escort.

" 'Now, major,' said he, turning to the other, who had several times broken in on Mr. S., 'I have only to say to you that both you and all your men are prisoners of war.'

"Even then the major could scarcely comprehend what had befallen him; for he again began to bluster and threaten. But Selden, at once cutting him short, ordered him away; when they both left the house together. I never saw creatures so puzzled and confounded as were Madge and Merry Skene. They neither knew what to say or how to act. As for myself, I could hardly hold in till the gentlemen had left the room, when I fairly shed tears with the laughter, which I could not repress, at the ludicrous scene I had witnessed. In regard to the valiant major, he will not, probably, make much more fuss about the affair to-day. To-morrow he will be considerably moved at the disaster; and by the next day he will have so collected his ideas and his wrath that he will be tremendously mad.

"They took the place about noon; since which we ladies have held our council of war. And it has been decided that we take our departure to-morrow morning for Albany, where we shall at present remain with a connection of the Skenes'. I should have certainly preferred, for myself, to go and reside with you. But I dare not name it to them; for the girls are already as jealous of me as witches; and I well knew that should I make such a proposition, it would be attributed to a secret wish to be where I could see more of Mr. S. And further, I am not quite sure but they might be so kind as to communicate their suspicions to father; for I have a father, who may claim a voice in some matters, as well as you. Now don't draw any inferences from that observation, Alma; because, positively, there are none to draw.

"Mr. Selden handed me your letter brought by Black Jack, till he fell into the hands of the powers that be. I read it with much interest—the more so, perhaps, as I thought of the possibility that we may yet have cause to mingle our sympathies.

"I shall remain with the Skenes till father returns —if he does return; for now we have war, I am rather uncertain what course he will pursue. Should he receive a commission that suits him, he may engage in the war. This, however, is doubtful. And I think it very likely he will remain neutral, as I suspect he thinks the government have not done him justice. At all events, I don't believe he feels very bitter toward the Americans; but if he does, I know of one who don't.

"P. S.—Mr. Selden is to escort us in person to Albany; and what is better the major is compelled to go with the other prisoners to Ticonderoga. His face is most unreasonably long at this arrangement—I think he will be crazy by to-morrow. Marge is secretly rejoiced, and I know another who is less sad about it than she might be. I have had a conversation with Mr. Selden alone, which has shown me that he can be serious when he pleases. But I have no time left me to state particulars. In my next I will be more explicit.

"Adieu, adieu!

"JESSY."

CHAPTER XX

"With pleasures, hopes, affections gone,
The wretch may bear, and yet live on,
Like things within the cold rock found
Alive, when all's congeal'd around."

DURING the week succeeding the stirring and important events which we have been endeavoring to describe, circumstances of both a public and private nature conspired to bring Miss Hendee in contact with her neighbors and acquaintances much more than usual. The recent change of masters at the fort having led to a new and frequent intercourse with the inhabitants of this section of the country, many of both sexes had called at the cottage on their visits to their friends, who were now members of the garrison. Business connected with her father's household concerns had also caused her to make several calls, during the period above mentioned, at the houses of the different settlers in the neighborhood. It could not reasonably be supposed, in a country settlement where people, in the absence of other employment of their leisure, are usually so curious respecting the affairs of their neighbors, and where every kind of gossiping always finds so ready a circulation, that the visits of so distinguished a young gentleman as Warrington at a house containing one so lovely and excellent as Alma Hendee had been suffered to transpire without being generally known and commented on by the inhabitants of the vicinity. Such, at all events, appeared not to have been the case in the present instance; for Miss Hendee soon discovered that her social intercourse with her lover, as limited as it had recently been, was well understood by nearly everyone of her acquaintance with whom she now happened to fall in company. And many were the jokes and banterings which she was compelled to meet on the subject. But there was one circumstance attending them which soon struck her as peculiar and uncommon in such kind of rallyings; and this was that, instead of the flattering and grateful approvals and happy predictions usually uttered on such occasions, they were now, in almost every instance, accompanied with some manifestations of regret or disapprobation at the conjectured intimacy —some hesitation of manner, some ominous shaking of the head, or some mysterious hinting at the dangers that would attend the connection, which none at the same time seemed to treat as one that would terminate in marriage. At first Alma paid but little attention to these intimations; but as they were repeated, they began to occasion her considerable uneasiness. And when she found them coming from all quarters, prudence would no longer permit her to pass them unheeded. And she began to busy her mind in trying to account for impressions which she supposed to be much too general to be attributed to chance opinions or personal prejudices. She felt satisfied that this feeling could not proceed from any wish to favor Sherwood's pretensions to her hand; for she well knew he was no favorite with the people at large. Nor could she perceive how it could arise from any ill opinion entertained against Warrington, who, as she had been told, was held in the highest estimation by the settlers generally, both for the signal services he had publicly rendered them and for the many excellent traits of his private character. Although delicacy of feeling, as well as prudence, prevented her making any inquiries of those who had introduced this subject, yet the amount of what she had gathered from them seemed to indicate the existence of some insurmountable barrier to the union to which she had recently engaged herself. But what the nature of this obstacle could be she was wholly unable to conjecture.

One day, after making one of her excursions among the settlers, she had returned home under an unusual depression of spirits, occasioned by some hints and warnings of a more pointed nature than she had before received, together with the mortifying reflection that her views and feelings in regard to her secretly contemplated union had found no response in the minds of her acquaintance. Although an easy credulity formed no part of the discriminating mind of Miss Hendee, yet prudence and discretion were ever among the leading traits of her finely balanced character. And these taught her the necessity of pausing in the path she had begun to tread, lest it, indeed, should be found to be beset with dangers which had been concealed from her view. She recalled to mind some insinuations thrown out by Sherwood at his late visit, by which she now, on reflection, supposed he intended she should believe that Warrington was not only a libertine but that he had by a clandestine marriage, entered into with one of his victims for the purpose of accomplishing his designs, put it out of his own power to contract a legal marriage with another. Considering those insinuations at the time entirely false and malicious she had instantly rejected them from her mind, without paying attention enough to them to examine the import of the words by which they were conveyed. But now, on recurring to the subject, and comparing Sherwood's words with the dark hints she had since received from others, she could not but be startled with the coincidence she perceived in all the different intimations that she had heard. And the more she reflected on the various remarks of her acquaintance, all seeming to tend to the same point, and to be strangely corroborative of each other, the more apprehensive she became of the existence of some fact which would not only level with the dust the fair fabric of prospective happiness she had lately been rearing but would place her in no enviable position before the public, when the step she had taken should become known.

While Miss Hendee was revolving these distracting thoughts in her mind, that had now reached that state of uncertainty and fluctuation which peculiarly fits it for the reception of questionable statements, her reflections were interrupted by the entrance of a man, who announced himself as a tinker, wishing to know whether there were any wares in the house which required the aid of his profession. Being answered in the affirmative, he pulled off his pack, and, producing his tools, went to work on such utensils as were brought him for repairing. He was a man of a loquacious turn; and he had scarcely become seated at his work before his tongue was going as rapidly as his hammer. Being somewhat amused at the remarks she heard him make to Ruth, the domestic of whom we have before spoken, Alma soon quitted the adjoining room, where she had seated herself, and, entering the kitchen, took a seat and fell into conversation with the talkative stranger, occasionally asking a question herself, and good-naturedly answering the various questions he put to her, as he rapidly roved from subject to subject, in so disconnected a manner that it would have puzzled a philosopher to have traced the association of the man's ideas.

"Your fort over here has lately changed masters, I learn," he carelessly observed, after he had started and dispatched every other topic which he apparently could think of as connected with the affairs of the neighborhood. "I wonder who has the command of the place under the new order of things?"

"Major Warrington, I believe," replied Alma, as a slight tinge overspread her fair cheek.

"Major Warrington—Warrington, did you say?" said the man inquiringly, repeating the name; "not Charles Warrington of Bennington way?"

"Yes, the same, sir," replied the other.

"Now, I want to know! Do tell us if he has got to be major?" half exclaimed and half inquired the seemingly surprised tinker.

"Is he a former acquaintance of yours, sir?" asked Alma, turning with a look of interest to the man.

"Lord, yes!" exclaimed he with great apparent simplicity. "Why, ma'am, I have known him ever since he was knee high to a toad—used to live in the same town with him and his father's family, in old Connecticut, before they moved to the Grants, and have seen Charles there often since, on his visits back among his relations—and—and old sweethearts," he continued, looking up roguishly to Alma, as if to see how the last remark took with her, but perceiving the uneasiness of her looks, he jocosely added, "Why, I spose the girls know that the young men will have sweethearts, don't they?"

"I pretend not to know young gentlemen's business, sir," replied Alma in a voice tremulous with suppressed emotion.

"Well, well, I meant no offense," rejoined the tinker, seemingly abashed at the poor reception of his rally.

"You have given me none, sir," timidly remarked the other. "But I think you said you had kept up your acquaintance with Mr. Warrington, and you may know whether—that is, you——" and she paused, unable from the fluttering of her heart to proceed with an inquiry, the answer to which would probably involve her every hope of happiness for life; for she felt that this plain and apparently honest man, with his intimate knowledge of Warrington's previous life and character, would be able to furnish her testimony which would remove her apprehensions, or confirm them and seal her doom forever.

"May know what, marm?" asked he, after waiting patiently a while for her to proceed.

Alma made an effort to go on; but so great was her agitation that she could not utter a syllable, and she remained silent.

"Yes, I know all about Charles Warrington as well as any other man," resumed the fellow, after he saw the other was not likely to go on with her inquiry. "A considerable of a chap he is, too. In fact he is a smart fellow; and a lively one, too, in the main. I never knew but one mean trick about him in my life; and that was shuffling off and deserting that poor simple wife of his, that he married kinder privately there in Connecticut, a year or two ago."

Had a winged shaft from an Indian's bow at that instant been driven through the heart of Alma Hendee, the convulsive start, the sudden contraction of the muscles of her face, and the fearful death-gasp would have been scarcely more visible than was the effect of the last words of the speaker. She sat a moment as if suddenly paralyzed in all her senses. Presently commenced the twitching, nervous motion of her fingers, as she rapidly handled over the work in her lap. Then suddenly rising, she went to the window, and gasping for breath, stood an instant vacantly gazing out upon the landscape, with a face as white as the bloodless marble. She then turned quickly away, and, with hurried, unsteady steps, rushed out of the room. Reaching her own apartment she again stopped short, and remained several moments mute and motionless as a statue, while the woe-stricken expression of her countenance and the silent workings in the muscles of her blanched and beautiful features, as she stood, like a tearless Niobe, with her anguished eye upcast to heaven, and both hands pressed tightly against her heart, told more forcibly than language can express the mental agony with which she was contending.

After Alma left the room the miserable wretch who had so cruelly inflicted this dreadful blow upon her feelings hurried through his work, received his stipulated wages, and departed. No sooner had he turned his back than the faithful Ruth, who had noticed and understood all that had passed, hastened with looks of visible concern to the apartment of her idolized young mistress.

"Alma!" said she, tenderly placing her hand on the now burning brow of the suffering girl, who had flung herself upon her bed, where she was lying, with one hand pressing her closed eyelids and the other her side: "Alma, your forehead is very hot. Shall I bathe it?"

"No, no, Ruth," faintly murmured the fair sufferer, "it is no attack of disease. My head, I know, is some fevered, and my eyes are sore, very sore, but the trouble is here!" she added, indicating the spot by lifting and replacing her hand upon her heart.

"I was aware of your feelings in some measure, Alma," replied the other soothingly, "and being, like yourself, deceived in the character of the man of your secret choice, I confess I did not disapprove of your partiality. But now, Alma, should you not be thankful that you have made this discovery in season to retrace your steps and escape the danger?"

"Yes, and I am, I certainly am; but oh, Ruth, Ruth, you little know how much I loved him! and oh! how cruelly—cruelly has he repaid my lavish affection."

With this the sealed fountain of her tears suddenly opened. And as the pearly drops flowed thick and fast over her lovely cheeks, she breathed more freely; and the torture, the scorching, tearless agony that she had felt withering both heart and brain was removed, giving place to the mitigated suffering of ordinary sorrow, in which she long, long indulged, while her faithful domestic, in character of nurse and friend, watched over and comforted her.

The next morning when Miss Hendee arose she was calm and composed, though looking extremely pale. Her appearance very plainly told that the struggle she had passed through had been a fearful one; but it told, also, that she had not struggled in vain for the mastery over her feelings. Though her heart had been pierced and lacerated, she seemed to have succeded in silencing its throbbings. There was a decision in her looks and movements that indicated the stern and unwavering resolves she had made. And in pursuance of the course she had marked out for herself, it was her first object to dispatch such a notice to Warrington of her determination as should effectually deter him from attempting any renewal of the intercourse. Accordingly, after she had superintended, as usual, the household affairs of the family for the morning, she retired and penned the brief note:

"MAJOR WARRINGTON:

"Our intimacy is forever ended. As no explanations need be given, so none will be received. I trust, therefore, that no further communications on your part will be attempted.

"ALMA HENDEE."

Sealing the note, she summoned Neshobee to her room, and with the same desperate sort of calmness which she had exhibited through the morning, though with a slight tremor in her voice, she said to him:

"Here, Neshobee, take this to Major Warrington

without delay, if you can find him within twenty miles of this place. But I understand that there was a vessel, with several boats filled with troops, arrived from the south last night; and he probably came with them, as he has been absent from the fort, I am told, for the purpose of enlisting more men. Go, give it him; and do not stay an instant for an answer, or to give him a chance to question you."

The Indian, who perceived both in her words and manner that some sudden change had taken place in the connection which he was aware existed between her and his friend Warrington, threw a keen, inquiring glance upon the face of his mistress, and seemed to hesitate and linger as if for an explanation of so unexpected an errand. But receiving only an impatient motion of her hand for his immediate departure, he turned away and, with an air of mingled wonder and regret, left the house in silence, and proceeding to his skiff at the landing, rowed directly over to the fort. When he arrived there he found all in bustle and commotion, preparatory to an expedition to Canada. Allen, Warrington, and Arnold had arrived, as before intimated, the evening previous, with a schooner and a number of bateaux filled with a considerable body of troops, collected for the contemplated expedition, all of whom were now on the point of embarking—Arnold in the schooner, with such Massachusetts troops as had arrived since the capture of Ticonderoga, and were now properly under his command, and Allen and Warrington, with the remainder of the forces, in the bateaux. As soon as the Indian reached the shore he sought out Warrington, and put the note into his hand. Receiving it as one who might be expecting a favor of the kind, the latter carefully put the supposed prize into his pocket, and informing the messenger that he had one for him to take back to his mistress in return, he turned to finish the directions he was at the moment engaged in imparting to his men.

When he had completed the business immediately on hand, he turned to look for Neshobee that he might take him into the fort to receive the letter he intended to send back by him. But after searching for him in vain among the men, he cast his eye on to the lake, and to his surprise and vexation he beheld the native rapidly pulling for the opposite shore and already out of hailing distance. Still supposing, however, that the messenger had misunderstood his request, the impatient lover hastened to a solitary room in the fort for the purpose of reading the precious paper alone, and adding a postscript to the one he had written, that he might dispatch it by a special messenger before he embarked. As soon as he was alone he eagerly broke the seal of Alma's brief note and read, with the most unmingled pain and astonishment, its unexpected contents. Hastily rising from the seat he had taken, he for many minutes rapidly paced the room in silence, while the agitation visibly depicted on his manly countenance plainly bespoke the depth and bitterness of his emotion.

"Yes, noble girl," he at length mournfully said, "incapable of intrigue and meanness yourself, you have, in some way, unsuspectingly become a victim to the snares of a villain! It is—it must be so. A deception has been practiced upon you—a gross deception could alone have prompted to a measure so sudden, so cruel, so inconsistent, and so destructive, as I know it must be, to your own happiness. Well, well, I have no leisure now, even if I would, to enter the lists with this despicable plotter of mischief, who has thus entered our Eden and turned its happiness to sorrow, in trying to ferret out his villainies, or compete with him in his low game of intrigue and deception. I must leave you, too credulous girl, to discover for yourself the arts by which you have been duped, and the injustice you have done me. Till then, farewell—till then, be my country my heart's only mistress."

Before another hour had elapsed Warrington had embarked with his troops and, with the gallant and warlike array with which he was borne down the lake, had passed from the scene of his love and disappointment on his way to fields of blood and glory.

It comes not within the scope of our design to accompany our Green Mountain Boys through the eventful campaign that followed their present embarkation, or to attempt to trace the varied fortunes of their gallant leaders; the daring, talented, and chivalrous Allen, who, in his heroic attempt on Montreal, was taken prisoner and carried to England in irons, and there kept through a long and doleful captivity, which deprived his country of the aid of one of her most energetic sons during the most trying period of the war, the skillful, cool, and intrepid Warrington, whose conduct soon won for him the admiration of his country; the gay and gifted Selden, whose sword and pen were alike successfully wielded in the cause; and the jolly and fearless Jones, who became known as the most sagacious and trusty scout-leader in the northern army. These, and the brave, resolute, and patriotic men under their command, who soon, by their courage and success in battle and their fidelity to the cause of freedom, rendered the name of Green Mountain Boys a terror to their foes and an appellation of honor among their admiring countrymen, we must now leave to struggle with their enemies abroad, while we remain on the spot we have chosen as the scene of our story, there to wait their return to make the place once more the theater of glorious conflict.

From this time, for a period of about two years, there was a pause in the action of our story. Although the events which formed its commencement were intimately connected with those attending its catastrophe, yet nothing occurred, during that interval, particularly to vary the aspect of the one or to hasten the other. And the relative situation of all the different individuals of our *dramatis personæ,* from this time separated and scattered in various directions, remained nearly unaltered till the tide of war, combined with other circumstances, brought them again together to figure on the scene of action where we have thus far described them. We propose, therefore, to pass lightly over this interval, and with a few observations, by way of noticing the situation and progress of affairs in the Hendee family in the meanwhile, we shall proceed at once to the closing period of our story.

From the hour of her supposed discovery of the duplicity and base conduct of Warrington, life was but a joyless blank to Alma Hendee. Although by the fortitude and firmness of her character, aided by female pride, which had been deeply wounded by the mortifying development, she had succeeded in her determined efforts to keep from sinking under the cruel disappointment, yet she could not but feel that the young affections which she had thus lucklessly suffered to entwine round her heart and root themselves in its very core were withered, never to be revived to their original freshness at the bidding of another. In the unbounded confidence of her youthful love, she had squandered her heart's best treasures on one from whom neither pride nor principle would longer suffer her to accept a return. And she was deeply conscious that she could never gather them again to bestow them on a more worthy object, or where they would yield her the earthly happiness to which she had begun to look so fondly forward in her anticipated connection.

It is an interesting and beautiful trait in the character of woman's affections that she never truly worships but at one altar. If that remains to her, though no new attraction be added,—no new inducement offered to insure the continuance of her devotion,—she asks no more, but worships on and on, more deeply and fervently, till the heart that offers the homage ceases in death to cling to all earthly objects. But if that is destroyed or removed, the incense of her heart passes away with it. She may, indeed, sometimes be found kneeling at another shrine and offering up the forms of devotion, but the life, the spirit of the worship is forever gone.

After the rupture between Miss Hendee and Warrington, Sherwood became for a while unusually constant in his visits at Captain Hendee's, and quite assiduous in his attentions to the listless girl to whom they were offered. At his first call after that event, he soon and with a malicious satisfaction discovered that the arts he had put in practice had been crowned with success. This he not only read in her pale face, in which the settled air of gloom and disappointment were visibly depicted, but also in her altered and more respectful manner toward himself, which, without any change of opinion respecting his general character, she very naturally, though unconsciously, perhaps, exhibited toward him, as to one whom she now exonerated from the particular charges to which she believed him obnoxious. Having satisfied himself of this state of things, he at first cunningly forebore to renew his former pretensions to her hand. In a short time, however, he began again to make professions of attachment and, without asking of her any other than the tacit acquiescence she had formerly yielded, talked of their engagement as of a settled business, and as if nothing had occurred to alter the relation formerly existing between them. These addresses Alma rather suffered than received; and the affair between them was in this manner allowed by her to fall into much the same train in which it was moving on Warrington's appearance. And yet she still had but little thought of uniting her destinies with those of Sherwood; but continuing to hope that something would eventually occur to save her from the dreaded fate, she permitted the affair to glide along as she had formerly done, solely out of regard to the feelings of her father and the interests of the family. And indeed, now more than ever did it seem necessary that the family should avoid a rupture with Sherwood, as they were becoming more and more dependent on his assistance. With the breaking out of the Revolution, the half pay which Captain Hendee had before regularly received, and which had constituted his main dependence, ceased to be transmitted. And he was therefore driven to avail himself, from time to time, of the offers of Sherwood to loan him money to meet his exigencies. In this manner Miss Hendee wore away about two years of her dull and joyless existence, finding nothing in the present to console or cheer her desponding mind, and seeing nothing but clouds and darkness in the future, when an incident occurred that threw a new light upon her dark and cheerless path, and produced a revolution in her whole views and feelings as sudden and complete as the event which caused it was singular and unexpected.

CHAPTER XXI

"A sudden joy lights up my loneliness."

It was a soft and balmy evening in that loveliest of all months of the year in our northern clime, delightful June, when two ladies were seen issuing from the Hendee cottage to wander abroad to enjoy the beauties of the evening and hold in the solitude of the fields that confidential communion on the subjects of mutual concern which is ever interesting to friends who have just met after a long separation. One was in height something above the ordinary standard of women, but with a form as faultless as the chiseled marble. Her carriage and general demeanor, though easy and graceful, were yet not of that light and joyous kind which generally bespeaks corresponding lightness of heart, but were marked rather by that serious, drooping cast that tells of secret cares and sorrows; while an air of deep and pensive thoughtfulness rested in her dark-blue eyes and overspread her somewhat pale, though exquisitely molded, features. The other female was a trifle smaller, and as volatile as a child in her movements. The very reverse of her companion, she seemed to be the creature of joyous impulses. Though both possessed far more than an ordinary share of personal beauty, yet their beauty was of an entirely different order; for while the appearance of the former was calm, intellectual, and commanding, that of the latter was sprite-like and playful, partaking largely of that certain prettiness, that eccentric will-o'-wisp sort of witchery, which men generally pursue eagerly rather than worship profoundly. They were both old acquaintances of the reader, and we will, therefore, allow them to announce themselves by the conversation that now ensued between them.

"Now, tell me, Alma," said the smaller girl, "for, in spite of all the dogged silence you have shown in your letters on the subject, I determined I would know the first time I saw you—tell me, I say, what was the true reason of your dismissing Warrington."

"There are some things, Jessy," replied the other, "which involve such imputations on our own prudence and discernment, and are of themselves so humiliating to our feelings that we can hardly bring ourselves even in thought to recur to them, much less to reveal them to others. And this is the main reason why I have never apprised you of the fact you seek to know."

"Yes; but I shall not let you off on such a reason, you may depend upon it. Come, come, girl, I will be your confessor; and the more crossing to your feelings the confession, why the more it will be for your good, if the Catholic priests are in the right of it."

"No, Jessy, let us forget the subject. I will not again disturb my feelings by recalling to mind the man who once caused me so much sorrow. It is enough to say that I was grossly deceived in his character."

"Deceived! How deceived? Now, I tell you, Alma Hendee, I will know; and, as I am to live with you till father returns from England, I will thorn you night and day till you tell me."

"Well, then, Jessy, if you must know, the cause of my discarding him was the best of all causes—because he could never be lawfully mine; for, whatever his heart may have been, his heart belonged to another. And while he was vowing his hand to me, he was the husband of a living wife in Connecticut. What say you to a deception like that, Jessy?"

"Why, monster! if so; but how know you that fact, Alma?"

"I received intimations of it from various sources, which I disbelieved, when a man called here who was well acquainted with Warrington's whole career, and he confirmed all that I had heard."

"Warrington—the high-minded and brave Colonel Warrington—guilty of baseness like that? Impossible! Are you quite sure that there is not some mistake or some intended deception about this, Alma?"

"Yes, yes; think not that, with my unbounded confidence in the man, I should have been brought to believe this easily. And oh! if you knew what the discovery cost me!"

"But did you apprise him of this discovery?"

"No!"

"Why?"

"Simply because, as I was fully satisfied of the fact, all attempted explanations would not only fail to mend the matter, but make it worse, by continuing a correspondence which would be ruinous to me and disgraceful to us both."

"Alma Hendee, I can hardly believe this strange story. I fear you have been deceived. I wish I had known it before. Neither Colonel Warrington nor Captain Selden have the least idea that such were your reasons for the sudden, and to them unaccountable, step you took. I have conversed with them both on the subject; and they both believe, I imagine, that you were either coerced by your father or were laboring under some misapprehension. Mr. Selden, I know, believes this; and he told me on our way here that if you would keep yourself from becoming entangled with Sherwood, the affair might yet be reconciled between you and the colonel, who yet cherishes for you all his former sentiments."

"It never will be reconciled, however, Jessy."

"Why, you have not seriously determined to marry Sherwood, have you?"

"I can hardly bring myself, I own, to think seriously of such a sacrifice," said Alma mournfully. "I certainly never should harbor the thought a moment if I had now any other object to live for than to render my infirm and embarrassed father as happy as possible. This I see but one way of doing. And as my own hopes of happiness are gone, should it not now be my duty to attend to his in the only way I can accomplish it? At best, it is but a dark and dreary prospect that lies before me, Jessy. And let us turn from it now to your own, which has at least hope to brighten it."

"Yes, hope, faith, and resolution, come what will, except such a damper as you received. By the way, Alma, did not you think that your father was a good deal taken with Selden for so brief an acquaintance as his short stay with us to-day afforded?"

"I did, indeed, and with great pleasure, notice it. And well my father might be pleased with him, for I know no gentleman whom I——"

"Take care! take care!" briskly interrupted the vivacious Jessy. "Be cautious how far you proceed with your praises, miss!"

"I will be moderate rather than alarm you, then," replied Alma, smiling.

"Well, see that you are, or I'll be jealous as sure as you live. Besides, I don't care a fig about obtaining your praises for him. But Captain Hendee's good opinion of him is a point gained with me; for my father, you know, has placed me, and my destinies, too, for aught I know, in the captain's hands for the present. I wish I could get a peep at that letter of instructions, as

I suppose it was, which I brought from my father to yours. What cautious old things these papas are about us girls, are they not, now?"

"Your father, then, suspects your attachment, does he?"

"Why, that is what I am myself puzzled to decide. Selden contrived right cunningly to get introduced to my father, soon after the old gentleman arrived at Albany where the Green Mountain troops, with their officers, have been posted the past season, you know. They have since met several times, and by the fact of my being intrusted to Selden's care in coming on here, I know father considers him a man of honor at least. But whether he has ever suspected the truth about us I have been wholly unable to ascertain. If he has, and disapproves it, he has studied out some sly, indirect way of breaking up the connection without recourse to open opposition, which I have often heard him say made ten matches where it broke one."

"But did not Major Skene, after his exchange and return, or his sisters, inform Colonel Reed of their suspicion, most probably?"

"They would have done so, perhaps, had they continued as jealous as at first; but since my engagement with Selden we have both acted in concert to blind them, and I think they are in the dark themselves."

"And how have you disposed of the major in the meanwhile?"

"I laughed him out of countenance—jeered and joked him about his valor at Skenesboro' before the officers, ridiculed him in every way I could devise, till at last the fellow became so sore under the torment that he fairly avoided me as if I had been a viper; and that is the way I advise you to take with your eternal hanger-on, who, like the major, was never man enough to cease his attentions when he knew they were not agreeable. But where is Sherwood now?"

"We don't know. He has been absent several weeks. He told us he was going to Albany. You heard nothing of him there, did you?"

"No; but if he was there, he would hardly show himself in public, I think. Did you know they strongly suspected him of being a Tory?"

"I knew not that he was suspected by others. But from his standing aloof from the contest when our bleeding country required the aid of every friend, from the character of his associates, and among the rest that despicable Darrow, and more especially from one or two secret journeys which I feel satisfied he has lately made into Canada, I have for some time known that he was anything but an American patriot."

By this time our fair friends, having wandered down the slope toward the lake, had reached the shore, and seated themselves on a little grassy elevation near the landing, where they were about to resume their conversation when a skiff containing three men, whose approach from the south had been screened from their sight by intervening bushes, made its appearance and put in for the shore. The girls instantly arose and were hastily retiring when they were hailed by the leader of the party, after he had risen in his boat and looked intently a moment at those on shore. On turning round, Alma at once recognized him to be the tall woodsman with whom she first became acquainted as the messenger of Warrington.

"If you'll agree not to be scart much at such a beauty as I be, gals," said Pete, leaping ashore and striding up the bank, "I should like well enough to have one of you stop running away long enough to have me tell you what one of you wants, that is, if I haven't forgot the face that used to belong to her."

Jones, now advancing to the spot from which the girls, with hesitating steps, were slowly retreating, pulled out a soiled and crumpled letter and offered it to Alma. But the latter, supposing it to be from Warrington, shook her head and declined receiving it.

"Well, now," said the scout, a little disconcerted at the unexpected refusal, "by hoky! if this aint the first time I ever knew a body that wouldn't take a letter that belonged to 'em! Well, I've done all that the fellow who asked me to bring it could expect of me, I consider."

"From whom did you receive the letter, sir?" asked Jessy, who easily apprehended the reasons of her friend for declining to receive it.

"Well, now, marm," replied Jones, scratching his head, "that is asking a notch more than I am very well able to answer. I partly hinted to the man to tell me his name, but he kinder screwed round in his talk so that he kept clear of telling me. Howsomever, it was an honest-looking fellow enough, that I fell in with at Skenesboro', where we stopped for breakfast this morning."

"Oh, it is not from any in the army, then," rejoined Jessy, throwing a significant look at her companion, intended to convey a sly joke for her overcautiousness.

"Any in the army?" said Jones, repeating the words of the other, as he began to assume his old comic twist of features. "No, unless you might call him a kettle-drummer; for, now I think on't, when we first came into the house where we found him he was at it hammer and tongs upon an old brass kettle, making clatter enough to crazy a small nation."

"I beg your pardon, Mr. Jones," said Alma courteously. "I was under a misapprehension in regard to the source of this letter; I will receive it now, sir, if you please, and thank you kindly for your trouble in bringing it," she added, extending her hand and taking the proferred paper.

"Are you direct from Albany, sir?" asked Miss Reed, preparatory to some other question, apparently.

"We started from there about twelve last night, and in a bit of a hurry, too," replied the scout, turning and looking upon the face of his fair interrogator, whom he now for the first time seemed to recognize. "Why, now, if I aint beat, to find that queer fighting bird again—beg pardon, marm—I didn't mean it for offense; for I don't calculate to be very sarcy to folks, except to the Britishers. And I kinder guess you aint very stiff for that side, after all, or you wouldn't allow yourself to be caught by the Green Mountain Boys so easy and often."

It was Jessy's turn to be disconcerted now, and, blushing to the very temples, she turned confusedly away, and pretended to be looking for wild strawberries in the grass, while Alma, smiling to see the discomfiture of her friend at the honest but sly hit involved in the remark of the woodsman, now addressing the latter, asked:

"Has any late intelligence of the enemy's movements been received at headquarters that has caused you to be dispatched in this direction so hastily?"

"I rather expect there has, marm."

"Any threatened invasion? I know there have been fears of one from Canada, but, hearing nothing of it lately, we had begun to believe it a false rumor."

After looking Alma earnestly in the face an instant, Jones motioned her to step a little farther from her companion, when, in a low tone, he observed to her:

"You used to be true blue—I wonder if you are now?"

"If you mean a friend to your cause, who can be trusted, you may count me as one."

"I rather thought so. Well, we fear there will be hot work in this quarter in a very few days from this. A British deserter, who was taken up over on Winooski River, and sent on by Captain Baker, arrived at headquarters yesterday, and gave us the information that

General Burgoyne, with an army of ten thousand men, had already reached St. John's on his way through this settlement to Albany, if he can get there. Colonel Warrington and his regiment of Green Mountain Boys were to march this morning to re-enforce St. Clair at Ticonderoga. And General Schuyler's whole army, before this, are on the move for Fort Edward, as the place where the grand tussle is to be had, if the enemy are not stopped before. I and my scouts in the boat there are now on our way to reconnoiter and watch the progress of the regulars as they come on. Now, this last part of it you must keep dark about to all where there is the least chance of its getting into the wind. If I get along back as far as here I will try to call and let you and the folks in this quarter know when the enemy may be expected, that you may be all out of the way before they arrive. But I must be off, for we must row ten good miles further to-night before we encamp. Good-nighty, marm."

Having given this exciting piece of information, imparted with more seriousness and directness of manner than anything of equal length he had uttered, perhaps, for years, Jones turned on his heel, bounded forward to the shore, and leaped into the boat, which the next instant shot by the landing and disappeared.

Knowing that the scout's secret would be as safe with her companion as with herself, Alma immediately called her, and repeated the startling news she had just received. And the solicitude and trembling apprehensions which filled the bosom of each, as they thought of their respective friends in connection with the approaching danger, for a while swallowed up every other feeling. Even the letter, the delivery of which had occasioned the call of the scouts, was forgotten till the girls had retraced their steps more than half the distance to the house. It being then recalled, however, Miss Hendee seated herself on a hillock, opened and began reading it with an air of listless curiosity, which showed how little she expected to be interested in its contents, while Jessy knelt before her on the grass, watching the varying expressions, from simple curiosity to eager interest, and from that to deep emotion, which successively passed over the countenance of the other as she proceeded in the perusal. The letter was without signature, and ran thus:

"Miss Hendee, I guess, will remember how, a year or two ago, a man came to your house and mended the things; and how he made some statements about Charles Warrington, the colonel that now is. Now, what I said at that time has worried my feelings a great deal most ever since. Though I then really thought what I said was justifiable, even if it was not quite true, as I was made to believe it to be for your good. But I soon after found out what I told you was not so, for I didn't know myself, and only said what I was asked to say. This was the story of it: As I was going from house to house, working at my trade there in your part of the settlement, I fell in with a plausible sort of a man—I don't think I had best call him by name—and we, after a while, got to talking about Warrington, whom I had seen often enough, though I knew nothing of his private affairs. Well, he in a smooth kind of way said there was one thing that hurt his feelings, and that was that Warrington was doing the wrong thing by a relative of his, a very likely girl, that he pretended to be courting for the sake of getting her family on his side in the York quarrel, when to his certain knowledge he had a young wife that he had deserted down country. He said it was a great pity to have the girl so deceived, and he would give two gold guineas to anyone who would break up the courtship. But he said it would do no kinder good for her relations to try; and they were very anxious someone else should undertake to do it. He then told me his plan was that he and I, if I would agree to it, should first kinder secretly tell folks this story about the deserted wife, so that it should get to her, and make her begin to believe it; and then I should go there, and pretend to come from where Warrington used to live, and let drop somehow, before the girl, that I was knowing myself to that business about his being married. Well, he kinder drew me into his plan, and I, being poor, consented for the money to do as I did. But I soon mistrusted that this man had some wrong design, which I found out to be the case, and I feel very sorry, and ask pardon for what happened; and shall feel very bad if I done any mischief by it, as I think Colonel Warrington a very likely man. I think I shall feel easier now in my mind, but I guess, considering, I shan't sign my name, though I am not ashamed of it, or at least I never was in any other affair since I was born.

"Your well-wisher to serve."

The first feeling that pervaded the bosom of Miss Hendee on reading this humble epistle, the truth and genuineness of which she found it impossible to doubt, was that of unmingled indignation at the base and detestable conduct of the man who had instigated the deception that had been practiced upon her with such complete success. The whole of that transaction, together with all the dark hints and warnings she had previously received from her acquaintance, now stood explained before her. She found no difficulty in tracing all to the same source, and she saw at once the motives which had actuated the subtle author of this piece of refined villainy in the course he had pursued. Her next feeling was that of deep and unfeigned regret for the injustice she had unintentionally done one whom, but for this erroneous belief, she would have held, of all on earth, the most dear and honored. At last came the heart's rich gushings of returning love. And from the overpowering force of these mingled emotions she sat down and wept like a child.

CHAPTER XXII

"And how felt he, the wretched man
Reclining there—while memory ran
O'er many a year of guilt and strife,
Flew o'er the dark flood of his life,
Nor found one sunny resting place,
Nor brought him back one branch of grace."

In the environs of Albany, at the period of which we are writing, stood an ancient-looking tenement, originally designed, as its general appearance indicated, for a common farmhouse, though the grounds around it seemed lately to have been left almost wholly uncultivated, while dilapidated fences and an unchecked growth of rank weeds springing up everywhere about the premises told anything but of good husbandry in the occupant. Indeed, there was an air of solitude and decay about the place which might reasonably have been taken by all as an evidence of a corresponding decay in the circumstances of the owner but for the fact, known to many, that he had brought large sums of money, which he must have increased, as he had ever lived on an economical scale and husbanded his treasures with the most miserly care, ever speculating upon the necessities of others, and loaning his money at exorbitant usury. Since the commencement of the unsettled times of the Revolution, however, he had been busily engaged in drawing in his funds, while he began to talk of pretended losses, and to feign the appearance of approaching poverty, by suffering his farm to run to waste, as if through inability to bestow upon it a proper cultivation. This was attributed by many to actual impoverishment; but those who knew more of his affairs set it down at once to his unwillingness to trust out his property in such fluctuating times, and his fears of being compelled to loan or otherwise part with it for maintaining the American cause, to which it was suspected he was not overfriendly. He had ever been a man of few friends and still fewer confidants. And for the last year or two he had almost wholly withdrawn himself from society; while, as was noticed by those who occasionally saw him, his health appeared to be gradually undermining, and his countenance wore an air of deep dejection, arising, it was surmised, as he had no visible grounds of sorrow, from remorse of conscience or other mental inquietudes, the causes of which he had never divulged.

To this cheerless spot we would now invite the reader, for the purpose of introducing one to whom allusion has been several times made, the father of Jacob Sherwood. The unhappy old man had been for several weeks rapidly failing, and he now lay stretched on the bed of sickness with the full consciousness that the end of his earthly career was fast approaching; while a retrospect of his life began to fill his mind with terror and alarm, in view of the retribution which his guilt-stricken conscience told him was at hand. Although, by the constant exercise of that peculiar cunning and cautiousness which were leading traits in his character, he had always contrived to steer clear of the penalties of the law, yet there had been certain secret passages in his life the memory of which now turned his dying bed into a couch of thorns, and drove him to think of making some atonement for the injuries he had inflicted before he dare go to his final account.

With this, among other views, he had the week previous sent a special messenger for his son, and he was now anxiously looking for his arrival. But the lingering days passed on and he came not, till the wretched invalid, warned by his failing strength that he could hold out but a few days longer, dared no more delay the act of justice which his guilty fears had urged him to perform, to those who had been the victims of secret villainies. But let us now enter his gloomy abode and proceed to his bedside. He had been lying about an hour in a troubled sleep, from which he had several times suddenly started up with a wild, apprehensive glare and a few incoherent mutterings that gradually died away on his working lips as he relapsed into his uneasy slumbers. He now, however, became thoroughly awakened, and, turning his face to the nurse in attendance, a wrinkled old crone, who, with an ignorant, clownish-looking boy, made up the rest of the family at the present time, he eagerly inquired if his son had arrived. And being answered in the negative, he sunk back on his pillow with a look of blended woe and disappointment which told the utter wretchedness of his feelings.

"Oh, when will he come? when will he come?" at length muttered to himself the hapless old man. "I shall die before he arrives! No, no! I must not die, I cannot die, till I see him—till he promises. But if he should not come! Or if he come and would not promise, or promising, would not perform, would there be the reparation? I fear—I fear him, with so much interest at stake! Oh, why have I delayed this so long! Why have I carried this dreadful weight till now! If I had but strength to write it! Perhaps I have. I will try—I will! Nabby!" he continued, calling to the deaf old woman; "I say, Nabby! bring me here pen and paper."

"Eh? Oh, ay!" replied the crone, bringing the required implements.

"Now, bolster me up on the bed, and lay that old ledger open on the bedclothes before me. There! that will do."

Having been a ready penman, and deriving a temporary strength from the excitement of his sudden resolution, the invalid succeeded in writing out a brief statement or confession of the misdeeds which lay heaviest on his troubled conscience.

"There! there!" he exclaimed in a sort of unnatural glee, "it is on paper! it is down—thank God, it is down! I feel easier now—relieved; some of the poison has passed from my heart to the paper." And he read over and continued looking some time upon the lines with a wild, exulting satisfaction, muttering at intervals, "Yes, thank God, it is down!"

He then, having again called the nurse and directed her to seal the paper securely, superscribed it to Captain James Hendee, giving the woman strict orders to give it to his son when he arrived, or to some other person who would promise to deliver it to the person to whom it was addressed. After this he fell back exhausted, and lay some time in silent meditation.

"Yes, that is something," he said at length, resuming his soliloquy; "but will it bring back the lost or dead? No! Will it restore the property I took from them? No! not a shilling without a suit; and then Jake will find some way to defeat it; and then the letter may be lost—he may mistrust what I have written, and destroy it. It won't do. I must make a will and place it out of his hands; I must—oh, I must and I will do it—I will do it now! Ezra! Ezra!" he continued, speaking with nervous rapidity; "Nabby! tell Ezra to come here in a minute!"

The ill-clothed and more ill-favored boy soon made his appearance.

"Ezra, you go over to Esquire Vanderpool's, and tell him I want he should come here as quick as possible —run! run!"

The man who was thus summoned, and who was an attorney whom the old gentleman had sometimes employed and consulted, on account of the prudence and secrecy with which he conducted all matters submitted to his charge, in a short time entered the apartment and quietly seated himself by the bedside of the sick man. The old nurse was then ordered to leave the room.

"I am going to die, squire," said the old man feebly.

"I hope not," replied the attorney, casting a scrutinizing glance at the pallid face of the other, but without betraying the least emotion.

"I know best; and I have thoughts of making a will. Can you draw one that will hold?"

"None of my making have ever yet failed."

"So I suppose; and I believe you honest and to have a mind of your own, or I should not have sent for you. But can it all be kept secret till the will is proved in court?"

"Who is to be executor?"

"I have been thinking of that. So much money is a great trust; but if you are not honest, who is? I must have you."

"All can be managed, then."

"Yes; but will it be done? Will you promise? I have reasons. You know Jacob—will you not let him buy you up?"

"Never!"

"Write me a will, then; and be quick—quick—bequeathing a thousand pounds to Captain James Hendee of the New Hampshire Grants, and all he now owes me; another thousand to his daughter. That will make them good for what I——"

"That is right! Make a clean breast of it, Mr. Sherwood," observed the attorney encouragingly.

"I will—God forgive me for taking that amount from the property left with me to manage. Put it down in the will 'reparation.' "

"I will. But the rest of the property?"

"All to my son. Write on—be quick!"

The attorney, with an acquiescing nod, proceeded diligently with his task, while the restless invalid again muttered to himself:

"It will be an inducement for Jake to marry the girl, which I fear he means to avoid. But he probably will do it now and then nothing will be lost by this; and if he don't, why he has enough without it. Yes, this will do. I shall feel better—better."

The will was very soon completed, witnesses were called, all the requisite formalities passed through; when, after receiving from the testator many additional injunctions, the attorney departed with the important instrument in his pocket.

As soon as this business, for which the sick man had summoned all his failing energies, was accomplished, he again became as helpless as an infant and lay several hours in a state of exhaustion and stupor. At length his malady began to assume a different and more threatening aspect. The pains of approaching dissolution set in, attended with mental anguish even more fearful in appearance than his bodily agony; and to the wretched old man a night of horrors succeeded. While his limbs were writhing with pain, and he seemed to be grappling in bodily effort with the king of terrors, the most fearful images appeared to rise continually before his distracted mind, to complete the horrors of his situation. At one time he seemed to be contending with desperate fierceness against troops of fiends that stood palpably before him, reaching out their long, skinless claws to drag him from his bed, while "Keep them off! oh, keep them off!" would burst in the accents of despair from his lips. At another time the images of those he had injured appeared to rise upon his troubled fancy and stand before him, giving, even by their quiet presence, unspeakable tortures to his feelings.

"Leave me, Brother Hendee, oh, leave me!" he would piteously exclaim, waving his hand for the other, whom he fancied to be standing by his bedside, to depart. "Away! away! I cannot look on you. You forgive me? What is that to me, so long as that great burning eye is looking down so fiercely upon me? Oh, don't smile upon me! Don't, Brother Hendee! It stings—it kills me! There! that is right—kind. He is gone now. But what is that coming? Oh, what is that?" he continued, starting up with a look replete with horror and distress. "See how he reaches out his little hands as they carry him off into the woods, crying, 'Uncle, save me, uncle, from the Indians!' It is a lie! I say I am not your uncle! You are an imp—a fiend come to torment me! There! I told you so—I knew it! See! see! there! He is sending that troop of devils to drag me down into that dreadful black gulf! Oh, God! they have seized me! I won't! I won't go! Help! Murder! Oh, help! help!" And with the expiring efforts of his delirious energies he rose up in bed and, throwing his arms wildly above him and uttering a fearful screech, he fell down on his face, and the next moment was a livid corpse!

Such was the fearful end of John Sherwood, who, with no penitence that could be acceptable in the sight of Heaven, thus thought to compound with his conscience and atone for his misdeeds by offering up a portion of that wealth which he had made the only idol of his worship through life—a life marked, indeed, with many acts of specious kindness performed toward those he had wronged, but always performed on the principle we have mentioned or to veil the secret injuries he had inflicted from the eyes of his victims and blind the public to his true character.

On the second day after the event just described, and but a few hours before the time appointed for the funeral ceremonies, Jacob Sherwood rode into the yard, and without any previous intimation of his father's death entered the house.

"How is the old gentleman, Nabby?" he asked, approaching and putting his mouth close to the ear of the deaf old domestic.

"Eh? Oh! Why, don't ye know? Han't they told you how he is dead?"

"No! Shocking! Why, when did he die?"

"Yester night—jest 'fore day. Desput sick, the old gentleman was that night. And he was in a terrible taking to see you, Mister Jacob, 'fore he died."

"What did he wish to see me for in particular, do you know?"

"No—not sartainly. But he was under some consarn of mind, I reckon. It was malagantly to hear him take on and see him act. Oh 'twas dreadful times with us that night. I and Ezra sot up. I hope the old gentleman never did anything that was wrong."

"Ezra, what did he say?" asked Sherwood, eagerly turning to the boy, who was present.

"Oh! he talked dreffful bad and scary 'bout somefing carrying him off. I's mortal 'feared, and went behind the door."

"Nabby—say, Nabby!" said the former, again addressing the old woman, "who has been here since father was taken sick besides the doctor?"

"Doctor! He wouldn't have no doctor—he took his own physics."

"Who, then, has been here?"

"Why, none but old Mrs. Chandler, to tell me about fixing his gruel and things, except the folks that came to lay him out, and Squire Vanderpool the day 'fore he died, and then the next morning, to carry off the papers and chests."

"Vanderpool! Papers and chests! What can all that mean?" said Sherwood in an undertone and with an air of concern. "But say, old woman, what did Squire Vanderpool and father do when they were together?"

"Don't know nothing no way about it, cause they sent me out—may be about some writing. La, now! I forgot the letter," added the woman, jumping up and bringing the letter the deceased had intrusted to her charge. "There! He told me to make you promise to give this to Captain Hendee."

"Certainly—I promise," said Sherwood, seizing the letter and putting it in his pocket.

After a few more inquiries, Sherwood retired to another room, when, taking out the letter and carefully breaking it open, so that it might be resealed if he saw fit to suffer it to go to its destination, he proceeded to read it; after which he rose, took out a pocket pistol, drew the charge, went to the fireplace and flashed the priming against the letter, which he held between his thumb and finger till it was entirely consumed.

"Well," said he to himself, as he replaced his pistol, "that piece of evidence is at rest, I think, and if all other matters can be managed as easily all will be well. But it is very evident that the old man has been making a will; and Vanderpool, who must be executor, I imagine, by his presuming to carry off the papers and money, is a hard customer to manage, I confess; though it must be done by some means or other—that is, if the old man's weakness and silly fears have led him to make any serious inroads on my prospects. And who knows how far he may have gone—devil! if he has been willing away my property! But that he could not do. He could only dispose of his own—the lesser half I think it must be. Well, that is mine, too; and I won't go it.

So, if he has been willing it away, curse me if I don't find a way to suppress or break the will. Let's see—Vanderpool is rather poor. That is lucky; for a cool hundred is something of a tempter. But if that fails, then here are the deaf old haddock of a woman and the doltish boy, ready with their humbug stories to swear the old man insane at the time. Good! I'll make it traverse somehow. But the first thing is to see Vanderpool; and I may as well do it now. No; I forgot. The time of the funeral is at hand, and I must be rigging up and putting on a sorrowful face—sorrowful! As if it was a matter of special grief to come into possession of a clear ten thousand!"

Thus soliloquizing and settling his plans for repairing the rent which he feared his father had made in his fortunes, the heartless heir dressed himself, and joined the domestics and others who had now come in to assist in making arrangements for the approaching obsequies. These being made, and the hour appointed for the funeral now arriving, the ceremonies were performed by a small train of the nearest neighbors, including the executor and one or two other individuals from the city who had sustained some connection with the deceased in business transactions. Though the demeanor of all present was marked with the decency and sobriety natural on the occasion, yet none of that emotion which the ties of heartfelt friendship severed by death usually produces at such times was visible among the company. Not a sigh was heard, not a tear was seen to bedew a single cheek, as they followed the old man, who had never exhibited any feelings in common with them, unwept and unhonored to his long home.

That evening, and as early as he thought decency would permit after his father's remains were consigned to the earth, Sherwood repaired to Vanderpool's office. And, after what he deemed would be considered some suitable observations upon his recent bereavement, he carelessly remarked:

"My father made a will in his last sickness, I understand."

"Well, the old gentleman undoubtedly had property to dispose of, I think," replied the attorney evasively.

"You drew it, I am told," observed the other, cautiously approaching the point at which he was aiming.

"Drafting instruments of that kind is part of my trade, you are aware," remarked Vanderpool, still evading any direct answer to the question implied by the other's observation.

"You will not deem it improper, I presume," said Sherwood, "for me to inquire what are the provisions of the instrument, since I am the person most interested?"

"Why, sir," coolly remarked Vanderpool, "whether you are the *most* interested, I should think, must depend entirely upon the will whose provisions you seek to know. And as regards the propriety of your making inquiries respecting those provisions, I am not aware of any impropriety in your asking; but whether, in the case you assume, it would be proper for me to answer, for the present, would depend solely on the condition imposed on me and the instructions I have received."

"Oh, certainly! certainly! Mr. Vanderpool," rejoined the other obsequiously, though he was evidently not a little startled at the ominous import of some of the attorney's remarks; "but what possible motive could my father have for enjoining secrecy in such a case?"

"Why, that, Mr. Sherwood, is undoubtedly a question that the interrogator is no less competent of answering than the interrogatee," replied the imperturbable attorney.

"Why, surely, Mr. Vanderpool," said the baffled heir, in a tone of expostulation, "you do not think I wish to do anything wrong, I trust. But if the will be a just one, there can be no good reason for keeping its provisions a secret the short time that intervenes before it must be openly proved; and, on the other hand, if it be an unjust one, a delay can be of no benefit to the legatees of a will which can be so easily broken."

"Broken! How?"

"Why I suppose you must be aware, sir, that my father was not in his right mind when he executed this pretended will, as can be proved by the family."

Being a little nettled at the imputation involved in the last remark, that he had assisted in the making of a will when he knew the testator to be incompetent, the conscientious attorney, with considerable spirit, replied:

"Whose testimony, think you, sir, would weigh the most in such case, two, good, honest, intelligent witnesses (to say nothing of myself), who were present and heard the testator converse, or a stupid old woman, so deaf as not to hear one word in ten of an ordinary conversation, and a more stupid boy, who was rarely in his presence?"

"Oh, I am no lawyer, sir," rejoined Sherwood with affected complaisance; "that must be left to gentlemen of your profession to decide. I merely repeated what was told me. And the only motive I have in making these inquiries is to obtain such knowledge of the will as shall enable me to make my arrangements for the future, since I am compelled to return immediately to my post in the Grants. And now," he continued, cautiously veering round on another track, "I really don't see how I can go without knowing something about the disposition of this property. It is a-going to be such a disadvantage to me! Why, I would not begrudge a hundred pounds. Indeed, in my peculiar situation at this time, it might make more than that difference in my circumstances."

"Ah! indeed?" observed Vanderpool, beginning to

suspect the drift of the other, but wishing to see how far he would venture to go if encouraged a little.

"Yes; that is really the case, squire," said Sherwood, thinking he had now hit upon a right course; "and if there are some nice rules among your profession to prevent your showing this will yourself, in obedience to such very singular instructions, why that can be easily got along with. The will can be left, for instance, on yonder shelf, or somewhere, so that, should I come in to-morrow to write a letter or the like, it might be glanced at, and still no blame could fall on you—even if the instrument should be afterward missing. All would come right between you and I, squire, depend upon it. Now, I should suppose that one live client, with my means and with my friendship, would be worth a dozen dead ones, shouldn't you, squire?"

"Why, that might depend," gravely replied the attorney, willing to alarm the other by way of punishing him for his insulting proposals; "that would depend, I should think, somewhat on the question whether the live client had means enough left him by the dead one to make good his promises."

"What mean you, sir?" hastily asked Sherwood, turning pale at the intimation.

"Oh! I am merely making suppositions by way of answering your inquiries; you must put your own constructions upon them," replied Vanderpool, with a look so equivocal as still to leave the would-be tempter in doubt how to proceed.

"Well, sir," said Sherwood, after a hesitating pause, "what am I to understand you are willing to do in this business? Really a hard case for me, squire. What do you say, upon the whole?"

"Upon the whole, then," replied the indignant attorney, looking the other sternly in the face, "I say, sir, that it does not follow that I am a villain and unworthy the trust reposed in me because others may think they can make me so. I am sole executor on your father's estate. The real estate, which is but a small portion of the property, you can take possession of as soon as you please; as to the rest, I shall take and keep charge of it for the present. I know my duty, both toward you and others concerned, and you may depend I shall do it. My supper waits. Good-evening, sir."

So saying, and taking his hat, the independent and incorruptible attorney turned his back on the other and immediately left the office.

Vexed and discomfited at the failure of his attempt, and alarmed at the startling intimations which had fallen from Vanderpool, Sherwood turned his steps homeward. Reasoning from his own principles and feelings, he supposed that the attorney would never have withstood the different temptations which had thus been placed before him unless he knew that the property was about to pass into the hands of others whom it was now more his interest to serve. And joining his argument, unanswerable to one who could scarcely conceive of actions not prompted by interested and selfish motives, with the contemptuous bearing of the attorney and the intimations he had dropped, the partially deceived, though justly punished, heir arrived at the maddening conclusion that his father must have bequeathed the greatest portion of his property to others, and in all probability to the Hendee family, to whom, besides being his only near relatives now left, his penitent and remorseful feelings would naturally direct his mind. And in addition to this he was not without strong apprehensions that his father had imparted to Vanderpool the secret which was contained in the letter directed to Captain Hendee, and which in case the son of the latter was alive, would greatly multiply the chances of losing the other part of the property also. And no sooner had he become confirmed in these conclusions than he made up his mind in regard to the only alternative which he believed was now left him for securing the property. Accordingly, after making a few brief arrangements with a neighbor for managing the farm, he started that very night and proceeded with all possible expedition to the New Hampshire Grants, where we will endeavor to meet him in another chapter.

CHAPTER XXIII

"Oh! what a tangled web we weave,
When first we practice to deceive."

After a rapid journey by land, Sherwood arrived at his house in the Grants, inauspiciously for his present object, on the very evening on which his base and execrable maneuvers to cause the dismissal of Warrington had been discovered by Miss Hendee in the manner we have described. And, deeply intent on carrying into execution his project of a union with her, whom he supposed to be still the dupe of his machinations, believing this now to be his only resource for securing the property, and being determined to accomplish it, if possible, before the provisions of his father's will should be made known, to lessen his chances of success, he early the next morning repaired to her residence for the purpose of urging an immediate fulfilment of the engagement which he now chose to claim as having for several years existed between them. And from the well-known wishes of the father, on whom he counted for a strong ally, and the late acquiescent manner of the daughter, he had the fullest confidence that he should be able to bring about his object with very little difficulty or delay. When he arrived, however, he soon saw indications which considerably lowered the tone of his assurance. In the first place, he was not at all pleased to find, as he unexpectedly did, that Miss Reed had taken up her residence in the family, believing that she, from the connection which he suspected she sustained with Selden, the friend of Warrington, would naturally exercise her influence against one of whom she had doubtless received unfavorable impressions. And in addition to this his quick eye detected a change in the manner of Alma herself toward him, which he fancied had reference to the subject of his present anxiety. And even in the demeanor of the father he thought he perceived a want of cordiality which never before had marked his receptions. But notwithstanding all these discouraging appearances, he determined on persevering in his original purpose. And, carefully abstaining from all mention of his father's death, he early sought a private interview with Miss Hendee, who, with a sort of business-like promptitude, and with the air of one who is fully prepared for an *éclaircissement,* immediately assented to his proposal.

"Mr. Sherwood has something particular to offer, I conclude?" inquiringly said Alma, with a most freezing dignity of manner, as soon as they were seated in a room by themselves.

"Why, you know, Alma, my attentions to you have ever been particular," replied Sherwood with what he intended for an endearing smile.

"Enough so, certainly," was the equivocal response.

"Well, I am happy," rejoined the other, purposely construing the remark in his own favor, "that you acquit me of any neglect in my attentions to one who is so worthy of them, and one in whom I have ever felt so deep an interest."

"You have manifested but little lack of interest in me or my concerns, I am free to acknowledge, sir," remarked Alma in the same equivocal manner.

"I hope I am not doubted in this respect," said Sherwood, with the air of an arraigned schoolboy attempting to put an immaterial issue, in order to escape or delay a blow, which he sees the disposer of his fate is preparing to give him.

"Oh, not in the least, sir," replied Alma in a tone and manner still more ironical and significant than before; "for I have lately received a sufficient proof of the interest you have taken in my affairs, in the confessions of a certain tinker, whom you may recollect having consulted on the subject on a former occasion?"

"Why — now — really!" stammered Sherwood, utterly disconcerted at this cutting allusion to a transaction which he supposed was known only to himself and the immediate actor in the affair; "really, Miss Hendee, I have not the happiness of understanding your meaning."

"Would further disclosures be likely to increase your happiness in that respect, sir?" asked Alma coolly.

"I did not seek this interview, Miss Hendee," rejoined the other, now recovering his assurance, "to listen to a recital of all the slanders that may have happened to reach your ears; but I sought it on more important business."

"I will not hear your propositions, sir," said she, without deigning any further reply.

"Why, surely, Alma," observed Sherwood in an expostulatory tone, "I know not how I have had the misfortune to offend you, as from your manner I fear I have. I had fondly anticipated a different reception. I had at last arranged my business so that I felt myself, for the first time since our intimacy, at liberty to settle down in life; and, accordingly, I came to propose a consummation of the engagement which has been so long settled between us."

"I wonder, sir," said Alma, "you had not first made known your intentions to my father, with whom the engagement you claim to exist was made, I believe.

Perhaps you might meet with better success in that quarter."

"You seemed disposed to trifle with my feelings, Miss Hendee," rejoined Sherwood, growing restless. "I wish for a direct answer, whether you will or will not fulfill your engagement with me."

"A direct answer, sir, then you shall have; and I will add, I feel not a little grateful for being, for the first time since my acquaintance with you, allowed the opportunity of giving one. Mr. Sherwood, I shall never voluntarily unite my destinies with yours."

"Surely you would not break a solemn engagement?"

"A passive acquiescence—a tacit consent, wrung from me by the force of circumstances, is, as you well know, sir, all the engagement that you can claim of me. And even that, your conscience must tell you, you have long since forfeited by your own conduct."

"Are you prepared, miss, for the consequences which may follow the step you seem determined on taking?"

"You do well, sir, I acknowledge, to remind me of that consideration," bitterly retorted the indignant maiden; "for I am aware that it is no light matter to brave the revenge of one who could instigate the assassination of a supposed rival."

Sherwood started as if stung by an adder, at the damning truth of the allusion. His face became fairly livid with suppressed rage and chagrin, and biting his bloodless lips, he rose and slunk out of the apartment, as would a demon from the presence of some pure being from the skies, without uttering one word in his own defense, or even lifting his eyes to the withering countenance which was bent upon him with a look of mingled pity, abhorrence, and contempt. Leaving the house, the discomfited villain immediately sought Captain Hendee in an adjoining field, for the purpose of instigating the old gentleman to measures of compulsion upon the refractory daughter, in furtherance of his designs. But here, also, he was unexpectedly doomed to disappointment and defeat. Upon Alma's return to the house, after the receipt of the communication exposing the baseness of Sherwood, she had sought an interview with her father, read him the letter, frankly confessed her own feelings, and disclosed all she knew, not only the course and conduct of Sherwood, but also that of Warrington, for a part of which she was indebted to her fair companion, who in turn received it from her lover, Selden, the intimate of Warrington. And among the rest, she had made known to the astonished father the magnanimous conduct of the latter in regard to his ownership of the land on which they resided, the circumstance of which she herself had never been apprised till that very evening. And although the old gentleman had listened to her disclosures without uttering a single word in reply, from which she could learn his opinions on the subject, her communications, nevertheless, had produced a deep impression on his mind and feelings, that were now fluctuating back and forth, like contending currents of the wind, when but a slight impulse is required to turn them back in fury in a direction exactly the reverse from that in which they commenced blowing.

"I little expected, Captain Hendee," said Sherwood with the air of an injured man, as he approached the other, "I little expected, sir, when I arrived here to have met with the reception which I have just received from your daughter."

"Why, what's the matter, sir—what's the matter?" replied the captain, with an air of indifference.

"The matter, sir? Why, your daughter refuses to fulfill her engagement to me, sir."

"Ah! what reasons did she give for that, sir?"

"No good reasons, sir. She has been listening to the tales of slanderers—some enemy has been prejudicing her mind against me, by falsehoods—utter falsehoods, sir!"

"Or has she not heard rather more truth about your maneuvers than you intended should have reached her ears? Come now, be honest, Jake, and tell me."

"Are you, too, in the league against me? Am I to understand that you, too, justify her in this course?" hastily demanded Sherwood, nettled at the cool, indifferent manner of the other, as much as at the blunt severity involved in his question. "I had little expected this from you, sir! I should have supposed the interest of your family would prompt you to a different course."

"Hinging on my obligations, are you, sir?" said the captain, turning fiercely on the other, with eyes flashing indignation. "Look ye, Jake Sherwood, I have, from the very first, used all reasonable exertions with my daughter to reconcile her to this match. And even more, I have done that which, when I have looked upon her fading face, and knew that she was martyring her own heart to please me, has smitten my conscience for years. And now I am resolved to leave her to make her own decisions, unbiased by word of mine. And as to your threats, sir, all I have to say is, go, and do your worst! Take all there is here to yourself, if that will satisfy you; or go join the enemies of your country, as I have long suspected you intended, and bring them down upon us to murder and destroy, if you choose. But don't think to buy and bribe me to sell my own flesh and blood! And don't come here again, sir, with accusations against us, till you can come with cleaner hands. Good-morning, sir!"

So saying, the indignant old man unceremoniously turned his back on his abashed and astonished guest, and hastily hobbled off to his work; while the latter, after standing mute and motionless on the spot several minutes, and leering on the receding form of the other with the concentrated malice of a fiend in his looks, slowly turned away, muttering between his clenched teeth, "Revenge! revenge! I wonder if they will cheat me out of that too?"

Feeling no desire of returning to the house, or again encountering any of its inmates, Sherwood now struck across the fields and directed his course toward Snake Mountain, at the particular spot which we have before described as the encampment of the Green Mountain Boys; but which was now occupied by another and far different company. To this place we will now take the reader, preceding the baffled intriguer a short time, to take a glance at the party there assembled.

Sherwood had secretly been in the interests of the Royalists for nearly two years previous to this period of our story; and more than a year before he had received a captain's commission, with directions to raise a company in the New Hampshire Grants, in which, he had represented to the British officers with whom he privately kept up a communication, were to be found many faithful adherents of the Crown. And Darrow, through Sherwood's influence, had also been commissioned as lieutenant of the contemplated company. But with all that this pair of military worthies were able to effect, they never had found more than about a half dozen men in this settlement to whom they dared to propose an enlistment into the king's service. These, with about an equal number picked up within the borders of New York, they had at length enrolled and organized into a fragment of a company, which, for the first time, had been called out a few days previous to this time, with the view of co-operating with the invading army of Burgoyne. About a dozen in all, they were now encamped on the ground formerly taken, as before mentioned, by Warrington and his companions, and were waiting in concealment the approach of the

British hordes that were now pouring down upon the devoted settlement from the north.

At the time we would introduce this group to the reader, Darrow had just arrived from the British camp, whither he had been dispatched by Sherwood, when the latter was on the point of setting out on his recent visit to Albany. And having taken some refreshment, the lieutenant was now sitting on a rough bench near the entrance to their shanty, enjoying a little repose after the fatigues of his morning's march. He had fallen into a doze and appeared to be lost to all external objects; while the men within, mostly morose, sullen-looking fellows, were some of them playing cards, some telling stories, and others talking over the plans they had formed to revenge themselves upon certain families in the settlement against whom they entertained private grudges, as soon as they should be let loose upon the inhabitants, at present wholly unprotected by any military force within their borders and but little aware of the dangers that awaited them.

At this moment Sherwood, having passed the line of sentries posted at intervals round the encampment, more to guard against being seen and reported to the inhabitants, than any expected attack, approached his sleeping subaltern and tapped him lightly on the shoulder. But the latter not awakening, the other grasped his coat collar and gave him a rough, impatient shake, at which the sleeper, suddenly starting, leaped on his feet, and dashing away the grasping hand of his superior, fiercely exclaimed:

"I'll be d——d if you shall! You have come before your time; be off! be off, I say! Oh! ah!" he continued, rubbing his eyes, and beginning to distinguish between the reality and the image that appeared to have been haunting his dreaming fancy: "Why, captain, it is only you, after all, is it? Well, well, now!"

"Why, who did you suppose it was, Darrow, I should like to know?"

"Oh, no matter, now—I was in the middle of a cursed dream, and thought a different character had waited on me to do a little business in his line—though not so very different, perhaps. But let the humbug go —what is the news?"

"Everything that is bad," replied Sherwood morosely. "The very devil himself, I would not have believed, could baffle me so much in my plans as I have been since I saw you."

"Why, what now, captain? You seem rather out of humor—what has happened?"

"In the first place the old man is dead. He died the day before I arrived."

"Well, what of that? He did not carry off his money with him, did he?"

"No, but he got penitent before he went off, and wrote out a confession of that old affair, in a letter to Hendee."

"And you let it reach him, hey?"

"Not so big a fool as you think. I gave it to the flames, before it was read by anyone but myself, I think."

"Very well, where are your great troubles, then?"

"Why—why——" replied Sherwood, hesitating to inform the other, as he was about to do, the particulars about the will and the extent of his fears respecting the disposition of the property, lest the minion might consider it for his interest to betray him to the Hendees: "why, I did not think to name it," continued the artful dissembler, deciding the question he had been debating in his mind in the negative, "but, upon the whole, as you already know so much about the affair, I think I will. Well, getting home last night, I thought I would go down to Hendee's this morning; so I went, and soon found the devil to pay. That sneaking tinker had been there and confessed all and the girl fairly spurned me from her presence; while her father—curse the old dotard! he, though owing me for half his living for years, had the audacity to insult me—yes, insult me, Bill. But——" and he nodded significantly.

"But what?"

"I can help myself, Darrow."

"Well, I would do it, Jake, without any more puttering with the proud minx."

"I will. My plans are fixed. When did you return from headquarters?"

"Not two hours ago—I left them early this morning."

"What is the news?"

"The whole army have moved on to the mouth of the Boquet where they are now encamped. A large body of Indians joined them yesterday, and General Burgoyne distributed presents among them, made a speech to fix them for fight, and wound off by giving them a grand war-feast. Hell and thunder! what whooping and yelling there was there last night! one would have thought that all Tophet had been emptied upon the earth, and that the world was alive with devils!"

"Good! just the instruments for our purpose in punishing the doubly damned rebels of this settlement. But did not the general send me any direction?"

"Yes," replied Darrow, taking a letter from his pocket, "he sent you this, and also," he continued, stepping within the shanty and bringing out a thick package of papers, "and also this bundle of proclamations, to be immediately distributed over the settlement."

"Well, let us first see what the general has written me," said Sherwood breaking the superb seal, and reading the contents of the letter, a very fair specimen of the official fustian of its doughty author, who, it may be recollected, was a fop in literature as well as a braggart in arms. The communication ran thus:

"J. SHERWOOD, ESQ., *Captain of His Majesty's Loyal Americans in the New Hampshire Grants:*

"It is one of the felicities of soldiership, and of the gratifications of a commander, to award the meed of approbation to fidelity in a common cause, and fealty to a common sovereign. This meed, sir, I deem it no flattery to say is yours, speaking, as I do, from personal acquaintance, and on the voucher of Colonel Beverly Robinson, a Loyal American officer, of worth, and zeal, and activity.

"The army under my command will now in a day or two move southwardly, mainly by water, but partly by land on either side of the lake. To you, sir, and the brave and loyal men whom you have, and may yet further induce to act with you, we look for a hearty co-operation in all that can be effected on the eastern shore, and, by the blessings of God, I will effect much, while we proceed to the investiture, and consequent capture of Crown Point, Ticonderoga, and all other opposing obstacles, on our victorious march to Albany. I send you by the bearer, Lieutenant William Darrow, a package of proclamations, issued by me, and signed by the same, and countersigned by Robert Kingston, Esquire, Secretary. They are addresses to the deluded and suffering people of your settlement. I anticipate great and universal effect from this appeal, made irresistible, as it is, by offers of royal mercy to the penitent, arguments of ineffable potency to the deceived by rebel sophistry and falsehood, and by the palpable shadowing forth of the sword of justice, in the contingent action of our red allies, to the perverse and stubborn. You will cause one of these, my proclamations, to be immediately left at every cottage and hamlet, if possible, in the settlement—to the protestations of which proclamation, together with such pecuniary inducements as you may deem it expedient to offer toward redeeming the land from the disgrace and ruinous anarchy of an unnatural rebellion and restoring a government of laws, of honor, of legitimate and happy sovereignty, you will add your own attestations.

"With sentiments, believe me,

"My very dear sir, of esteem,

"J. BURGOYNE."

"There! what think you of that, Bill?" exultingly exclaimed Sherwood, as he concluded the perusal of the precious document. "Is not that a handsome thing for a man who stands so high at the British court to say to and of us?"

"Why, yes, captain, what he means is well enough, I spose; but if a British general had not writ it, I should have called some of it nothing but d—— flumididdle."

"Oh, it is a feather in our caps, Darrow; depend on't. Burgoyne is hand and glove with the king and ministers, besides being a noted warrior. He will conquer all the northern colonies. The rebellion, indeed, is as good as crushed already. And then the country will be divided off into lordships, and those who have been most active in subduing the rebels will all receive rich rewards out of their confiscated estates. Bright days are before us, Bill. And while we are thus making our fortunes, what a glorious chance to pay off old scores upon these rascally settlers? You can safely act out nature now, Bill, with a vengeance. We will have our revenge, and the beauty of it is that others must father our deeds and pay us well into the bargain for what it is only a happiness to perform."

"What are your plans, captain?"

"You or I must go this very night over to the British camp and get Burgoyne to let us have fifty redskins to make up our company. We shall want them soon, and perhaps I may, for the first purpose."

"D—— it, Jake, you are *too* thirsty," said the minion, looking keenly at the other, and comprehending the purpose of which he spoke: "they are your own flesh and blood. You don't mean to let those red devils loose upon them, do you?"

"No; but leave me to take care of them. They need not be harmed, but prisoners they shall be till that haughty jade's pride is brought to begging terms. And this is the first case, Darrow, to be attended to."

"I am not quite sure but there is another case for you to attend to, also Jake."

"What is that?" asked Sherwood, turning to the other, with a look of blended curiosity and apprehension.

"Why, perhaps it is all nothing but a notion, after all. But I will tell you the wrinkle that's got into my head, and how it got there. In coming from headquarters to-day I ran my canoe generally close in to the shore of the other side of the lake, and, on arriving within about a mile of Crown Point, and about as far as I intended, before crossing over to this side, I took it into my head I would go up into the woods, climb a tree, and try to get a peep into the fort, as the general asked me very particularly about the number of the garrison there. Well, I went on a piece into the woods, when I heard the steps of someone crossing my course ahead and taking his way to the fort; so I squatted down in an old tree top, where I could remain unseen till he passed by. His course brought him within a few rods of the spot where I lay; and when nearly abreast of me, he mounted an old log, and, without discovering me, took a sort of leisurely survey of the woods around him, turning his face so as to give me a fair view of his countenance—and——"

"Well, what more about it—who and what was he?"

"Why, though not in full uniform, I think he must be a young rebel officer, who had been out with his gun for game. Though he must have arrived at the fort quite lately."

"But who do you mistrust him to be?" asked Sherwood, with evident uneasiness.

"That is the question that has been bothering my brains ever since. Jake, don't you think it possible for a man to wear about the same face and look that he did when a boy, so that one who had never seen him from four or five years old, would know him again when grown up?"

"Yes, barely possible; but what the devil are you coming to, Bill? What has that to do with this case?" demanded Sherwood with an agitation which he was unable to conceal.

"Maybe a good deal. There was something in this fellow's looks that struck me—that made me ready to swear I had seen the same countenance before, though somehow, not just the same neither. Well, he finally went on, and I, forgetting all about spying into the fort, went back, and struck off for this side, this fellow's countenance all the while haunting me, and working up a devilish strange, streaked kind of feeling, that I can't very well describe. Well, as I was crossing over, still bothering on the subject, I happened to cast my eyes up the lake, when I caught a glimpse of old Hendee's house through the trees; and by Heavens! it came across my mind, like a flash of lightning, who the fellow must be."

"What mean you, Darrow?" exclaimed Sherwood, seizing the arm of the other with a convulsive grasp, while his face became as pale as ashes.

"I mean," replied Darrow, looking his agitated companion full in the face, and speaking in a low, measured, and decisive tone, "I mean, Jake Sherwood, that if Captain Hendee's boy lived, he is now among us!"

Long and earnestly communed these worthies in conjectures about the person concerning whom Darrow had made, as he felt confident he had, so startling a discovery. Who could he be? By what name now known? Could he be aware of his own family history? Had he discovered his relations? were questions which were raised by them, but without finding any satisfactory answers. The two last questions, however, were at length settled in the negative. And, after some further discussion in regard to the best means of ascertaining more about the private history of the unconscious object of their deliberations, and the most feasible way of disposing of him, if the information gained rendered it probable he was the person they feared him to be, they broke up their conference, Darrow retiring to rest, and Sherwood, with two of his men as attendants and oarsmen, setting off for headquarters, fifteen or twenty miles distant from the Tory encampment.

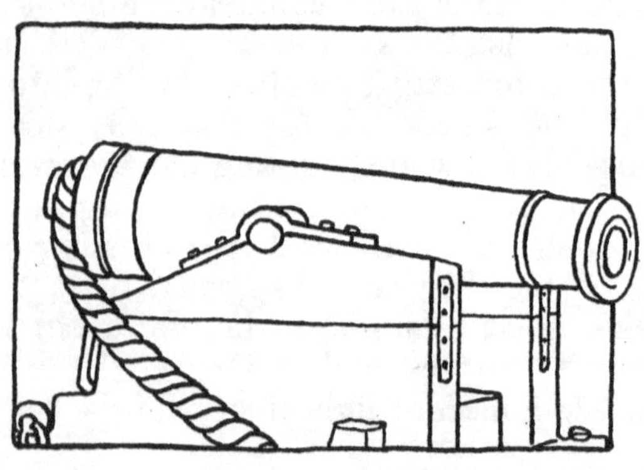

CHAPTER XXIV

"Sounds from the waters, sounds upon the earth,
Sounds in the air, of battle! Yet with these
A voice is mingling, whose deep tones give birth
To faith and courage."

The storm of war which had been gathering for some weeks in the north, almost unnoticed by the Americans, now began to roll down upon their frontier settlements with a rapidity as alarming as it was unexpected. Although the leaders of the Continental army were aware of the landing of a large British force at Quebec in the month of May, from which an invasion was expected, either by way of Oswego, as had previously been given out, or through the valley of Lake Champlain, yet, counting on the same dilatory action by which all the movements of the enemy had been characterized ever since the battle of Bunker Hill, they supposed it might be late in the summer before the hostile army, should they take the eastern route, would reach the military posts on Champlain. But whatever might have been the errors of other British commanders in the respect just named, none of that kind certainly could be chargeable on General Burgoyne. The navigable waters of the north had scarcely burst their wintry fetters before he landed at Montreal. And in another week he was pouring the disciplined bands of his proud and numerous army along the western shores of Lake Champlain. The American generals were, in a great measure, taken by surprise by this rapid advance of the enemy, and having delayed to strengthen their defenses, they were but illy prepared to meet the first shock of so powerful a force. And if those whose duty it was to make themselves early acquainted with the enemy's movements had thus been kept in the dark respecting the important one in question, still less, as may well be supposed, were the inhabitants of the country apprised of the time and extent of the coming invasion. The settlers of the New Hampshire Grants, who were directly in the route of the enemy, were consequently almost wholly ignorant of the dangers that awaited them till the storm was nearly ready to burst on their defenseless heads. And their surprise, therefore, was only equaled by their dismay, when the American scouts, who had been dispatched to gain intelligence of the reported invasion, returned and spread the startling news that a British army of ten thousand regulars, with several thousand savage foes, was within a few miles of their borders, ready to spread death and devastation over their whole settlement. This information, which many still hoped might be false or greatly exaggerated, was fully confirmed the next morning after it was received by the scouts, by Burgoyne's proclamations, which, through the activity of Sherwood's band of Tories, had been left during the night at the door of every house through all the northern section of the country. This pompous and gasconading document, however, with all its promises and threats, had, notwithstanding its author's anticipations, no other effect on the inhabitants than to bring them to the determination of driving off their stock so far into the interior as to be out of the reach of the enemy, and of commencing active preparations for fleeing themselves before the invading army.

With these general observations on the situation of affairs at this particular juncture, we will now return to the Hendee family, to follow their fortunes through the fearful trials which were now shortly to await them.

It was not till night, after the signal failure of Sherwood at their cottage, that Miss Hendee had an opportunity of ascertaining what had passed between that personage and her father in their recent interview. That evening Captain Hendee, on his return from the labors of the day, entered the room where Alma happened at the moment to be sitting alone, and silently took a seat at the open window. A frown was upon his brow. The uneasiness which a man of high spirit may be expected to feel from a sense of obligations to one he secretly despises, combined, in the present instance, with the mean advantage taken by such obligations by Sherwood, had all the afternoon been operating upon the old gentleman's irritable temperament; and he was now evidently in no very pleasant frame of mind. At the first glance his daughter detected in his countenance the unfailing indications of a storm; but on whom it was to burst she was unable to determine. From the circumstances attending the interview between Sherwood and her father, she felt satisfied that she herself had been the subject of their discourse; and although extremely anxious to know the result of that conference, yet she almost feared the knowledge she wished to obtain. And with trembling solicitude, therefore, she awaited in silence the announcement which she saw from her father's mood would not long be withheld. After sitting some minutes puffing away rapidly at his pipe, and knitting his brows with an angry, flashing expression of countenance, he suddenly drew the implement from his mouth, and by way of knocking out the ashes, gave it so spiteful a rap on the window-sill as to shiver it to pieces in his hand. Hastily dashing the broken fragments out of the window, he turned abruptly to his daughter, and said:

"Alma, what did Jake Sherwood say to you to-day?"

"Why, many things, father. Would you wish me to repeat all he said?"

"Yes. I don't hold to prying into such matters, for a general rule, but I have particular reasons for wishing to know now."

Still feeling uncertain on whom the resentment of her father was about to fall, Alma, with some agitation, proceeded to detail the conversation in question, giving the words used by Sherwood and the substance of her own replies.

"Threats to you, too, hey?" said the captain, after listening attentively to his daughter's relation of the affair. "Why didn't you drive the pitiful puppy from the house with your broomstick?"

"You astonish me, father!" replied Alma, looking up into the face of the other with an expression of joyful surprise.

The old gentleman made no reply, but again relapsing into moody silence, sat some time without uttering a word. At length he brought his foot to the floor with an angry, decisive stamp—and while the tears which were brought to his eyes by his keenly conflicting emotions were glimmering on the quickly moving lashes, he again turned suddenly to his expecting daughter and asked:

"Alma, are you willing to become a slave?"

"For my own and your support, I could cheerfully become one, dear father. But a slave to a villain I can never be."

"Nobly said! spoken with the spirit of a Hendee! Would to God I was more worthy of such a daughter!" exclaimed the passionate old man, choking with emotion. "Come here, Alma, I have been wrong and you have been right,—come, come to me, my child, forgive and kiss me."

In another instant the father and daughter were locked in each other's arms, intermingling their tears, and giving themselves up to the gush of feelings which was overflowing their hearts at this return of mutual love and confidence to their long-estranged and distrusting bosoms.

"I did not make any reply to you, Alma, when you laid open to me the conduct of that base and intriguing villain," at length observed the captain, releasing his daughter from his embrace, and regaining his composure, though the other continued weeping. "But it was not because I doubted the truth of what you told me, or because I had it in my heart to try to restrain you any further. It was because I felt self-condemned, guilty—guilty for what I had already done in making war upon the happiness, and I know not but upon the health, of my own, and only child. Oh, don't weep so—don't, my dear daughter! Thank God, we have both now cut the ties by which we were held in bondage, and are free. The Sherwoods may have all; and we won't trouble them neither to drive us off: we will leave this place, Alma, for the southern part of the settlement. As old and infirm as I am, I can still work. Our faithful Neshobee will also stick by us, and work as much as an Indian will ever work, for you know the Indians are a lazy race, and we must make allowance for him. But at all events, as poorly as we may fare, our poverty will be happiness compared to the slavery that Jake Sherwood would now impose on us if we remained. Yes, Alma, we will go—that is, if you are willing. What say you, my daughter, are you ready to relinquish this pleasant home, and go with me, penniless, indeed, but with the proud and happy consciousness that we are free?"

"Oh, yes, yes, indeed, my dear father," eagerly replied the other, with a look of joy and gratitude that beamed brightly through her still fast-falling tears; "and never could an eastern slave leave his gilded fetters behind him with more pleasure than I shall quit this place. Yes, yes; and, believe me, my father, however hard my lot—however menial I had known would be my employment for support, I have not seen an hour for the last two long and joyless years but my heart would have leaped to hear you make such a proposal. And if such then were my feelings, judge what must now be my pleasure to hear your announcement."

The conversation was here interrupted by a light rap on the door, and while the captain and his daughter were pausing for a repetition of the sound, uncertain whether it proceeded from someone wishing for admittance, the door was partly opened by a man without, and the queer visage of our old friend Pete Jones was protruded with a comical, inquiring look into the room.

"How are ye?" he said, after glancing from father to daughter a moment, with a half-sheepish, half-roguish expression, indicating his consciousness of having on a former occasion played a little upon the credulity of the old gentleman, of which he felt slightly ashamed, though still inwardly tickled at the recollection of the trick: "how are ye, captain? Sarvant, marm!"

"It is Mr. Jones of the army, father, the person who gave me the news I imparted to you respecting the expected invasion," observed Miss Hendee, noticing that her father did not recognize the scout.

"Ah! the tall gentleman that called here once—I recollect. Did you try my remedy?—but no matter, now—walk in, walk in, sir," said the captain.

"Why, no, tankee," replied Jones, leaning his long body on his arm, and swaying it to and fro by the play of the door on its hinges, as he grasped the handle, "I guess I'm rather too much in a hurry about these times."

"You called on some errand, then?—to give us some news, perhaps?" rejoined the captain expectingly.

"Why, yes—that is, if you would like to hear it—that is, if you han't heard it already."

"Speak on, sir."

"Well, I thought I'd just pop in my countenance, as I came along back, to see, that in case the devil was at your heels, whether you would like to know it?"

"You speak in riddles. How shall I understand you, sir?"

"Well, I an't particular, how."

"You said the devil?"

"Yes, and his name is legion. Why, to be plain about it, captain, a British army of ten thousand, with as many redskins as one would wish to see, will most likely be here before to-morrow night."

"You astonish me, sir! Has any news of this reached the other settlers in this quarter?"

"I have just sent a brother scout up the road here, to tell them they may as well be driving off their cattle, and jogging along south themselves in the course of to-morrow. I just come from the fort over here, and they've pretty much concluded to pack up there, and be off for Old Ti to-night; so the redcoats and Indians will have full play along the shores till they get to Ti, where there will be something of a brush likely."

"You would advise us women and cripples, then, to beat a retreat, would you?"

"Why, yes, that's rather my notion, considering. Though Burgoyne says—haven't you seen his proclamation?"

"No."

"Well, you will soon, I guess. The Tories have scattered 'em as thick as bumblebees along north of here. Burgoyne says, as nigh as I can English the high-flown concern, stay at home, sell him your cattle, and he will protect you. But if you budge an inch, he will let loose the redskins to act at their pleasure upon you.

And what that will be, you know as well as any man, they say, captain."

"Yes, I know enough of their tender mercies. And I know also that Burgoyne, whatever he may promise, can no more restrain the hell-hounds after he has once let them from their slips than he can crupper the whirlwinds. Montcalm tried that experiment, on that dreadful day of blood and horror, at Fort William Henry—at least, I think he tried to avert the catastrophe: for Montcalm, though an enemy that troubled us much, was yet a brave man; and as a general rule, my friend, you will never find a truly brave man either cruel or treacherous. The great sin is in employing the Indians. And this circumstance will do much, in the present case, to hasten the destruction of Burgoyne. Even the dead, almost, will rise up to bear arms against him. All New England in a week will be in motion. In another week, as he passes along up the lake, they will be hanging like an angry thunder cloud on his flank. And, mark my word, sir, this general will find, before he reaches Albany, that neither his numbers nor his proclamations will save him."

"The Lord grant you may prove a true prophet, and I think, upon the whole, you will. Howsomever, captain, it will be considerable of a chore to bring it all to pass. And while we are fixing for it, I rather guess you, along the northern parts here, may as well make yourselves scarce a little."

"We intend it, sir. Indeed, as regards my family, we had already determined on a removal soon. And now we shall follow your advice immediately, with many thanks to you for calling. Let me see—our first move shall be for Rutland, where we can probably safely remain a few days, to conclude on a place for a more permanent residence."

"Will you, sir," said Miss Hendee, with a slight blush, as she perceived the scout was about to depart, "will you apprise our friends in the army of the destination we think of taking?"

"Will you take this, sir, to the person to whom it is addressed?" said Miss Reed, who, during the latter part of the conversation, had been nimbly plying her fingers over the blank leaf of a little volume which she had been reading in an adjoining apartment, when the scout's voice and anticipated errand brought her into the room. "You see, Alma, I am not afraid to write to my beau; now I will leave it to the captain to say, who is the bravest?" she added, turning to the latter with an expression in which roguish defiance and fear of disapprobation were queerly blended.

"Ah, girls!" said the captain in reply, after a moment's hesitation, which seemed to end in a conclusion to treat the matter good-naturedly, "you may be setting your caps for men that will be swinging on the gallows in three months: for you know, in attempted revolutions, men are only patriots and heroes when they succeed, and are but rebels and traitors when they don't."

"We prefer, however," replied Alma, with spirit, "to set our caps for men who *may* be hung on that principle, rather than for those who *should* be hung on every other."

"Is not there a law, Captain Hendee," asked Jessy archly, "that a man may be pardoned on the gallows, if a lady can be found who will step up and marry him on the spot?"

"Why, I have heard such stories," replied the captain, laughing, "but supposing there was such a provision, in this country, you little quiz?"

"Why, in that case," replied Jessy, casting a roguish look at Alma, "I think there are certain officers in our army who need not be under any great apprehensions of being hung at present."

"Now, that is what I call grit," observed Jones, who had been looking on the two beautiful and spirited creatures before him, with an admiration equaled only by his surprise. "The colonel and captain know considerable well what they have been about, after all, I see. Well, I must be jogging, I guess, captain, so goodnighty. And you, gals, may the Lord bless ye, and keep you steadfast in your resolution! If I had a hogshead of blood, it should all be shed for ye, and the like of ye. Trol, lol, lol, lol de larly!"

During that night and the following day all was bustle and commotion throughout the northern part of the settlement. "To arms! to arms!" resounded in every direction. And nearly all the able-bodied men, promptly responding to the call of General Schuyler, whose expresses were seen furiously dashing along the roads to rally the hitherto slumbering settlement, seized their rifles or muskets and hastened off to join their countrymen in arms, leaving the old men, invalids, and boys, to take charge of their families, in removing from the scene of danger. The stock was collected in droves, marked with the initials of the owner's name, and started off for the south; while the inhabitants, taking with them all the articles of value which their respective modes of traveling would permit, collected in small companies and soon followed. The party whose destinies more immediately concern our story, consisting of Captain Hendee, Neshobee, the two young ladies and their respective female domestics, in the course of the day bade adieu to their pleasant cottage and mingled in the general flight, which by nightfall, brought them in safety to the house of a hospitable friend nearly twenty miles distant from the home, to which, as they supposed, they were never more to return.

CHAPTER XXV

> "Not all so much for love
> As for another secret, close intent,
> By marrying her, which I must reach unto,
> But yet I run before my horse to market;
> Clarence still breathes: Edward still lives, and,
> When these are gone, then must I count my gains."

Several unforeseen circumstances connected with the removal of their effects, together with the impression that they were now so far south as to be in no very immediate danger from any incursions of the enemy, having induced our party to accept the invitation of their kind entertainer to remain a few days at his abode, nearly a week had unfortunately been suffered to elapse without resuming their journey. Aroused, however, at length by the news that Burgoyne had reached Ticonderoga, and closely invested the fortress, while a party of Tories and Indians were ravaging the country to the north of them, both the families of Captain Hendee and his host determined on an instant departure for a place of more safety. Accordingly, with a few hasty preparations, they started in their respective carriages about the middle of the afternoon for Castleton, which they were under the expectation of being enabled to reach by daylight. The day being excessively sultry, Captain Hendee, after traveling a while at rather a brisk pace, checked his horses and suffered them to fall into a moderate walk, during which the other party, who were in advance, and who seemed less disposed to slacken their speed, passed entirely out of sight, and soon became widely separated from their more tardy fellow-travelers. When our party had proceeded several miles in this leisurely manner, and while the captain, to use a quaint and somewhat curious expression of the poet Parnell, was "deceiving the road" by the relation of one of his old war stories, they were met by a stout built, though an ordinary looking, and slovenly dressed man on horseback, who, after closely scrutinizing the company a moment, stopped his horse, indicating at the same time, by his looks and gestures, a wish that the others should stop also. Supposing the stranger was desirous of making some inquiries, Captain Hendee instantly pulled up his horses, and sat waiting, with an air of expectation, for the man to proceed with what he might have to propose.

"I was thinking what your name mought be, mister," at length began the horseman, with a bold, saucy air. "It kinder seems to me I have seen you somewhere or other."

"Very possibly, sir," replied the captain, in a manner sufficiently cool and repulsive, as he thought, to check the intrusive familiarity of the other.

"Well, I knowed I had," rejoined the stranger, not at all abashed by the coolness with which his advances had been met, "and yet I don't know as I can quite call you by name."

"My name is Hendee, sir."

"Ah! oh, yes; you live down there against Crown Point?"

"Yes; or at least we did till within a few days. But how happens it that you are going to a part which, at this time, the settlers are so generally deserting?"

"Why, an't it safe traveling that way?"

"It would be for some, doubtless," replied the captain significantly.

"Well, I spose you've hearn of me," observed the stranger, evidently disconcerted at the suspicions which he perceived were beginning to be entertained of him, "my name is David Remington. You are acquainted in Castleton, an't you?"

"Yes, with several individuals in that town."

"Well, that's where I live, when I'm to home. Do you know Mr. Woodward there?"

"I do, sir."

"I want to know? Well, now, he is one of my near neighbors. Here's a paper he gin me t'other day. Jest read it, will ye?"

Captain Hendee, with an air of curiosity, not unmingled, however, with surprise, at an offer so gratuitously made to an entire stranger, took the paper, which the other now extended to him, and read as follows:

"This may certify that David Remington, the bearer hereof, is thought to be a true friend to the States of America.

"Joseph Woodward, Com. of Safety.*

"Castleton, June 2, 1777."

"This appears to be genuine, and should be sufficient," remarked the captain musingly, as he handed back the paper. "Have they received any news at Castleton within a day or two, sir?" he added, with more

* A literal copy of the original certificate, lodged in the public archives of Vermont, and accompanied by another from the noted Tory, Colonel Philip Skene, certifying that Remington had taken the oath of allegiance, and was a true Royalist. These papers, together with a receipt signed by "J. Sherwood, Captain;" for two heifers procured for the British, by Remington, all dated about the same time, are supposed to have been found on the person of this or other Tories, when subsequently slain or taken prisoners.

freedom of manner than he had before exhibited toward the other.

"News?—from where?"

"From our forces at Ticonderoga, I mean, of course."

"Oh, yes, I spose so—why, I came from there myself, last night."

"Indeed, sir? Well, what is the prospect of St. Clair's being able to cope with the enemy, so as to put a stop to their progress at that place?"

"Cope! hum. He will be lucky if he don't get coped himself, I guess."

"What, sir? The garrison are in no danger of being taken themselves, surely?"

"Well, sir, I don't pretend tō know nothing about it; but I shouldn't be surprised if the folks about here heard news, within twenty-four hours, that made 'em stare."

"Impossible? But what is the situation of affairs there, that leads you to this conclusion?"

"Why, sir, the situation is that General Red Hazle,* with his Jarman brigade, has got possession on this side of the lake, up as far as East Creek, where he is now posted; while General Burgoyne has entirely inclosed the fort on the t'other side. And what is still more, he has cut out a road, and drawn up a whole slew of cannon clean to the top of Mount Defiance, which he will have all mounted, and ready to pour hell and thunder down on 'em in the fort before they dream of it."

"Is it possible that St. Clair can have suffered Burgoyne to get possession of that commanding spot for such a purpose!" exclaimed the captain. "I knew," he continued, "that most of our officers in the old war used

* From original papers, still preserved, written by those whose spelling was evidently guided solely by the common pronunciation of words, it appears that General Reidesel went, to a considerable extent at least, by the name of *Red Hazle*.

to consider that mountain inaccessible with artillery. I, however, always thought differently, and agreed, in this respect, with Major Putnam, who, I well remember, suggested the project of getting cannon up this eminence to General Howe, as our army was approaching the fort the day previous to the battle which cost poor Howe his life. And had that gallant young nobleman, who was the only lord of common sense whom the British ever sent to America, been spared, the thing would have been done, and we should have taken the fortress, instead of drawing off our army without effecting anything. But, as I said, is it possible that St. Clair can have permitted this in an army approaching from the north, and wholly unacquainted with the surrounding localities?"

"It is true, anyhow; and if they don't find themselves in a pickle, there in the fort, by to-morrow morning, I lose my guess," replied the other, with a satisfaction which he was unable wholly to conceal.

After a few apparently careless inquiries respecting the destination of our travelers, and their expectation of reaching it, Remington seemed suddenly to become convinced that it would not be prudent to proceed any further in the landlooking excursion, which he stated was his business to the north, and announced his intention of immediately returning. Accordingly, wheeling round his horse and bidding the company good-day, with the remark that he should probably ride rather faster than their team would travel, he rode off at a moderate trot, till the intervening bushes at the first turn of the road screened him, as he supposed, from the sight of those he had just left, when he applied his whip, and dashed forward at full speed.

"What opinion did you form of that man, father?" asked Miss Hendee, after they had ridden some distance in silence.

"Why, but for the certificate of so true and vigilant

a friend to the cause as Woodward, who undoubtedly signed it, I should certainly have had strong suspicions that the fellow was some designing Tory," answered the captain indirectly, and with the tone of one still doubting over evidence which he could not reject, nor yet receive as wholly conclusive.

"I know not," rejoined the other, "that I can give any good reasons for my impressions; but there was a certain something about the man, which, from the first, struck me unfavorably. And is it not possible, that he may be secretly in the interest of the enemy, notwithstanding his certificate, which, without being asked, he was so ready to show?"

"I noticed his readiness to show the paper," again replied the captain, without any direct answer to his daughter's question. "And it also occurred to me that he appeared to be far better acquainted with the movements of the British than with those of our own army."

"And did not you think, Captain Hendee," observed Miss Reed, "that he betrayed a secret pleasure when relating the perilous situation in which he stated the American forces to be placed?"

"I don't know that I noticed that in particular," said the captain; "but if he be a Tory, and has told us the truth, I fear he has too much reason to rejoice. I cannot, however, think that St. Clair would fail to keep open a way for retreat, so that the garrison shall not be taken in any event."

"Here, Neshobee," said Alma, as the Indian, who had traveled mostly on foot, keeping generally a few rods in advance of the horses, now fell back to the side of the carriage; "you have sometimes shown yourself a shrewd guesser; and we will have your opinion in this case. What did you think of the man father was talking with just now?"

"Me guess him have two tongue—mean something no good," replied the native, in his usual quiet manner.

"Him no think me see him through the bush, when him ride away slow—then look back for find out we see him, then whip—off a gallop!"

"So much the better," remarked Jessy, "for the faster he goes, the further he will get from us."

"Neshobee, perhaps, would draw a different inference," said the captain.

"Why should he, father?" asked Alma.

But the other, not willing to alarm the ladies by naming his secret apprehensions, which, after all, might prove groundless, made only some evasive or indifferent reply, and became silent.

"He can have no immediate communication with the Tories and Indians, by going in that direction," resumed Alma. "They, if we are rightly informed, are still far behind us."

"They *were* behind us," observed Captain Hendee, relapsing into silence, in which his example was soon imitated by the rest of the company all of whom seemed oppressed by that undefined sense of impending danger which is sometimes felt without the inclination—on account of conscious inability, perhaps—of communicating it to others.

It was now drawing toward sunset; and our party had yet nearly ten miles to travel before reaching their proposed destination for the night. They had been, for some miles, passing through a dark, continuous forest, whose unvaried gloom soon began to be increased by the shades which, before the usual hour, were slowly stealing over the wilderness in consequence of the broad and deepening masses of vapor now gathering along the western horizon. And presently the low, deep rumbling of distant thunder, heralding an approaching shower, reached the ears of the company, and increased their anxiety to gain some opening, at least, before storm and darkness, to say nothing of their secret apprehensions of more terrible foes, should overtake them. Casting an uneasy glance at the lurid and threatening aspect of the heavens, Captain Hendee applied the whip, and was urging on his horses to renewed efforts of speed, when his arm was suddenly seized by the convulsive grasp of his daughter:

"Stop! stop! father!" she exclaimed, in a low, hurried tone, "look at Neshobee! There is danger near us!"

All eyes were at once directed toward the Indian, who was now about a dozen rods in front of the carriage. He had turned round, and with quick and eager gestures was motioning them to halt. Instantly reining up the horses, and bringing them to a stand, the captain, with the rest of the company, continued, with intense interest and alarm, silently to watch the motions of the native, who seemed to be still in considerable doubt, either of the nature of the apprehended danger or of the exact point from which it was to proceed. After standing a short time, however, in the attitude of listening, slowly turning his head, as his eyes were keenly searching the woods around him, he hastily started back, and, pointing to a dark thicket nearly abreast of the carriage, leaped nimbly behind a tree and seemed awaiting some expected result. The next moment the shrill, quavering sounds of the terrific war-whoop, issuing from the coverts in every direction, announced to the appalled travelers the fearful character of the foe by which they were surrounded. And in another instant a score of painted savages leaped from the bushes and, menacingly brandishing their tomahawks aloft, closely invested the carriage. Knowing it would be utterly useless to attempt any resistance, the old veteran put up the pistols, which he had drawn out on the first alarm, and, while the shuddering females, with a terrified glance at the frightful group around them, were burying their faces in their hands, very coolly proceeded by signs and such phrases as he supposed might be understood to signify to his assailants that he yielded himself and family as prisoners.

The captors, having ordered out their prisoners into the road, immediately fell to work with their knives, in cutting the harness from the horses, each of which, when released, was mounted by one of the enemy and ridden off into the woods, while the carriage was run into the nearest thicket and concealed. The prisoners, including Neshobee, who, in attempting to escape, had been seized and brought in, were then placed in Indian file, alternately with a sufficient number of their captors to guard the whole, and marched out of the road the same way in which their horses had been previously taken, which soon brought the company into an old, overgrown path leading through the forest in a westerly direction. In this manner our party were urged forward at a rapid pace for nearly an hour, during which not a word was uttered by either captors or captured, with the exception of Captain Hendee, whose irritable temper occasionally broke out in a half-suppressed anathema as he jarred a rheumatic limb while hobbling along the rough and frequently obstructed path. At length, to the great and unexpected joy of the wearied captives, the cheering light of an opening broke upon their view, affording hope that the fatigues under which they were nearly ready to sink were now to be terminated for the night; and that they were to be favored with quarters in some kind of a house, instead of an unsheltered bed of earth in the wilderness, as they had anticipated. The opening, consisting of thirty or forty acres of land, and containing two small log tenements, with a barn of similar construction attached to one of them, was situated along the margin of a picturesque pond, embedded in a forest of majestic pines. On entering the clearing, Captain Hendee instantly perceived from appearances about the cabins that they had reached the headquarters of the gang, who, as he rightly concluded, had taken possession of the place since its desertion by the inhabitants. His horses, that had arrived before him, had been turned out and were now quietly grazing in the field; while a large number of the enemy, nearly equaling that of the party who had been engaged in the capture, were scattered about the place, some bathing in the pond, some fishing, some pitching quoits, and others lounging about the buildings. As he approached this portion of the enemy, the captain soon noticed a difference in the appearance of many of them, as contrasted with that of such of his captors as had come under his inspection, which, with his acquaintance with the peculiar motions and demeanor of the natives, immediately led him to suspect that a considerable part of the band, though painted and habited like Indians, were white men in disguise. And he now readily understood that he was indebted for his present misfortune to the traitor Remington, who, being secretly connected with this band of Indians and Tories, had doubtless been employed by them to bring intelligence of the approach of such families as should be passing along the road; though why his own family should have been thus particularly marked for capture, while others were suffered to escape, it did not at that time occur to him.

When our party, with their captors, arrived at the first cabin, which they reached about dark, they were halted at the door, while a consultation was held at some distance aloof between two or three, who appeared to have the control of the band; after which, one of them came forward, and, having first caused Neshobee to be taken to the barn, motioned to the rest of the prisoners, except Miss Hendee, who stood in the rear, to enter the house. Perceiving it was intended to separate her from her friends, the alarmed maiden suddenly darted by her immediate keepers, and attempted to reach the door at which her father at that moment was entering. A rough hand, however, was instantly extended, and grasping her arm, rudely pulled her back.

"Kill me, if you will," she exclaimed, "kill me, but let me die with my friends."

"Prisoners can't always be choosers, my proud one," said the apparent savage in good English.

"It is Darrow!" said Alma, with blanching features, and with a look of alarm, which the brandished tomahawk of the Indian had failed to call forth. "I see it all, and know the design. Death I fear not; but such a fate! Oh! as you value the innocence and eternal peace of your daughter, protect me, my father."

Comprehending the meaning of his daughter, and appreciating all her apprehensions, even before she had done speaking, the maddened father hastily drew a pistol from his pocket, and discharged it full at the head of Darrow. The bullet grazed the temple of the astonished ruffian, and his locks were slightly singed by the burning powder; but he escaped with no other injury. Recovering from the shock of the explosion, he hurriedly pulled out one of the heavy pistols which hung in his belt, raised it to the breast of his unflinching opponent, and, with the look of a fiend, was in the act of taking deliberate aim, when the heroic girl who was the innocent cause of the strife suddenly threw herself between her father and the weapon leveled for his destruction. After holding the deadly implement in the same threatening position nearly a minute, as if deliberating whether he would send the bullet through both father and daughter, for the sake of wreaking his vengeance on the former, the balked villain with an angry movement thrust the pistol into its place, and turning to his men, fiercely exclaimed:

"Seize the d——d old dotard! Secure him, and let him wait for my revenge till I have disposed of this silly jade. She will soon find out, I guess, what she has gained by the rumpus," he added, again grasping the arm of his recoiling victim, and, regardless of her shrieks, roughly dragging her off to the other cabin;

while, in obedience to his orders, his painted minions proceeded, with demoniac glee, to bind the old gentleman, and thrust him with the rest of the prisoners into the house. With the assistance of his men, several of whom he ordered to attend him, Darrow soon succeeded in forcing his half senseless victim to the other cabin, situated on the shore of the pond near the western extremity of the clearing; when, opening the door, he gave her a spiteful push which sent her reeling through the entrance, at the same time gruffly exclaiming:

"There, madam! there are your quarters for the present. And let me just inform your ladyship that the less fuss you make about this matter the better it will be for you."

With this he drew the door to and, after posting a guard round the house, returned to the main body of his band, who were now assembled round the first mentioned house, busily engaged in cooking their suppers in the open air, or patching up the leaky roof of the log barn, to protect those from the threatened storm who should be compelled to take quarters in it, in consequence of the arrangement which the leaders had seen fit to make of placing the prisoners in separate houses.

After being left alone, Miss Hendee made an effort to regain her composure. And having succeeded in a good degree, she proceeded, by the dim twilight yet remaining, to examine the interior of the house, containing but a single room on the ground floor. Three or four old chairs, a rough pine table, and a straw bed laid upon a rudely constructed bedstead, with a couple of coarse blankets for covering, constituted all the visible furniture of the cabin. With these observations, she seated herself in a chair, and endeavored to think coolly on the novel and alarming situation in which she now found herself placed. From Sherwood's known connection with Darrow, the apparent leader of the present band, she had but little doubt that the former was in fact the commander of these marauders, or at least the instigator of the seizure of herself and family. And in either case, she was at no loss to understand that the possession of her person was the main, if not the only object, of the present capture. Nor did she doubt, for similar reasons, that Sherwood must be near,—probably already on the ground. And from the circumstance of her being separated from her friends, and confined alone, she felt but too fearfully certain that a fate was in reserve for her on which, at the best she could hope for, she shuddered to think. After she had remained in this situation a while, listening to every movement from without, and starting at the sound of every footstep, lest it prove the herald of a visit from Sherwood, which she now every moment expected would be paid her, and to which she looked forward with a dread that the anticipated presence of no other foe could impart, the door was thrown open, and a man unceremoniously entered. She hastily rose from her seat and threw a look of alarm toward the intruder. A second glance, however, told her that he was not the dreaded visitor, but only one of the disguised Tories come to bring her lights and refreshment. Placing the torch which he bore in the chimney, the man silently advanced, and set a trencher of coarse food on the table; after which he turned and departed, neither questioning nor questioned. Feeling no inclination to taste the food, the hapless girl resumed her seat, and again gave herself up to the distressing thoughts which her situation was so well calculated to inspire. The last gleams of twilight had now faded away, and night had fallen upon the earth with almost Egyptian darkness. There was a low, rushing sound abroad, betokening an approaching conflict of the elements. The attention of Alma being arrested by these renewed indications of the storm, which, for several hours, appeared to have been slowly concentrating its forces in the distance, she arose and went to a narrow window that opened upon the dark waters of the forest-girt pond. The ominous sounds before heard had given place to the more audible murmurs of the troubled air, which in fitful and variant undulations now moaned dismally along the ground, and now piped, in brief and broken strains of melancholy music, among the tops of the neighboring pines. Large, black masses of jagged clouds were hurrying through the heavens, which were occasionally made visible by slight, quivering flashes of the electric fires, partially disclosing the broad outlines of the convolving vapor above, and dimly lighting up the dark landscape of wilds and waters beneath. While the maiden was looking abroad upon this scene of gloomy magnificence, which seemed strangely to harmonize with the kindred gloom of her own sad and desolate bosom, a bright but far-off flash gleamed fiercely athwart her vision. Turning her eyes to the quarter whence it proceeded, she beheld a distinct, attenuated, and ribbon-like flame approaching from a distant part of the horizon, and describing in its apparently slow and crinkling movement, as it came, an arch of fearful splendor across the illuminated heavens. The next instant it fell upon the top of a towering dry pine, standing on the opposite shore of the pond, and hurled the blazing fragments of its giant trunk in every direction over the woods, and far into the hissing and bubbling waters around. A single stunning report followed, and all without was again dark and silent. Recoiling at the shock of the deafening concussion, and almost blinded by the intensity of the flash, the astounded girl turned suddenly from the window and attempted to grope her way back to her seat. Before reaching it, however, a slight noise within the room arrested her steps. Pressing her hand upon her eyes an instant to enable her to discern the objects in the dimly lighted apartment, she sent an apprehensive glance toward the door, when, to her unspeakable dismay, she encountered the basilisk eyes of Sherwood, who was quietly standing within the entrance and looking upon her with an expression in which guilt, effrontery, and triumph were singularly blended.

"Leave me!" she exclaimed, as the other now began to advance toward her; "leave me, sir!" she repeated, with all the firmness and decision of manner she could command, while she gradually retreated to the opposite side of the room.

"Why should I leave you, captious girl?" he responded in his usual and affectedly meek and plausible manner, "why should I leave you, or you desire it, when I am the only friend to whom you or your family can look for intercession with those into whose power you have fallen? Having heard of your misfortune I hastened immediately to the spot and have but this moment arrived."

"Base dissembler!" said Alma, with an indignation which, for the instant seemed to overpower every other feeling, "will you pretend, sir, that these are not all your doings?"

"Why—why, I admit," he replied, considerably disconcerted at the question and pointed manner of the other, which led him to suppose that she had by some means received a much more certain knowledge of his connection with the band than she really had; "I admit that these men belong to a company which I have a commission to command. But I protest; I have had nothing to do with your capture. And why should you always be imputing to me the worst motives for every action I may perform? Here, now, I come to befriend and save you; and you receive me only with insults!"

"I will put the sincerity of your professions to the test, sir," promptly rejoined the other. "If you really came to befriend me and have the power, as you admit, let me go instantly to my father and friends."

"Why, the time has arrived, it strikes me, when I am under no very particular necessity of being further dictated to," sneeringly replied the villain, now throwing off the mask, which he perceived was serving him but little purpose. "I have a certain condition to propose, and when you comply with that, neither you nor your family are longer prisoners."

The heart of the wretched girl sunk within her, but she made no reply.

"You have not forgotten, probably," resumed the other, "our late interview, when I proposed the fulfillment of a long settled engagement. Well, if you have, I have not, nor the manner in which my overtures were then treated. But notwithstanding all the scorn and abuse I have received both from you and your father, I still feel disposed to allow you a chance to fulfill that engagement, which, as a prisoner and in my power, is more than you could reasonably expect. I am still willing to make you my legal wife; but it must be done on the spot. I have a clergyman within call to perform the ceremony. Will you consent?"

"Never!" replied the indignant and yet unconquered girl. "What! consent under such circumstances —under the menaces here held forth and the feelings here exhibited? I would as soon unite myself to a fiend! Consent to such a mockery, intended only to disguise violence and outrage, under the sacred rite of marriage? Never! While death can be my alternative, oh, never!"

"But supposing death cannot be your alternative, you foolish girl?" said the miscreant suitor in a taunting tone. "You will do well, perhaps, to bear in mind that your person is already in my power; and that I am the one to name your alternative. And I shall name one, too, in which I shall be likely to dispense with the services of the parson."

"Monster!" exclaimed the aroused maiden with an energy which insulted virtue alone could have excited, "begone with your polluting presence, lest the thunders of heaven, which are now angrily rolling over our heads, strike you to the earth in vengeance for your meditated villainies!"

With all the innate baseness and disguised effrontery of his nature, Sherwood could not help quailing under the withering scorn and almost unearthly majesty which accompanied this bold rebuke; and unable to summon the hardihood to proceed any further at present, he turned toward the door, muttering as he went:

"Well, we will soon see who is to be balked this time! Two hours," he added, pausing at the threshold and looking back, without, however, venturing to raise his eyes to the face of the other, who still stood fearlessly confronting him,—"just two hours shall be allowed you to conclude which of the two alternatives you will embrace, and in making up your mind, you may as well take into consideration that your father attempted the life of my lieutenant, who will require such an inducement as I alone can offer him to make him relinquish his purpose of revenge."

After the first glad and grateful sensations of relief which came over the feelings of our heroine on being freed from the dreadful presence of her relentless persecutor had passed away, all the moral energy that had sustained her through her fearful trial forsook her, while, with it, her overstrained nerves, which so powerful an excitement had braced for the exigency, gave way; and weak, exhausted, and despairing, she tottered across the room and throwing herself upon the miserable pallet, yielded herself up for a while to the dread certainties of a fate which now even ever-flattering hope could suggest no way of escaping. For her family she felt no great apprehensions of any fate much more severe than that which usually falls to the lot of ordinary prisoners; since the present contest, as she was aware, had so far been conducted, wherever the Indians had been employed, on altogether different principles from the preceding wars in this country. And contenting themselves with plunder, the savages had generally, on making prisoners, delivered them over unharmed to their white allies, when such only as had been found in arms were retained, while the rest, especially females and the young and aged, were soon dismissed for their homes. Nor could she believe that either Darrow or Sherwood really intended, as they had threatened, to make her father an exception for an act which, however hasty it might have been, had resulted in no injury. But all these considerations could, in her present peculiar situation, be of no avail to herself. An immediate escape or some sudden rescue were apparently the only means of snatching her from the impending doom. And yet how were either of these to be effected? Any attempt to get from the house, guarded as it was by posted sentries, the sound of whose footsteps frequently reached her ear, she knew would be utterly useless. Equally futile also must be the hope of any rescue till long after her fate would be decided. No other resource, therefore, remained to her but to face the danger, as terrible as it was to her, even in the least abhorrent of the alternatives which had been set before her, and persevere in the determination she had already announced of resistance unto death. And she earnestly besought the great Protector of the innocent and injured to arm her with strength and fortitude to meet the coming trial, or interfere, in His mercy, to save her from its terrors and perils.

While the mind of the almost frantic girl was thus painfully engrossed, as she was reclining on the bed with her face buried in the clothes, a noise, differing from anything she had before heard, and proceeding from some point above, but seemingly neither exactly within nor without the building, had several times reached her ear. And now it became too distinct not to attract her particular notice. Startled, though as yet not seriously alarmed, she hastily rose and endeavored to ascertain the nature of the sounds that had disturbed her. The rain, which had now for some time been heavily pouring to the earth, had extinguished the fire, and while utter darkness pervaded the room, nothing was to be heard but the ceaseless roar of the descending torrents. At length, however, the noise was repeated. It appeared to proceed from the flue of the chimney, down which it soon became evident that something possessing life and motion was slowly and cautiously descending into the room; but whether it was a man or wild beast she was unable to determine. Presently the mysterious object seemed to reach the hearth. And in a short time the dark outlines of a seemingly shapeless figure became discernible to the perplexed and now thoroughly frightened maiden. Her excited imagination instantly took wing, and in the bewilderment of the moment the motionless object swelled into a ferocious monster, preparing to clutch her in his horrid embrace. A strange feeling of undefined fear and dread took possession of her bosom and seemed to paralyze all her faculties. She tried to speak, but could utter no sound—to move, but her limbs refused to do their office; while a peculiar, cold, curdling sensation, commencing with the crown of her head, settled over her, converting her whole system into a helpless, inanimate, and frozen mass, alike incapable of thought and action. At that instant a vivid flash of lightning lit up the room with the brightness of the noon-day's sun and broke the spell that had so strangely enthralled her senses; for, equally to her joy and surprise, she beheld, in the object of her alarm, no other than her faithful friend Neshobee, who, uncertain whether the room might not contain some of the enemy as well as his mistress, whom he knew to be confined here, had squatted in the fireplace, after his descent, with the view of ascertaining the fact before he should speak or advance.

"Umph?" uttered the Indian, apparently nearly as much relieved as his mistress at the mutual disclosure. "Missus Alma speak very no loud," he continued, in a half whisper, as he glided noiselessly forward to her side and laid his hand on her arm in token of caution. "Them three Tory, what stand for watch, all gone fore side for get out of the rain, and so no see Neshobee climb up back side and come down chimney. But missus talk soft, them stand close up side, hark um, hear um, catch um Neshobee."

"How fares it with my father and the girls? Are they still in the other house and yet unharmed?" eagerly whispered Alma.

"All um there. Them Tory and Indian all in the barn when the rain come. Leak down, make um jump, crowd thick, so no see Neshobee creep away. Me go back side tother house, peep through crack, see um there when flash come bright. Cappen hands all tie tight. Him look sorry. Three other girls lay on straw in corner—cry much—all look very scare."

"And what is to become of us, Neshobee?" asked Alma mournfully, as she brushed away a tear elicited by the Indian's brief but graphic and touching description of the situation of her friends.

"Neshobee no get in there for help cappen and them. But me help Missus Alma up chimney, get out, and they no hear so long the rain pour hard."

"No, no, Neshobee, it is impossible," replied Alma, after reflecting a moment on the proposal of her friend, who had run such risks to rescue her. "Could I succeed in getting out upon the house, my light dress, if nothing else, would betray us to the guards, and we should both be taken. And even could I escape, how could I withstand an exposure all night in the woods to this dreadful storm? No, Neshobee, leave me to my fate, which will probably be decided long before you can be the means of our rescue. But my poor father and the girls you may perhaps be instrumental in saving. Then go, Neshobee. If you succeed in escaping from this place, proceed directly to our army at Ticonderoga and tell them that we are prisoners to Sherwood and Darrow, with a band of Tories and Indians. Tell Colonel Warrington or Captain Selden that father's life is threatened—that I—— Oh, Heavens! but let my situation be passed over. And should they send a force to deliver us, as I know they will, you can guide it to the spot. Now don't hesitate to leave me, my faithful friend,—to leave me to the care of Heaven," she added, laying her hand on the other's shoulder and gently pushing him toward the avenue by which he had descended into the room. "Don't delay an instant. Go, and I will ask the blessing of a good Providence to speed you on your way."

"Me go," laconically responded the native, vanishing from the sight of his mistress in the darkness and silently ascending the chimney.

After anxiously listening a few moments to the cautious egress of her messenger, and satisfying herself that he had reached the ground and escaped undiscovered, the unhappy girl once more returned to her homely couch,—not there, however to find repose or any alleviation of the woes that so deeply oppressed her feelings. The distracting apprehensions, from which her mind had been in some measure diverted by the presence of her humble friend, now, on his departure, returned with tenfold force to her mind. And a feeling of utter loneliness and desolation took possession of her desponding bosom. Conscious that the time set by Sherwood for his return, to execute one of the dreadful alternatives with which he had brutally menaced her, was now nearly at hand, and her feelings becoming at the maddening thought too intense to permit her to remain longer quiet, she arose and again took her station at the little window. The storm cloud still girt darkly and heavily the whole visible horizon; and the elements were in fearful commotion. The howling of the blast, as it swept over the vexed wilderness, attended by the crash of falling trees, the deep but varying roar of the deluging torrents of wind-driven rain, and loud over all, the terrific peals of bursting thunder, preceded by flashes of lightning that seemed to envelop earth and heaven in a blaze, came mingling on the senses in awful tumult. And yet the scene, as awful as it was and would have been to her under ordinary circumstances, had no terrors for the wretched captive now; nay, as the forked lightnings were leaping from cloud to cloud, and darting to the earth in terrific gambols around her, she felt a strange pleasure in their fearful proximity. And regarding them as the instruments of Heaven, which might perhaps be commissioned for her deliverance, she often during that dreadful hour, under the wild impulses of maidenly terror and despair, with which the recurring thoughts of her situation filled her, involuntarily stretched forth her hand toward the deeply charged clouds as if to invoke the fatal shaft to descend and snatch her from a doom to which death was a boon of mercy. But that Heaven to which she was looking to relieve her thus had reserved her for another fate; the storm rolled heavily away, and left her beauteous form unscathed. The rain at length ceased; and the lightnings, as they played along the black parapet of clouds that lay piled in the east, shone with less dazzling fierceness, and only to show the ravages which the tempest had left behind. As, mute and desponding, the lovely captive stood with her eyes still vacantly riveted on the receding storm, she, during the continuance of a bright and lingering flash of lightning, cast her eye obliquely toward the quarters of her enemies, when she caught a glimpse of a man picking his way along the half-flooded path leading to her cabin; whom she instantly recognized to be the dreaded Sherwood. A deadly sickness came over her, her brain began to whirl, and she sunk senseless on the floor.

CHAPTER XXVI

"For freedom's battle once begun,
Bequeathed from bleeding sire to son,
Though baffled oft, is ever won."

WHILE the incidents last described were transpiring, an event occurred which spread consternation and alarm over all the neighboring country. This was the unexpected evacuation of the important fortress of Ticonderoga, to which the Americans seemed to have confidently looked as a barrier which was to interpose an effectual check to the further progress of Burgoyne in that quarter. But whatever may have been said of the remissness of General St. Clair, in suffering the enemy to gain those advantages which compelled him for the salvation of the army to evacuate that post, and whatever disasters were immediately occasioned by the movement, the final consequences which resulted from the event proved highly auspicious to the American arms: for while it inspired the British general with an undue confidence of success, and caused him to push rashly into the heart of the country, it at once aroused the Americans from the apathy with which they seemed to have viewed the approach of the invading army and kindled up the flagging spirit of patriotism to a pitch of enthusiasm that soon brought the rallying bands of the hardy yeomen of the north to the post of danger, and led to that series of brilliant achievements which terminated in the entire overthrow of this formidable array of British power.

Scarcely had St. Clair succeeded, under cover of darkness, in reaching the eastern shore of the lake and getting his army in motion for the interior, before an active pursuit was commenced by General Frazier, with a large detachment of British regulars, followed by General Reidesel with most of the Brunswick forces. The Americans, however, kept some miles in advance of the enemy through the day; and St. Clair, with the main body of his troops, pushed forward that night as far as Castleton, leaving the rear guard of the enemy, consisting of about a thousand men under the command of Colonel Warrington, on the road some distance behind, where he encamped at a farmhouse within three miles of the place which was the same night occupied by the lawless gang of Sherwood and their unfortunate captives, all parties being equally ignorant of their vicinity to each other.

With this glance at the situation of our army, with whose movements were more or less closely linked the destinies of all those whose individual fortunes we have undertaken to follow, we will now go on with our tale, which the crowding events of the next twenty-four hours were destined to bring to its catastrophe. And after leaving our fair and persecuted captive in the happy state of insensibility, in which we last described her, we will now follow her trusty messenger on his adventurous way to the American army, which both he and his mistress supposed was still posted at Ticonderoga, some twenty miles distant.

Happily succeeding in leaving the cabin and gaining an adjoining field undiscovered by the guards, Neshobee, after stopping a moment to pitch his course, plunged directly into the tangled and dripping wilderness lying along the northern borders of the pond. Pausing at every considerable interval of darkness that still almost impenetrably shrouded the earth, and darting forward by the views which the fast flashing lightning afforded, he threaded the difficult mazes of the forest with a rapidity rarely attainable by any but natives of the wilds. Passing round the western extremity of the pond, and bending his course in a more southerly direction, an hour's traveling brought him to the great military road leading directly to the lake. The storm having now ceased, he hastily stripped off his drenched garments, wrung out the water to enable him to run with more expedition, reinvested himself, and again set off at a long trot down the road toward his supposed destination. It was to be his fortune, however, to travel but a short part of the distance for which he had prepared himself: for, after proceeding about a mile along the now unobstructed way with a speed to which his feverish anxiety lent wings, he came to a large opening, which presented the unexpected appearance of numerous dimly burning fires scattered through an extensive field. Stopping short at a spectacle so unusual under the present circumstances, the cautious native immediately put his ear to the earth, and listened long and intently. A low, mingled hum, as of a hushed and reposing multitude, rose in a scarce perceptible murmur on the air; and soon the slight jar of measured footsteps, resembling the distant tread of slowly pacing sentinels, became distinguishable to his acute senses. No longer doubting the presence of an encamped army in the opening, but wholly ignorant of its character, he cautiously crept forward, rising, from time to time, to discover, if possible, without exposing himself, whether it was a friendly or hostile force which he had thus unexpectedly encountered. Keeping within the range of a stump, or some object by the roadside, to screen his approach, he crawled along about a dozen rods, and again paused for a more careful observation. The clouds were now rapidly breaking away, and in the increasing light he was soon enabled to trace the outlines of a sentry, standing motionless as a post in the middle of the road, but a few rods ahead. While he thus lay, tasking his vision to discover something in the dress, arms, or appearance of the man from which the fact he sought to know might be inferred, the waning moon shone out through the parting clouds and disclosed to the startled Indian the British uniform of the sentry, and at the same time the numerous tents of the enemy dotting the fields in the distance beyond. The first thought of Neshobee, on making this alarming discovery, was to secure a retreat from this dangerous vicinity to the sentinel, though he was wholly at loss what course he should now take to find those to whom he had been dispatched for succor. But his doubts in this respect were set at rest by information he the next moment obtained from an unexpected quarter: for, while he lay anxiously watching a cloud that was nearing the moon, and promised in a few moments again to obscure her light, which now made it hazardous for him to move from his position, a soldier approached to relieve the one on guard.

"Well, Tom," said the soldier just arrived, "you have had a devil of a drenching this bout, haven't you? Why! what! has the man turned to stone? Say, Tom, why don't you answer me?"

"Oh, yes, yes," replied the other, arousing himself from his stupor, "yes, wet enough—a ghastly time I've had of it, Jerry, since I've been out here. Hang me, if I haven't got quite enough of this chasing the Yankees into the bush. I wish 'twas over. But do you know the orders for to-morrow?"

"Why to chase the d——d rebels till we take them, be sure. Our captain has just returned from General Frazier's quarters, and he says they have a sort of go-between, by the name of Remington, who came directly from the Yankee camp, and brought word that the main body of the rebels have got about ten miles ahead of us, while a regiment or two, under a Colonel Warrington, are encamped within a league of us on the road. And the plan is, I believe, to move on, at daylight, to the attack of the nearest force. And if the main body return to the rescue, why, we have General Reidesel, with plenty of Hessians, a few miles behind, to back us; so very likely we may get a tolerable bush fight of it, before it is over, particularly as this Warrington, they say, is a fellow of grit; and his men are mostly Green Mountain Boys, who have more of the regular-built bulldog about 'em than anything the Yankees have got in their ragamuffin army."

"Well, Jerry," replied the other, in accents partaking somewhat of the doleful, "I can't exactly tell how 'tis, but if we do have a battle, I have a notion I shan't live through it."

"Why, what makes you think so, Tom?"

"Oh, I don't know—I feel it creeping over me, and that ain't all, I am very sartin—'deed I could swear to it—that I saw a shape out there in the road yonder, a little while ago, that rose up right out of the ground, and then stood kinder quivering a minute, and vanished. I expect it was my spirit, Jerry."

"Pooh, man! your liver must have got water-soaked here in the rain, to make you so down in the mouth about such whimsies. Here, take a suck at my canteen. There! now back to your tent; your pluck will be up by morning."

Animated by the cheering intelligence he had gathered from the conversation above detailed, every word of which had reached his attentive ears, the native slowly and noiselessly withdrew from the spot in the now favoring darkness, till fairly beyond the sight and hearing of the guard; when he began rapidly to retrace his steps along the road toward the American encampment, to which we will now repair in anticipation of his arrival.

It was a calm and cloudless morning that ushered in the day so long remembered in Vermont for the sanguinary conflict of Hubbardton, which proved so destructive to the boastful and haughty foe, while it widely scattered the weeds of woe throughout her infant settlement.* The sun had just burst over the long range of eastern mountains, whose broad, empurpled sides lay looming in the distance, and a thousand sparkling exhalations were rising from the storm-beaten encampment of the Green Mountain Boys. Though deeply worn and fatigued by the forced march of the previous day, and drenched to the skin through the night, yet the troops were already in motion, eagerly engaged in preparing themselves for whatever emergency might follow, and while hastily snatching their morning's repast, many an eye was turned anxiously toward the quarters of their gallant commander, where it was understood a council of war was being held, to determine whether to continue their flight after the main army or to remain to give battle to the pursuing enemy. At length the officers were seen emerging from the quarters in question, and with quickened steps returned to their respective corps, while the increased activity which succeeded throughout the camp indicated the importance of the result now communicated.

"Well, Captain Selden," said Warrington, as, rous-

* There was no engagement in our Revolution, perhaps, which exhibited such determined energy and resolution on the part of the Americans as the battle of Hubbardton; and yet there was no one of which the results are more obscurely or indirectly stated by our leading historians—most of them making our loss from 200 to 300, and that of the British from 100 to 200. But if they had reversed the statement they would not even then have done justice to our gallant troops. Ethan Allen, in his narrative, says: "Our loss was about 30 killed, and that of the enemy amounted to 300 killed, including a Major Grant. The enemy's loss I learned from the confession of their own officers when a prisoner among them. I heard them likewise complain that the Green Mountain Boys 'took sight.'" After a diligent inquiry I am satisfied that Colonel Allen's statement is substantially a correct one.

ing himself from the reverie into which he had fallen after the council had broken up, he looked around and observed that his confidential friend now remained with him in the apartment, "what do you think of the argument of Hale, and those who so strenuously opposed our proposition of making a stand against the enemy?"

"Quite as well of their arguments as their patriotism, colonel," promptly answered the person addressed. "Shakspere never better evinced his knowledge of the human heart than when he put into the mouth of one of his secretly craven boasters the salvo argument that 'discretion is the better part of valor.'"

"The inference is a sharp one, captain, but, I fear me, too well deserved. There was one thing, however, which gratified me: not a single officer from the Green Mountains opposed the proposition. And it is so with the troops of my regiment. I was out among them this morning by daylight to gather their feelings on the subject; and, though the poor fellows were wet, weary, and war-worn, I found our Green Mountain Boys universally burning for the encounter."

"There is no doubt of it. But after all, colonel, I fear these preachers of prudence were prophesying by instinct, when they told us we had a bloody day's work before us. The force we are sure to encounter is, perhaps, more than double our own; and we know not how many more are on their way to re-enforce them."

"I am aware of all this. But as soldiers can we longer endure the thought of being driven before the foe?—as citizens and settlers of these our mountain homes, can we see the enemy marching into the heart of our country, and strike no blow for its protection? As little as the people expected our evacuation of Ticonderoga, much less will they expect us to continue a flight which will soon leave the whole settlement exposed to the ravages of the merciless minions of Burgoyne. With my own regiment alone I can make a successful stand against the force which immediately menaces us with an attack; and if more arrive, the re-enforcements which St. Clair will surely send us, when our express shall reach him, will be in season for the rescue."

"General St. Clair *may* send us a re-enforcement, but——"

"May? He must! And if he does, and will send another force around into the rear to cut off the enemy's retreat, they are all ours before sunset. Think you Ethan Allen would be found longer skulking before the foe, or, if in St. Clair's command, would suffer a man of them to return to the lake alive or uncaptured?"

"Never! But Ethan Allen is not our general. And the man who suffered the enemy to get possession of every commanding post round Ticonderoga, till we had good reason to evacuate, may still, like some of his humble imitators in our council just now, think it prudent to take care of himself and leave us to do the same."

At this moment the sergeant of the guard entered the door.

"Colonel," said he, "we have taken a prisoner this morning, who came from the direction of the enemy; and, though he professes fair and pretends business with you, yet, having no pass or papers of any kind, and refusing to give any further account of himself, we have kept him under guard till we thought you might have leisure to examine him."

"What is he—a British soldier?"

"No—an Indian, or part Indian, I should think."

"Bring him here instantly," said Warrington with an expression of interest.

The sergeant accordingly left the apartment, and in a few moments returned with Neshobee by his side, when, upon an intimation from his superior, he withdrew, leaving his prisoner and the two officers by themselves.

"Neshobee, my good fellow!" exclaimed Warrington, advancing to the native and shaking him cordially by the hand, "I hope they have not misused you; but how came you here?"

"Me come for purpose find you. Missus Alma ——"

"Alma Hendee! Where is she?" eagerly interrupted the colonel.

The Indian then related to his astonished auditors, in his peculiar manner, the particulars of the capture of the Hendee family, and all of the subsequent occurrences which had come to his knowledge till he reached the American encampment.

"Execrable villain!" exclaimed Warrington, with unusual bitterness, after a few questions and answers respecting the number and equipment of Sherwood's gang had been rapidly exchanged between the excited officers and the native; "execrable villain! but his triumph shall be a short one!"

"God grant it!" responded Selden with the same spirit. "But what do you propose, colonel?"

"To proceed instantly to their camp, storm it, and rescue the captives within this hour—if possible, within this very hour!"

"And you are willing to risk, even at this emergency, the absence of men enough to accomplish it?"

"I must—as much as we may need them, I must risk it. And would to God that my duties would permit me to head them against this farrago of fiends incarnate. Will you perform the service, Captain Selden?"

"Most joyfully!"

"Go, then. Take your company, including Jones and as many of his scouts as you think best. If you succeed, furnish the family with an escort to a place of safety, or bring them to the rear of the army, as circumstances shall dictate. Stay, Selden—a moment," he continued, approaching the side of the spirited and impatient young officer, and speaking in a low, confidential tone, "I am well aware that this may be a day of danger—of death to many of us. Tell that lovely girl her frank and noble explanation has been received and appreciated; that my heart has ever been and is now doubly hers; that if I survive I will soon be by her side, and if I fall my last thoughts will be upon her."

At that instant the quickly successive reports of a dozen muskets in the direction of the expected enemy broke the stillness of the morning, announcing a collision between the opposing outposts, and the battle at hand.

"To arms!" exclaimed the commander, rushing out into the open air and leaping upon his charger, that, caparisoned and ready for his gallant rider, stood impatiently pawing the ground at the door; "to arms! instantly to arms!"

As the loud and thrilling tones of the well-known voice of their idolized leader rung through the camp, falling upon the ears of the aroused and excited troops, every man sprang for his musket, and the busy quiet that one moment before had reigned through the tented lines, was at once changed into the noisy din of preparation. Captain Selden, in accordance with the arrangement just settled between him and his superior, hastily formed his company, briefly informed his men of the object of their proposed expedition, and, amid the clangor of rattling steel and rolling drums, mingled with the stern, brief words of command, filed off rapidly across the field toward the northern forest, and, with Neshobee as guide, soon disappeared within its borders.

Let us now return to the captured. The first object that saluted the eyes of our hapless heroine, on recovering her consciousness, was the dimly seen figure of Sherwood standing in the doorway, in the attitude of one whose attention on entering had been suddenly arrested by some unexpected sight or sound behind him. The next instant a man on horseback came dashing up furiously to the spot. Hastily closing the door behind him, Sherwood immediately advanced to the side of the halted horseman, when the following dialogue distinctly reached the ears of the eager listener within:

"Captain Sherwood—ain't it?"

"Yes—Remington, I believe, from the voice? Well, what news?"

"Important—great—glorious!"

"Aha! What is it?"

"The rebels have evacuated Ti!"

"The devil!—and all escaped?"

"Every scoundrel of them; but their race is nearly up."

"Why? How? Where are they?"

"St. Clair, with the bulk of them, made shift to push on to Castleton by dark. Warrington, with a regiment or two, now lies encamped at Seleck's farm, right against us over on the military road. General Frazier, who followed hard on their tracks through the day, lies at Lacy's camp with his brigade; and Red Hazle and his Jarmans are but a few miles behind."

"And what is Frazier's plan?"

"To move upon Warrington at daylight; and he told me to tell you to be on hand when the attack was made, flank the rebels in the woods, and keep on ahead of them to cut off their retreat. But the order needn't interfere with your business here," added the traitor with a knowing chuckle, pointing toward the house with one hand and giving his master a significant nudge with the other. "There's no need of your marching before break of day; so you see you'll have time to——"

"Hush! Speak lower, you prying devil—she'll hear you."

"Well, well; but what is to be my share for this night's job?"

"British gold—Burgoyne will see to that."

"Yes, I know that; but I mean what share of the same kind of coin that you are about to make free with? You understand me, hey?"

"That's asking more than you have any right to expect, Remington."

"The h——l it is! I know there is game to be had, and if I can't have my share, when my betters are helping themselves, I'll know the reason why, by ——."

"Yes; but don't get in a passion about it. Something of the kind may be effected for you, perhaps. The Scotch girl is promised to Darrow; but there are two maids. It can be managed, possibly——"

"To-night?"

"Why—why, not very conveniently; if you will delay till to-morrow night—but hush! hush! Who is that? Who is that coming in such haste?" hurriedly exclaimed Sherwood, as, startled by the sound of rapidly approaching footsteps, he looked around and distinguished the figure of someone hastily making his way toward them.

"It is the lieutenant's gait," observed Remington, whose situation on his horse enabled him best to determine the point in question. "And it is Darrow, too, ain't it?"

"Yes, I am the chap," responded the ruffian, striding up to the spot. "Where is the captain? Oh, here! Jake, the devil is to pay!"

"What is the matter?" eagerly asked Sherwood.

"Why, it may be matter enough for us soon, if what Remington here says about the rebels being so near us is true—Hendee's cursed Indian has escaped!"

"Hell and furies! Bill, who suffered that?"

"The lubberly curse that you set to guard the red scamp in the corner of the barn got asleep, I spose; and the confusion and crowding caused by the storm prevented anyone else from seeing to it."

"How long has he been gone?"

"These two hours, for aught I can ascertain."

"Did you see anything that could be taken for the imp on your route, Remington?"

"No, captain. As soon as I found that the rebels were on the road, I rode several miles round in byroads to reach the British camp."

"Well, Darrow, we must move," said Sherwood, after musing a moment; "I know that fellow well. He will know what to do without being told, and will be as cunning as Satan in bringing it about. In beating about for help to rescue the family, he will learn Warrington's position, which ten to one he has reached before this. You as well as I can guess what will come next. Within an hour a hundred of Warrington's bulldogs may be upon us, with ambuscades in every direction around us. We must march, and that instantly. Our private plans, Bill, must be deferred until another night. And by that time, I am thinking, there won't be enough left of the d——d scoundrel or his men to trouble us. We will take to the hill on the south end of the pond yonder. The moon is coming out, and this breeze will shake the water from the trees, so that we can make our way comfortably. Go forward, Darrow, and be mustering the men. Remington, let me mount that horse till we enter the woods. Guards, ho! you may close up round the house now, and in a few moments we will relieve you of your charge."

If ever an offering of unfeigned, unmingled gratitude ascended to Heaven from the lips of mortal for boon bestowed, it was that of Alma Hendee, as on bended knees she poured out the incense of her gushing and grateful heart to her Divine Preserver for this temporary deliverance from the perils that so nearly threatened her. She had scarcely risen from her devotions when a messenger from Sherwood's quarters entered and summoned her to attend him to the other cabin. She obeyed with cheerful alacrity, and in a few moments more was in the silent embrace of her friends, receiving the low, murmured caresses and blessings of her overjoyed father, on whose bosom she lay sobbing till interrupted by the stern, harsh voice of Darrow at the door, commanding them all to come forth, to be taken with the band in the movement which had been so hastily concerted by the alarmed leaders.

On emerging from the house the prisoners found the entire band of their captors drawn up in the yard, waiting only to receive them before commencing the contemplated march. And, after the former had been ordered to take their places near the center of the line, separated from each other by the alternate intermingling of guards, as on the afternoon's march, the whole moved silently forward across the pasture in the direction previously mentioned by their leader. When they arrived at the outskirts of the clearing, Sherwood relinquished the horse, upon which he had thus far superintended the march, to Remington, and, after sending off the latter on some secret destination, took his station at the head of the forces and plunged directly into the forest. After many windings through the pathless and still dripping woods, for the purpose of confusing or misleading their enemies in any attempts which might be made to follow the trail, they bore down upon the pond, and soon struck into an old Indian path running along the margin of the water toward the south. In this they slowly pursued their dark and often difficult way till daylight, when, arriving at the southern extremity of the pond, and being here, as they believed, out of the reach of any immediate danger from pursuit, they withdrew a short distance from the vicinity of the water, and halted to wait the operations of the hostile armies, being now within a short distance of the clearing in which the action was expected to take place.

After the scouts had been dispatched to watch the movements of Warrington's forces, and some time spent in inspecting their arms and preparing them for instant service, the band, at the intimation of their leaders, proceeded to partake of a hearty repast, consisting mostly of bread and dried meats, which each produced from his own knapsack, with the exception of the officers and captives, for the supplying of whom one of Captain Hendee's horses, loaded with provisions and tent-cloths, had followed in the rear. A scanty portion of this kind of food, with a gourd-shell of water, was after a while sent to the faint and wearied prisoners by Sherwood, who seemed studiously to avoid coming himself into their immediate presence. The meal was partaken by the captives in gloomy silence, which, except here and there in the ribald jest of a Tory, or the low guttural grunt of a savage, was imitated by the mongrel gang of ferocious and brutal-looking fellows around them.

Scarcely had they finished their homely repast when a rattling peal of distant musketry, followed by the sound of rolling drums furiously beating to arms, came booming through the forest, awakening the echoes of hill and dell for miles around, and startling both captives and captors by the sound, now well understood by all as the herald of the approaching conflict.

"To the hills! Forward to a station on the hills!" loudly shouted Sherwood, now for the first time openly exercising the command in the presence of the prisoners.

Hastily forming a line of march, Sherwood with quick and eager steps led his men up the rugged steeps toward his proposed station, leaving the brutal Darrow, who had charge of the rear, in which the captives were now placed, to goad on the infirm old captain and the tender and already exhausted females to keep pace with the rest. After a rapid and fatiguing march of half an hour, at almost every step of which the forest around them was resounding to the roar of thickening conflict on the plains to the right, they reached the summit of a wood-covered hill which overlooked the extensive opening to the west now occupied as the scene of action by the contending armies. Immediately detaching about a dozen of his most trusty Tories, with Darrow at their head, to guard the prisoners, Sherwood, with the remainder of his force, proceeded some forty or fifty rods down the hill and took his station in the bushes bordering the opening, to wait a favorable opportunity to co-operate with his British friends. The guard, on the departure of Sherwood, wishing to take a stand themselves where they could witness the battle, ordered the captives forward to the brow of the hill, and permitted them to take seats upon the edge of a cliff which afforded them, through the opening of the overhanging foliage, a distinct view of the field of conflict. A grand and thrilling spectacle now burst upon their view. At the distance of less than a mile, in the broad field beneath them, stood the plain and hardy sons of liberty, unflinchingly engaged face to face, and often arm to arm, in deadly strife with the gorgeous and disciplined bands of their outnumbering foes; the fluttering standards and glittering arms of wheeling squadrons now flashing in the morning sun, and now enveloped in clouds of eddying smoke, as the fires of a thousand death-tubes blazed fiercely along the opposing lines; while hill and forest around seemed rocking responsive to the deafening thunders of the embattled plain. With an interest equally intense, but with emotions widely different, was the scene witnessed by the little group of captives; for while Alma and Jessy gazed in silent awe upon the fearful spectacle, trembling and amazed at the tremendous din that rose from the spot, and with bosoms painfully beating with secret anxiety for the fate of betrothed lovers, engaged, as they believed, in the hottest of the strife, and exposed every instant to the missiles of death, or already weltering in their gore among the dying and dead; while, with such agitating emotions gazed they upon the scene, Captain Hendee watched the progress of the contest with the experienced eye of a soldier, and with a view to its general results. For nearly an hour the battle raged with unmitigated fury. Alternately driving and driven, the contending foes, without any permanent advantage to either, fiercely disputed for the mastery of the field; while volley after volley, bursting in rapid succession along the serried lines of the opposing fronts, continued to sweep the plain with the leaden tempest, covering it with heaps of the dying and the dead. At length there was a momentary lull in the din of battle. Even the "stormy music" of the shriek-drowning drum for an instant ceased to send up its monotonous roar from the field of conflict. And all beneath the broad and veiling cloud of smoke that hung over the spot at first seemed as silent as if that cloud had been a pall for an army of the dead. The next moment, however, a sound reached the quick ears of the female captives, more fearful than the thunders of battle.

"List! What is that?" asked the girls, with a simultaneous exclamation and looks of horror, as the piercing and mingled wail of many voices came wafting on the breeze with awful distinctness to the ear. "Oh, father, what dreadful sound is that?" repeated Alma, with a shudder.

The old gentleman, whose less acute organs had not been affected by the sound, without replying turned an ear toward the fatal field. The same hideous, though low and distance-mellowed screech, came up again from the spot with the succeeding undulation of the fitful breeze, but was the next instant lost in a fresh burst of martial music, which once more sent its swelling roar over the surrounding hills.

"It is the cries of the wounded," said the captain, turning to his unheeding auditors, for they sat with their hands tightly pressed upon their ears to exclude the abhorrent sound. "But it is over—it is over now," he continued, motioning them to withdraw their hands.

Understanding the gesture rather than the words, the girls hesitatingly unstopped their ears, and turned a mute and startled look of inquiry upon the captain.

"It was the groans of the wounded," resumed the captain. "It is, indeed, a dreadful sound to one not inured to the horrors of war. The first time I ever heard it, I well remember, it made my hair rise upright on my head, and filled me with more terror and dread than the bullets of the enemy. But it does not often occur, and should never, as it disheartens the men; yet it will sometimes happen, when some sudden change in the order of battle is taking place on both sides at the same moment."

"And do you suspect any important change is about to take place in the present battle, father?" anxiously inquired Alma.

"I do, child. I can perceive there is a movement going on among our troops. There! do you see that officer dashing at full speed along the lines, as he occasionally appears in the openings of the lifting smoke? He is rallying and forming for a fresh onset, and is probably the chief in command, who you understood was to be——"

"It is! It is he!" exclaimed Alma, with trembling eagerness. "Yes, it is he! and yet spared, thank Heaven!" she added, checking herself, and sinking her voice into an almost inaudible whisper. "But, oh! the perils which the next moment may surround him!" and she buried her face in her hands to conceal her emotion.

"Well, whether Warrington or another," observed the captain, "the officer in command there is winning glory for himself and his country. I have never seen a defense against a superior force conducted with more ability than he has displayed, nor a field disputed with more determined intrepidity than this by the men under him—at least by all those who have yet engaged. But there is one battalion standing aloof by the copse yonder, whose movements I neither understand nor like. I wonder who they are?"

"That is Colonel Hale's regiment," said a voice from the rear. "We have no great fears of him or his men; but them dare-devils in the thickest of it there, are Green Mountain Boys, and I'll own—but they've got to knuckle soon, for Red Hazle can't now be more than a mile or so off and then——"

The captain turned his head, and beheld in the speaker the traitor Remington, who had arrived unperceived, and now stood unblushingly, and with a malicious and exulting leer looking him in the face. The double-faced villain, however, was met by the old veteran with such a withering look of scorn and contempt as caused him to pause in his remarks and soon to slink away behind the guards.

Muttering a few deep and bitter curses upon the object of his aversion, on whom he looked as the despicable instrument of his present misfortunes, Captain Hendee again turned to watch the progress of the battle.

"Keep your eyes on the field, girls," said the old gentleman, after closely scanning the appearance of the belligerent forces a moment. "They are evidently on the eve of some important evolution. There! see there! There goes the fire of our whole line upon them in a single blaze! Ah! that fire must have told dreadfully on the enemy!" he continued with an exulting air, while waiting for the dispersion of the smoke that, curling its wavy folds over the American lines at this terrible volley, concealed for an instant both them and their foes completely from view. "Yes, dreadfully—as they acknowledge by not returning the fire. There! you can just see their scarlet lines now—and in confusion—staggering and recoiling in confusion as I live! And, by Jupiter! see how like lightning the black masses of the Continentals are throwing themselves into columns. They charge! they charge! Heavens! what a clash of encountering steel; but no wavering in the charging column yet! On they move! And, by the Lord of Heavens! the redcoats give way before them! They reel—break and run—yes, see! see! the poor beaten devils are fairly taking to their heels! ha! ha! Hurrah for the Green Mountain Boys! ha! ha! ha! ha!" And the excited old veteran, breaking the restraint which his situation as a closely guarded prisoner had imposed, leaped up and clapped his hands in gleeful exultation.

"Stop that d——d old fool's gab!" shouted the nettled and chafing Darrow, who, having taken a separate station in the bushes some rods distant, stood deeply absorbed in the movements of the field when the old gentleman's exclamations reached his ears. "Stop his gab, I say! Or spit him on your bayonet and hurl him over the cliff! H——l! Here, let me come! I may as well have my revenge now as ever!"

As, with angry growls, Darrow was hastening through the bushes to the spot, the nearest guard brought down his piece and drew back for a thrust at the captain with his bayonet; but in the act he suddenly started, dropped his musket, gave a convulsive screech, sallied back, and was on his way to the earth when the sharp and stunning report of a dozen rifles from the back of the hill burst upon the ears of the startled captives and their no less astonished captors, who, in their eagerness to see the action, had neglected to keep watch against a surprise from pursuing enemies from the woods.

"There! take that, d—— you!" exclaimed Darrow, as, more intent on accomplishing his meditated revenge than attempting a defense, he sprang forward the instant he perceived himself attacked, within a rod of the captives, discharged his pistol at Captain Hendee, and, without waiting to see the effect of his shot, which his eager haste had luckily rendered a vain one, jumped off the cliff, and, venturously leaping from shelf to shelf down the precipice, disappeared in the direction of Sherwood's station at the foot of the hill.

The surviving Tories, for four of them had been stretched lifeless upon the earth by the shot of their assailants, discharged their guns at random toward the covert of their yet unseen foes, and fled along the cliff to the south, to gain the gorge where Sherwood and his party had descended. But they were a moment too late to effect their object. The movement having been perceived by Selden's party—for, as the reader has doubtless already anticipated, the assailants were no other—they suddenly closed up that end of their line and cut off the retreat of the fugitives, who, quickly tacking about, commenced their flight back toward the captives, with the view of escaping along the ledge to the north of them.

"Aha! ye scampering Satans, you can't go that this time!" exclaimed the sharp and rattling voice of Pete Jones, who, with a dozen sturdy fellows at his heels, at that instant burst through the bushes, and came down like a whirlwind upon the baffled Tories, in time to prevent them from gaining the thicket in the rear of the captives—"spread out, there, boys, and be ready to give 'em the lead at the word," continued the scout, motioning to his men, who, promptly complying, cocked their rifles, and throwing themselves into a half circle, continued with hasty steps to advance upon the affrighted wretches, now standing huddled together on the brink of the precipice, and looking wildly around them for some chance to escape.

"Now, ye painted devils," resumed Jones, still

drawing up with leveled rifle, "now you have got to jump, or take it."

Misunderstanding the real intentions of the scout, which were to frighten, and then give quarter, and expecting to be shot down the next instant, the Tories threw down their guns, and with one consent plunged madly from the cliff!

"Blood and bayonets! who would have thought that?" exclaimed the woodsman, in tones of mingled horror and surprise, as he stepped up and peered over the brink, from which, down a broken but nearly perpendicular descent of over an hundred feet, this desperate leap had been taken. "Now I'll be blamed, if it don't make me feel ugly. Only see 'em there!" he continued, gazing down upon the mangled wretches at the foot of the precipice, with an expression of the deepest commiseration, "only see! three or four lay there in a heap, panting and quivering at the last gasp! And there's the rest, just crawling off into the bushes like snakes with their backs broke! Howsomever," he added, turning away with an effort to shake off the feeling, "we can't very well afford the poor devils a great deal of lament, for the same sarce would have been ours if we'd fell into the hands of their sort of cattle, jest as sure as Tory is their name, and infarnal their nater."

In the meanwhile Selden, followed by the rest of his company, had reached the spot; and the former having flown to the side of his overjoyed Jessy and her friends, the now liberated captives, was exchanging those hasty and heartfelt greetings which the circumstances were so well calculated to call forth, when a new and startling war-cry rose from the thicket below, where he had just learned from his rescued friends that Sherwood with the main part of his band was posted.

"Do you hear that, my brave fellows?" exclaimed the young officer in a tone that rung through the forest, as he burst from the group of his embracing friends, and, with a look of kindling enthusiasm, leaped forward toward his men, "do you hear that rallying shout below! But let them come! The redcoats are flying in confusion before our friends in yonder field. Let their scurvy minions here in the bush be taught the same lesson. Every man to his post!"

Responding with hearty and reiterated cheers to the words of their gallant leader, the men flew to their stations along the ridge to await the approach of their foes, who were now evidently rallying for a rescue.

At this instant a shower of bullets struck the crags at the very feet of the captives.

"Jones, your assistance!" shouted Selden, rushing back to the group who had thus narrowly escaped death, and pointing him to Alma, as he himself grasped his own affianced girl in his arms, and with rapid steps bore her back, nestling and trembling on his bosom, to a place of temporary safety over the screening ridge in the rear.

Comprehending the other at a glance, the scout bounded forward to the side of Miss Hendee, at that instant engaged in trying to quiet the alarms of her less self-possessed domestic, when, concluding to give the order of his superior its most liberal construction, he gave a swoop with his long arms, and, gathering both mistress and maid in his grasp and lifting them high from the ground, bore them, blushing through their alarms at their novel situation aloft, over the hill, occasionally pausing in his monstrous strides over rock and log, to give a wink to Neshobee to follow his example with Zilpah, the only female now left on the spot of danger.

"Guess you catch um first," tartly observed the yellow maiden eluding the hesitating grasp of the bashful gallant, and darting forward like an arrow toward her friends.

"Where is my father?" inquired Alma, with a look

of concern, the instant she was released from the arms of the scout.

"Your father, mum?" replied Jones. "Oh, didn't yer see him? Why, that careless shot of the enemy there among you jest now seemed to raise the old captain's dander right up, and, seizing the gun of that dead Tory, that my old Trusty here brought down in such good time for the old gentleman, I'll be blest if he didn't hobble off like the very mischief to help the boys man the cliff. And your tame redskin has concluded to do the same thing, I reckon, seeing as how he got the mitten," added the scout, tipping a knowing and saucy wink to Zilpah.

A general discharge of rifles and musketry by Selden's party, along the top of the ridge to the south, here interrupted the conversation, announcing that the enemy had made their appearance on their way up the hill toward the accessible points in the ledge.

"That must be a feint," observed Captain Selden; "they cannot be serious in any attempt to mount the ridge in the very teeth of our death-dealing rifles, can they, Jones?"

"No captain, that aint no part of their calkerlation, I'll swear to it. Neither need we have any fears of their flanking round the ledge to the north of us, as that might bring 'em between two fires, one from us, and another from the field. So, while a few of 'em are showing themselves, and firing just enough to keep up the sham, the main part will push round at the other end of the ridge, about a half mile or so to the south of us. And I shouldn't be surprised if the lead was flying considerable thick along here in the matter of twenty minutes from now. But suppose you put the women a-jogging, captain, and let me be looking to the sarpents a little," added the scout, glancing uneasily around him, and showing signs of impatience to be gone.

"You are right, Jones," promptly replied Selden,

"and there is now but one course to be pursued. The ladies must pass down the hill, and, striking for the open field, endeavor to gain the rear of our army. I must attend them, leaving the command of the men with you to cover our retreat. Can you do it?"

"Why, I rather guess I mought; that is, if you will clear with the women—the sight of them kinder clogs a fellow, you know."

"Call in Captain Hendee, then. He is not nimble enough for a bush fight. Send us also Neshobee, and two of my men as an escort."

"Ay, ay, captain," cheerfully responded the scout, loping off at a rapid pace to his charge; "ay, ay, we'll fix it about right, won't we, old Trusty? Trol, lol, lol de larly."

Within five minutes from the disappearance of Jones the family were all collected and in rapid motion down the hill. Nor was the expedition with which the movement was accomplished uncalled for by the event: for scarcely had they proceeded a furlong on their route before the cracking and irregular reports of rifles behind them announced an attack by the foe, in a manner just predicted by the sagacious scout. Passing onward with all the speed they were capable of making, they paused not in their course till they reached the spot where they and their captors had halted in the morning. There, after taking charge of Captain Hendee's horse, which had been left tied to a tree, and ascertaining from the direction and distance of the firing at the scene they had just left that Jones was at least maintaining his position on the hill, they turned short to the west, and made their way immediately to the opening where the main action, as was evident from the heavy discharge of artillery that occasionally came pealing through the forest, was still kept up by the slowly retreating enemy. On arriving at the borders of the woods our party entered the mouth of a ravine, which, while it protected them by its screening banks from the view of any spies whom Sherwood might have posted on the hill, luckily led up and opened upon the plain, directly abreast of the position now occupied by Warrington's regiment of Green Mountain Boys.

Passing hastily along in Indian file up this ravine, till fairly beyond rifle-shot distance from the woods, and arriving by this time at an elevation where, still unseen, they could easily obtain a glance over the scene of action, the company halted for the purpose of ascertaining, before proceeding any further, the exact position of the American forces, and the prospect of maintaining the temporary advantages which they had evidently already gained over the boasted brigade of the gallant, but now mortified General Frazier.

A misty veil of undissipated smoke still hung over the field of battle, and prevented Selden and Captain Hendee, who mounted the bank for the purpose, from ascertaining anything more than the general positions of the hostile armies. The Americans, having pursued their routed enemies a short distance, had fallen back upon the ground occupied by them at the onset; while the British, having collected and rallied their broken and disordered forces, had made a sullen stand about a half a mile distant.

"Our troops have beaten the redcoats and driven them from the field of attack, it is evident," observed Selden musingly, as he ran his eye anxiously over the field, "and yet, I fear, their temporary victory has been bought too dearly to permit them to avail themselves of the advantages they have obtained."

"I fear so, too," replied Captain Hendee. "Nor do I exactly like the aspect and motions of the enemy yonder. See! they are now deploying off toward the woods against our left wing. They are either preparing for a fresh onset in a new form, or opening for a re-enforcement large enough to form a center; and I am apprehensive of the latter, as, now I bethink me, I heard a treacherous scoundrel who came near us a few moments before you arrived for our rescue making the boast that a fresh body of Burgoyne's German hirelings were about a mile or two distant, and in full march for the field."

"God forbid!" exclaimed Selden, with a look of anxiety and alarm. "But this must instantly be seen to. Perhaps our officers are not aware of it. I must immediately forward to Warrington. Keep your position here, my friends, till I return, which shall be soon, better informed how to act and with some plan for your disposal or escape," added the young officer, as, leaping down into the valley, he seized the horse from the hands of Neshobee, mounted, and, waving a hasty adieu to the ladies, dashed forward at full speed over the plain to the American lines.

Captain Hendee, still retaining his post of elevation, continued anxiously to watch those movements of the enemy which had raised his suspicions of an approaching re-enforcement. Nor had many minutes elapsed before his worst apprehensions were confirmed by the appearance of Reidesel who, with flying colors and rattling drums, and all the pomp and pride of military array, came pouring the numerous troops of his well-trained brigade across the field, and bearing down in solid columns directly upon the American center, which stood calmly awaiting their approach; while at the same time Frazier with his whole force, a little in advance of the Germans, moved rapidly along under the woods to the south against the extreme left of the Americans, mostly composed of the doubtful regiment of Hale. A few moments of awful suspense followed; and again the flash of a thousand exploding muskets enveloped the encountering hosts in clouds of rolling smoke and shook the earth and heavens with the fearful concussions that followed.

At that instant Selden, accompanied by a soldier with two horses, emerged from the smoke and came galloping to the spot.

"Prepare for instant flight!" he exclaimed, hastily dismounting, and urging his horse down the bank toward the little grassy nook on which the females stood instinctively crowding together in mute consternation at the fearful noise and commotion of the plain above. "Ten minutes delay on this spot may again make you prisoners, and in the hands of a brutal and exasperated soldiery."

"There is no hope, then, that our troops can long withstand this fresh and formidable onset?" said Captain Hendee, coolly preparing to mount the horse allotted to carry him and his daughter, in the manner in vogue among the settlers of carrying their females behind them on horseback.

"Scarcely longer, perhaps, than to allow us time to gain the forest," replied Selden, placing Jessy on the crupper of his own horse, and springing himself into the saddle before her, while the little cavalcade, the two maids having been placed on the back of the third horse, began to move slowly down the rocky and frequently obstructed ravine.

"I feared so," said the former; "but where in the name of Heaven is St. Clair all this time, that he sends no re-enforcement?"

"Well may you ask that, Captain Hendee," said Selden bitterly. "Within hearing of our guns, with a full knowledge of our attack by a superior force, and with more than two thousand troops at his disposal, all impatient to be with us, he allows not a man to come to our assistance. God forgive him! I can't."

"Nor I; but what of that dainty-fingered colonel, whom I noticed from the hill standing aloof and idle with his regiment at a distance on the left?"

"Hale? * Eternal infamy on his name! Having looked coldly on, and without lifting a finger in assistance through the whole of the first assault, he, on the approach of Frazier in this last onset, hoisted a white flag—even before it could be seen by the enemy, and disgracefully surrendered his regiment, with all the chance in the world to save it by retreat. And by this craven act he has thrown all that important part of the field into the possession of the British, who are already sweeping past us and securing the roads to the south, leaving our brave friend Warrington with his regiment of heroes (scores of whom are stretched bleeding or lifeless on the field), and the gallant Colonel Francis, with his battalion of Massachusetts troops, to contend with a fresh force of more than double their numbers. But they must soon give way—not to retreat in a body, for every pass by which that could be effected is now closed against them—much less to surrender themselves as prisoners, but to break, scatter, and save themselves as they best can, to rally again in some appointed place round the standard of their lion-hearted leader."

"And which way do you and Warrington propose for our flight, after reaching the forest?"

"An old byroad leading from the head of yonder pond directly across the country to Otter Creek, and there intersecting the creek road to Pittsford and the older settlements. One of our guards, here, must be dispatched to call in Jones with a dozen trusty men to guard us on our way, while the rest of my company shall keep the accursed Sherwood and his gang, if possible, engaged, that he may have no way to discover the route we have taken till we are beyond the reach of his malice. But hark! 'tis a shout of triumph from the British line!

* It is but justice to say that though this was the version put on Hale's conduct at the time by many, yet his family wholly deny its correctness, and affirm he demanded a court-martial, but died before obtaining it.

Forward with all possible speed—for God's sake, forward to the woods!"

Dashing onward at the word, the whole party in a moment more gained the confines of the forest and quickly disappeared within the recesses, thus escaping the danger of the field, where they had been nearly involved in the general *mêlée* of dispersing pursued and pursuing combatants that ensued at the close of that fierce and bloody conflict, but escaping only to encounter other perils, in their flight through the woods, of a still more fearful and dreadful character.

CHAPTER XXVII

"The hour of fate draws on."

THE setting sun was throwing its parting beams of rich and mellow light, in a thousand variegated hues, over the intermingling foliage of the deciduous and perennial forest that deeply clothed the mountain slopes to the eastward of the sluggish Otter. The hardy and heroic woman whose lot had been cast in the wilderness on the banks of that stream, and whose curious abode we have already described in a former chapter, still fearlessly maintained her post, in spite of all the terrors and dangers of an invasion which had driven every settler to the north and west of her from his home, and laid open all that section of the Grants, to her very doors, to the unopposed ravages of British and savage foes.

Her toils for the day being over she was now sitting at the door of her rude cabin, enjoying with an anxious and thoughtful brow the grateful coolness of the evening air, while her hopeful brood of embryo foresters were lolling upon the grass or gamboling in childish freaks around her.

"Oh, mother! what was it that I seed over yonder, that twinkled kinder white in the bushes, just now?" exclaimed one of the younger boys, starting up with excited looks, and pointing to the opposite side of the creek at a spot some distance up the stream, where the clearing, extending to the water, afforded a fair view of the forest-lined banks of the western side of the river.

The mother started, and threw a quick glance in the direction thus indicated, but perceiving nothing, she sank back into her seat and observed, "I doubt whether you saw anything, my son; but if you did, it was probably a flock of pigeons, or some other birds rising from the ground."

"No, it wasn't, mother," replied the boy confidently, "it wan't birds! It was something coming proper fast along this way, by an open place in the trees, and looked just like folks running with white clothes on."

Aroused by this last remark, as well as by the eager and confident manner in which it was made, Mrs. Story hastily rose, advanced a few steps, and sent an anxious and scrutinizing look along the opposite bank in search of the object that had so excited the boy's attention. That object was the next moment disclosed to her in the partial view she obtained of a small company of both sexes on horseback, urging forward their smoking and jaded steeds with all possible haste toward the landing on that side of the stream. She had been accidentally apprised that the Hendee family were on their way south the day previous, and having heard a distant, heavy firing in the direction they had taken, the fore part of the present day, and coupling the circumstances with the hurrying and alarmed appearance of the approaching company, a painful apprehension now flitted across her mind; and, with an air of deep concern, she stepped inside the door, took down her rifle, and began to proceed at a hurried pace toward the creek. Some doubt, however, seeming to arrest her steps, she stopped short, and again gave eye and ear to objects before and around her. The report of several rifles some hundred yards up the stream, followed by the distant shout of skirmishers, at that instant reached the spot and at once resolved her doubts. Turning hastily to her children, now huddling with looks of alarm around her, and ordering them into the house, she flew down the path through the woods to her landing, drew out her canoe from its concealment, and springing in, pushed out boldly for the opposite shore, at which she arrived just as the fugitives, with soiled and torn garments, and way-worn and troubled looks, came hurrying up to the spot.

"God bless you for this timely promptitude, Mrs. Story," exclaimed Selden, leaping from his horse and assisting the females and the infirm and sadly jarred old veteran to dismount.

"You are pursued?" eagerly asked the widow.

"We are," answered Selden, "and have been every step of the way from the red fields of Hubbardton. We did not, however, intend to have brought peril to your house. But striking across the country to the creek, with the hope of escaping up the road to Pittsford, we discovered the road to be ambushed by a party of our outstripping foes, and, as our only hope of escape, turned down-stream to find refuge at your abode. And even this we never should have reached alive, but for the protecting rifles of that noble fellow, Pete Jones, and his brave and trusty scouts, who are still keeping four-fold their numbers at bay till we can cross."

"Well, Heaven be praised for your deliverance so far," rejoined the widow, who still sat in her boat, heading it up against the bank for the others to enter, "but come, girls, jump in here, we will take you over first."

"Ay, ay," said Selden, "there is not a moment to be lost. And here, Neshobee," he continued, as the native, who had followed his friends on foot, now arrived, "throw down your rifle, dash in there, and swim across to bring back the boat, while I lead the horses into a thicket—perhaps they may be saved. At all events, there is no chance to swim them over here."

"The canoe will not carry us all safely," said Alma in a quiet and sorrowful tone, as her companions, who had first entered, seated themselves in the boat

"Oh, no danger—not the least; step in," said the widow encouragingly.

"No, let me remain," replied the former. "There will probably be no danger till the boat can return. But if there should be," she added, in the same plaintive and desponding accents, "if there should be, what matters it to me?"

"Alma Hendee!" said the widow, looking up at the other with an air of mingled surprise and expostulation, "how is this? Where is your fortitude?"

The grief-stricken maiden made a slight effort to speak, but the utterance died away on her quivering lip, and the bright tear drops stood in her eyes.

"What has happened to her?" asked the widow, looking round on the company with an expression of wonder and concern.

"Warrington has fallen in battle," replied Selden, with an unsuccessful effort to speak without emotion.

"Now, Heaven forbid!" exclaimed the widow, in accents which plainly told the shock which the sad announcement had imparted to her feelings.

"Yes, the gallant fellow has left us," resumed the other. "The melancholy tidings were received from a soldier who joined us in our flight, and who said he saw him fall dead from his horse in the last moments of battle. But do not allow yourself to despond, my dear Miss Hendee. You had better go over now," he added soothingly, as he approached, and gently urged the mutely sorrowful, but now passive girl into the boat, which was instantly headed round, and, under the strokes of the strong-armed widow, sent surging toward the other shore.

Stopping no longer than to see the females under way, Selden sprang up the bank, seized the horses by their bridle and, whipping them into a lively trot, led them into a neighboring thicket, tied them to saplings, and flew back to the shore. The active young Indian, who had readily undertaken to swim the stream, had already returned with the canoe, taken in Captain Hendee, and sat impatiently waiting, with unlifted oar, to push again from the shore.

"There! now lay to with a will, my lad," cried Selden, leaping into the boat, just as the scattering fire of several rifles, quickly returned by that of a much larger number, a short distance beyond burst from the bushes at a point now not more than a quarter of a mile up the stream apprising them that the enemy were rapidly driving in Jones and his party, who, as previously concerted, were retiring before their pursuers in three divisions, each in turn coming in front, discharging their pieces from their coverts, and scudding on to the rear of the others, to reload and wait the approach of their foes.

"If we can get one boatload of men safely over," resumed Selden, "we shall be able, I trust, to protect the rest in crossing; and when we all are over, I hope to keep the rascals on their own side of the river."

"That may be done till dark, perhaps," observed Captain Hendee, "but with our small force not after, I think. No, Captain Selden, unless the disposition of these Tories is less devilish than I rate it, and the nature of their Indian allies has changed since I used to deal with the hell-hounds, we may as well prepare for a siege."

"Let it come then," replied the other determinedly —"with the widow's 'tother world' for a concealment and stronghold for the women and children, and those impervious logs of her cabin to protect us while we fight, many a Tory and redskin must take a leaden supper before they capture us. But here we are, safe ashore. Neshobee, will you take back the boat, or shall I?"

"Me go—no 'fraid," answered the native, again pushing out into the stream.

"Very well—I will remain to superintend the transportation of the men. And you, Captain Hendee, had better proceed immediately to the house, and, if you will, be looking a little to the means of defending it. An old soldier like yourself will need no instruction in that duty. Hold out bright hopes to the ladies, but see that they retire from the upper world in season, and while they may undiscovered, if their passage to the lower, with which I am unacquainted, is likely to expose them to the sight of the enemy."

"Ay, ay, I will see to it," replied the other, hurrying off with unwonted activity to the cabin, where he was met at the door by the widow.

"What is the prospect, captain?" she asked, in a low, eager tone.

"The men will get over, I think, with few or no losses but——"

"But what?"

"Those untiring fiends are after blood! Our men have already to-day made a heavy inroad on their numbers and they are determined on revenge. I have no hope but that they will find means to cross the creek and besiege us, as soon as it is dark."

"Nor have I the least, since Alma has told me the particulars of your disasters, and the conduct of that wretch who has caused them. Hendee, I have long known that Jake Sherwood, and have wondered at your course."

"I was duped—deceived, Ann Story, but I have been an egregious old fool, even at that, I will own—besides treating my own flesh and blood like a tyrant and a brute. Furies, I could beat my own brains out!

If you were a man, and connected with me as you are, you ought to curse me to my face. A good round damning from a friendly source would seem to relieve my feelings. But where are the girls?"

"All within here. They have taken a little refreshment, and seem getting up their spirits a little."

"Well, we will not dampen their feelings at present; but they and you, with your children, had better be on the move for your underground refuge."

"That is easily gained now."

"Why, you enter the creek as formerly, don't you?"

"No, I have made an improvement this summer. Come, attend to me, and you shall see."

"I will, but must first glance at the means we shall have of defending the house, which we must make our fortress, for beating off or weakening the enemy. Your place of concealment below must be the last resort of the men, if they enter it at all."

They now entered the house, and were met by the anxious and inquiring looks of the girls, who sat silently waiting to hear the news which the captain might have brought from the scene of action.

"Has he——" at length commenced Miss Reed, unable longer to repress her anxiety, but stopping short and blushing at the exclusiveness of the inquiry she was about to make, "has—that is, is the danger over?"

"We hope so," replied the captain, "at least, there can be but little danger for you females. Captain Selden trusts to prevent the enemy from crossing. He commands without, and I, for the present, within; and I hope to find in you a brave garrison."

"Jessy, at least, will prove no coward for herself, I suspect," remarked the widow, a little archly.

"Well, both she and Alma are soldiers' daughters," resumed the captain, "and should danger beset us tonight, I trust they will bear themselves as they have already done for the last twenty-four hours, with firmness and fortitude. But now for the business on hand," he added, turning to the hostess, and glancing round the walls of the house.

"Very well, sir, and, to begin, here is my double plank door—bullet-proof, I think, and the fastenings abundantly secure."

"Yes, I have noticed; but what loop-holes shall we have to fire from, besides that window?"

"Here," answered the widow, stepping up to one of the walls, and pulling out a nicely fitting block from a cone-shaped embrasure cut through one of the logs; "there are two of these on each side and end of the house, and as many more just below the eaves in the chamber loft above."

"Just the things for us—and now if we had but a long, square block to fill that window——"

"You have it at hand, with a loop like the rest, in that block on which the children are sitting there."

"Admirable! a regular fort, by George! Ann Story, you ought to be the wife of a general. Let us now proceed to your unfindable fastness below."

"In an instant," said the widow, going to the fire and blowing up a torch. "Boys, lift that door," she added, pointing to a trapdoor in the corner of the room, that opened into the cellar.

Followed by the captain, the widow now descended through the trap in the floor on a short ladder into the cellar, and going to the western side and removing a bundle of straw standing against the wall, disclosed the entrance of a narrow, upright passage leading off into the earth in the direction of the river.

"Come on!" said the prompt and energetic woman, plunging with torch in hand directly into the dark, vaulted way before her.

After proceeding several rods through this straight and narrow passage, all smoothly cut through the solid earth some distance below the surface, they came to a lateral excavation, forming an arched room about a dozen feet square.

"This is my halfway house—my innermost recess," said the widow, stepping into the center of the room and holding up the light that the other might see to examine. "This is a much stronger place than the outer or western room, which you have been into before, I believe, as the earth is here much thicker above us, owing to a swell in the surface, over which, to make it still more difficult to dig through, spread the widely branching roots of several large maples."

"True," replied the captain, "and one man at each entrance might defend the place against hundreds. Ah! I plainly see that we old soldiers have got to yield the palm to you, Ann. In all my experience of twenty years among these northern forests in fighting and dodging the enemy, and planning, building, or seeking out places for forts, defenses, and refuges, I never saw or thought of anything like this establishment of yours."

"I can think of no way by which our foes can rout us from this," rejoined the widow, "unless they storm us or smoke us out. I believe I shall curtain off this room with blankets for the children and girls to-night, while we give up the other room, if needed, to our defenders. But you have seen enough of this; let us pass on."

They now entered the remaining part of the passage, which, after running a few rods in a different line, and then winding around to the left, brought them into the large partitioned room we have formerly described.

"This you have seen before," said the widow, pausing as they entered the room, "and there is nothing new to show you here, except my stores; those barrels," pointing to two casks standing just within the entrance of the smaller room, "contain provisions, which, on the rumor of the approaching invasion, I employed my neighbor, just before he left us, to purchase for me at Crown Point."

"Well, it is not impossible that we shall need them," remarked the captain thoughtfully.

"Famine often follows closely in the footsteps of war," resumed the other; "so I thought I would supply myself in season. Nor do provisions constitute the whole of my supplies; for it occurring to me at the same time that something like the present emergency might happen, I made another purchase, which may be still more important to us."

"What may that be?" asked the other.

"Stand back to the mouth of the entrance, take and hold up this torch, and I will show you," answered the woman, proceeding to the opposite side of the room, taking down a broad piece of bark, which had been snugly fitted into the mouth of a little, low chamber or recess excavated in the earthy wall, and disclosing to view the ends of some half-dozen strongly bound casks, to which she now directed his attention with her finger.

"What have you there, Ann, so mysteriously hid up?" said the old gentleman, with a look of mingled curiosity and surprise.

"Gunpowder, with an abundance of lead behind there to serve."

"Indeed! but not all your own, surely?"

"No; only one is mine. The rest belong to the settlers who live north of this, and who, expecting that a stand would have been made against the enemy in this vicinity, had, it seems, amply provided themselves for the crisis. But, finding that resistance would be useless, they concluded to flee; when, getting wind of my stronghold, they brought their munitions, which they were unable to carry with them, to this place for safe-keeping till they should return or send for them."

"Faith, that's lucky!" exclaimed the captain. "It may be wanted to supply the powder horns of the men, and—and——" he continued, partly to himself, as he glanced about the room, with a look of wild and exulting joy at the thought which seemed to strike his mind, "and with the chance which these underground rooms and passages afford, as a last resort, of blowing that infernal gang nearer heaven than they will otherwise ever get. But time enough to think of that when other measures fail."

"What measures?" asked the widow, who, having been busy replacing the door of her magazine, had not heeded the remarks of the other, except two or three words at the close.

"Oh, nothing of any present moment," answered Captain Hendee, with an air of one willing to let the words pass without being understood; "but let us now see how you have fixed the outer entrance."

Resuming her torch, the widow immediately led the way through the passage to the entrance at the bank of the creek.

"There! Having no further use for this entrance, I have fastened it up," said she, pausing as she approached the end of the avenue, which was blocked up by a single layer of square short timbers, placed horizontally across the passage and let into the earth at the ends. "It can only be opened on the inside as you perceive, or at least not easily; and I have considered it a safe barrier, though, to be sure, by considerable digging on the outside—but hush!—hark! Do you hear that shouting out upon the creek, or on its banks?"

"Ay; and it sounds as if there's trouble afoot, too. Cannot this top timber be removed without danger of exposing the entrance to the discovery of the enemy from the opposite bank?"

"I should think so, as the mouth is pretty thickly overhung with bushes."

"Let us lift it out, then, that we may see, or at least hear, what is going on."

The timber was accordingly carefully removed, when, through the crevice thus formed, a tolerable distinct view was obtained of a long reach of the creek above and a short one below. The last boatload of Selden's men had gained the middle of the stream, and were pulling with all possible speed for the hither shore, on which all those who had crossed were posted behind their coverts, keenly watching, with cocked and leveled pieces, for the first head that should be raised on the opposite bank, to fire upon the boat. The boat's crew, as they had been ordered, were all seated save one man, who had inadvertently risen on his feet to point out to his companions on shore the object which had caused the noise and stir that had reached the ears of the widow and her friend. The man's arm was still extended up the river, with the motions of one trying to count a series of some moving objects.

The widow, having the most favorable position for the purpose, instantly turned her eyes in the direction thus indicated.

"What can you see as the cause of the commotion?" asked the captain, after the other had gazed an instant in silence.

"Well, I confess I don't know exactly what to make of them," replied the woman, as with a puzzled expression she still kept her eyes riveted on the spot. "Something is evidently crossing the creek nearly as far as I can see up the stream. At any other time I should think it must be a flock of cranes with their long necks only above water."

"It is the Indians!" exclaimed the captain in low, startled accents; "it is the Indians swimming the creek on their backs, and holding their guns upright on their breasts. I have seen their tricks before to-day."

At this instant a stream of smoke, accompanied by the sharp crack of a rifle, shot out fiercely from an old tree-top on the opposite bank, while at the same time the man standing in the boat fell over backward into the water and sunk, to rise no more, beneath its bubbling surface. An exclamation of horror rose to the lips of the captain and the widow; but before it could be uttered, and while the echoes of the last shot were yet ringing among the neighboring hills, the stunning report of another rifle, bursting from the bank directly over their heads, and followed by a hollow groan and a floundering in the bushes on the other side, told that the death of the victim was avenged.

"There, Jim Townley!" exclaimed the well-known voice of Pete Jones on the bank above; "'Old Trusty' has done the business for your murderer, I guess; though if he hadn't tore his coat so as to make a white spot in his back, as he was slinking away, I never could have got an aim worth firing for. Well," he continued, soliloquizing, as he appeared to be reloading his piece, "that is the way with the best of us. Jim was a fellow of first-rate grit, and I'd rather gin anything but old Trusty—yes, and that, too—than to have him gone so. But if spirits can hear and see things, as some think, it will be a grand comfort to one of Jim's spunk and pride, on his way along up, to know the bloody rascal didn't live to brag on't."

The survivors of the boat's crew, now reaching the landing, sprang upon the bank, and took their station among their comrades along the shore, to watch any further appearance of their foes. But none daring to show themselves after the lesson just received, a silence of some minutes now prevailed. The calm was not destined, however, to last long. Another cry of alarm was soon raised by one of the men, eagerly calling on the rest to look down the stream.

"Oh, the divils! the divils!" cried the shrill voice of Jones; "they have stole our horses, and are swimming them across down there, with two of the lubbers on the back of every horse. By Judas, what a chance to plug them, if I was only forty rods nearer! Say, Captain

Selden, what if I take two or three men and send them down that way a little?"

"No, Jones," replied Selden, "our force is too small to scatter. The Indians in a few minutes more will be upon us from above. Besides, we have not a man to lose in open fight. Let everyone, therefore," he continued, raising his voice to a tone of command, "retire from the bank, and, keeping a tree in his range, repair directly to the house. Then let them come with a welcome."

"Well, the hour of trial is at hand," observed the widow with a sort of desperate calmness, "and may God be merciful unto us! Assist me, Captain Hendee, to replace this timber; and then I must instantly back to bring down my children and the girls. The men will reach the house by the time we can get there ourselves. There! that will do—all safe, I think. Now, follow me as fast as your crazy old limbs will let you; come on—faster—faster; come on—come on!" And with the old veteran taxing his powers of speed to the utmost to keep up, the fearless woman, though anxious mother, with her torch streaming behind her, rather flew than walked till she had gained the cellar, and sprang up the ladder leading up into the room where she had left the objects of her solicitude.

"Here!" she exclaimed, raising her head through the trap, and glancing round the room, where the females, ignorant of what had taken place without, were unconcernedly sitting, with the children sitting about their chairs; "here, to the cellar, every chick and child of you, to the cellar! And you, girls, must follow without a moment's delay," she added, seizing the little urchins by the waist, and lifting them one by one in rapid succession down the pass-way, as, alarmed by the startling tones of their mother's voice, they ran huddling to the entrance.

"Is there any immediate danger?" asked Alma

calmly, though with an expression of some surprise at the rapid and agitated manner of the widow.

"Not for us, if we are out of the way; but the Tories are crossing below, and the Indians on this side above are by this time, perhaps, within gunshot of us in the skirts of yonder woods."

"And Selden and his men?" eagerly said Jessy.

"Will be here in a moment to make this room their fortress, for their own and our protection. And a shower of balls, through that open door and window, will probably salute them as they enter."

"True, true," observed Captain Hendee, who, having crowded by the window on the ladder and gained the floor, now stepped to the door, hastily shut it, and proceeded to bring the block for closing up the window; "true, this danger to the girls and children did not occur to me, as it seems it did to you, by your leading my rheumatic legs such a deuced race through the passage from the creek. Yes, girls, down with you all, and on to the middle room, and have no fears but that we will defend you."

"But you, father," said Alma, looking back as she was descending, with an expression of solicitude, "you are surely not to remain? You are too old—infirm——"

"I am young again, girl. The thought of our treatment, and the fate which our foes evidently design for us still, make me a soldier again. Go down, my daughter, and may God be with you and strike for us all!" said the old veteran, letting down the trap upon the last of the retiring party.

Scarcely had the mingled voices of the women and children died away, as they retreated along the passage to their refuge under the earth, before Selden and his men came scattering along into the house, fortunately not, however, with the danger which the widow had anticipated. As soon as the whole company, now numbering but twelve, including Captain Hendee and Neshobee, had gained the room, they immediately proceeded to barricade the door and put everything in the best possible condition for a defense.

While they were busily engaged, unmindful of the severe fatigues of the day in the excitement created by the alarming prospects of the night, which was now about to set in, the trapdoor was pushed up, and the provident widow reappeared, ascending the ladder with a large loaf of bread and a haunch of dried venison under one arm, and a pail of water, in which floated the accustomed gourd-shell, slung on the other. With many a blessing on the widow's head, and many an oath to defend her and hers to the death, the famished and wearied soldiers eagerly fell upon the grateful repast, after which they repaired with renewed spirits to the several stations allotted them, above and below, along the walls.

"I wish the rascals would make themselves manifest, if they are round us, as I suspect," observed Selden, after the company had stood some time at their respective loop-holes, silently awaiting the appearance of the enemy.

"That they will be cunning enough not to do till the approach of darkness," replied Captain Hendee. "Then you will hear from them, I'll warrant you. And as they can have but small hope of perforating these logs with their bullets, they will probably attempt to beat down the door or burn the house over our heads."

"They will find the latter a difficult job, I imagine," responded Selden. "These bare logs, after the heavy rain of last night, and that, too, at the distance at which we can manage to keep the knaves, cannot offer much inducement for an attempt to ignite them with lighted arrows."

"True," replied the other; "but you forget the roof—these bark coverings are rather combustible."

"No, I thought of that," rejoined Selden, "and was about to remark that if they fired the roof we must tear it off."

"That can be done, perhaps," replied the former. "At all events, it will be time enough to think of it when they arrive for the attack; for I doubt whether there is now one of them within a quarter of a mile of us."

"Now, I've a notion there is," said Pete Jones, who, in the meanwhile, had been keenly watching every appearance within the scope of his vision; "and I shouldn't be much surprised if some of those stumps and log-heaps over in the widow's grass yonder, if they could talk, would be willing to swear to it."

"Have you actually seen any of them, Jones?" asked Selden.

"Why," answered the scout, with his peculiar comic twist of features, "I have actually seen a sign or two, that I have never known fail, except in the dryest of times. And with your leave, Captain Selden, I have thoughts of an experiment by way of putting the question at rest and doing something more, perhaps, into the bargain."

"Well—very well——" said Selden, pausing for the other to explain the nature of his proposal.

"Here is at it, then," said the scout, choosing to answer by actions rather than words the inquiry which the manner of his superior implied, while he proceeded to strip off his coat, button it up, and, with the brush of an old broom that stood in a corner, distend the body, running the short handle into one arm to keep the artificial limb thus made in a horizontal position.

"What are you a-going to do with your scarecrow now?" asked Selden who, with the rest of the company, stood looking on, anxious to learn the character of the proposed stratagem.

"I'll show you in a minute," replied Pete, now

getting the poker and suspending his contrivance on one end of it. "There, Captain Hendee, I want you should take charge of this concern—you'll know how to manage it—while the rest of us, who have keener sight for aim in the dusk will attend to our rifles. But, mind ye, I have first got to deliver a little bit of an oration for the benefit of the gentlemen outside, if so be that they're within earshot as I surmise."

The scout then, after pulling out one end of the block in the window a short space, that his voice might the better be heard by those whom it was intended to reach, commenced and carried on by himself a sort of ventriloquial dialogue, purporting that a discovery had suddenly been made that they were out of bullets and were wishing to obtain a bar of lead that had been left standing outside under the window while the question seemed to be who should expose himself by reaching out his hand to get it; but one at length appearing to be found hardy enough to undertake the task, the speaker suddenly dropped the discourse and turned to the company present.

"There, boys, have your muzzles to your loops and your eyes on the lookout for game," he said in a low, eager tone. "And you, Captain Hendee, be ready to pass the figure up to the window, which I am about to lay open, and which all, as they value the union of body and soul, must keep out of the range of. Don't fire till I give the word. All ready? Well, here goes, then!" he added, swinging out the block and stepping quickly to his loophole.

Captain Hendee now proceeded immediately to execute the part he had been requested to perform. And while the company were waiting with breathless interest the result, he moved along the effigy toward the window, so as to show only one arm and a portion of the bust to those who might be watching without, skillfully imparting to the figure the cautious and hesitating motions of a living actor, who might be supposed to be conscious of the hazard incurred, though determined to approach. Scarcely had the protruding arm entered the narrow opening, bringing one side of the body in fair view to the supposed lurking enemy without, when a bright flash suddenly gleamed through the window, and, with the almost simultaneous report of a dozen guns, bursting from the surrounding coverts, a shower of bullets passed through the effigy and buried themselves in the logs of the opposite wall. There was again a momentary silence, when, with the lifting smoke along the line from which the fire proceeded, several dark forms became visible, peering out from their respective coverts and quivering and dodging about in the dissipating vapor. Then came the sharp word of command from the watchful scout:

"Fire!"

Eight well-aimed rifles from the loops along the walls above and below instantly spoke in response; and the mingled screech of a half-dozen voices, followed by a yell of rage and disappointment from the whole band of the besiegers, plainly told the result of the stratagem.

"Now, by hokey! if I don't keep this coat to brag on—six bullet holes right through the body, and the owner still alive and kicking!" exclaimed the scout, picking up the riddled garment and feeling out the bullet holes with his fingers, as the loud shout of exultation and defiance which burst from the little band on the occasion died away in the surrounding forest.

For nearly an hour the besieged, who had closed up their window and resumed their respective posts, now strained both ear and eye in vain to catch some sight or sound indicating the presence of the foe around them. Being fully aware of the desperate and wily character of those with whom they had to deal, they determined to suffer none of their vigilance to relax. And but a short time elapsed before they made a discovery which taught them the wisdom of the resolution. As all stood watching at their posts in silence, a low, short exclamation from the young Indian testified that something suspicious had at length attracted his attention.

"What now, Neshobee?" softly asked Selden, stepping noiselessly toward the native, who was lying on the floor in one corner, listening through a crevice which he had found between the lower logs.

"Me no see nothing, but hark um scratch um buttons; guess um lift something," was the somewhat hesitating reply.

"I'll grant you the best 'harkum,' as you call it, boy," said Pete Jones, who stood near, and, on the exclamation of the Indian, had renewedly taxed his vision to discover the cause; "but as to eye-shot, you have got to knuckle to me, for I can see them; and they are at some bobbery, too; though what in the name of reason it can be," he continued, pausing and hesitating, as he turned his head one way and then another, to obtain a more distinct view; "what it can be I am dubious whether the devil himself can tell—unless he contrived it for 'em. They are moving down the path this way, I believe; yes, and in pairs, too, like new-married geese. What? No—yes, they have got something upon their shoulders; I should think it was one of the corpses we made for 'em, which they were carrying to be buried, only it is as long as a sea-sarpent."

"Aha! I understand it!" cried the young leader; "it is some long timber which they intend to use as a battering-ram to beat in our door. And thank Heaven for the timely discovery, but for which, ten to one, we had been lost; and even as it is there is danger enough. Stand to your guns, boys," he continued in a low, thrilling tone, though sufficiently raised to reach every man within; "if we can but drop two or three of the foremost, the whole, probably, will be carried down by the weight of the timber. Cock your guns; keep a steady eye on the advancing column, and be ready for the word."

Slowly and with noiseless tread did the performers of this new mode of attack approach along the path, staggering under the weight of the long, heavy pole, or rather the trunk of a closely trimmed tree, which they bore on their shoulders, till within three or four rods of the house, when, squaring round, and pointing the butt end of their formidable implement directly at the door, they began to bear it forward with mighty force toward the object of its aim, which the next instant must have given way before the tremendous impetus which it was gathering for the blow. At that critical juncture Selden gave the signal to his impatient men, and every gun that could be brought to bear was discharged upon the assailants. A cry of agony rose from the spot, followed with a shout of "Hold on! for God's sake, hold on!" Then was heard the sounds of floundering footsteps, and in another breath the whole came thundering to the ground. Once more the house rang with the triumphant shouts of the Green Mountain Boys, and all again was silent.

Another long respite was allowed our little band, and during the hour succeeding the last onset nothing could be seen or heard to betray the presence of the enemy anywhere in the vicinity of the spot. They had evidently retired to some distance to hold a consultation and arrange some new method of attack. At length, however, the occasional cracking of a dry stick, as it broke apparently under cautiously moving feet in the fields and woods around, apprised the intently listening band within that the twice baffled foe were again stealthily drawing up to the spot, still bent on renewing in some shape or other the assault. After appearing to approach to their line of coverts, reaching within five or six rods of the house, a dead silence of many minutes ensued, leaving the besieged still wholly ignorant of the form in which the threatened attack was to be made, and even, at length, in some doubt whether it was to be made at all. All at once a tremendous outcry broke through the surrounding gloom, and the thrilling yells of the savages, mingled with the hoarser shouts of the Tories, resounded in one unceasing din through the forest. Startled, but not dismayed, by this sudden outbreak, the Green Mountain Boys instantly cocked their pieces and stood straining their vision to catch a glimpse of the foe. But they watched in vain. No living object was to be seen, though the noise, which seemed not to be the regular war-cry sometimes raised on the eve of an onset, but a promiscuous clamor, was continued without the least intermission. And together with the war-whoop and shout, the rattling of guns and ramrods, the crashing of dry brush, the beating of clubs against trees, the mimic hooting of owls, the howling and bellowing of wild beasts, with all imaginable noises, seemed to unite to swell the strange uproar.

"Well, now, if I ain't beat!" exclaimed Pete Jones, as usual the first with his comments on the occasion. "I wonder if the foolish Satans expect to throw down our walls of hard maple logs, and well locked together at the ends to boot, by racket and roaring, as the Jewish militia did those of old Jericho, that I've read of in the Scripter? I rather guess they will find it a hard go, unless they blow them down with horns of powder, as I've sometimes kinder reckoned must be the meaning of the Good Book in that business I've just spoke of, seeing as how it was jest as easy for God to make 'em gunpowder to do it with as 'twas manna to eat."

"I think it must be a feint," replied Selden, "to cover some design of a more dangerous character than mere noise. An attack of some kind is doubtless in preparation for us; but in what manner or place the storm is to burst I am wholly at a loss to conjecture. Keep a keen eye abroad, boys. And you, Neshobee, go immediately down through the passage to the western entrance, where you heard Captain Hendee say he would repair when he left us a short time ago. Tell him to keep a strict guard in that quarter, and, if beset, send instantly for a re-enforcement. And now, my brave lads," he continued, turning to his men, "a crisis may be at hand which will require your coolness and—but stay! what means this? Do my eyes deceive me, or is it growing lighter in the room?"

"It is—it certainly is!" responded several.

"The moon—the rising moon!" suggested others.

"You needn't go to blaming the moon for this," coolly observed Jones, "for, according to my reckoning, it won't be up this two hours."

"True," said the leader, "though evidently reflected light, it is not from the moon. See! see! how rapidly it increases!" he continued, as a sort of flickering suffusion of light, weak and scarcely perceptible at first, but growing stronger and more distinguishable every second, as if reflected from a steadily kindling flame in some unseen point in the heavens, now began dimly to light up the grounds around the house, and even render objects in the room visible. "This light was never made by the enemy to enable us to shoot them. There is mischief afoot somewhere. Let every man, then, stand to his post, and let every eye be strained to discover the cause."

At that instant the appalling cry of "Fire! the roof is on fire!" resounded through the loft above, revealing at once to the startled inmates below the character of the expected danger and the meaning of the mysterious uproar which had, it was now evident, enabled the enemy to approach the house, mount it at the corners, set fire in different places to the roof with their ready-prepared combustibles, and descend and escape unheard and undetected.

"Cut the fastenings of the outside binders of the

roof, and stave off every bark of the covering that the fire has reached," shouted the excited leader to the men above.

"It will expose us to certain death from the shot of the enemy to make an opening while we remain here," was the reply.

"Rip up the floor between us, then," promptly said Selden, "to give us a chance to do it from below here—off with the fastenings! up with the floor! Hand us down two or three of those longest planks for our purpose, and descend yourselves to our assistance. Lively, my men! As you value our salvation, be lively!"

In prompt obedience to the command the men tore up the loose boards composing the floor and, after passing down to their comrades below such as might be needed, hastily threw the rest together at the ends of the loft, leaving all the inside of the roof open to the lower floor; when, swinging themselves down by the bare beams, they joined in the operations already then in rapid progress upon the frail covering above. The long boards having been reared up endwise, and each one placed in the hands of two strong men, were now thrust forcibly against the roof at the different points where the fires were supposed to be burning on the outside; and several breaches were made; all expecting that, by the removal of a few of the barks, the flames might be extinguished. But appearances soon taught them that their hopes of thus conquering the element were wholly delusive. The light above, instead of dying away, as portions of the burning roof were removed, continued rapidly to increase. Small tongues of the lambent flames began to show themselves through the lateral crevices in the covering in numerous places, quivering and leaping from point to point along the inner surface, while a general crackling above plainly told them that the fire had already spread nearly or quite over the whole of the outside of the roof. Perceiving that nothing short of unroofing the whole building would stop the progress of the flames, they now proceeded with renewed vigor in their operations. Piece after piece of the broad barks were beat off and hurled blazing to the ground. And the work was continued with unabated energy till the last vestige of the burning material had been removed, and nothing but the naked rafters intervened between the lower floor, on which all our little band were now assembled, and the starry heavens above them.

"There, thank Heaven, we are freed from that danger at last!" exclaimed Selden, in tones of gratulation, as he threw down the implements with which he had been assisting the men in their labors.

"That's right enough," observed the scout, whose attention for some moments seemed to have been arrested by some appearance he noticed through a loop-hole. "All that is right enough, mayhap; but while we are putting up thanks for deliverance from one danger, I am a little suspicious whether or no we hadn't better join to 'em a small bit of a prayer to be delivered from a worse one that we've got to see soon, I've a notion. Jest look here, captain."

Selden turned to the spot occupied by the speaker, who stood silently and successively pointing to the different loop-holes along the walls, and the words of the latter were explained. Flames, rising from the ground on the outside, began to be visible, and their flickering points were already darting up in fitful leaps athwart several of the apertures, announcing to the dismayed inmates that a fire was in rapid progress on the outer walls of the house, from combustibles which had been piled up against them, doubtless, at the time of firing the roof, and which had been kindled by fire placed there by the enemy, or by burning fragments of bark falling down from above. All saw at a glance that it was utterly impossible to arrest by any means now left them the spreading conflagration, and that, consequently, the house must soon be relinquished to the devouring element. And but a few more moments had elapsed before they were warned by the spouts of crackling flames now beginning to shoot up above the tops of the roofless walls and by the sensibly increasing heat in the room, to prepare for their retreat to their last refuge in the subterraneous abode of their provident hostess. At that instant the voice of Sherwood, the leader of their foes, was heard, above the roaring of the flames, loudly calling on the besieged to yield themselves as prisoners and come forth, lest they should perish in the fire.

"Is there a possibility of getting a glimpse of that demon through the loops?" asked Selden in a tone of concentrated bitterness. "If there is, let a rifle bullet take back his answer."

In pursuance of the suggestion of their leader, the men made an attempt to get a sight of their foes, who, now sensible of their advantage, were heard shouting within a few rods of the house. But it was useless; for the walls, by this time, were so completely enveloped in fire and smoke as wholly to intercept the view of every object without. "Let us beat a retreat, then, for the widow's stronghold below," resumed Selden; "but let us pause a moment to send a glance over yonder tree-tops, lest they contain eyes which will discover, in our movement, what I trust those exulting fiends do not and will not suspect—that this is not our last nor best resort for baffling their hellish purposes."

The last speaker had scarcely ceased before Jones, who seemed to have anticipated the object of his superior, raised his rifle to his shoulder, preparatory to an aim, while his eye continued intently fixed on the body of a large hemlock standing eight or ten rods from the house.

"What now, Jones?" said the former, who noticed the sudden movement of the scout.

"Hold easy!" replied the other, "there's something that acts mightily like a redskin going up the back side of that tree yonder. But he's so pesky delicate about showing anything better than toes and fingers—stay——stay," he continued in a low gleeful chuckle, "there's a large limb just above him, which, if he's fool enough to try to pass it, must throw his body out of the track so far that—and, by Jethro! he is a-going to try it. Now hold still as thunder, all, and I'll be the chap to speak to the red divil."

Every eye now glanced anxiously from the long and steadily poised tube of the scout to the tree in question, and a moment of breathless silence succeeded; when the sharp report of the piece rang through the forest, and the dull, heavy jar upon the earth that instantly followed told that another foeman was added to the long list of victims who had fallen beneath the murderous bullets of the unerring Old Trusty.

"Down! down with you all, before the smoke of the piece rises," exclaimed Selden, as he now, after hurrying his men through the trap into the cellar, hastily descended himself and let the door down after him.

CHAPTER XXVIII

> "The waves a moment backward bent—
> The hills that shake, although unrent,
> As if an earthquake pass'd—
> The thousand shapeless things all driven
> In cloud and flame athwart the heaven,
> By that tremendous blast."

LEAVING the burning building to its fate Selden and his men immediately entered the dark avenue below, when, after blocking up the mouth as well as they could with earth and stones taken from the cellar wall, to keep out the smoke, as well as to secure it against the discovery and entrance of the enemy should they break into the house before the progress of the flames in the interior should prevent them, they proceeded directly to the middle excavation. Here they met their hostess walking with restless steps and anxious looks to and fro before the curtained apartment containing her family.

"Well, Mrs. Story," said Selden, as he approached at the head of his followers, "I regret to inform you that your house is irrecoverably on fire. We have done our best to avert the catastrophe, but have wholly failed, and even have been driven to retreat to your refuge for our own safety."

"I know it," replied the widow, "I have been up to the mouth of the passage to listen every five minutes, and know all that has happened. But let the house go —all—everything, and I am content if my treasures here," she continued, with a slight tremor of voice as she pointed toward the curtained recess—"if my treasures here can but be spared me. The little fellows, thank Heaven! are now all asleep and know nothing of the dangers that hang over them. And God grant that they may remain so till the hatchets of the hell-hounds now yelling above us shall,—if it is so ordered of Heaven,—shall be buried in their——" Here, choking with emotion at the horrid thought which her imagination began to suggest, she stopped short and was for a moment silent.

"Captain Selden," she at length resumed, "were my own personal safety alone concerned, I think I could follow you to the cannon's mouth without flinching. But when I find the lives of my children at stake, the mother instantly prevails within, and I become, in spite of all I can do, a poor, trembling coward. But enough of this. Have you any reason to suspect the enemy are aware of our place of refuge?"

"None whatever; and even at the worst, we think you have but little to fear. But where are the girls?"

"Alma and Jessy are in yonder room guarding the hollow stub through which the smoke of our fireplace escapes, lest some of the enemy should discover that avenue to the room and attempt to descend."

"Nobly employed! But the duty shall now be done by fitter hands," said Selden, as, followed by his men, he passed on to the main apartment.

On reaching the room they found the girls, as the widow had named, stationed before the rude fireplace. Alma was sitting upon a block in an attitude which would enable her to hear the least sound connected with the hollow trunk above; while her more volatile companion, having chosen the part of sentry, was silently walking back and forth before the hearth with the widow's rifle in her hand. Nor was this weapon their only dependence: a quantity of loose straw was lying in the fireplace, and a slow burning torch was at hand to apply and set the combustible material into a blaze the instant anyone should attempt to enter the cavity above.

"Bravo, ladies!" exclaimed Selden, as he approached. "I don't now remember me," he continued, eying Jessy archly, "to have seen so heroic a display of this character since whilom at the bloody siege of the Lower Falls."

"Now, Captain Selden," replied the other with a half resentful, half deprecating look, "if you ever mention that affair again, I will never—positively—never forgive you. Besides, how can you feel like joking at such an hour as this?"

"For ourselves we tremble not," interposed Miss Hendee, rising and turning to Selden with her usual calm dignity of manner; "but think of that distressed mother and her helpless family, upon whose heads we have brought this fearful peril!"

"Heaven forbid that we should be unmindful of them!" rejoined the young leader seriously; "and believe me, Miss Hendee, there is not a man—not a single man of us here who, if need be, would hestitate to shed his heart's blood in her defense. But we will now relieve you of your charge here, ladies. Retire then, and, if possible, to rest and slumber; for I well know your exhausted systems must, by this time, require both. Go, girls," he added, conducting them to the entrance of the passage leading to the apartment of their hostess, "go—keep up bright hopes, and rely on our disposition and ability to defend you."

As soon as the ladies had retired a guard was selected to supply the place they had just relinquished, and another was ordered to relieve Captain Hendee and his faithful attendant at the western entrance. The remainder of the men, glad to seize every moment offered them for rest, mostly threw themselves upon the earthy floor and fell asleep, while Selden and Captain Hendee, willing to leave them to what repose they might thus snatch from the duties to which they were liable the next instant to be called, repaired to the small partitioned room adjoining, to hold a consultation and be ready for any movements which might be made by their persevering foes. A brief period of comparative silence now succeeded, in which nothing was to be heard below but the deep heavy snoring of the wearied men and the low, dull roaring of the flames above. Slight jarrings of the earth, however, showing that the enemy were again in motion, at length began to be perceptible below; and soon the unexpected sounds of the blows of axes or hatchets were added to other indications of some fresh project about to be attempted by the besiegers, the nature and object of which the besieged had now no means of ascertaining.

"Now that just settles the question; for I'll be blest if I stand it any longer!" exclaimed Jones, who had for some time been manifesting signs of uneasiness as he sat listening to the movements above ground, and who, as the last sound struck his ear, sprang upon his feet and began with restless steps to pace the apartment. "To be cribbed and holed up here like so many hunted foxes, with forty devils over our heads, who may be preparing to send down one of those great hemlocks to smash us like midgets, for anything we know, or fixing some other contrivance for us not much better, and all without allowing us the least chance to know the how, when, and whereabouts, is a thing I don't fancy. And if I can get out there at the creek, I swow by Lucifer's red taffeta jacket, I'll jest know what they are up to there above ground."

"What do you propose to do, Jones?" asked Selden, who, overhearing part of the scout's soliloquy, now entered the room; "not to go out, and alone, surely?"

"I reckon I jest do, captain—that is, unless you swear right down I shan't."

"But consider the danger of its leading to a discovery of our refuge, and the fearful personal risk you must encounter."

"And then again consider the chance that the Satans have smelled out that secret already, or, at the best, that they will, when the house falls in, and they find we ain't there. And as to my own risk in the matter, I think you hadn't ought to grumble much, if I don't, considering," said the scout, taking the other's remarks for a consent to his proposed excursion, and moving toward the entrance.

"Jones, you shall not go alone—it shall never be said I suffered that," said Selden, calling after the scout, snatching up a rifle, and following him into the passage.

Although Selden had given way to the proposal of the scout with a mind nearly balanced between the dangers which might be averted and those which might be incurred by the measure, yet, having once decided to permit and take part in it himself, he threw aside all his doubts and proceeded to carry it into instant execution. And having ordered the guard at this post to be doubled, and leaving the command with Captain Hendee, to act as circumstances should dictate, the two adventurers removed a portion of the block-work at the mouth of the passage sufficient for an egress, crept cautiously and silently out into the open air, and soon gained the top of the bank above unmolested. Here they paused a moment to listen and reconnoiter; and perceiving no signs of the presence of any enemy, except in the immediate vicinity of the burning tenement, and being thus relieved from their fears of an ambush at this spot, which they considered the greatest personal hazard that they would be likely to incur, they again set toward the scene of action by separate and slightly diverging routes, under the agreement that each should return by himself, and as speedily as possible, after obtaining the best knowledge of the situation and movements of the enemy of which the case would admit. Carefully keeping within the shadow of a tree or bush, lest the light of the conflagration, which was brightly illuminating every open space in the woods around, should expose him to the view of the enemy, Selden, after leaving his companion, crawled noiselessly on to the border of the woods, where he soon succeeded in gaining a position in a thick clump of low evergreens, which luckily afforded him every chance he could wish for observation. The greater part of the enemy were still at their stations, a short distance from the house, where they stood, peering over their coverts, with their guns leveled at the door, which they were evidently each moment expecting to see thrown open by the besieged, whom the flames, they supposed, must soon drive from the house. A small band was busily engaged in the edge of the woods, some eight or ten rods to his left, in trimming out with their hatchets a small spruce tree, which they had just cut down, and which he at once concluded was to be used as another battering-ram, the former one being found by them, probably, too unwieldy for their purpose. While Selden stood making these observations he heard the steps and voices of persons in the open grounds, apparently approaching from the spot at which the engine was preparing, and turning his head, he was soon enabled to see two men coming from a nook in the clearing some rods to his left, of which his situation had not permitted him a full view. Passing along near the woods, they soon came between him and the burning pile, when they slackened their pace; and finally coming to a stand a little to his right, they turned their faces toward the fire. With the first flash of light that fell upon their features Selden instantly recognized in one of them Sherwood, the leader of the band. The other he rightly judged to be Darrow, the reckless minion of the former. Selden's rifle was instinctively brought to his face, with an aim at Sherwood's heart, and his finger was feeling for the trigger when prudence overcame the temptation of ending the life of the villain, and slowly and reluctantly lowering his piece he gave his attention to the dialogue which now ensued between these two worthies.

"Yes, the tables are now turned, Darrow," were the first words that became distinctly audible to our listener. "We have now, singularly enough, chased them round nearly to the spot where this same accursed Selden was one of the foremost of the gang to have me tied up and whipped like some scurvy thief. And if he is the same fellow you saw in the woods, near Crown Point——"

"That I can swear to."

"And if you are right in your suspicions as to the other particular——"

"I am more and more convinced of it, Jake."

"Well, I got one glance at his features to-day, and, come to look at him with that object, I swear I believe you are right; and if so, both interest and revenge demand his death while he is in our power. But I should prefer to have this brought about before they surrender; and that was the reason of my particular orders to the men to pick him off as soon as possible."

"Yes, and how the devil it has happened that he has so long escaped the effects of that order is more than I can tell. I have had four fair shots at the fellow myself in the course of the chase to-day; and two or three of the men say they have tried it with the same luck. He stands fire like a salamander," added the ruffian with a ferocious grin at his own wit, "and, by h——l! I am beginning to think they are all of that sort of animals, to stand out there in the flames at this rate."

"Well, the worst is their own, d—— 'em," rejoined

Sherwood with a demoniac laugh; "and if they do get baked a little, it is no more than they deserve. But the fact is they must have been driven out long ago, if they had not contrived some way to keep out the flames—the one, probably, which I suggested, that of bringing earth from the cellar, and strewing it over the upper floor."

"And still they must know, that in fifteen minutes more they will all be buried beneath a blazing log-heap."

"True; and I am surprised, I will own, that they don't throw open the door, and call for quarter. But we will now very soon save them the trouble, as I see our men are just starting with their battering pole to beat in the door."

"I see; and I am glad they have got it under way, at last; for that will tell the story devilish quick; and to tell the truth, Jake, I am plaguy suspicious of some trick about this business."

"Well, if there is, this will be the best way to discover it; but had not you better go and take the command?"

"No; Remington will know how to manage."

"Have you given him and the men their orders?"

"Yes—to let drive at the door with all vengeance."

"And in case they rush out?"

"Why, shoot down the men, and spare the women for our use."

"And supposing they cry for quarter?"

"Remington is to grant them; but three or four of such marksmen as he shall select are not to understand the order till they have dropped Selden on your account, the old captain on mine, and that long-legged devil who has settled the fate of so many of their companions to-day on their own."

"All right, Darrow; but come, let us move a little to the south, where we can get a fairer view of the door, when they make the trial, and where, at the same time, we shall be out of the range of the bullets, should the rascals be desperate enough to attempt to fire upon us again."

It was with no small effort that Selden restrained himself from taking immediate vengeance on the black-hearted villain before him, as he listened in silence to the foregoing dialogue, and discovered the extent of his diabolical designs. The consciousness, however, that the lives of many—and among them, one whose life was dearer to him than his own—might be endangered by the act, enabled him to master his feelings to the end of the discourse. And the objects of his indignation having now withdrawn themselves from his view, he gave his attention, in common with his foes, to the operations about to be commenced on the house, being anxious to witness the result, to see to what discoveries it might lead, and to what new movements it might give rise, among the enemy, before retreating from the ground: nor had he to wait long for that object. The new battering implement, when once fairly placed upon the shoulders of the party immediately in charge of it, was borne round to the front side of the house, where it was transferred to the shoulders of those selected to employ it against the door. For the next succeeding moment, as the engine was being poised and directed to the object of its aim, a breathless silence ensued, broken only by the sharp clicking of cocking rifles, now heard in every direction, while the dark forms of the enemy were seen slinking behind the different objects of the lighted landscape, and protruding their long, death-commissioned tubes, in readiness for the expected rush of the besieged from the house, the instant the interior should be laid open.

"All ready? Ahead with it, then!" now shouted the infamous villain to whom the command of the assaulting party had been intrusted—"ahead with it, as if the devil drove it on end!"

Starting at the word, the men shot forward the butt end of their engine with a desperate effort toward its object. It struck; and the massy door flew nearly to the opposite wall of the blazing interior; while the sides of the fabric, already loosened, and about to separate at the corners from the action of the fire, after tottering a moment at the violent jar imparted by the blow, gradually swayed inward, and finally came down in a mass of red ruins over the cellar, sending up to the tops of the neighboring trees a broad gush of flames that flashed far and wide over the surrounding wilderness.

The enemy, to whom this result was wholly unexpected, looked on in mute astonishment, not unmingled, apparently, with some feelings of horror, at the terrific fate which they took for granted had befallen every soul of the besieged.

"The devil!" at length exclaimed Sherwood, awakening from the stupor of the surprise into which he seemed to have been thrown by the event—"so they have all gone to hell together!"

"That don't follow, by a d——d sight!" bluntly replied Darrow.

"What do you mean by that, Bill?" asked the former, turning hastily, and with an air of concern, to his minion.

"They have escaped, Jake!"

"In the name of h——l, how?"

"Don't know; but depend on't they have. Why, do you think them such cursed fools as to stay there to be roasted alive, when the worst they could fear from rushing out would be the tenfold preferable death by the bullet? Never! I tell you they have found some way of escape—probably by a drain or passage from the cellar into the woods. It began to creep through my hair some time ago, but you was so confident——"

"Damnation seize me for a dolt!" exclaimed the enraged leader. "Ho! there, men, the game has slipped through our fingers. To the woods! to the woods, for the trail!" he added, springing forward himself to take the lead in the execution of the order. And so sudden and unexpected was the movement, that before Selden had become fairly aware of the dangers of his situation, Sherwood and Darrow had entered the woods but a few rods to the south, and were rapidly approaching the spot where he stood concealed. Deeming it impossible now to retreat for his refuge undetected, and thinking there might be a chance that they would pass by without discovering him, which would still l ave him time to escape before others of the enemy could arrive, he prepared his arms, and silently awaited the approach of these two deadliest of his foes. They came nearly abreast of him and were passing by, when the motion of his shadow, which was cast by the bright flames of the burning pile across their path, caught their sight and caused them to stop short. Turning round for the object, their eyes fell upon the other, and they gazed at him an instant in evident doubt and surprise.

"The very fellow, by h———l!" eagerly muttered Darrow, in an undertone to his companion.

All three simultaneously raised their weapons and fired. But in taking a hasty step forward, Selden's foot, as fortunately for him, perhaps, as for one of his foes, became entangled in a small bush, and in the act of discharging his piece he fell to the ground. The bullets of his foes whistled harmlessly over his head, while his own, for the same reason, missed the object of its aim. Leaping forward in the smoke, the desperadoes both grappled with their unprepared antagonist before he could gain his footing, and throwing him back upon the ground, drew their knives to dispatch him. As Selden was about to shut his eyes in anticipation of the fatal blow, he caught a glimpse of the well-known figure of the tall scout coming with tremendous bounds to the spot. And the next instant Darrow, as he turned and was starting up at the unexpected apparition, received a blow over his head and shoulders from the clubbed rifle of the former that sent him reeling to the earth; while Sherwood was seized by the same powerful hand and dashed against a tree with a force that laid him nearly senseless by the side of his disabled companion.

The surprise of Jones was equaled only by his joy, as Selden, whom he supposed at least badly wounded, and whom he was about to grasp and bear off in his arms, now sprang upon his feet unhurt, and drawing his rapier, turned to add the finishing blow to his two still prostrate, but fast reviving antagonists.

At that instant the shout of rallying foes hurrying to the rescue, and already entering the border of the woods, not twenty yards distant, broke upon their ears, warning them of the necessity of immediate flight.

"By Moses! we must leg it, captain," said the scout, as, reluctantly relinquishing their object, they both darted away from the spot and, throwing each a tree in the range behind him, commenced a rapid retreat toward the refuge they had just left. In another moment they had reached the creek, thrown themselves over the bank, entered the passage, and were in the embrace of their alarmed and anxious friends, while the woods above were resounding with the hideous yells of the disappointed foe, running about in search of the missing objects of their rage.

Our band, having but little reason to hope that their retreat would now long remain undiscovered, immediately set about such preparations as were deemed necessary for its defense. The short timbers composing the barrier near the mouth of the passage were more firmly secured, while convenient loop-holes were formed by raising some of the upper timbers and inserting, at intervals, flat stones between them. An efficient guard, with muskets and fixed bayonets, were then stationed at the spot, the charge of which was intrusted to the brave and trusty scout. This and the other arrangements being completed, they awaited in silent anxiety the approaching crisis of their fate, all intently listening, from the different stations allotted them in the rooms or along the passages, for some sound which should indicate in what shape and direction the expected assault was to be made. They were not long in suspense. The sound of suppressed and eager voices, and cautiously treading feet, fast gathering on the bank above, soon apprised them that the entrance to their retreat was discovered. For some time, however, the enemy seemed wary and fearful about showing their persons in front of the passage. But, after appearing to listen a while, first one, and then another, ventured out abreast of the barricade across the passage, which was situated about a yard from its mouth.

In the meantime Jones and his men stood within, holding their breath in motionless silence, with their bayonets in their loops, and their eyes eagerly fixed on their marked victims, who, feeling their dark way with the muzzles of their guns, were slowly and cautiously approaching within reach of the murderous blades of those of whose dangerous proximity they were wholly unaware. The assailants, now striking the barricade with their guns, paused, and seemed to hesitate; but, after again listening a moment, they withdrew their pieces, and, coming up to the timbers, were beginning to feel with their hands, apparently to ascertain the nature of the obstruction, when the death-doing bayonets were suddenly thrust forth, and with horrid shrieks the pierced and recoiling wretches sprang back and fell over with a heavy splash into the water below.

Warned by the fearful reception of their comrades, the enemy ventured not again to appear before the mouth of the passage, but soon retired from the bank, and for a long time gave the besieged no further cause of alarm. So profoundly still indeed was all above, that our little garrison at length entertained a strong hope that their assailants, grown wise by the lessons they had already received, had given up their design and made a final retreat from the place. The soldiers gradually relaxed from that stern and determined air which the exigencies of their situation had thrown over their war-worn visages, and began to exchange the careless remark or sportive jest. Mrs. Story and the other females, venturing from their secluded refuge, came out into the main room to hear from their gallant defenders a recital of the various occurrences of the night, to the deadened and imperfect sounds of which they had been listening for many hours with the most painful anxiety. These were accordingly narrated. And every individual feat accomplished, or peril encountered, was made the theme of praise or gratulation to the different actors of the occasion; while to wind up, Pete Jones, with his characteristic waggish gravity, displayed to the astonished ladies his bullet-riddled coat, as a proof that his case afforded a climax to all the hair-breadth escapes of the night. As the attention of the company was thus engaged, and at the instant when the eyes of all, including those set to guard against the descent of the foe down the hollow stub before described, were turned upon the scout, a savage warrior dropped silently upon the hearth, and rearing himself partially from his crouching attitude, and throwing a keen, rapid glance around the apartment, glided swiftly through the assembled group, and darted into the dark passage leading into the interior room, where the children were left unguarded. So sudden, so noiseless and shadow-like had he entered, passed through them, and disappeared, that few heeded, and still fewer became fully aware of the character of the apparition. The eagle-eyed vigilance of the mother was not, however, thus to be eluded. She caught a glimpse of the flitting form of the savage as he entered the passage; and, with the heart-rending exclamation, "My children! Oh! my children!" she sprang forward like a maddened tigress, and disappeared in the passage after him.

"A light! follow instantly with a light!" shouted Selden, drawing his sword, and rushing into the dark avenue to defend or rescue the frantic mother and her periled children from the deadly knife of their merciless foe. He had scarcely passed the entrance, however, before he was met by the intrepid woman, dragging back, with resistless force, the struggling savage, who had been overtaken while groping his uncertain way onward, and seized round the waist from behind by the desperately grasping arms of his captor. He had just succeeded in unsheathing his knife, which was fiercely glittering in the light of the advancing torch, as it rose and fell in quickly repeated, but, as yet, ineffectual passes at her body. A glance sufficed to show the young leader the imminent danger of his unheeding hostess, and, with the next breath his weapon was sent to the hilt into the body of the screeching foe.

"Thank God! thank God!" hurriedly ejaculated the nearly breathless and exhausted woman, casting from her, with a shudder, the gasping and gory corpse, which, as she now turned and hastened back to comfort her alarmed but untouched children, was drawn away, and covered up in a corner.

While this was taking place Jones had placed a quantity of the combustible material, already prepared for such an emergency, in the fireplace, and applied the torch. And by the time Selden had taken breath after his exploit, so as to turn his attention to other objects, the rapidly kindling flames were beginning to flash and roar along up the cavity above.

"That was well thought of, Jones," said the latter, approaching the scout, who had dropped on one knee in the corner of the fireplace, and was intently listening to such sounds as he could distinguish in the chimney above, amid the roaring of the fire,—"well thought of; but what do you hear up chimney?"

"Why," replied the scout, rising at the approach of his superior, "I got down there to see if I could find out whether there were any more of these visitors coming down the hollow, thinking that the way they would scratch and scrumble up back again, when the smoke and blaze met 'em, would be a curiosity."

"And what did you discover?"

"Jest nothing but unsartinty. Though from some noises that reached me, I rather guess there was one or more of the scamps at the top of the stub, harking down, and waiting to see how the first one got on, before venturing; but that wan't what I was at, when you spoke——"

"Well, what was it, then?"

"Why, I should rather guess there was a considerable party standing not far from over us, now, kinder consulting, or mayhap waiting to have some contrivances made, as the rest appear to be at work with their hatchets round in the woods as busy as the divil in a gale of wind."

"Ha! what now—felling trees upon us?"

"No—lighter work than that—and I'm thinking whether it an't sharpening stakes, or possibly hewing out wooden shovels. But hush! hark!"

Every voice was instantly hushed at the ominous words and manner of the scout; and as the room became silent, the sounds that had attracted his attention became distinctly audible to the whole company: at first was heard a distant trampling of feet, apparently approaching with slow, irregular movement, from all directions toward them. Nearer and nearer they came, pausing every few steps, and stamping heavily upon the earth as they continued gradually to close up to that portion of the surface which extended over the room where our intrepid little band stood silently awaiting the result of this new movement, the object of which, they soon conjectured, was to ascertain, by sounding the earth, the exact position of their place of concealment before attempting to dig or otherwise effect a breach through the surface. In a moment more the advancing lines reached the verge of the solid earth, on either side, and began to step over the boundary upon the hollow ground above the room; when, seeming to become aware of the fact, they suddenly paused, exchanged a few words, and commenced a furious stamping over the whole space covering the excavation beneath. As the trembling earth gave back the hollow sound, thus affording unequivocal evidence that the place of their search was at length discovered, they raised a fierce yell of exultation, and fell to work with their hatchets, and such rude implements as they had hastily prepared for the purpose, in cutting away the roots, and loosening and removing the earth in such places as they had selected for effecting openings.

As soon as it was fairly ascertained that the enemy had commenced operations for effecting a breach through the earth above, our band, with one consent, ceased listening, and began to prepare for action. Everyone seemed fully sensible that a fearful crisis was now indeed at hand, and carefully examining their arms to see that everything was in readiness for instant action, they arranged themselves at the command of their leader, in lines around the sides of the room, while in the compressed lip and sternly knitting brows of each was depicted the deeply breathed resolution to fight to the death in defense of themselves and the fair and tender ones whose only hope was now in their bravery.

"Give me a place among you," cried the intrepid widow, at this moment emerging from the inner room, armed with her rifle and equipped for battle, "give me a place, and see whether I am the first to desert the post of danger."

"But madam, dear madam," began to expostulate Selden, "do you know the peril that now awaits us? Do you hear the sound of those busy fiends, belaboring the earth above to break through upon us? and there! do you see those fragments falling from that jarring and trembling ceiling? Are you aware that in ten minutes——"

"I have heard all—I see and know all," interrupted the woman, in tones of desperate calmness; "I am prepared for the worst. I can never live to see my children murdered before my eyes. Here," she continued, planting herself at the entrance of the passage, "here I will remain, and if the enemy enter here, it shall be over my dead body. Nay, not a word, Captain Selden, I will not be denied."

At this moment Miss Hendee and Miss Reed glided past the widow into the room, and with looks yet unmoved by the danger, which they well understood now menaced every individual of the company, presenting themselves before the admiring gaze of the soldiers.

"Ah, girls! you missed the tread of your sentinel, did you? I meant to have escaped you unnoticed," said the widow with a melancholy smile.

"Aware that the hour decisive of the fate of us all had arrived, we came to see if we could be of any service here, or elsewhere," replied Alma in a firm, but serious tone.

"God bless you, noble girls!" said Selden, with emotion, advancing to the side of his lovely and heroic friends. "God bless you for this fortitude and self-sacrificing bravery!"

"Oh! let me die by your side," murmured Jessy, dropping her head on Selden's bosom.

Touched by this exhibition, so gratifying to his feelings as a lover and to his pride as a soldier, the hero, gently putting her from him, gazed an instant on the slight symmetrical form, and the beautiful and soul-speaking features of the fond and spirited young creature before him, with the mingled look which imagination would naturally ascribe to a worshiper of the goddess Beauty, while kneeling at the shrine of her image, and proffering the strangely blended adorations which the nature of that worship must necessarily have inspired.

"No, no, Jessy!" he at length replied, arousing himself from the momentary entrancement. "No, girls, you two, at least, may not—must not remain. To say nothing of the perils you must encounter, your presence here might more embarrass than aid us. Retire, then, and trust to us, under Providence, for your deliverance."

"Is your father asleep, Alma?" asked the widow, as the young ladies were leaving the room.

"He is," was the reply, "for, though when he came to our room and threw himself down among the children to try to get a little sleep, he desired me to awaken him on the occurrence of any new danger, I yet could not find it in my heart to disturb him so soon."

"Let him be instantly awakened," said Selden, "I would have his counsel."

In a few moments Captain Hendee, who, nearly ready to sink under the fatigues of the day, had retired to the inner room in the interval of quiet which followed the repulse of the enemy at the western entrance, had made his appearance. A glance at the ceiling, now visibly shaking in two different places under the rapidly progressing operations of the foe above, enabled him, with the hasty intimations just imparted by his daughter, to comprehend at once the situation of both besiegers and besieged.

"This is a strait to which I both feared and expected we should be finally reduced," he remarked coolly, after a momentary pause, "but let no man despair; I have been in situations more hopeless than this, and yet escaped."

"We can at least sell our lives dearly," responded Selden.

"True," replied the old veteran thoughtfully, "even in the method of defense which I see, from your arrangement, you propose to adopt—that of shooting the assailants as they attempt to enter the breaches that they make. But will you be able thus to repel them long? Every foot of this earthy covering, which now protects us from their bullets, may be removed, or beat in upon us, before we can bring our guns to bear upon them with effect. And every surrounding tree-top will, by that time, conceal a foe ready to send us death from above; while firebrands and combustibles will be hurled down upon us by those remaining on the ground. And if we retreat into our narrow passages, as we must, the same game will follow us there."

"All these hazards, Captain Hendee," replied the young leader, "I am fully aware we may encounter. But what other mode of defense can we adopt? A sally from the western entrance, which is now doubtless closely guarded by the enemy, with the expectation that we shall soon be driven to make it, must prove fatal to all who shall attempt it; while the entrance to the other end of the passage is blocked up by a red mass of burning ruins. What other expedient, then, is left for us?"

"I had thought of one," said Captain Hendee with some hesitation. "I had thought of one, as our last resort, in an emergency like this. It may not be without risk to ourselves, I am aware, but"—he continued, with fiercely flashing eyes—"but it must be swift destruction to the accursed gang above, who are thirsting for our blood!"

"In the name of Heaven, declare it, then!" eagerly cried Selden, casting an uneasy glance at some fresh demonstrations of the progress of the foe in the covering above.

"I will—here, this way," replied the former, as stepping across the room, he opened the concealed recess in the wall, and disclosed the widow's magazine to the wondering gaze of Selden and his men, who, ignorant of its existence, did not at once understand the nature of its contents, or perceive the old gentleman's object in displaying it. "There!" he added, significantly pointing to the heads of the casks thus brought to view, "there, that explains my plan."

"How? What do those barrels contain?" rapidly demanded Selden, with the varying expression of doubt, surprise, and alarm.

"Gunpowder!" was the emphatic reply.

"Good God! Captain Hendee, do you consider our case so desperate that, Samson-like, we should all perish with our foes?"

"It does not follow that we shall perish with them. I have seen somewhat of the operation of exploding mines, and cannot believe that the effects in the one proposed can reach far into that winding passage, to the further end of which, if thought safer than the inner room, we can all repair."

"I'll be blest if I don't think the old thrash-the-devil is about right, Captain Selden," exclaimed Pete Jones, leaping about and snapping his fingers in great glee. "Jest place them in that corner beyond the fire there, and it must be a sort of powder that I'm not much acquainted with, if it turns at a right angle very far into that passage after mischief. Well, now, the Lord be thanked for putting this into your noodle, old friend. I had about agreed to say gone dogs for us all, but now I can see a considerable sprinkling of hope through them barrels of thunder yonder."

"And you, Mrs. Story, whose stake is the greatest in the result," said Selden, turning to the widow, after hastily running his eye over the different parts of the room, as if calculating the probable extent to which the explosion would affect the earth laterally; "what do you say to the measure?"

"I don't know—I don't know," replied the distressed mother, who had been mutely listening to the startling proposition in a sort of wild amazement. "The work of the element will be terrific—perhaps fatal to us—but the work of the exasperated foe, unless thus destroyed, will be, I fear, for all we can do, no less dreadful. I leave it to you, and may God direct the course which shall be for our good," she added with a shudder.

"It is a fearful experiment, but it shall be tried," said the young leader, turning away to begin the required arrangement.

At that instant a large fragment of earth was suddenly ruptured from the ceiling, and fell heavily to the floor, scattering dirt in every direction around, and disclosing in the place from which it had been detached, the point of a huge sharpened stake, protruding several inches into the room; while the wild and exultant shouting of the foe above, as the stake was drawn up, and the redoubled fury with which they renewed their exertions, all loudly warned our band that there was no time to be lost in preparing for the execution of their purpose.

"Clear the room instantly!" cried Selden, in low, but startling accents, "back! back! every man of you, but Jones, to the further end of the passage. No remonstrance—no offers!" he continued, as urging them with drawn sword from the room, several began to persuade him to permit them to incur the hazard of exploding the fatal mine, "not a word! the match shall be applied by my own hand."

As soon as the room was fairly cleared, Selden turned, and with rapid steps proceeded to the recess, drew forth the barrels, and, carrying them to the corner opposite to the entrance of the inner passage, placed them firmly, and pulled out the bungs, allowing a quantity of the powder to run out from each on to the ground. He then laid a small, continuous train of dry powder, extending from the barrels across the room into the entrance in question; while the scout, by his orders, after having removed the light to a safe distance, wet a cartridge upon the contents of his canteen, and hastily converted it into a slow match, to apply to the end of the train.

"There! now leave the rest to me, Jones; take care of yourself, and see that the passage is kept clear for my retreat," said the leader, receiving a torch which was brought him by the other, and taking his station to await the fearful moment of firing the train.

The enemy in the meantime were making rapid progress. Two breaches were already made through the earth into the room, and these, as was evinced by the almost constant falling of heavy masses of dirt, were every moment widening; while from the trampling of feet, all gathering up to the spot, the mingled shouts, curses, and commands of the infuriated gang and their leaders, it was obvious that an attempt to descend was about to be made. At this moment they seemed to perceive that the besieged had deserted their room, and retreated further into the earth. Grown madly desperate by being already so long baffled and doubly infuriated by the discovery that their intended victims had still a further refuge, they were now heard hastily throwing aside their tools and resuming their arms, preparatory to entering the breach to follow up the pursuit, little dreaming, in the hellish joy of their anticipated revenge, that the torch was even then suspended over the train, and waiting only their first movement to send them, in an instant, with all the passions of fiends raging in their bosoms, unannealed into the presence of their God. But while the foe-trampled earth was jarring to the hideous tumult above, the silence of death prevailed through the hushed vaults beneath. The agitated mother was breathing hurried ejaculations over her clasped children. And near her might be seen the huddling forms of her shuddering female companions, with their fair hands tightly compressed over both ears and eyes, as if to shut out from their recoiling senses the noise of the now momentarily expected explosion; while the men in the dark passage beyond stood motionless and silent, listening in the attitude of intensely excited expectation for the awful *dénouement*. Selden, in the meanwhile, hesitating between his fears that the train would get disturbed by the entrance of the foe into the room, and his anxiety to have the band gather over, or so closely around it, as to bring them all within the reach of the explosion, still held the torch suspended in his extended hand over the train, now lowering the point of the low flickering brand nearly to a contact with the powder, at some indication of the expected descent, and now hastily withdrawing it, as other and less decisive sounds reached his ear. His hesitation, however, was soon ended; at that instant a loud yell at the western entrance, and the sounds of thickly trampling feet that followed, told him that the enemy had forced the barrier at the end of that passage, and were rushing into the room; while another hurrah from the Tories above, and the heavy and quickly repeated jar of feet striking upon the floor, which accompanied it, further announced that the latter were beginning to leap down the breaches to join the former in the assault. At this critical instant, and before the mingled war-cry of the savage and Tory had died away in the echoing vaults beyond him, the young leader applied the brand to the fuse, and rapidly retreated along the passage toward his friends. Having reached the curtained recess containing the women and children, and here encountering Captain Hendee and Jones, he turned round, and with them awaited, with palpitating heart and suspended breath, the fearful result. With the low, hissing sound of the slowly burning match came a cry of horror from the scrambling foe, over whose minds, now for the first time, seemed to flash the dreadful truth. But too late. The next instant, with a concussion that almost threw Selden and his companions from their feet, the earth yawned and opened along the passage overhead nearly to the spot where they stood; when through the long vibrating chasm was displayed to their appalled vision the broad space of tree-covered earth over and around the room beyond, leaping, in disrupturing masses into the air, along with the diverging column of fiercely shooting smoke and flame, in which were seen, commingling with rocks, earth, and the limbs and trunks of uprooted and swiftly revolving trees, a score of human forms, wildly throwing out their arms, as if for aid, and distending their mouths with unheard screeches, as, with blackened and distorted features, and dissevering limbs, they were borne upward with amazing force in the flaming mass to the heavens. The chasm slowly closed over the astounded but unharmed band, and shut out from their reeling senses the deafening din that was breaking in crashing thunders above. A momentary stillness ensued, when the returning shower of ruins came thundering to the earth; after which all again relapsed into a deathlike and unbroken silence.

Once more the morning light was springing in the golden chambers of the east, heralding the approach of the fiery coursers of the day-god up the glowing pathway of the sky. More and more brightly broke the suffusing radiance over the mountains, darkly gleaming, at first, upon the quiet surface of the gently flowing Otter, and then, gradually lighting up, one after another, the bolder features of the altered landscape, till the whole scene of the last night's thrilling drama and its awful catastrophe stood revealed to the sight. The humble tenement of the lone widow, which the last setting sun left standing unmolested in her toil-wrought opening in the wilderness, had disappeared; and in its place lay a pile of black and smoldering ruins. Fences were thrown down and scattered in every direction; while the growing crops in the fields around, reared by the hard labors of the indefatigable occupant, and constituting her sole dependence for the future sustenance of her numerous family, were scorched and withered by the falling cinders thrown up from the burning house, or prostrated and beat into the earth by the trampling feet of reckless foes. The breath of war had, indeed, passed over everything, and her little all in one short night had perished.

Near the banks of the stream, where stood a thick growth of trees, over and around the main apartment of the subterraneous abode, now yawned a huge, black chasm in the ground, in which scarcely a trace of the late regular room was discernible; while the burned and discolored bark and foliage, marking the standing forest around, and the broken, splintered, and uprooted trees, which had been hurled outward and prostrated with the earth for many rods in every direction from the spot, and which were now lying strewed over the ground in wild disorder, intermingled with smoking rubbish, all told the fearful power and extent of the terrific explosion. Half buried among the wide scattered ruins lay the torn, mangled, and blackened corpses of savage and Tory—the fated victims of the mine which had so suddenly, so unexpectedly sprung beneath their feet, sweeping them, in an instant, indiscriminately away, with the cries of anticipated victory and vengeance on their lips, like chaff in a whirlwind of fire.

As the increasing daylight began to fall more broadly upon this scene of death and desolation, two human forms might have been seen cautiously breaking through the loose earth that closed up the mouth of the long passage into which our little band last retreated.

The small, topling head, cranelike neck, long body and limbs, and the peculiarly rapid and shambling movements of the one, as now crouching, now rearing his tall form aloft, and throwing quick and wary glances around him, he glided round beneath the sides of the broad, black pit into which they had emerged, sufficiently announced him as the incomparable scout. The swarthy and immovable features, the short figure, and deliberate air of the other, proclaimed him also to be an old acquaintance of the reader, the trusty and faithful Neshobee. Creeping out of the excavation, the two separated and quickly disappeared in opposite directions in the woods and bushes along the banks of the creek. After the lapse of half an hour, in which they had apparently made a reconnoitering circuit round the opening, they reappeared on the banks of the excavation, communed a moment, and, throwing aside the air of caution that had marked their movements, approached, with bold and confident steps, toward the choked entrance through which they had forced their way into the open air.

"Hurrah, there below!" shouted Pete, dropping on one knee, and poking his head and long neck into the dark hole before him, "hurrah! ye poor, half-smuddered divils—asking the captain's pardon for the freedom—do you hear?"

"Ay, ay! what report—what news from the regions above?" responded several voices from the dark and till then silent recesses within.

"The coast is clear as a hound's tooth," replied the scout. "Yes, all clear, and that, too, with what I should call a considerable of a vengeance: so just troop along out here, and see what God put it into men's heads to make gunpowder for."

This announcement seemed to produce an instant effect. A lively bustle was immediately heard among the party below. And in a few moments more the men, followed by the women and children, came creeping, one by one, from their crowded and uncomfortable retreat, looking worn, haggard, and pale from fatigue, and more especially from the want of fresh air, with which they had but imperfectly supplied themselves by digging, with their bayonets, small holes through the earthy covering of their refuge, to the surface above. After reaching the open air the company stood a moment on the banks of the chasm, viewing in silent horror the awful spectacle that was here presented to their sight; when at the suggestion of Selden the females, accompanied by himself and all but the common soldiers (who were busy in searching for guns and other spoils among the ruins), hastened to leave a scene so revolting to the senses. And making the best of their way over the tangled mass that everywhere encircled the spot, with many a shudder at the disfigured and sometimes limbless bodies of the slain, for which they were often compelled to turn aside in their route, they proceeded toward the open grounds in front of the site lately occupied by the house.

"Umph! look! jus look um up there!" exclaimed Neshobee, eagerly pointing up the trunk of a large dry hemlock, which, standing some half dozen rods from the seat of the explosion, the company were unobservantly passing.

Arrested by the unusually excited manner of the Indian, the whole party suddenly paused and looked upward in search of the object to which he was so earnestly directing their attention. About halfway up the tree, the doubling body of a man hung dangling in the air from a short, pointed limb, upon which he had evidently been thrown from the earth, and literally impaled through the middle by the force of the explosion. His cadaverous face was turned full toward the company, and a glance at the peculiar cast of his death-set features explained at once to Captain Hendee and the girls the cause of the wild and gleeful interest manifested by the native. It was the traitor Remington,* who first betrayed the family to their enemies, and who was afterward discovered to be in full league with Sherwood and Darrow, and, to the last, in active co-operation with them in the black designs which they supposed themselves on the eve of accomplishing when thus awfully arrested in their guilty career. Awe-struck and appalled at the strange and dreadful fate of the villain, the company with one consent turned away from the sickening sight, and, hastening from the spot, pursued their way in thoughtful silence till they had passed, as they supposed, beyond the scene of these multiplied horrors. Another trial, however, though of a different and mingled character, still awaited them; a deep groan, issuing from a small covert on their left, now reached their ears and caused them again to pause in their steps.

"It is a human groan," said Selden, "and doubtless that of some poor wounded wretch who has crawled away from the scene of action. Perhaps his life may yet be saved," he added, as, beckoning to Jones, he promptly set out for the place from which the sound had proceeded. As the two passed round to the spot, they discovered a man lying in a state of almost utter exhaustion in the weeds behind a long log, by which he had apparently been arrested in his course while trying to reach a small brook a few rods beyond. His face, with every other exposed part of his person, was thickly besmeared with dirt, gunpowder, and blood, which last was still freshly oozing from his mangled and broken legs; and it was only by his hair and the remains of his burned and tattered dress that he could be distinguished as a white man. He seemed to be aware of the presence of others, and the lips began to move with some inaudible request.

* The last of his Tory family, consisting of several brothers I am informed, was sent to State prison a few years ago.

"The poor creature is begging for water," said Selden, lowering his ear over the face of the invalid; "let us remove him to the brook."

Raising him carefully in their arms, they accordingly bore him to the bank of the rivulet, and having placed him in a sitting position, with his back against a large stump, they applied a gourd-shell of water to his lips, of which he drank eagerly and deeply. They then washed the blood and dirt from his face, when he considerably revived; and, opening his eyes, he looked up in evident surprise on our party, all of whom, having gathered round him, now stood reviewing his gory and lacerated limbs in silent commiseration.

"Why! it is Darrow—the wretched and guilty Darrow!" exclaimed Miss Hendee, starting back in surprise and with an expression of mingled pity and abhorrence.

"Ay, guilty enough, doubtless," responded Selden, "but as deeply dyed in guilt as he is there is another still more guilty. Wretched man, what has become of your master?"

"He escaped unhurt from your accursed mine," feebly muttered the wounded ruffian in reply.

"And has fled?" asked the former.

"Yes, fled like a craven brute," said the other with an angry scowl; "fled with the few who were as lucky as himself, leaving me and the rest of the wounded, with our cries for assistance ringing in his ears, to die like dogs alone here in the woods. And they have died—some of their wounds, some by crawling into the river and drowning, and some by plunging their knives into their own bodies to put themselves out of misery. Yes, all gone but me; and I——"

"But perhaps your leader went off after a re-enforcement, expecting soon to return with better means of serving you," interrupted Selden, with the view of gathering from the other such information as would enable him to judge of the probability of Sherwood's return to renew the attack.

"No, d—— him!" exclaimed the wretch bitterly, "he supposed, as I did, that all of your band, as well as most of our own, had perished in the explosion. No! the infernal villain intended I should die," he continued, with an expression rendered fairly diabolical with rage, combined with the bodily anguish he was enduring. "But he did not dream I should fall alive into your hands, else he had finished me on the spot to prevent it, the black-souled devil! for he is well aware that I know enough of him and his father before him to make my revenge as ample as it will be sweet."

"What do you know of his father?" asked Captain Hendee, stepping forward with looks of eager curiosity and interest.

"Enough," replied the other—"enough of both, to my sorrow; for, between them, they have worked my ruin and death. In aiding the old man in his villainy I damned my soul; and in abetting that of his son I have lost my life; for I feel that I must go now soon, though I might have been saved. Yes, and what have they done for me? What can they do now? Nothing! The old man has gone to his place; and Jake—perdition seize him!"

"What do you mean?" sharply demanded the captain. "Is John Sherwood dead? Why, Jake told me, before he turned devil to us, and not more than a week since, neither, that his father was alive and——"

"And what if he did," interrupted Darrow, growing restless and impatient from the pain, which was now evidently beginning to invade the citadel of life—"what if he did? The old man made a will—too much in favor of your daughter here, or you, he suspects—and all was to be kept dark till he could bring certain things about."

"Man, man, you are deceiving me!" cried the other warmly.

"Father, I believe he is speaking the truth," interposed the daughter, to whose mind the late conduct of Sherwood, before inexplicable, was now explained.

"Truth — truth! Alma Hendee," resumed the wounded man, now breathing thick and speaking with increasing difficulty; "it is only the beginning of truths, that concerns you all, that—that I could—that I must and will tell, if—if soul and body will hold together long enough for me to expose——"

"Expose what? What can you reveal? Go on! Speak—speak!" exclaimed the old gentleman, impatiently breaking in on the other in a tone and air of feverish excitement.

"Wait—wait," resumed Darrow, grating his clenched teeth and writhing about in a fresh paroxysm of anguish. "I will—will tell all—but wait till this is over—oh, that pain! Oh, God! that pain, that pain!" and the poor wretch gasped for breath, and wildly threw about his arms in the insufferable pangs of his agony.

"Captain Hendee," he faintly and in a softened tone resumed, after the desperate paroxysm had subsided, "did you ever mistrust that John Sherwood played you foul in respect to your property, which you was blind enough to intrust to his management?"

"Why, I thought it strange," replied the other, "and yet I could not detect—but was he dishonest, then?"

"Yes," exclaimed Darrow; "in that final settlement he defrauded you out of more than half of what was honestly your own: and, as the main instance, you recollect a large landed lawsuit he brought in your behalf?"

"I do," said the captain; "and, finding he must fail in it and subject me to ruinous costs, he compromised, by paying a small sum, and withdrew the action, as I understood."

"Well, now, it is God's truth, captain," rejoined the former, "that instead of paying anything, he received a large sum—his adversary and not he finding he must fail."

"The faithless villain!" exclaimed the astonished captain, "may the wrath—but I will not curse him, now he is gone."

"No; for you can revenge yourself more effectually," said the other. "The man with whom this compromise was made is still alive and, though it was agreed that the transaction should be kept a dead secret, there is no doubt he will swear to the amount he paid Sherwood, as he was not privy to the fraud on you."

"But how know you all this?" asked the captain, some new doubt seeming to arise in his mind.

"You will know directly," replied Darrow—"that is, if—if I tell you the rest," he continued, pausing and hesitating, as if irresolute whether to proceed; but at length seeming to make up his mind, he resumed: "Captain Hendee, you once had a darling son, who was lost?"

"I did, I did," responded the other with visible emotion.

"And you have heard," continued the former, "that he was last seen with a young man in John Sherwood's employ? Did you ever see that young man?"

"No," said the captain, "nor do I know what became of him, or whether he is now living."

"He is still living, but will not be long," said Darrow. "You see him in the miserable, shattered, and dying creature lying before you, Captain Hendee."

"You! you!" wildly and fiercely exclaimed the old man; "but what of my son? Wretch! did you murder the boy?" he added, raising his voice almost to a frantic scream, as the suspicion flashed over his anticipating thoughts.

"No, I was spared that," answered the other, "though my instigator, who was no other than that same John Sherwood, expected it of me, I think. No, I came across an Indian, who, for a bottle of rum, was willing to take the boy where his friends should never hear of him again."

"And you agreed with the hell-hound to do it, did you, monster!" again fiercely demanded the captain.

"Yes, I did that— I own it! I own it! ay, I confess it!" exclaimed Darrow, eagerly repeating the words, as if he had brought himself to this act of penitence by some mighty effort. "There!" he added, wildly and menacingly brandishing his fist at some imaginary presence, as he began to draw up his limbs and glare deliriously around him under another and fearful attack of his pains, "there! I have confessed it, you black fiend!" and with a terrible yell of seeming exultation and defiance, he fell back convulsed from head to foot; and for many moments he appeared to be wrestling terribly with the angel of death.

At length, however, he became calm, and again opened his eyes upon the horror-stricken, but intensely interested company.

"I can't live through another like that—so let me speak while I can. You would know more of your son?" faintly said the reviving wretch, turning his glazed and blood-shot eye languidly upon the captain.

"Yes, yes," replied the other in a softened and imploring tone, "yes, if you have strength to go on, tell me, if you know, for God's sake, tell me, whether there is any hope for a bereaved and sorrow-stricken old man? Did you ever hear of the boy? Do you think he is still living?"

"If that boy lived to grow up," said Darrow, in reply, "if he be still among the living, Captain Hendee, I believe he is now standing by your side."

Wholly unprepared for a development so unexpected and improbable, the company stood silently gazing at each other a moment with looks of mingled doubt and astonishment; when Selden, who was obviously the one alluded to by the confessant, and who had appeared thoughtful and abstracted during the latter part of the conversation, now turned to the other, and, with the air of one trying to recall some indistinct image of other days, observed:

"I have some strange dim recollections—but what circumstances can you name to warrant the belief you have just expressed?"

"Why, if I am right," answered Darrow, "as I still think I am, you must have had, for many years, if you have not now, the proof on your person! For before I parted from the boy I pricked two crossed arrows, with lasting ink, into his skin near the elbow."

A flash of joyous intelligence instantly broke over the beaming countenance of the young officer, and, as quick as thought, his arm was bared and held exultingly aloft, disclosing the still visibly impicted arrows to the astonished and delighted group around him.

For one full minute not a word was uttered, and the mute eloquence of the speaking countenance alone told the springing emotions of those most interested in this unexpected but happy *dénouement.*

"My son!" at length convulsively burst from the trembling lips of the overpowered father; "God bless—bless—bless"—and his voice died away in whimpering murmurs, as father, son, and daughter rushed into one long sobbing embrace.

Aroused in a short time from this absorbing scene of gushing affections by a noise from the wounded man, the company turned toward him. A change was passing over his face, and with the low muttered words, "REVENGED—REVENGED ON THE DESTROYERS OF MY SOUL AND BODY, AT LAST!" he gave one long, quivering gasp and expired.

On the proposal of Selden, for such, for convenience, we will for the present continue to call him, the company now left the spot and proceeded to an open and unencumbered space by the road side, where the whole band were soon assembled preparatory to a final removal from the scene of action.

At that instant a band of twenty armed horsemen burst suddenly from the woods and came pouring, in gallant array, along the road from the south toward the spot. From their equipments and general appearance they were instantly discovered to be a detachment of mounted riflemen from the Continental army, headed by a field officer of considerable rank.

"You are the day after the fair, my hearties," gayly remarked Captain Hendee, whose over-mastering feelings at the recent joyful discovery had now settled down into a fine flow of spirits. "But I am glad they have come, for I want the whole world to know how proud I feel of my new-found son."

"Ay, but when they hear," replied the young officer in the same spirit, "that we owe this victory, and with it our lives, solely to the old veteran's plan of blowing up the enemy by wholesale, ten to one they don't say that the son has far the more reason to pride himself in the happy discovery. Seriously, however, the arrival of these men at this moment is most opportune, as some of them, doubtless, will give up their horses to convey you, the females, and children from the place. But what ails our merry friend Jones yonder?" he added, pointing to the scout, who stood in the foreground, eagerly and with mouth agape, looking at the advancing cavalcade, and holding his cap in his hand as if about to hurl it into the air in some joyous outbreak.

"He is about to welcome them with a few cheers, I suspect," replied the captain. "And hang me, if I don't join him; for if I don't give vent to my feelings in some way, I believe my old broken shell of a heart will burst for very joy, like some old rusty howitzer charged to the muzzle with gunpowder."

"No, no, father," rejoined the other good-humorerly, "joy rarely proves as explosive as that I imagine. But I must forward to attend to this reception myself. Jones," he continued, advancing to the front, "let us ascertain their object, and a little more exactly who they are, before we make up our mouths for much of a hurrah on the occasion."

"Well, that's jest what I'm at, captain," said the scout; "and I calkerlate I have about two-thirds found out both them particulars already; for, if twenty-four hours ago I had seen a chap riding toward me, with the make and bearing of that officer, who sits so splendid in his saddle yonder, I would have sworn, with a quarter of this bothering, that it was—and, by the living Lazarus! I'll swear it is now—so here's hurrah for the unshot colonel! Hurrah! hurrah!" he added, throwing his cap thirty feet in the air and leaping, in the ecstasy of his joyous emotions, a yard from the earth at each of his stentorian shouts; in the last of which he was heartily joined by the whole band of his delighted comrades, as their beloved commander, the heroic Warrington, whom they had mourned as slain, now came dashing up to the spot, bowing low in token of acknowledgment of this flattering mark of their esteem.

"Had you dropped down from the clouds before our eyes, Colonel Warrington," said Selden, after the noise and bustle of this enthusiastic reception had a little subsided, "your presence could have scarcely more surprised us."

"Indeed!"

"Yes, you was reported to have fallen in the last moments of the battle."

"I must, then, have been mistaken, I think, for Colonel Francis."

"Has that noble fellow then indeed been added to the honored catalogue of martyrs in our glorious cause?"

"I grieve to say it. He fell covered with wounds, bravely fighting at the head of his regiment."

"But you, and your men."

"We yet mostly live to give Burgoyne a thrashing. But here, overpowered with numbers, by my own orders, we broke, scattered, and fled, to meet again at Manchester. Reaching Rutland last night, and guessing at your course and at your danger, I collected this small force and hastened to the rescue. And now, captain, for your report, which, with these evidences of a conflict before me, I should dread to hear but for the merry looks of the men and the sunny faces of my fair friends whom I notice yonder in the rear."

"All in good time, my dear colonel; but come, first go along with me," said Selden, with a significant and slightly mischievous smile, as he took the arm of his superior and urged him forward to the spot where the interesting group to which he had just alluded still stood, in the agitation of their joyful surprise, with sparkling eyes and happy and fluttering hearts, eagerly waiting to greet him.

But over the touching and tender scene that followed, marked as it was by the reuniting of long estranged hearts, like the rushing together of kindred waters, the surprising announcement of Selden's recently discovered relationship, and the mad pranks of the excited old veteran, now clamoring for the curses of Warrington on his own head for his blindness and folly, and now eagerly bestowing the hand of his daughter as a compensation and reward, with many a sob-broken ejaculation for blessings on the happy couple—over all this we will drop the curtain, not caring to trust the pen to vie with the reader's outstripping fancy in filling up the picture.

Before another hour had elapsed the whole were mounted and in motion, on their unmolested way to the older settlements in the southern part of the Grants.

CONCLUSION

THE rolling seasons had nearly completed their annual round since the stirring incidents which we last narrated transpired, and nature was again enrobing herself in the leafy glories of summer. The great struggle on the Northern frontiers was over. The battle of Bennington had been fought and won, immortalizing the name of the Roman Stark and covering with deathless laurels the brave Green Mountain Boys. The whole of that proud army, indeed, that swept the last season so vauntingly along these desolated shores, had felt the vengeful arm of young Freedom and withered at the touch. The inhabitants on the borders of Lake Champlain, who had fled before the tempest of war, had mostly returned and were now in possession of their unmolested homes. The seat of their country's strife was removed to a distance. And the husbandman was again following his plow in the field; the peaceful sounds of the axmen were heard in the woods, and the hunter once more roamed his deer-trod hills unsuspicious of hostile ambush.

At the pleasant, and no longer desolate cottage of Captain Hendee, a company, evidently much larger than the usual family circle, were assembled. The old veteran, as was formerly his wont, was sitting in his easy-chair before one of the open windows of the parlor, solacing himself with his old companion, the pipe. The other window was occupied by a fine-looking military person, now in the full bloom of vigorous manhood, richly dressed in the lace-trimmed uniform and the surmounted badges of a field officer in the Continental army; while by his side sat a peerless girl, whose simple, but rich and tasteful array of spotless white, surmounted by the emblematic rose of the same color, instead of the dumb, unspeaking jewel, told of bridal preparation. They were gazing out upon the glittering expanse of the breeze-ruffled waters of the lake, and the gratified eye of the officer was resting on the bright folds of his country's flag, which was again proudly waving in the distance over the walls of the opposite fortress; while the delicately blended fondness and respect that marked the blissful look of each, and the tender pathos of their low, intermingling voices as they exchanged the occasional remark, betokened the presence of mutual confidence and love. There was another maiden in the room, scarcely less beautiful than the one just mentioned, but though arrayed, like her fair companion, in the bridal garb, yet she sat unmated and alone, now listlessly running over the leaves of a little volume in her hand, and now anxiously and impatiently glancing through the window along one road to the south, as if expecting the appearance of someone from that quarter. The only other person at present in this apartment, with whom the reader has been made acquainted, was a modest, staid-looking female, who, though comely and not greatly faded, had yet evidently outlived by many years the freshness and bloom of beauty's most favored period. She was sitting quietly in a corner, partly screened from the rest of the company by the door that swung inward. She, also, had been companionless, and had not, like the restless fair one last described, appeared to expect to be otherwise.

But at this moment a singularly tall, woodsman-looking fellow came stooping through the door-way from the adjoining room, where part of the company still remained; when, after throwing a half-sheepish, half-mischievous look around him, apparently to see if his movement was particularly noticed, he sidled around the swinging door with a sort of hesitating, stealthy air, and sunk by degrees into a chair beside the demure-looking damsel of whom we were speaking.

"Well, now, if this aint a curious fix!" were his first words. "I vow to Never-come-Jack—a sort of Saturday in the afternoon-chap that we used to swear by in the army—if it aint too bad! Don't you think so, now, honestly, Miss Ruth?"

"What is it that you complain of as so bad, Mr. Jones?" replied the girl, with a good-natured and encouraging smile, which seemed instantly to reassure her somewhat flustered companion, as he replied:

"What do I complain of? Why, to be invited, as I was, by the colonel and Alma there, to be here at two o'clock to see three weddings; when now it is well along toward night and one bridegroom don't get on according to agreement and no parson come to fix them that are here and ready for it. Now, I like to see folks put out of their misery in some kind of season, and so do the rest of them, I've a notion; only jest look at the old captain yonder! He is getting out of sorts at the delay, rather rapid, a body would guess, by the manner he is puffing away at his old comforter there. And there is the Scotch bird, too; may I miss my next aim on Old Trusty, if I don't believe she'll fly away if Major Selden, as he has now got to be—Major Hendee, I spose, you'll call him here—don't come soon."

"Jessy does, indeed, appear rather uneasy," observed the other, "and I really wonder Edward didn't come, myself. He sent us word that he expected to get the Sherwood property all settled so as to start from

Albany yesterday morning. But you said three weddings, didn't you?"

"Three, did I say, Ruth?" said Pete with waggish gravity. "Well, two then—that is, if there aint raaly any chance to be another, no way."

"Why, what other could there be?" said Ruth quite innocently.

"Well, now, I can't exactly say, but I was thinking it was rather a pity there shouldn't be another match worked up here somehow?" replied the scout, with a look at the other so significant that it brought the blood into her cheeks. "You hold to save time and expense, don't you?"

"Why, it is well enough to think of that in some cases, perhaps," muttered the doubtful and confused girl.

"Then, suppose, when the priest comes," said the other, with a roguish squint at her glowing cheeks and downcast looks, "suppose you jest stand up with—with—with old Captain Hendee to be noosed the same time his children are?"

"Oh, nonsense! Mr. Jones," replied the girl, greatly relieved, and yet evidently disappointed at this turn in the scout's remarks, which she supposed were to terminate in proposing one much nearer home—"Captain Hendee! why, he is old enough to be my father! Besides, he would not have me."

"Yes, he would."

"No, he wouldn't."

"Well, if he should flummux at such a chance, I know of a chap—and not too old, neither—who'll agree to take his place."

"Really, Mr. Jones, I think you must be trying to trifle with me?"

"Mayhap you're mistaken, now," said Jones, with the air of one about to make some hazardous push, but looking keenly about for some chance to secure his retreat.

"Then how am I to consider what you say?" asked the other seriously.

"Why—why," said Pete hesitating, but finding himself at a point where he must back out entirely or proceed directly with his object, he added, with a sort of desperate resolution: "Yes, I will—so here goes for dead ruin—you may consider it, Ruth, as good and earnest an offer as ever a man stuck an ax in a tree."

"Why, surely, Mr. Jones!—this is so sudden—so unexpected, that you cannot expect me now, as you have never before spoken to me on the subject——"

"No; but I've looked at you on the subject, Ruth; and that an't all—I have thought on the subject, and that, too, ever since I left off sogering, after we had used up that old trooper Burgoyne, last fall. But I didn't know how to get at the bothering business. And now I have got at it, I want to do it all up while I've got the knack of it. Now, all I've to say for myself, by way of recommendation, is jest only this: I have a farm, and can love like a two-year-old. And, if you can go it on that, let us agree on the spot and go off with the rest."

"Impossible, Mr. Jones—that is now—if—if I had a little time for reflection—perhaps——"

"Good! grand! glorious! I'll give you time, till the parson comes—a good half hour, I'll warrant you," exclaimed the woodsman, leaping up, in his ecstasy, and, with a sudden bolt through the door, bounded off into the fields, and giving vent to his delighted feelings in his old chorus, "Trol, lol, lol, de larly!"

At that moment a horseman rode hastily into the yard, leaped from his saddle, and, with a few light and joyous bounds, landed on the threshold.

"My brother!" exclaimed Alma, rising and rushing to the door.

"My son, God bless you!" said the captain, hobbling forward, with extended hand. "But how came you to be lagging at such a juncture as this, you truant?"

"Oh, Edward!" cried Jessy, bursting from an adjoining room, to which she had a few moments before retired. "Oh, Edward!" repeated the joyful but wayward girl, flying to the open arms of her betrothed, now dashing her hands about her to clear the way among the advancing group, and now shaking her slender finger aloft, in affected menace, as she went, "now, if I don't punish you for this, sir! Back! back! all of you, till I deal with the villain for his conduct."

"Fairly a prisoner, sir; you may as well surrender, major," gayly observed Warrington, to the laughing young officer, now inclosed on every side by besieging friends.

"Ay, ay, colonel," blithely replied the latter; "but I shall be upon my parole in a moment, I think; when I will pay my respects. I have a glad secret for your ear, Warrington."

"A secret! a secret to be kept from us at this hour!" exclaimed both of the girls at once, summoning a storm of affected indignation to their pretty brows.

"Ah! you little tyrannizers!" said the major jocosely, "you are wise to make the most of your power now; for your reign is short. I saw the parson falling into the road behind me, about a mile back."

The last intimation seemed to produce an instant effect on the young officer's fair assailants. And releasing him at once, they fled, in maidenly dismay, to their private apartment, to compose and prepare themselves for the happy, though half-dreaded crisis.

"Now, my son, tell us, in a word, what success you have met with at Albany," said Captain Hendee, turning to his son, as the girls disappeared.

"Very fair; the business is all definitely settled at last."

"Right glad to hear that; but first, I am curious to know with what kind of a face that black-hearted imp of mischief, Jake Sherwood, met you, after all that has happened?"

"It was not till after many fruitless efforts and a long negotiation, carried on with him by a go-between of his own kidney, that he could be induced to come from his lurking places to face me at all. And when he did, it was with the same fawning and cringing, the same dissembling and falsehood that has marked his whole career."

"And what kind of a treaty did you at length conclude with the arch villain?"

"Better than he had any reason to expect from those who had both the right and the power on their side; for, after taking from the estate that part which Jake had counted as his own by uncle's will when I was considered as disposed of, and which, of course, became mine on establishing my identity as your son—and after deducting also the legacies which old Sherwood's conscience wrung from him in favor of you and Alma, together with the sums which the indefatigable Vanderpool had found evidence of having been embezzled by the old man out of your property—even after counting your legacies as so much restitution—after deducting all these, there would have been a mere pittance in equity, and, nothing, probably, in law, left for the miscreant. And as he had been apprised of this by Vanderpool, whom he could neither intimidate nor corrupt, he chose to throw himself on my mercy rather than contend with us in law."

"Well, as skillfully as this web of iniquity was woven, it is all unraveled then, at last. But what did you finally allow him?"

"A thousand pounds; for while I despised I could

not but pity the abject wretch. He signed acquittances, received his portion, in money and drafts, and the same day, as I accidentally learned, started off to join his Tory brethren at the south.

The conversation was here interrupted by the arrival of the parson, who had scarcely been ushered into the house before yet another guest was announced. This was the amazon widow, who now rode into the yard, attended by Neshobee, each having a brace of her hardy urchins, disposed of behind and before, on the cruppers and necks of the captain's thus trebly burdened horses, which had been kindly sent for that purpose early in the morning.

"Not at the eleventh hour after all," said the woman, as with stately tread she came sweeping into the room and gave her hand successively to each of the assembled guests, who rose, and with looks of mingled cordiality and respect advanced to meet her. "Well, I am gratified to find I am not too late to witness the ceremony, though another motive mainly prompted my coming."

"Another motive?" said the captain, "what might that be?"

"Gratitude," rejoined the widow feelingly—"to offer, in person, the thanks and blessing of the widow and fatherless to these brave and generous young officers for their undeserved gift of fifty pounds."

"Not undeserved, especially from us, permit me to say, Mrs. Story," replied Major Hendee. "And our only fear was that it would not even requite you for the losses you sustained on our account on that fearful night, which none of us can ever forget."

"Not requite me? Oh, more—doubly so," replied the woman, mastering her grateful emotions and resuming her naturally free and easy manner. "Why, gentlemen, if you would but visit us there now you would see a new house worth two of the old one; flourishing crops, and a well-provisioned and happy family—and all from your bounty."

"Our pittance, if you please," observed the colonel, "and that, too, under the management of one, who, I must say, of all women——"

"Has the least patience with a flatterer, colonel," interrupted the widow with good-natured bluntness, jumping up and going to the window, as something seemed suddenly to occur to her mind. "Now, I should like to know, if you gentlemen can tell me," she resumed, gazing out on the lake a moment, "I should like to know the meaning of the great stir I noticed over at the fort as I came down the road. One would think they were preparing for a battle."

"We heard a firing in the direction of Ticonderoga an hour or two ago, which we could not account for, but have noticed nothing unusual over here, I believe," said Captain Hendee, looking inquiringly at the two officers.

"Ah! your promised secret, major?" cried Warrington, perceiving a knowing and mysterious smile upon the countenance of the other.

"You shall have it now—the rest of the company will know it soon," replied the major, approaching his superior and whispering in his ear.

"God bless you for the news!" exclaimed the colonel, with a look of joyful surprise. "But where did you meet him?"

"At Bennington, where he arrived but three days ago amid the roar of guns and the shouts of a rejoicing people. I persuaded him to come on with me, as he did, to Skenesboro'; when he took the water, while I came by land, having first dispatched a runner to notify the garrisons at the two posts of his approach."

"Heaven be praised!" rejoined Warrington, "and let the Green Mountains rejoice!"

"They will, soon; for yonder he comes, by Jove!"

exclaimed the major, eagerly pointing out upon the lake.

At that instant the house shook and trembled to the reverberating roar of a twenty-four pounder, belching forth a cloud of fire and smoke from the gray walls of the opposite fortress.

The surprised and startled company instantly rushed into the yard. A light sailboat had just made her appearance on the lake from the south, and with bellying canvas was now scudding rapidly before the freshening breeze, with her course evidently let for the fort. As she neared, a tall, erect, military figure appeared conspicuously standing on the forecastle, with folded arms, gazing steadily forward toward the works, around whose ramparts were seen the long rows of the expectant officers and soldiers of the garrison; while, at momentary intervals, came the welcoming peal of the deep-mouthed gun. At length the sails of the vessel were furled, and she swept round and lay to, directly abreast of the fort; which, the next instant, was suddenly enveloped in a springing cloud of smoke, while the tall forest around nodded to the united roar of a dozen cannon, among the broken echoes of which, as they rolled from shore to shore and died away among the far responding mountains, was heard the noisy salute of drums, and the reiterated cheers of the soldiery, once more making the welkin ring with the name of "Ethan Allen!"

After a brief interval of silence the same little craft was seen, with hoisted sails, emerging from the lifting clouds of smoke and making her way directly across the lake toward the cottage. And in ten minutes more the hero of the Green Mountains, unexpectedly returned from a long and painful captivity, was received and ushered into the house amid the warm and unfeigned congratulations of the rejoicing party.

"Well, Colonel Allen," said Captain Hendee, scanning the thin and worn person of the other, as they all became seated in the room, "they have rather worsted you in your captivity, I perceive. You are now hardly the stanch and iron-bound fellow you was three years ago, when eight or ten armed hirelings came here to seize you as a York outlaw, but were fairly cowed out of the attempt till they supposed you asleep, and a little worse off than that, too, perhaps."

"Aha! my old friend, do you remember that foolish scrape?" replied Allen. "No, no, captain not the man I was then," he added, glancing over the huge raw bones of his shrunken frame with a melancholy smile. "No, the British could never forgive me for taking Old Ti; so with characteristic magnanimity to a fallen foe, they took their revenge by battering, hewing, hacking, and starving the old body till there is scarcely enough left of it to furnish a habitable tenement for the soul, which remains as whole and sound as ever; for that, thank God! they could neither kill nor bribe."

"Bribe! bribe! Did they really try to do that?" exclaimed the young officers, laughing at the thought of an attempt to buy up Ethan Allen.

"To be sure, did the infernal fools!" said Allen, "and that more than once; though the last, and perhaps the best offer I ever had to induce me to damn myself, that is, to become one of them, was made me by a high dignitary of the crown, who, in behalf of his prince, as he said, offered me nearly half the lands in Vermont if I would enter his service against my countrymen!—the Christless knave! It was well for him that I was handcuffed at the time."

"And what answer did you give him?" asked Warrington curiously.

"Answer?" replied Allen, smoothing his dark brows, which had become fierce and stormy at the remembered insult, "what answer? Why, I told the royal ape to go and tell his master that he reminded me, in his offer to give me lands in America, of a certain other prince mentioned in Scripture who took the Saviour up into a high mountain and, showing him all the kingdoms of the world, offered to give him the whole of them, if he would fall down and worship him—when the fact was, the poor devil had not a single foot of land on earth to give!"

The subject was here dropped by common consent; when, after a brief pause, Major Hendee turned a significant look upon his father, who seemed readily to understand what was now expected of him, and he accordingly observed:

"I suppose you have been apprised, Colonel Allen, of the happy occasion upon which, after all our troubles, we have been permitted to assemble?"

"I have, sir," gallantly answered the other, "and I felt, that my peculiar notions, relative to the certainty of the earthly rewards of bravery and virtue, were strikingly confirmed when I learned that my two friends here were about to draw such rich prizes in the lottery of life."

"Ah, Colonel Allen!" exclaimed Jessy archly, "you, too, caught playing the flatterer? I had thought well enough of you to believe you an exception to the generality of men, in that respect. But I'll expose you, my brave colonel! What did you say and predict at the time you captured Ticonderoga, respecting the intimacy which you were then accidentally led to suspect existed between your then Lieutenant Selden and Colonel Reed's daughter?"

"Why, the deuce is to pay!" cried Allen, taken rather aback by his fair antagonist—"there has been treason here, somewhere. I recollect something about my misgivings in the matter. But I am not a-going to be tricked out of my compliment, at all events: for if the daughter of a British colonel has the independence to marry a Yankee rebel, she must be, to him, at least, a prize richly worth the winning."

"She is not married yet," observed Captain Hendee, with well-assumed seriousness: "for before that is suffered to take place, I, who stand as a sort of sponsor for the girl, must be heard in the business: and to this end, I beg the leave to read a little from my letter of instructions from her father; which I have never before made known," he added, producing a letter, from which he proceeded to read to his surprised and wondering auditors the following extract:

" 'Wi' regard to the wayward bairn o' mine, an' that Mr. Nabody, her rebel lover, as I became satisfied he was, it is out o' the question I should be consentin' to a match of sic a sort. Na, she must be cured, an' in some sic way as I named to you. An' that being done, then her old lover, Major Skene, will come in for an easy conquest. But in your moves to this object, let me again caution you to beware how you forbid this intimacy; forever since mother Eve's dido wi' the apple, the moment you forbid, the Diel taks the woman.' "

"Father, how is this, and at this late hour?" exclaimed the astonished son, glancing from the former to the no less surprised girl at his side, who also began to open her lips in remonstrance, when, detecting a lurking smile on the old gentleman's countenance, she stopped short.

"Perhaps we may as well read a passage from another letter of a more recent date," said the captain, opening another paper, from which, after slyly enjoying the perplexity of the party interested, a moment, he read:

" 'So you sly old Yankee, you an' Jessy hae contrived to checkmate me at last! This comes o' leaving a daughter in a land o' rebellion: nathless I canna but say I regret that circumstances will not permit me to be present to take my stoup on the merry occasion, which you say, wi' my consent, is to tak place early the coming summer: weel, you may tell the younker, wi'out hinting my good opinion o' him as aboon written, that, upon the whole, I will own him as a son-in-law, provided he will take the crap o' wild oats which the chick, frae sa plentifu' a-sowing, must now hae ready for the reaping, as a portion o' the wife's dowry.' "

"Gad! I begin to like the humorous old fellow," said Allen, "and that stoup which he regrets he cannot take with us, I will drink to his health as an extra bumper after the ceremony. Though before that takes place, I would ask if there are no more cases which might be settled at this time?"

"We know of none," replied the captain and his son, to whom the last part of the speaker's remarks had been addressed in an undertone.

"I don't know about that," rejoined the former, "I have been looking about me a little, and it strikes me that there are materials enough, at least. If you will make me master of the ceremonies, with powers to draw out the parties——"

"Certainly, certainly, colonel," replied the others, laughing, but shaking their heads dubiously at the well understood suggestion.

"No faith, eh? Well, there is nothing like trying," rejoined Allen. "Jones," he continued, now turning round to the scout, who had resumed his seat by the side of Ruth, "Jones, you have been a brave fellow—how is it that you are not to be rewarded, at this time, as well as the rest?"

"Well, I've jest been thinking, colonel," replied Jones, screwing up his phiz, now queerly streaked with blushes, "that it was rather a hard case, considering, that I shouldn't have any share in the loaves and fishes.

But the fact is, that the fish I've had in my eye," he added, casting a sheepish glance at Ruth, "won't quite say whether I'm to be in luck to-day or not."

"Aha! just as I thought. But she shall say," cried Allen, advancing a step toward the confused and blushing maiden, on whom all eyes were now turned in surprise, at this development of a courtship so little expected; "she shall give you an answer, at least, or by the wrath of Cupid! she shall be punished for her cruelty by running a kissing gantlet through the company. And I'll have the first one," he added, still further advancing, as if to suit the action to the word.

"It is so ridiculous!" stammered the shrinking Ruth.

"Perhaps you had rather say yes to my worthy friend, here?" said the former, his lips slightly curling with a sportive smile.

"I should—that is, I—I should," replied the girl, dropping her head in confusion.

"Do you see that?" exultingly said Allen. "I have succeeded in spite of your faithlessness; nor do I believe my triumphs need end even here."

"Ah! I will knock under, colonel," observed the captain, laughing.

"Ay, ay," responded the major gayly, "we must now acknowledge your prowess in the court of Cupid, as well as in the camp of Mars. But be not overambitious, lest your zeal be dampened by a failure. Where will you find materials for another triumph?"

"Here," answered the other, pointing to Neshobee and Zilpah, who, for reasons best understood by themselves, had also paired off in a corner together. "I have been reading eyes, which are about the only book I ever read where we are sure of the truth; and if those who control these persons should have no objections——"

"Never mind that, colonel, if you have faith for

the trial," exclaimed the old captain, entering into the full spirit of the game.

"Upon my word, Colonel Allen, I think you a most incorrigible meddler; but you may proceed, for aught I care," said Miss Reed, pouting most beautifully.

"Ah, don't laugh, ye wise ones, till you see," said the jovial matchmaker confidently. "Well, Miss Zilpah," he continued, familiarly addressing the half-blood, "you see which way your young mistress is about to travel—now, as you intend to follow her fortunes, don't you think it would be more pleasant and suitable for you, to have some such brave and trusty companion on the road as Neshobee here would make you?"

"Ki!" exclaimed the girl, with a blush which brought her cheek to a fellow redness with that of the young Indian by her side. "He! you queer man! But Neshobee, he no hab me."

"Good!" cried the former, "there is a challenge for you, my red friend. She says you won't marry her!"

"Umph!" uttered the still grave, though evidently delighted native, "me never know Zilpah tell lie before."

"There! you unbelievers," exclaimed Allen, looking round triumphantly upon the company, "see what a man can do. Now parson, do your duty!"

Reader, our story is told, and, with a word upon the subsequent career of those in whose destinies we trust we have been able in some degree to interest you, we will bid you adieu:

Of that singular, bold, rough, versatile, yet honest and strong-minded man, Ethan Allen, little more need be said. The remainder of his public life was devoted to the accomplishment of that object for which he had so fearlessly contended before the Revolution, the independence of his State. And her history sufficiently attests to the importance of his services.

The gallant young officers, after their twice extended furloughs had expired, leaving their lovely and loving wives at the cottage of Captain Hendee, to cheer and soothe the old veteran in his declining years, and, in due time, to render his second childhood anything but companionless, returned to their posts in the army in which, honored and distinguished, they remained till they had witnessed the achievement of their country's independence; when they retired to their homes in the Green Mountains, to receive from their fellow-citizens those substantial memorials of their esteem which may still be found recorded among some of the early acts of the Legislature of Vermont, granting valuable tracts of land to certain individuals for important public services.

Pete Jones and his staid spouse immediately repaired to their little opening in the woods, where, having renewed his acquaintance with his rusty ax, he caused the forest to melt away before his powerful arm till his labors were rewarded by one of the best farms on the borders of the lake; while his wife became one of the most notable of housewives, having never had cause to regret her abrupt connection with the eccentric though amiable woodsman, as may be inferred from the opinions she was often heard to express in favor of long men and short courtships.

Widow Story remained on her farm, cultivating and enlarging it with her own hands for many years; when, her oldest son having at length been enabled to butt his mother, to use a chopper's phrase, that is, to get off his cut first, in a trial of skill on the same log, she concluded to betake herself to household duties, giving up her farm work to her sturdy little band of foresters, who in the process of time let in the sun on extensive tracts of some of the finest lands on Otter Creek.

Neshobee and his yellow rib continued to reside on the farm of Captain Hendee, in a log hut built expressly for them, till the old gentleman's death; when they removed to the woody shores of the Horicon, where they spent their days in a ceaseless warfare upon the beautiful trout of the lake, and the deer, bear, and other wild animals of its surrounding shores.

And lastly, the miscreant Sherwood, who, through the inscrutable ways of Providence, was permitted to live Cain-like to old age, found his way at the close of the Revolution to the common refuge of American Tories in Canada, where he finished his days in poverty and disgrace, always obtaining credit by flattery and falsehood, always abusing it by fraud and treachery, and living, indeed, abhorred by men and seemingly accursed of God.

THE END.

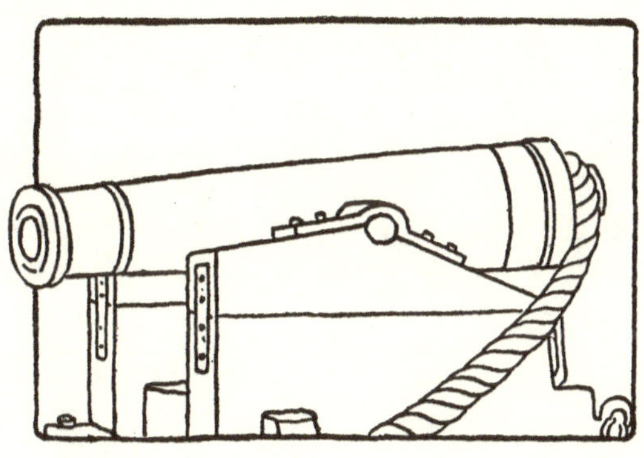

Honor

www.ingramcontent.com/pod-product-compliance
Lightning Source LLC
La Vergne TN
LVHW050911080826
845145LV00001B/49

* 9 7 8 0 8 7 7 9 7 3 5 9 1 *